ACTS

OF

CUPIDITY

E. S. Drake grew up in Bedford, a natural daydreamer as a child, penning poetry by moonlight and escaping into her imagination. She later moved to Bodmin Moor to dwell among the wild things, exploring different genres of writing while building a business teaching archery and survival skills. The darker aspects of her past have been her main motivation for creating flawed and complex characters to encapsulate the pitfalls of humanity, attempting to navigate our vulnerability with humour and compassion. *Acts of Cupidity* is her debut novel.

ACTS OF CUPIDITY

E S DRAKE

ZAFFRE

First published in the UK in 2025 by
ZAFFRE
An imprint of Bonnier Books UK
5th Floor, HYLO, 103–105 Bunhill Row,
London, EC1Y 8LZ
Owned by Bonnier Books
Sveavägen 56, Stockholm, Sweden

A CIP catalogue record for this book is
available from the British Library.

Hardback ISBN: 978-1-80418-619-0
Trade paperback ISBN: 978-1-80418-885-9

Also available as an ebook and an audiobook

1 3 5 7 9 10 8 6 4 2

Typeset by IDSUK (Data Connection) Ltd
Printed and bound in Great Britain by Clays Ltd, Elcograf S.p.A.

MIX
Paper | Supporting
responsible forestry
FSC
www.fsc.org   FSC® C018072

Zaffre is an imprint of Bonnier Books UK
www.bonnierbooks.co.uk

For Roly, the T-800 to my John Connor,
and for my inner child, we never gave up

1

Bleeding Heart

SOMEWHERE LEFT OF THE BISTRO on Greville Street, perched on a red-brick roof, stood a figure in the chill of the January air. The sound of London traffic below mingled with the rhythmic cooing of pigeons that fluttered from ledge to ledge.

'Bleeding Heart, eh? How appropriate,' Erron muttered as he fixed the limbs of his bow to the riser, before flicking the stub of his cigarette onto the puddled rooftop. His black hair ruffled in the wintry breeze. Despite years of wisdom, he never aged beyond his thirty-one years, and despite the bitter wind, he was blessed with a youthfulness that tinged his pale skin with a warm glow. Only a faint scar on his cheek added a hint of lived-in imperfection to his face.

'There's no loss of irony these days.' A second man joined him, handsome, also early thirties with sandy blond hair tied into a ponytail. 'Poetic, almost. It's a pleasant little café, to be fair. Lovely croissants.' He was almost a foot taller than his companion, a looming six feet four but his slim frame removed any element of intimidation from his height.

'It's too cold for your chirpy observations, Casey.' Erron deftly fixed the string to his bow, his long black jacket slapping against the backs of his legs as the wind picked up.

'No need to be like that.'

Erron rolled his eyes in response and rested the bow on the ground, searching his satchel for his assignment card.

'Well, *I* think it's beautiful,' Casey went on, gazing down wistfully at the corner restaurant.

'You think everything's beautiful. Or marvellous, or delightful.'

'Isn't it?'

'Not from my perspective.'

Erron studied the card and slipped it back into his bag. 'Twelve forty. We have twenty minutes to spare.'

Casey paced back and forth along the edge of the rooftop, turning his face away from the sharp breeze. He regretted his choice of attire that morning, only dark grey suit trousers and a thin blue shirt, thinking they wouldn't have been waiting in the cold for quite so long. He usually favoured a more bold or formal look, right down to his favourite fifties grey trilby and red braces, but the assignment needed a cover agent on the ground, and he had to look casual. The streets of London below were reaching the lunchtime humdrum of people rushing back and forth, ducking into coffee shops and cafés before hurrying back to the nine-to-five grind.

'Quit daydreaming and check your card, will you? There's a discrepancy.' Erron wrung his hands together, trying to warm his freezing fingers.

Casey plucked his card from the back pocket of his trousers and read the brief details on the reverse. 'Van to the left, cyclist, cyclist, target?' His gaze looked over the disgruntled look on

Erron's face and then followed where he gestured to a roadblock being set up for a temporary diversion.

'Ahh ... Well, you know the agency have certain variables-procedures. We haven't been diverted yet, so stick to the plan.'

Erron, quite the opposite to his colleague, was the stubble-faced brooding type and was busy shielding his lighter from the wind as he lit another cigarette. 'Get yourself down there, then.' He nodded to the street with a slow exhale of smoke, flickering the metal lighter closed. 'Make a good impression.' He winked.

'You know, you really *must* quit those things,' Casey scolded.

'Why? They're hardly going to kill me.' Erron took a long drag, the tip of the cigarette glaring against the grey sky, his voice drawn out with a Cockney twang.

'They just ... *aren't very nice.*' Casey huffed and walked off down the length of the rooftop. Things that *weren't very nice*, in Casey's world, ranged from people who left chewing gum on the seats of public transport to those dreadful types that held people hostage at a bank hold-up. Anything beyond that became *very inconvenient* or *rather awful*, depending on the circumstances.

Erron checked the courtyard on the other side of the roof for onlookers, only finding two ladies huddled out of the cold in a shop doorway, one of them speaking frantically into the phone about a business deal gone awry. The roadworkers were too preoccupied to see Casey unfurl his wings, immense, white-feathered limbs, which carried him swiftly off the roof and gracefully to the floor.

Ten minutes later, with a blare of horns and shouting, a van was held up at the roadblock and penned in, unable to reverse. Two cyclists whizzed by just as a young brunette stepped into the street, her hair whipping against her face in an updraught of cold air. Casey emerged from the side street and grabbed her arm, pulling her from the path of the van that had been shunted from behind by another, sending cones flying.

Wide-eyed in shock, she swivelled to face him. He smiled warmly and put on his best act. 'Are you all right, miss?'

'Huh? Yes, sorry, yes. Thank you.' She gripped a coffee cup in gloved hands which trembled slightly. In the jolt of being pulled away from the van, she'd spilled most of her drink.

'Close call, eh? I think it would be best if you sat down for a minute. Let me buy you another drink,' Casey said in his soft, sing-song voice.

'No, it's fine, I have to be getting on. Thank you though.' She broke into a smile, though she still appeared rattled.

'Just five minutes? I can't leave you like this until I know you are OK. Shock can do funny things, you know.'

Casey had the genteel charm of a young, softly spoken English teacher, his kind smile inspired confidence in even the timidest women, and the brunette nodded and followed him across the street to the Bleeding Heart bistro.

Twelve minutes to go.

'Tea? I like a good cup of tea.' Casey gestured to the counter.

'Oh, oh no, thanks.' She held her coffee cup up as explanation. 'A latte would be nice though.'

'Of course.' He pulled out a chair for her and ordered their drinks.

They made small talk and she told him her name, though he already knew it. Cassandra Highfield, a twenty-three-year-old trainee nurse. She explained that she was on her way to the hairdressers for an appointment but hadn't been concentrating after having worked overtime all week. Casey looked

4

to the door ten seconds before twelve thirty-seven and counted down to when a young man in a Parka jacket walked in, carrying a messenger bag. He spoke briefly to a server, handed over a small envelope and took a signature before leaving.

Casey knew everything he needed to know about the man. Twenty-eight-year-old Ryan Connor, bike messenger with his own start-up firm in the pipeline, sharing a flat with his older brother and desperate to make it in the world.

'Anyway, miss, I must get going. Don't you need to get to your appointment?' Casey cut her off mid-sentence and stood abruptly.

12.39.

'Oh, yes, yes. Thank you again.' She wrapped her scarf back around her neck and pulled on her gloves, letting him lead her out the door. 'I didn't get your name?'

'Milo,' Casey lied, guiding her to the doorway.

Ryan Connor unhooked the chain of his bike in the side street by the bistro and adjusted his bag, swinging one leg over and finding a pedal.

12.40.

The whistle of an arrow sailed down from the roof, through the windy courtyard and into the back of Ryan's jacket, disappearing on impact into a shatter of silver dust. Feeling nothing, he pressed hard on the pedal and pushed away, colliding with Cassandra Highfield as she came out of the bistro and landed in a heap on the cobbles. Casually, Casey stepped around her and made his way back to a hidden corner of the courtyard to soar back up to the roof, hearing the commotion as he left.

'Silver assignments are always a nice start to the day,' Casey said when he rejoined his colleague who was already packing away the recurve bow. 'She'll really help him bring his business plans to fruition.'

'Did you do that thing? That thing you always do?' Erron grumbled.

'What?'

'Look at their extended files, like you give a damn.'

'Don't you care? I think it's beautiful. I care, I always care.' Casey smiled as he watched the two people down below awkwardly exchange numbers and coy glances.

'I need a bloody coffee, you daft day-dreamy bastard.' Erron slung his equipment bags over his shoulder and crushed his cigarette under one polished boot.

'Back to the desk?'

'Yeah, back to the desk. Got to get these cards stamped.'

* * *

The agency building was cleverly disguised as an apartment block in Poseidon Court on the Isle of Dogs. As far as the neighbours were concerned, the people who came and went from the multi-storey building were just residents and were rarely seen doing anything out of the ordinary. But past the understated doors and bland security-controlled inner vestibule, three floors buzzed with the mid-London district employees of the Apollo Division. The crisp lighting burned all hours of the day and night as the building was rarely ever unmanned. Above the door hung a symbol of a stylised bow and arrow with a set of wings, surrounded by a ring of stars. All three floors of the building served a slightly different purpose, the ground floor being dedicated to equipment issue and repairs, the post room, changing rooms and security. There was also a smaller office used as a call centre, where agents could earn mortal money for subsidise their lives among mortals. The first floor was primarily occupied by the open-plan office of the dedicated night-shift agents, along with a basic kitchen for all staff to use. The second floor was the largest office, boasting the best views, and was used by remaining agents on days and late shifts. The division boss held a small side office on the second floor, backed by the arrow storage room and adjacent to the assignments desk.

Erron sauntered in, slinging his bow case and quiver down for security check-in. A burly man in his late fifties nodded at the two men and glanced over the bags, his security badge displaying the name 'Michael'. 'Back early, fellas?'

'Only one assignment for us this morning,' Casey answered, placing his own bag down for checking.

'All right for some, eh?' Michael teased.

'Can't complain,' Casey twittered.

'Have a good day, Agent Hart, Agent Grover.' Michael nodded them both through as he buzzed open the glass door.

'You too, Mike,' Casey answered.

Their desks were among others on the second floor. Erron's was strewn with paper and news clippings, a glow-in-the-dark plastic figure of Stay Puft from *Ghostbusters* holding down his stack of files with a cheerful, marshmallow grin. Casey's was more orderly; a stack of neat books and a tidy silver laptop sat next to a lolling peace lily. The large room was adorned with soft decor, inoffensive abstract art, and several colourful bean-bags in a relaxation area at the rear. Eclectic lamps offered a variety of bright and soft lighting and there was no shortage of exotic potted plants littering the empty spaces. The whole place had a relaxed, cosy feel. There were no other agents at their desks as most were out on assignments, the lunchtime rush being a peak time for work.

Erron made a beeline for a hatch window with a calligraphed 'Returns' sign on the glass sliding shutter.

'Mrs Murnard.' He addressed the squat, pinched-faced old woman behind the screen.

She took a moment to observe him with narrow eyes over her half-moon glasses. Without responding, she whipped the assignment card from his hand and scanned it over.

'Early for you, Mr Grover.' She raised an eyebrow. With a swift movement she stamped the card with a time stamp and marked it as complete. It was added to a pile on her desk.

'Afternoon, Margie.' Casey smiled widely at her while holding out his own card.

Her miserable pout unravelled into a warm smile as she took the card graciously. 'Thank you, Casey. I've put on a fresh kettle to boil. Come around the back and help yourself.'

Casey made small talk with her as Erron wandered off, rolling his eyes, and collapsed lazily into his leather swivel chair. Casey joined him ten minutes later, a hot cup of coffee and another four cards in his hand, two of which he passed to Erron.

'Ta.' Erron didn't look at the assignment details, dropping them on the desk as he sipped the drink, allowing its warmth to reach his inner depths. He pushed a small figure of a Dalek around among his scattered papers, his mind wandering to distant places.

'Erron, haven't you noticed? We have a gold assignment! First one of the year and it's only January. What was the last one, September?' Casey picked up one of the cards again and eyed the specialised gilded print, turning it so it glimmered in the light.

Erron glanced down. It was indeed a rare gold assignment, one of true love: the kind of concept poorly portrayed in films as being easily obtainable, when really it only existed in the rare fringes of life. Gold assignments were only given to the most experienced agents, and the arrows had to be signed for from the secure lockbox they were kept in, authorised only by the Apollo boss. Of their district, there were only six agents qualified to undertake gold assignments, Erron and Casey being two of them. 'We've got a few hours to kill before the gold one; it's in Farringdon station. The second is only ten minutes' walk away from that, but that's just a bronze. We'll have an hour in between.' Casey had already memorised the details.

Before Erron could respond, a door flung open from a side office, and their boss, Kendra Eckhart, hurried through.

'Grover, Hart, I need you in here.' She was short, slightly overweight and formidable. The wild, tight curls of her bleached-blonde hair framed a round face made up in bold cosmetics, reminiscent of the eighties party scene. She was no stranger to revelry; her nightlife was renowned in the office and she frequented concerts and clubs more than she ever slept. Obediently, the two agents got up to follow her, exchanging a silent look with raised eyebrows at her bold choice of a leopard-print jacket and tight black skirt, her shoulder pads almost meeting the dangle of her garish plastic earrings. She wasn't the worst boss by a long shot, but she had as much depth as a yoghurt pot.

'You've got our first gold of the year so we'll sort the arrows shortly. Other than that I've made sure you've got a quiet day overall,' she said, adjusting her skirt as she sat down.

'What's the catch?' Erron asked.

'We have a rookie.' Kendra tossed a new-recruit binder containing the basic details of each new agent at him. Erron caught it, opening it to the first page, which revealed a photo of a young woman with red hair and haunted eyes. 'They always look terrified in the staff photo,' she observed, letting out a half-hearted chuckle.

'Can you blame them?'

She dismissed his comment with a loose wave and carried on. 'Nikita Wolf. Twenty-nine. A journalist by trade. She's in her induction and processing currently. I need you guys to show her around; we're short on people who can train her currently. I'm working on getting her partnered up but you need to take her on for now.'

'Casey's got this. He's great with rookies.' Erron handed his colleague the file.

'You and Hart are a team, Grover. How many times do I have to remind you of that? Now come and sign for these golden arrows and start pulling your weight.' Kendra stood and beckoned them to follow her, all the while tugging on her skirt to keep it in place as she walked.

They entered a dimly lit back room where Kendra handed Casey two files that related to the gold assignment. A bright spotlight was pointed towards a heavy wooden cabinet, ornately inlaid with gold and pearl depictions of Greek gods surrounded by swirling clouds, great monsters and landscapes of intricate beauty. Kendra fetched a key from a separate lockbox with a combination code.

The cabinet emitted a warm glow as it was unlocked, and two thin steel tubular cases were removed and handed to the agents. 'Sign here.' Kendra produced a receipt book for them to write in before locking the cabinet once more.

Casey scanned the signatures. Their last gold assignment was as he thought, back in September, and had involved some precarious balancing on the boat ride at Legoland. He chuckled to himself at the memory.

'Right, I'm off to get some late breakfast after saying hello to the new recruit. I expect she'll be up here within the hour, depending on how many slides Jerry has on the projector.' Kendra hustled them out of the room. 'I'll let you know when I've rostered in a new trainer for her.'

'Can't Freya train her?' Erron huffed. 'We always get landed with the new ones.'

'We'll see that she settles in well,' Casey interjected with a warm smile, guiding Erron towards their desks.

'Suck-up,' Erron muttered out of earshot of Kendra.

2

Under Pressure

TWENTY-EIGHT OR SO HOURS PREVIOUSLY, the young journalist in question was stuffing papers haphazardly into a portfolio, while trying to wriggle her feet into a pair of slip-on shoes that were just about present-able enough for her job interview at an online news site that investigates cold cases. She was sceptical about some of their sensationalised reports of missing people and strange coincid-ences, but the pay was good and it would give her a leg-up into investigative journalism. She paused briefly to calm her nervous breathing; she hadn't had an interview in years and her stomach was a washing machine that had her lunch on a spin cycle. Her eyes looked over the chaos of her living room; her cluttered apartment was a mildew-plagued hellhole that she'd decorated with posters of her favourite rock bands from the seventies and quirky dinosaur ornaments to brighten up the drab wallpaper. She'd never got the hang of the IKEA lifestyle, where everything was muted and matched and perfectly assembled, but she made do with her eclectic taste. Books on mythology and witchcraft spilled over her crowded bookshelf, and she had more scented candles than was probably healthy for a flat with only two operational windows.

Nikita was desperate to climb the corporate ladder and drag herself out of the oppressive struggle of minimum wage. Sighing heavily, she pulled out her suit jacket, which was bobbled around the collar and had a subtle stain on the lapel, but it was all she had found in her size at the local Cats Protection charity shop.

Her phone buzzed three times, messages popping up from her friend Claire wishing her luck and telling her to sell herself to the point of dishonesty. Claire had already arranged for them to go for a Nando's that evening to discuss the interview regardless of how it went, as apparently being surrounded by well-seasoned chicken was the way forward. After a whirlwind of grabbing keys, her wallet and a wrinkled overcoat, Nikita wrestled to close the door of her flat. She imagined her elation if she got the job; it was certainly a step up from the trashy celebrity affair stories she was currently covering, despite there being the occasional UFO sighting or poltergeist story to invest-igate, which were clearly thrown in to grab attention. She allowed herself the luxury of imagining all the things she could afford if she was well paid, like new furniture, clothes ... Even being able to put the heating on would be a start ...

An hour later, she was gripping the steering wheel of her battered green Corsa as she edged onto a roundabout near Croydon. Despite the cold, her windows were rolled down as the twenty-five-year-old car was always steamed up on winter mornings. Though she was young, she had always resisted anything too modern, and enjoyed the feeling of the lack of power steering and having to manually wind down her windows. The best feature was the sunroof, which beat having air

13

conditioning hands down, as it was far better for watching the rain through when parked up in the leafy suburbs when she needed to clear her head.

A burst of movement caught her eye in the wing mirror as a cyclist dressed all in black careened between two cars, quickly coming up beside her and slamming into her driver's door. Next second, he was flung into the road in a heap.

'Oh shit,' she muttered and reached for the door handle, but the man was already up on his feet and apologising profusely.

He gripped her arm through the window and bent over. 'I'm so sorry. There's no damage. Not yet, anyway . . .'

Before Nikita could answer, he'd plucked the bike off the road, swung his leg over it and pedalled off in the blink of an eye. She had no time to think about it as horns blared behind her to move. Shifting into gear, she stuck her head out of the window to shout at the horn-blaring taxi and let her foot slip off the clutch. One and a half seconds ticked past as her car lurched into the pathway of a bus and she was killed on impact.

The cyclist had stopped up ahead and watched on, checking a card in his pocket, scribbling a quick note on it, before riding away.

She hadn't felt a thing.

Not until an intense light surrounded her and lifted her high above the wreckage of her car and the chaos of the roundabout, before gliding her across the city with nauseating speed. Too stunned to make sense of anything, Nikita felt herself slowing down and being ushered into a cool room, where the radiating light dimmed until it was dark, and a flow of icy air enveloped her. Pinpoints of light swirled in and out of her vision until they became a whole galaxy of neon stars, spiralling slowly towards her. With every fleck of brightness that collided with her, a surge of energy flooded into her core, until she pulsed with raw electricity and glowing light.

The surrounding cold pressed into her bones, or what she thought were bones. Her whole body felt jelly-like, as if she could slide around like oil on the surface of water. Had she the ability to lift her arms, she was convinced they would simply detach from her body and wibble away like two gelatinous gummy worms. She could see nothing but blurred light and shadows, could hear nothing but a medley of whispered voices. Indiscriminate time passed by until clarity returned to her vision. She was in a tank of ice water, but could barely feel a thing, completely submerged, her body rippling slightly from muffled sound waves that passed through her. She felt no need to burst to the surface to breathe, no panic to extricate herself from the icy depths, only a deep and relaxing serenity. Soft lamps glowed overhead and gradually she rose towards them, until all the water had drained away from her body.

'Replication successful,' a soft voice murmured, its owner outside of her field of vision. 'Time of life, 16.46.'

'Bring her round. Give her the good news.' Another voice, female, soothing.

Suddenly the room fell into crisp clarity. Sound fully returned, the piercing cold of the water assaulted her every nerve and air rushed into her lungs as she took a terrified gasp. Two hands gently pulled her up, perching her on the cold edge of the steel gurney she'd been lying on in the tank. Thick beads of freezing water dripped off her feet like condensation on a glass of lemonade in summer. A light sheet was wrapped around her naked form as a woman switched off the speaker that had been playing a song Nikita recognised from the band Nickelback.

'Hello, Nikita. Welcome to the afterlife,' the first voice said, belonging to a tall, round-faced man in hospital overalls. 'Well, the stopgap, at least.'

She stared blankly at his warm smile, his deep blue eyes examining her with professional efficiency. He had thinning hair, a wide nose and the countenance of a man who was eager to get his job done so he could get back home to his left-over takeaway in the fridge. He introduced himself as Dr Carroway.

'You're going to experience a whole host of emotional reactions,' he said with the same blandness that someone might use to explain the ingredients of scrambled egg. 'But you will get through them, well, because of who you are. It is one of the many reasons that you have ended up here. Now, let me explain. A few hours ago, you decided to French kiss the front end of a bus. Your face and chest were crushed beyond recognition, your car realised its dream of being a contender in a demolition derby and your soul was plucked from your body before you had a chance to even say, *Fuck this for a game of Monopoly*. Do you follow so far?'

Wide-eyed, she half nodded, trembling violently from the cold.

'Good. You died; our staff brought your soul here, not your body. We put you in a tank to replicate your living body and, much like a cake, we baked your soul for a few hours or so at gas mark three and popped you out when you'd risen again, like the Lord Jesus Christ Himself. Except, we don't cook, we cool. Freshly extricated souls solidify with coldness and pressure and take on the form they were used to in life. With a little help from Nickelback – we've found their music helps speed up the process. Please don't ask me why as I don't know, or care.' Dr Carroway handed her a thick booklet. 'Give that a read through. Our psychologist will give you some starter points to prepare you for the next bit.' He was already taking off his apron and heading towards the door.

Nikita looked down obediently at the booklet which was titled *Born Again – The Light at the End of the Condensation Tank*. The female attendant had been busying herself while Dr Carroway explained the bare facts, and once he'd left the room, she pulled a rolling stool across and sat in front of Nikita. She had kind eyes behind thick-framed glasses.

'I'd offer you a warm blanket, but we have to let you return to normal temperature slowly in case you don't solidify fully. It's a messy affair when that happens,' the woman explained with a grimace. 'We had one guy who warmed up too quick and he's still got a transparent knee.'

Nikita thumbed through the booklet blankly, her mind utterly unable to comprehend her situation.

'I'm Dr Rayne, the Reanimation Psychotherapist. You'll be in shock for some time, especially considering your exit from mortality – very sudden. But when that has passed, you are likely to want to ask a lot of questions, or get angry or sit quietly in denial, et cetera. Each phase will work its way out and you will restore yourself to full comprehension. From experience, most of our new additions take between six and forty-eight hours to process it. The booklet explains a lot of the physical and emotional experiences that you will undergo. The rest of your questions will be answered at your next stage of processing.'

Once Dr Rayne had calmly talked Nikita through the expected psychological impact of death and cold pressure soul-baking, she helped her into a standard hospital gown. 'This is the interesting bit now. Your soul is still settling, and currently you are able to function based on the initial jolts of synthetic stardust that you were given in the tank. But they will fizzle out soon, and you'll need to be given your new source of life. Or *afterlife*, if we're being pedantic.'

'Sorry, did you say stardust?' Nikita started to wonder if she'd inhaled some kind of psychoactive substance and was about to meet a white rabbit.

'It's complicated. But yes. Essentially, the same particles of energy that make up the entire cosmos, they're easy to replicate if you know how. Not everything works the same here as the world you were used to.'

The doctor helped her into a wheelchair and pushed her slowly down a dimly lit hospital corridor ending in a set of double doors marked as 'The Revival Ward'.

'Behind those doors is the beginning of your new journey. I can't go in with you, but I will be here once you have completed the process,' Dr Rayne said, bringing the wheelchair to a halt in front of the doors.

Nikita hesitated, still very confused. The initial pulses of energy were fading within her. Her limbs were beginning to feel heavy and sluggish, and her skin was growing clammy and blue. Gradually she was beginning to feel like she had some form of flu and her body was giving in to grim weakness. With wobbly legs, she rose from the chair and staggered towards the doors. Nothing but pitch blackness greeted her, and the distant voice of Dr Rayne urging her to keep going forward as the doors swung closed behind her. The room was a void, and she shuffled her bare feet forward cautiously, until the sensation of the vinyl underfoot faded away.

She had no sense of direction. Then, in a swirling motion, her body was lifted from the floor and suspended into vast nothingness by forces unseen. The swirling grew faster until she became aware that she was orbiting a tiny sparkle of light in the emptiness. More sparkles joined it, gathering their light together into a small orb of brightness. Nikita felt overwhelming peace with the gentle motion, marvelling at the brilliance of the light that was growing to the size of a balloon, throbbing with golden energy at its core. Without warning, it burst into a shatter of glittering specks, the force of the explosion knocking her backwards and filling her mind with thousands of images of life; immense forests, clouds, raging fires, animals, vast oceans of creation, colossal storms and untameable mountains. Her motion resettled, the blinding orb burned again central to the empty space, much smaller but this time surrounded by a scattering of colourful tiny stars, pulling Nikita into a gentle spiral towards it.

As the orb continued to throb, tiny tendrils of light crept from within it, reaching for her like tentacles of spun gold. As soon as they touched her skin, she felt a rush of adrenaline take over her body, the orb pulling itself towards her chest until it pushed right through her ribs and engulfed her body from within. It felt like the touch of a thousand gods, a white-hot lightning of ecstasy exploding through her body with the force of a universe, burning and pulsing and rippling.

Nikita closed her eyes, more overwhelmed and energised than she'd felt in her entire life. There seemed to be no passage of time, but her feet eventually felt the floor beneath them and the glow of a set of doors beckoned as the darkness crawled back to reclaim the space.

Dr Rayne smiled as Nikita emerged through them.

'It's beautiful, isn't it?' the doctor said softly.

Nikita was unable to answer, still in a state of awe.

Dr Rayne guided her to a recovery room, which was filled with glossy light and swathes of gossamer curtains. The room was sparse and cool, but not uncomfortably so, meticulously clean, and vacant of any other occupants. She was given a glass of ice water and shown to a clean white bed. If there were such things as hospitals in Heaven, she imagined they would look like this: otherworldly and calm.

'You have just received a Photoplasmiacelestioral Infusion, but we tend to call it the cosmic satsuma, just to make it easy. Essentially, your body is now running on living starlight. The cosmic satsuma sits where your heart is, feeding energy to your body via the circulatory system. You will still need to breathe, and if cut, you will bleed. But that's not quite a heartbeat in your chest, it's your satsuma pulsing now.'

'So . . . I am a zombie. That runs on starlight?' Nikita said slowly, narrowing her eyes in deep thought.

'Not quite. Unless you have a craving for brains?' Dr Rayne faked a sincere look before cracking a small smile. 'Let me try and explain. You aren't a ghost, an angel, vampire or any other undead being. You fall into a rare category of people, no longer part of the mortal world, but not completely impervious to harm. There is one drawback, you won't be able to bear children or have a normal hormonal cycle. Creating life in the afterlife is impossible by design.'

'So no periods then?' Nikita asked.

'No.'

'Can't say I'm exactly upset by that. I mean, I'm not particularly happy to be dead and all, but I don't see that as a drawback.' Nikita was glad she wouldn't have to spend one week a month in agony, working her way through a ten-pack of Cadbury Freddos in one sitting just to feel human.

'I'm with you on that. Look . . . there's no easy way to tell new recruits that their life is over, you understand.' Dr Rayne spoke wistfully, almost reminiscent of when she might have been told herself. 'It's best to just get the shock out there straightaway. I mean, sometimes, we have people who know they're dying. The terminally ill, those in accidents that result in hours before rescue, some people that have a few moments to fight for their life – the murdered, the drowned. They almost have a head start with acceptance. But you, you had it tough. No time to even comprehend it. Did you have chance to think of anything?'

Nikita exhaled slowly, drawing her knees up to her chest under the thin, heavily starched bedsheet. 'I think . . . I might have just managed to think, *Bastard*, because I didn't have enough time to think, *Oh shit, a bus*. But I guess I will never remember clearly.'

Dr Rayne cracked a smile. 'Well, from experience, *bastard* is certainly a good word to go out on. Strong finish.'

Nikita managed a smile herself. 'I'll remember that if I ever write another article.'

'Well, the good news is, you are nowhere near done with life now. You may have left your old one behind, but there's a whole new start ahead for you.' Dr Rayne folded her arms, a slightly triumphant look on her face.

'You said *recruits*. What do you mean?' Nikita's brow furrowed.

'Ah yes, that brings me on to the next bit. Like I said, you're rare, Nikita. Most people don't come here after death. Most, well, they go to other places. Everything will be explained in due course. You've been hand-picked. All of your hard work, your strength, your struggles, haven't gone to waste. You've been recruited into something utterly amazing.'

'Wait. You're telling me I was killed as part of the selection process *for a job*?' She felt a spike of hot anger rush through her chest.

'No, not at all, you were due to die. But you had been pre-shortlisted.' Dr Rayne stood and smoothed her hair down with one hand. 'I know it's complicated right now, but I don't want to overload you with information just yet.'

'You just told me my heartbeat is now a throbbing galactic orange. I'm not sure it could get much weirder,' Nikita challenged.

'Get some rest, it will all become clear in good time,' Dr Rayne soothed, before leaving the ward.

Nikita gazed emptily at her upturned palms, mesmerised by the fact that they appeared just ever so slightly translucent. Her entire freshly baked body was still setting, and held a glossy, ethereal quality. She waved her hands dreamily in front of the overhead lighting, bemused that the glow could be seen through her palms. She had lost track of time while exploring the visual phenomenon of her somewhat pellucid anatomy, only to find that, gradually, she was becoming more corporeal and opaque. Slowly, her mind nudged its way back into the realms of her untimely death, and more bizarrely, her sudden resurrection. By nature, she was fierce in her pursuit of the truth, so she began to compartmentalise her experience in the same way she would approach a piece of journalistic writing, pulling herself back to the start.

She'd been driving to an exclusive interview, one that would have cemented her position as a respected columnist, but more importantly, give her a lift towards the field of journalism to which she aspired. The pressure had been on, but she'd met it with a mix of strong will and terrible stomach butterflies. She'd made the mistake of wearing a second-hand suit that was uncomfortable, her hands were both clammy and cold on the steering wheel, the stereo playing Meat Loaf just a bit too loud, and the traffic hold-up clouding her ability to remain calm. The taxi had pissed her off, mainly because she'd just gotten over the adrenaline dump of the cyclist hitting her car. Oh, her poor beloved car, the little bean can on wheels hadn't stood a chance. Nor had her face, for that matter. A stupid, petty chain of events had ended her life and the memory of the bus rushed back to her as fast as the collision had happened. The finality of her situation dawned on her. Dead. Deceased. An ex-person. No more late-night shopping, no more career, no more early nights tucked up watching old films. No more Nando's with her best friend. No more Christmas dinners at her mum's house or opening birthday gifts with her family . . .

Hot tears sprang from her newly baked eyes and streamed down her freshly set cheeks. The quiet sobs became ugly, wrenching wails that surged from her body, folding her in half and giving her every reason to wrap herself in a death grip as she trembled with grief for all the small things in life she'd taken for granted, and all the things she would never get to do again. Her stomach hurt with the strain of her sobs and the sheer weight of realisation that she would never be able to say goodbye to anyone she loved.

When no more tears came, and no sound ebbed from her raw throat, she eased herself back on the bed, reverting to blankly staring at the far wall and occasionally checking whether her hands were still imperceptibly see-through. Her grief had not disappeared, it had merely become a numb, heavy stone set in the pit of her gut.

Dr Rayne returned, softly as a ghost, and took up a chair beside Nikita's bed.

'I promise it gets easier,' she said quietly, checking Nikita over for opacity. 'You are nearly set. Get some sleep if you can, your new body still needs everything your old one did, including sleep. I must warn you though, you need to look after your new body as best you can. If you die, there will be no version of afterlife for you, you will just cease to exist. You are a solid soul now, there's nothing else that can float off into a different state of being.'

'Well, that's comforting.' Nikita didn't like the concept of becoming a great big nothing.

'You'll be just fine. Before you know it, you will be collected for your induction.' The doctor pressed the cold chest piece of her stethoscope to Nikita's sternum, hearing the new cosmic heartbeat pulsing strongly. She nodded to herself before standing to leave.

'Are there no others?' Nikita said quietly, her eyes sweeping the empty room as the doctor was leaving.

'Not today. Try to sleep if you can,' Dr Rayne repeated, leaving the swinging doors rocking on their hinges in her wake.

3

Two Out of Three Ain't Bad

OUGHLY TWENTY-SEVEN-AND-A-HALF HOURS SINCE HER death, Nikita Wolf sat timidly on the edge of a hard plastic chair in a blank office space, dressed in the plain grey tracksuit she'd been given upon leaving the hospital, her fire-red hair pulled limply back in a scrunchie. She faced a thin man who was poring over a stack of notes. He was dressed in a mottled brown three-piece suit with a tired-looking red bow tie and introduced himself as Jerry Benson. A woman entered the room in a bold leopard-print jacket and a huge halo of blonde curls.

'Nikita!' The woman smiled warmly underneath her brightly coloured makeup. 'I'm popping in briefly to say hello. I'm Kendra and I'm the boss here, so if you need anything my office is upstairs.'

Nikita barely had a chance to finish saying, *Nice to meet you,* before Kendra excused herself with a clattering of her kitten heels on the laminate floor, claiming she had more urgent things to be seeing to. Nikita turned to face Jerry once more.

'Right, Ms Wolf. I'm just here to go through the legal side of your contract.' The drone of his voice matched the blandness of the room. 'You died yesterday morning due to a fatal car accident involving a bus, am I right?'

Still shaken and confused, she nodded.

'You've had your initial revival and explanation.' He lowered his glasses and eyed her over the rims. 'Though it seems you haven't yet fully reached acceptance. Don't worry, that's quite normal.'

He flicked through more pages, a long sigh issuing from his thin lips. 'You were a gossip journalist, writing for a publication called *The Eventmaster*, a contemporary news publication on all upcoming red-carpet events and their coverage, but you were heading for an interview for *Dark Matter*, which covers everything from true crime to crop circles. Why the change?'

'I was moving into investigative journalism and I needed experience in research topics. I wanted to write about more serious news,' Nikita answered softly.

He flipped further into the notes.

'You were never in love,' he stated.

'Yes, I have been, once,' she argued, confused. 'His name was Toby.'

'That wasn't a question, Ms Wolf. It was a statement of fact.'

'What is all of this? One minute I am in a hospital, the next I am sat in a review of my life. Why is any of this relevant?' She grew increasingly frustrated. 'If this is some kind of after-life, why am I *here*?'

Jerry ignored her outburst. 'It's not the reanimator's job to explain the recruitment, your new employment will commence with the Apollo Division this afternoon. You will be placed on full pay for a trial period. Once your training is completed you will be given your full licence and operative status. You have been secured new accommodation and your recoverable personal effects will be transported to the new address within seven business days. Your contract is here ...' He pulled a thick booklet from his desk drawer and dropped it on the desk in front of her. 'Once you have read the contract you will need to sign in the places marked by the cross and then your training will commence.'

'I'm not signing this! I don't even know what this is for, or what the Apollo Division *is*. This is bullshit.' Hot angry tears streaked down her face as she stood up to leave.

'Ms Wolf, please take a seat.' The droning man waited for her to calm down. 'All of your questions will be answered.'

She paced for a while before complying. 'And if I don't sign this? Then what?'

'Ms Wolf, you have been selected for this role and the other option should you decline is, well, I have a duty to show you.' He rose from his chair in the manner that a daisy would slowly open to the morning sun and pulled down a screen on the wall, before firing up a projector unit.

For the sheer volume of resources available at the agency, there were some sticking points which left several things far behind, approximately thirty years behind, much like the old whirring projector and its yellowed screen. It wasn't a *lack* of access to technology, it was more for comfort, as some of the agents were in excess of three hundred years old and weren't so fond of sudden modernisations. Even those who had come to terms with their reincarnation and indoctrination into a supernatural corporate body were often wary of the fandangled new officer stapler. Things took time to be integrated. There was almost an internal riot when laptops were voted in over the old ribbon typewriters. But everyone had to agree that a laptop is far easier to work on while sat on the Piccadilly line.

'Unselected people go to the Oblivion Fields.' He showed a slide of a vacant place, with otherworldly plants that looked parched, gripping loosely to the dry soil. 'It is neither day nor night, and the soul wanders the plains until they are judged. It can be many hundreds of years before this happens as processing time has increased significantly in the last few hundred years ... population has gone crazy, you see. From there, you will be placed in one of three locations, depending on how you lived your mortal life.'

He showed a sequence of slides, depicting a natural paradise of lush plants, blue oceans and gleeful people lounging in colourful gardens surrounded by bright butterflies and plentiful wildlife. Exquisite architecture rose from the forests, of gilded castles with cloud-topped turrets, rainbow walkways and soft floating lanterns in the sky. 'This is a snapshot of the most heavenly of places. Well, I suppose one might refer to it as Heaven, but the official name is Arcadia. Naturally, there is more to it: bookshops, flying horses, talking pixies, that sort of thing. It's all tailored to your personal view of Heaven. But they have every flavour of ice cream you could ever want,' the man explained, quickly skipping to the next set of slides.

It featured a bland landscape, neither ugly nor beautiful, filled with small, neat homes and plain landscaping, pleasant suburban greenery and everyday-looking folk. 'This is the Land of Mediocrity, where your average person goes. Sure, it's a comfortable afterlife, missing the element of sheer luxury and magic ... and it does have its own ice-cream van. But the only flavour is vanilla. You see where I am going with this?'

Nikita nodded slowly in comprehension.

He clicked the button to change the slides, landing on a chaotic and hellish nightscape of unknown creatures and people screaming in terror. 'Hell isn't quite like this; they were just late to the promotional print day, so we had to take a picture out of a library book. It's not all fire and brimstone and red devils or anything. They also have an ice-cream van, but they are always out of waffle cones and the only flavour is mint-choc-chip. No flakes ...' The man seemed lost in his own thoughts, shaking his head sadly. 'Never any flakes.' He snapped back to reality and clicked through a few more slides. 'Again, the official name for this place is Erebus ... Oh, this one is quite accurate: they do have a pit of boiling sludge, but the health and safety inspectors won't let you swim in it unless you have watched a long, and I mean *long*, instructional safety video. Believe me, there's a lot more health and safety policies in Hell than you might think. Lots of red tape and bureaucracy.'

When he switched off the projector, Nikita stared blank-faced at the empty screen.

'So that's it, years of endless wandering then finally a place-ment at one of those three?' she finally asked.

'Or this.' He waved the contract. 'Good pay, subsidised lodgings, free Oyster card.'

She eyed him suspiciously.

'Your own desk, flexible working pattern, twenty-five days holiday a year. And upon voluntary retirement you are automat-ically promoted to the best the afterlife can give you, provided you complete a minimum of two hundred years of good service.'

'So that's the motivation, is it? Work for two hundred years to guarantee a spot in Arcadia, or take my chances with judgement?'

'That's the bottom line. But consider this, Ms Wolf, those recruited into the agency aren't done with life yet. And most would not make it to Arcadia.' He gave what she thought was a slow wink, but he didn't pull it off well. 'Let me give you an overview of what we do here.

'Apollo agents are responsible for making the right people fall in love. Cupids, if you may. We also have Hades agents, known as Ghosters, though throughout history they have been referred to as Grim Reapers. They ensure that souls leave the body when a person dies.'

He explained that Nemesis agents were responsible for dishing out vengeance to rebalance the level of justice in the world. Lastly, there were Fortuna agents, who dealt out good and bad luck to people who were destined to receive it.

'I'm no expert here, but there's a lot of muddling of classic mythology in all this, any reason for that? Were the Greeks and Romans kinda right with all the gods and stuff?' Nikita folded her arms, still not fully convinced.

Jerry sighed a deep, exasperated sigh. 'The agency existed long before the myths of those civilisations were born. Believe it or not, the Greeks and Romans used our division names and created deities out of them. Back when agents were a bit too open with telling mortals what we got up to. Had people worshipping us back then. Of course, the Apollo Division went through three names, starting with Eros, then Cupid and then Apollo as it was a little more obscure in the modern world and not so easily mistaken for a dating site. Though sadly more people associate it with space than its real origin nowadays.'

'So I'm not going to be an astronaut then? That's a shame.' Nikita almost cracked a smile.

'No, you will be a certified Cupid,' Jerry replied blandly.

'Oh god, do I have to wear a nappy?' she said, mortified.

'No, no, not at all. Unless that's something you're into. We don't judge, just don't wear it on assignments.' He gave her a sideways glance. 'It's my duty to explain to you about agents of Chaos also. In the world that we live in, Fates control destiny. However, there is another realm: Chaos. For ever pitted against the Fates, the Chaos agents would love nothing more than to rule our world. But don't worry, they are kept in check, relegated to delaying trains and jamming office printers – anything that throws off the smooth running of life. Without them, life would get boring, but we don't actually *interact* with them. They are truly immortal and a pain in the arse. They were never human, you see; they were created at the start of the universe, when the Great Cosmic Sneeze happened.'

'The Big Bang, don't you mean?' She raised her eyebrow, unsure if her GCSE in physics meant anything at all at this stage.

'No . . . it was definitely a sneeze. There's some big old creature out there sneezing out galaxies every few years. I think it's one of the Fates' pets,' he said dryly.

'So . . . what do I do if I see one of these Chaos agent demon entity things?'

'They aren't so much demons, in the sense of the word, but not far off. If they had full power in our world, then maybe, yes, demons would be an appropriate term. You won't have to worry though. They can't access this world in the real form, and you wouldn't want to see them if they did. Only their reflection is allowed through, as it's almost powerless, like a shadow, and they manifest in ways unseen to the mortal eye. Occasionally they can possess pigeons or the like. Soulless creatures.'

'Pigeons?' Nikita was starting to wonder if the man had been left in his office too long.

'Oh yes, though personally I think pigeons are actually robots. Makes sense right? No creature's got any business bobbing its neck like that.' He looked into the distance, transfixed, slowly and subconsciously imitating the bobbing neck of a pigeon. He stopped himself and turned his attention back to her.

'So, what do you say then?' He nodded at the contract.

Slightly concerned, Nikita scribbled her name on the contract and slid it back towards him. 'Either this is the weirdest dream I have ever had, or I have a lot to learn. But if I've got to choose, being a Cupid sounds a lot better than a whole lot of nothingness. Or mint-choc-chip ice cream every day.'

'Welcome on board, Trainee Agent Wolf.' His solemn face raised a wan smile. 'Here is everything you need for the moment.' He handed her the promised Oyster card, an agency mobile phone and a small silver ear cuff. 'Pop that on your ear. It will be uploaded with your wages at the end of every month and it contains your new agency ID.'

She did as she was told, and the ear cuff fitted itself tight to her right ear. She turned the phone over in her hand, taking a moment to find the on switch.

'All the relevant office numbers will be pre-programmed into the phone, but feel free to use it as your own. You're welcome to buy your own elsewhere if you prefer, but this will be the number the office calls you on.

'Oh, before I forget.' He passed her a thick envelope. 'In here is your fake ID if you ever need it. It's rare but sometimes you have no choice but to pass as a mortal. It's linked to your new bank account. Speaking of which, there's also a small starting allowance in pounds sterling, to get sandwiches and stuff. Don't spend it all at once. Your Apollo wages are paid in novas, the universal currency for agency staff, and you will only have the opportunity to earn mortal money once you have completed your basic training, so make that last.'

Nikita peered into the envelope at the notes and counted approximately £120.

'Head on up to the second floor. You're expected.' He gestured for her to leave.

'Wait, is it all Apollo here then? Or are there Grim Reapers wandering about up there? Because I'm really not ready for that.'

'No, it's only Apollo here. Hades are over at Highgate, Fortuna in Kensington and Nemesis are near Southwark Crown Court. So you can relax.' Once again he nodded towards the door.

4

Cupid's Dead

CASEY WAS SIPPING TEA WHEN the confused red-haired woman walked in, clutching a folder of paperwork. He stood and offered his hand. 'Hello, Nikita.'

Her lip trembled, but she forced a weak smile.

'It's all a little overwhelming, isn't it? Don't you worry, we'll look after you,' he said softly. She shook his hand.

'I'm Casey Hart. And this is Erron Grover.'

Erron nodded vaguely in acknowledgement. He was fiddling with his own agency ear cuff and staring off into space.

'So, what happens now? I don't really understand any of this.' She glanced down at her folder.

'It'll take time. It always takes time. How about a drink?'

Nikita nodded and was offered a seat at a vacant desk as Erron strolled away to make her beverage.

'Let me break this down.' Casey pulled up a chair next to her. 'The legal induction and processing team don't answer questions very well.'

'I got that impression.' Nikita rolled her eyes.

'It's all corporate bullshit,' Erron said, as he arrived back and held a cup of coffee out to her.

'Well, they have their processes, Erron,' Casey said calmly. 'I will start at the beginning then. You have found out that your former life has … expired. As has everyone's who works for this organisation. You have been specially selected to be offered this role based on a long list of criteria that you have met during your former life, of which you would not have been aware. I promise you, it is a wonderful opportunity.' Casey gripped her shoulder gently, his angelic smile distracting her from the reeling thoughts tumbling over one another in her mind. 'Before I continue, do you have any outstanding questions? I will answer them straightaway.'

'OK, only about a million, but I suppose let me start with, if I am dead but wandering around, what if I bump into someone I know?'

'They won't recognise you; you will just be a memory of a person that they can't quite place. It's a clever illusion.'

Hot tears burned behind her eyes at the realisation she wouldn't be seeing her family or friends ever again, or at least, they wouldn't know if they ever crossed paths. 'So I'm walking round dead, and my mum would just pass me by as if I was nothing?' A tear overspilled and rolled down her cheek.

Casey squeezed her hand. 'That part never gets any easier, not until they join the afterlife anyhow. But be comforted that you'll be reunited again sometime far in the future. And you aren't wandering round dead. You're in limbo.'

She mulled it over for a few minutes, realising everything she thought she knew about death was fiction, and things weren't anywhere near as final as she had been led to believe.

The idea of being reunited with her loved ones gave her immense comfort and set her mind at rest. She dried her eyes on her sleeve and composed herself.

'Sorry, you said I was in limbo?'

'Yes. Your replicated body behaves in a similar way to your old one. You have a new circulatory system—'

'A cosmic satsuma,' she cut in.

'Well, I can explain how that works—' Casey began, but Nikita shook her head.

'Actually, do you mind if we change the subject? I'm struggling to take all this in right now.' She pressed her fingertips to her temples and squeezed her eyes shut.

'Sure,' he said softly. 'You know what, I had forgotten how radiant new recruits look, you are practically glowing.'

She blushed, glancing down at her hands and noticing that there was a definite unnatural radiance to her skin. She had noticed a feverish warmth taking over her and now her interest in finding out what was going on was being overshadowed by an intoxicating feeling she couldn't quite place. Of all the tumbling thoughts regarding her sudden transition into the afterlife rushing through her mind it clarified long enough for her to ask what would become of her worldly possessions left behind in her grotty flat.

'Don't worry, the Ghosters will have had their team in your flat before you even died,' Erron added.

'That's the Grim Reaper people, right?' She recalled from her earlier conversation with the recruitment guy.

'Erron, please ...' Casey held his hand up with indignation.

'Yeah, those are the ones. Hades Division, the people responsible for ending your life,' Erron replied bluntly.

'So, are you saying I was murdered?' Nikita took a long slug of the coffee and steadied herself.

'No. Your name appeared on an assignment card in their office. The card was passed to an agent, who found you and released your soul when the Fates cut your thread. If you want to believe in that,' Erron explained. 'They just do their job, just like we do. It was your time.'

'And you are Cupids, right?'

Casey took hold of her hands. 'Yes, unlike the Ghosters, here in the Apollo Division, we are the agents of love. We are responsible for the most beautiful of human emotions and making sure the right people find it.' He smiled dreamily as if recollecting every time he had joined two hearts together.

'What this sentimental bugger is saying is that we go out, shoot people with sparkly arrows and wait for them to fall in love. So, you know, I hope you like soppy romance and all.' Erron rolled his eyes. 'Oh, a word of warning. Over the next few hours, you'll start to experience an unnatural amount of hormone imbalances that relate to increases of ... things and ... stuff ...'

She gave him a puzzled expression.

Casey cleared his throat. 'Joining this division, you have suddenly been immersed in significant levels of dopamine, norepinephrine, oxytocin, serotonin and vasopressin and a couple of others. All the key elements for generating love, lust, attraction and attachment. It settles after a while, but don't be surprised if you start to ... erm ... develop a whole host of feelings for a whole host of people for maybe no reason at all. Don't beat yourself up over it, as the saying goes. It will settle soon; it usually lasts around twenty-four hours before you are back to normal.'

'They call it the Apollo Flush,' Erron said dismissively. 'You're gonna love it ... and hate it.' He gulped the remainder of his own stale coffee and made a tortured expression at the bitter taste. 'But it sure beats mint-choc-chip ice cream.'

'OK, what is with the ice cream?' she asked. 'Is that all anyone cares about?'

Erron snorted in laughter. 'Well, not entirely, but dear old Jerry in recruitment seems to think it's a key element. He comes up here once a year to give a talk on professional good practice, and ice cream seems to be a big motivator to him, so he assumes it goes for everyone. I reckon he must have been an ice-cream man in his for—'

Casey interrupted. 'The Apollo Flush will take effect very soon, so don't panic if you start to feel a bit giddy. I promise it settles. But its function is to help you with your job. You see, we often need people to trust us, so it's our innate ability to disarm them with an aura of natural charm, almost infatuation at times. It starts with what feels like a fever building, and a mental haze.'

Nikita had already noticed the feverish warmth, and the hazy thoughts, like she had been enveloped in a warm dreamy state, which might explain why she was so ready to accept just about anything she was told about her afterlife.

'Well, I'm not finding anyone ridiculously irresistible yet,' she lied, her thoughts had been rapidly morphing from the shock of her death, to desperately trying to stop wondering what Erron looked like naked, or whether Casey was a good kisser. It was a first for her, as she wasn't the type to let carnal desire get in the way of her logic. 'I just want to know who killed me,' she added quickly.

'The bus driver,' Erron replied bluntly.

'No, who took my soul. I want to know. Who was it?'

'It doesn't work like that. Besides, you *are* your soul, baked in a pressure cooker and solidified. Your body is in a morgue somewhere. The Ghosters just give you the touch of death.'

'Nikita, it would do you no good to know who helped you pass over,' Casey said softly. 'Those agents don't work out of this building, and they don't share their cases with anyone unless absolutely necessary.'

'OK. I guess some mysteries are best left buried,' she conceded. 'No pun intended.'

Erron exhaled audibly. 'Nobody really remembers who took their life. They are instantly forgettable. It would have been someone you saw during the day. Someone that brushed past you on the Underground, someone that handed you something you dropped, shook your hand in greeting. You were just a name and a time of death to them. But they do like to untie your soul from your body as close to your death as possible so they were likely someone you saw just before you died.'

'How many are there?' she whispered, racking her brain in an attempt to remember who she'd seen just before the bus hit her, but the details were foggy.

'In our district alone? Around two hundred and forty-five full-time agents, twenty or so special case operatives and a district manager.'

'They must be busy.'

'Well, yes, much busier than the rest of us,' Casey began. 'Let me explain. There are things in our world called fixed points. Not everyone that falls in love, gets lucky in life or receives justice needs to have an agent to orchestrate that. There are fixed points in time that need to be adhered to, certain decisions and situations that must happen for the future to progress how it is designed to. Unfortunately, death is always a fixed point, and with every death, a Hades agent gets involved. All fixed points have to be undertaken or dreadful consequences can result.'

'What if there's something awful like a bombing? How do they have enough staff to take all those souls?' Nikita questioned.

'They have something the rest of us don't,' Casey explained. 'They get blind cards, assignment cards with no name on them. They either stay blank, allowing the Ghoster to reap souls from whoever they are closest to, or sometimes a name appears if there is an agent unexpectantly caught in the crossfire. Essentially, agents don't have an end date, but we still have a soul – well, we *are* a soul ... so if something very unfortunate happens to us, the Reapers still have a job to do.'

Nikita sighed and slumped her shoulders, already losing track of all the information she'd had dumped on her. 'They did warn me about that. I don't like the idea of dying all over again.'

'Yes, but let's not dwell on that right now.' Casey squeezed her shoulder gently. 'What name did they give you for your fake ID?'

Glad to change the subject, she rummaged in the envelope and pulled out a small leather wallet with a fake driving licence and various documents to match. The photo looked like her, but slightly off. She read the name on the card. 'Oh ... Sasha Lovell. That's not terrible. What are yours?'

'Mine is Milo Casen,' Casey replied. 'And Erron's is Alexander Kyler.'

'Just Alex. Don't make it sound too fancy,' Erron grumbled.

'Try and remember it, as it'll come in handy when you need to interact with mortals. But if you don't need formal ID, just make up any old name, whatever feels easier. I like to mix it up a bit,' Casey explained.

'I tell you what,' Erron said. 'How about after our tasks this afternoon, we take you to Nightjar and you can ask all the questions you need? It's a jazz bar, great cocktails.' He got up and stretched.

'Is that wise?' Casey whispered, throwing him a look of contempt.

'Sure. We hang out there anyway. Give the kid a chance to grieve her own death. Lots of agents go there. It'll do her good to meet people from other divisions, loosen up a bit.'

Nikita raised an eyebrow to suggest she was well aware she was being discussed as if she wasn't even there. 'I'd like that.'

Casey smiled warily. 'Of course, of course.'

'So do all the divisions hang out together then? Or are we kept separate?'

'There aren't many formal social mixers as such, but we do tend to get to know some people from the other divisions. It's good to network, and a lot of us hang around the same establishments around the city for recreational purposes, if you will. You are allowed to enjoy your time off. It's not that strict,' Erron explained. 'Just be a bit discerning who you make friends with.'

'I feel like there's a story behind that warning,' Nikita said.

'Yes, there's one Hades agent that keeps pestering Erron here. She's got a huge crush on him.' Casey rolled his eyes. 'She latches on to us if she sees us out anywhere.'

'Let's show you your kit, shall we?' Erron bluntly changed the subject and walked off, knowing they would follow.

He led them down to the ground floor and through a swing door at the far end from the entrance into a vast locker room, lined with full-length lockers in various colours, each decorated in such a way that showed their owner's personality, or their colleagues' satirical perception of them. Changing rooms stood to the left for anyone who needed them. A plain blue locker with a ticket stuck to it stood ajar in the fifth row. Erron nodded his head towards it and leant on the locker opposite.

Her curiosity piquing, the new trainee pulled open the door and found a neatly stacked pile of equipment.

'Field boots, full field kit, quiver, basic training recurve take-down bow, equipment maintenance bag, and a whole bunch of other things the agency deem necessary to issue,' Erron said. 'You won't need any of it just yet. Apart from maybe this, because you'll need to take some notes.' He pulled out a standard office notebook from her locker shelf and a pack of pens and handed them to her.

She thanked him, turning her attention back to the array of equipment, which seemed a lot more special ops than the cute image of Cupids found on Valentine's cards.

Contrary to popular belief, Cupids generally didn't float around wearing oversized nappies with matching rosy cheeks. The Apollo agents came from all walks of life but, to date, none were openly known to frequent the adult baby scene, or to have a penchant for Hallmark clichés. They were, however, expected to carry a bow, as it was the easiest way they could complete assignments. The agency had trialled other methods, such as the Pea Shooter of Love (didn't have much range and one agent choked from improper use), the Musket of Infatuation (left an awful ringing in the ears and could easily startle local wildlife) and the Rifle of Adoration (had a terrible tendency to hit too hard and knock people off their feet . . . into rivers and in front of buses).

'Who pays for all of this?' Nikita questioned, inspecting some of the kit.

'The Fates. But, not in the same way our money works. These things are just . . . created.' Erron scratched his head.

The Fates, entities that were far superior to any agent of any division on Earth, and speculated on in many different mythologies throughout history, remained mysterious, even to those who undertook their bidding. Casey liked to believe the Fates were a glamorised version, like the Moirai of ancient Greek lore, a heavenly sisterhood of goddesses who spun the threads of human destiny while lounging in the clouds listening to the harp. Erron thought more of them as a bureaucratic rank of managers, idling away their time in conference calls, bickering over the last Bourbon biscuit and taking forever and a day to reach a corporate decision over their assignments, but not before discussing the annual executive pay rise. There was an element of truth in both ideas, but a tiny, grain-sized element that was far flung from the accuracy of the reality.

'We hitting the Tube for this Farringdon job?' Erron checked his watch. 'Gives us a bit of time to kill.'

Casey rolled his eyes. 'If we *must*.'

'Young lady hasn't got her wings yet.'

'Wings, as in real wings, or is that a euphemism for something?' Nikita asked cautiously, a tiny seed of hope growing in her that she heard that currently.

'Good things come to those who wait. But yes, real wings.' Erron smiled.

'Maybe we could give her the tour first?' Casey suggested, pointing upwards.

Erron considered it. 'Sure, we've got a few hours, right?'

'The tour?' Nikita asked.

Erron's eyes widened with the first bit of enthusiasm he'd had since she'd met him. 'We're going to introduce you to the agency, in the best way we can. We're going to Elysion.'

Nikita followed them out of the locker room, having closed her locker and pocketed the key. She had decided she already liked them both, even though she didn't have a lot of choice about who to make friends with on her first day. The well-spoken one seemed displaced from another era, where men would have bowed to a lady and settled their differences with pistols at dawn. The other one, from the scar on his cheek and rough-around-the-edges demeanour, seemed the type to never start a fight but always finish one. He was the kind of good-bad boy that she would have tripped over herself to get to know in her teen years. But from the primal heat of the Apollo Flush that was starting to rage through her body, she was pretty convinced she could indulge in the company of almost anyone right now provided there was plenty of physical activity involved.

She gave her thoughts a cold shower and tried to focus on all the questions she originally had tumbling around. The whole situation felt so bizarre and she was worrying that she'd accepted it all far too readily, but something told her it wasn't a dream her mind had conjured up following a night of eating too many Wotsits and watching reruns of *Round the Twist*.

5

Fly Me to the Moon

'**Y**OU'VE GOT TO BE KIDDING,' Nikita muttered as they approached an ice-cream van parked up in a side street in Greenwich. A pale, droopy-faced man was slumped at the window, looking bored.

'OK, so there is a theme here,' Erron admitted.

'Three 99 Flakes, please. Hold the cones.' Casey leant in close to order.

The bored man nodded, moved to the back of the van and opened the rear door, waving them inside. Dutifully, Nikita followed the two agents into the cramped rear of the ice-cream van. Casey, being over six feet tall, had to crouch down in the small space.

'I wish these things weren't so cramped,' he complained, knocking his head on an overhead storage shelf.

'Well, I think they're just right.' Erron grinned wryly, for once enjoying being five foot five. He nudged Casey playfully in the ribs.

'Which zone?' The ice-cream man interrupted, pulling down a shutter over the serving window.

'Crater Pass will do,' Erron replied. The man nodded again and pressed a button on a menu of ice-cream flavours three times. 'It's all yours.'

'Ta.' Erron opened up a hidden door on the Mr Whippy machine to reveal a swirling vortex with all the colours of the Northern Lights undulating within it. Turning to Nikita, he gestured to the chasm of space. 'Ladies first.'

Her jaw dropped at the sight of the impossible portal leading to god-knows-where. Before she could protest, Casey had taken her by the hand and pulled her through, with Erron hot on their tail. For a few seconds, she was accelerated to a speed where she felt like she might disintegrate down to an atomic level, with the sort of lurching sensation that comes from tipping over the edge of a roller coaster when your stomach tries to high-five your brain. Before she could take a breath, they came to a sudden stop, splashing down in what seemed to be a glittering lagoon of luminescence.

She took a moment to recover, before obediently following the other two as they climbed glossy marble steps out of the lagoon.

'What ... What was *that?*' she gasped, wide-eyed. 'And how are we *dry?*'

'It's the only way to access Elysion. And it isn't water, it's a pool of celestial energy.' Casey helped her up the steps as her legs wobbled beneath her. 'You'll soon get used to it; the first time is always a bit rough.'

She smiled, the warmth of his hand around her arm a comforting reminder that basic human kindness stretched beyond the grave. But her raging Apollo Flush hormones soon tainted any sense of platonic comfort and she gently shook him off.

The steps led up onto a large marble plateau. A soothing purplish glow hung in the air and low lamps of soft blue light lined the walkways. Casey guided her towards a spiral staircase that led to a pillared building, not unlike the Acropolis of ancient Greece, swathed in beautiful, ethereal vines that emanated their own soft glow.

'Close your eyes,' Casey whispered and took both her hands. He slowly steered her up the stairs and out to the far edge of the building until they leant up against an ornate balustrade. 'OK, you can look now.'

Tentatively, she opened her eyes, her breath catching in her throat at the view that met her. Sweeping below them was a magnificent metropolis of otherworldly buildings. They stretched upwards with gilded rooftops, interspaced with sparkling Venetian-style waterways and luminescent willow trees draping into softly lit streets. Fireflies danced in the air against the warm glow of thousands of windows, rich drapes of colourful fabric overhung doorways and the inviting sound of upbeat music rose up from a few streets away. Casey nudged her gently and gestured for her to look over the adjacent balustrade.

'Oh jeez,' she whispered. 'Is that Earth? We're not on Earth?'

'Elysion is on the moon. Well, the moon was actually made to give the agency some distance from the mortal world,' Erron explained. 'This place has everything you need. International conferences, shopping, training areas, ceremonies, restaurants, leisure facilities, soul visiting, nostalgia rooms. The works.'

Nikita couldn't take her eyes off the sight of the Earth aglow in the distance, surrounded by the remote glint of stars. 'Wait, what about ... like the moon landing?'

'It never happened . . . filmed in a studio. The Fates won't let humans reach the moon, we actually have our own contingent agents at every space station in the world, meddling with any attempt. They can go to space, but the moon is off limits.'

Nikita's knowledge of history was being rewritten faster than she could absorb the information.

'It might be easiest to explain it all this way.' Erron leant over the wall casually, flicking open his lighter and wedging a cigarette between his teeth. 'Being human is the start of a mass multiplayer game. Your character is new, easily hurt or killed, and it takes time to gain experience. But if you die and become an agent, you level up. You get to access new areas, get a whole host of new abilities . . . but there's still one more level above us, complete immortality. You just haven't unlocked that yet.' He grinned, puffing smoke out of his nose like a short, Cockney dragon.

'So, what extra powers do I get then?' She couldn't take her eyes off the city, encased in an immense shimmering dome that went from one crater edge to another.

'There are a few things, but the main thing is that you can charm people with your presence, as a result of the Apollo Flush. People will open up to you, tell you their innermost thoughts, trust you implicitly,' Casey explained.

'And have you ever wanted to fly?' Erron added.

She looked at him wide-eyed and nodded. He opened his wings and stretched them out, moving them slowly back and forth. 'You'll get wings, once you're ready. It's the quickest way to travel, and a mark of a full agent. Plus, they are invisible to mortals.'

'Oh wow!' Nikita gasped. 'You really weren't kidding about the wings.' She reached out tentatively to touch them, glancing at him to see if it was OK to do so. When given the green light, she cautiously ran her fingers over one of the swan-white feathers, which was over a foot long and in every way the same texture as a bird's.

'Shall we?' Casey gestured to a gap in the balustrade pointing towards the city, where a bundle of umbrellas stood in a brass urn.

The new agent followed them to the gap where a sheer drop below made her feel giddy once more. Casey passed her a purple umbrella and opened one for himself.

'Take my hand. It's much easier than you think; gravity isn't all that out here.' He stepped up to the edge, and once she'd popped the umbrella up, he pulled her off the side.

Nikita let out a scream as her feet dangled into nothingness but was pleasantly surprised when the umbrella sailed gently downwards and towards the city, as though it knew exactly where it was going. They landed with a soft bump in a busy street, right outside a croissant shop.

'You always land here.' Erron rolled his eyes as he dropped down next to them. 'We haven't got time for pastries. This is a whistle-stop tour, remember?'

Casey fought back the disappointment of being denied an Elysion croissant but conceded.

As they walked briskly through the city streets, aided by the bounding lightness from the low gravity, Nikita was overwhelmed by the beauty and diversity of the place, as though all the cultures of humankind had their best creativity and design on display. They passed by hundreds of agents, all happily bobbing about with everyday tasks. The atmosphere was an uplifting medley of music and light, more lively and cheerful than any human city on Earth. Down some streets ran the Venetian-style canals she'd noticed before, whereupon some agents were travelling in style sat atop pedal boats designed to look like graceful and glittering swans. Nikita was drawn to the faces of people she passed, the Apollo Flush taking over her completely as she was spoilt for choice with people that she was intensely attracted to, each of them having a unique set of features she suddenly found irresistible.

'Nikita, are you with us?' Erron waved a hand in front of her face as she smiled alluringly at every passer-by.

'Sorry!' She blushed and cast her gaze to the floor.

The enticing aromas of fresh coffee, hot coriander bread and lively jambalaya spices wafted from a corner restaurant selling a mixed menu of world foods. There was so much to take in as Casey rushed through an explanation of some of the stranger places that could be found, such as the nostalgia rooms, where you paid to revisit your own childhood memories in a sophisticated virtual reality style experience. Next door to that was the Hall of Unconscious Stories, where you could pay to live out your favourite nightly dreams, all preserved perfectly in the great cosmic web of energy downloaded during your soul regrowth. He explained that, in Elysion, you could automatically understand any language that anyone spoke owing to the abundance of cosmic energy connecting everyone on that plane, but that unfortunately didn't apply on Earth.

Nikita was most enthralled by the Valley of Flavours, a short walk-through of beautiful glowing willow trees, within which drifted bubbles of flavour that could be sampled by catching them in one's mouth. She managed to catch a strawberry cheesecake, a chocolate fudge brownie and a Welsh rarebit before they reached the end of the path and was thoroughly pleased with herself. She was pleasantly surprised that they weren't all ice-cream flavours for a change.

It wasn't long before they had to leave, and on the way back through the streets, Casey explained the currency in more detail. 'You get novas to pay for everything up here. It's basically agency money. You can get most of what you need, but there will be things you might want back on Earth and you'll need to pick up shifts in the Apollo call centre to earn old money, or pounds sterling for us. But you'll be shown that side of things later in your training.'

'OK got it. Making people fall in love gives me moon money. Answering calls gets me a Burger King.' She couldn't help but chuckle.

'You're getting it.' Erron nudged her playfully.

Erron checked his watch as they neared a shopfront that claimed to sell ice cream. 'We're getting close to time so let's take the portal back from here. No time to get back to the main entrance.' Erron jumped behind the counter and pressed three buttons on the wall to unlock a portal door then entered a destination on a screen next to it. A green light blinked above the door once the destination had been set, and Erron gestured for Nikita and Casey to hurry up and jump through. Nikita wasn't looking forward to the lurching sensation but had no choice, knowing she couldn't stay on the moon for the rest of eternity, no matter how good the bubbles tasted.

6

Passengers

THE JANUARY COLD STILL SWEPT the streets, ruffling discarded papers and reddening the faces of city folk as they bustled about their business. The portal had taken them back to the same ice-cream van in Greenwich and they made their way to the nearest Tube station, North Greenwich, where they took the Jubilee line to London Bridge and then hopped on the Northern line to Bank station. The buzz of the city grew louder and more hurried as people dashed about their daily tasks, filtering through the ticket barriers and jostling for prime position on the platforms. It was approaching rush hour and it was uncomfortably hot and crowded. Casey wrinkled his nose at the smell of the crowded tunnels and made a concerted effort not to touch anything as they boarded the first train that pulled up.

They had over forty minutes to spare, so instead of switching lines again, Erron suggested they get some fresh air and walk the rest of the way, influenced by the multitude of displeased looks Casey had been subtly displaying. They ended up at Bank station and decided to walk from there, at which point an occasional flutter of snow was on the breeze. Erron paused outside a small café that promised the best sandwiches in London.

'Case, you got much in the way of old money on you?' he asked, rifling through his pockets for change. 'I'd kill for a cheese toastie right now.' He pulled out a couple of pound coins and half a pack of Rolos.

Casey waved Erron's offering away. 'Keep your change. I'll get us all a sandwich.'

'I'll save you my last Rolo then.' Erron pocketed his change and as he opened the café door, a whoosh of warmth and the smell of cooking greeted them eagerly. The three huddled on stools at the tall counter by the window, watching the crowds shuffle by outside in the cold, the sky already dark from the early winter sunset.

A young blonde waitress sidled up to take their order, a bored look on her face. After she'd gone, Casey asked Nikita how she was feeling.

'It all still feels like some bizarre dream. I keep thinking any minute I will wake up in hospital and be told I was sleep-talking about going to the moon in an ice-cream van.' She cast her eyes to the floor, part of her hoping that maybe it was all a dream, and that she would go back to her old life and see her family again. Pangs of grief lay like stones in her gut, despite her now knowing death was just a new adventure. 'I mean, if it is real, at least I know there is an afterlife, and maybe I will see everyone again one day,' she added, deep in thought.

'Like I said earlier, you will get to see your loved ones again. It's all just a matter of time,' Casey said softly. 'It's a real gift to know that death is not the end, and that everyone gets reunited eventually.'

Erron snorted. 'Well, that depends where they end up.'

'It doesn't matter. Those of us that do our time in the agency get to retire in Arcadia. And that means we get an access-all-areas portal pass to visit loved ones in the other places. Twice a year in fact.' Casey folded his arms triumphantly.

'What if all my family go to the Land of Mediocrity and I'm stuck on my own in this Arcadia place?' Nikita asked. 'Doesn't sound that good at all.'

'You can choose to join them, if you don't mind giving up your pass. Or so I've heard,' Erron said. 'But that's ages away yet. Don't start planning for retirement on your first day.'

'So is Arcadia even better than Elysion then?' Nikita couldn't imagine going anywhere more beautiful than the city on the moon.

'I haven't been so can't say. But once you're there, you don't have to fanny about making people fall in love, and you don't have to pull double shifts in a call centre selling god knows what to earn human currency either. Essentially, Arcadia is like Elysion but with free time and loved ones and hobbies and not having to worry about keeping your cosmically charged meat-sack safe from harm.'

They talked quietly until the waitress slid three toasted sandwiches in front of them, dripping with grease and smothered in bubbling cheese.

'I still need to eat then,' Nikita stated. 'I haven't felt hungry at all.' In truth, she *had* felt hungry, but her cravings were not for anything strictly edible. A light blush rose to her cheeks as she swatted away ideas of other things she wanted to put in her mouth.

'Your body will run very efficiently with its new cosmic power pack, but you will need to stop and eat. And sleep of course, much like your old self,' Casey explained. 'My goodness, girl, your face has gone the same colour as your hair. Are you feeling OK? Was it something I said?'

Erron nudged him and winked. 'It's the old ... you know.' He mimicked a cartoon heartbeat with his hands.

'Oh ... oh! Sorry. Yes. Anyway, Nikita, it's all perfectly normal. Within a few hours that side of things will pass, but you'll still want breakfast.'

Accepting of this, she tucked into her sandwich with new enthusiasm, turning her crimson face away to watch out of the window, where faint drifts of snowflakes gathered in the gutters to join most of her thoughts.

7

No Leaf Clover

SOFIA CARTER, A YOUNG, CONFIDENT woman of Bangladeshi descent, was ambling around the edge of the platform at Farringdon station, where a number of stationary food huts were tempting her with the aroma of their wares. Her stomach was knotting, not so much from hunger, but because she was only a train journey away from meeting her biological father for the first time since she was adopted as a baby to a childless couple in Surrey. She settled on buying a sandwich – salmon and cucumber on thick seeded bread – before making her way to where her train was due in. She perched on a low wall, and as she ate, she stared at a photo of her father, Dhanajit Hasan, trying to burn the image into her mind so she could easily pick him out in a crowd.

The Fates had matched her with Jagdev Ali, who was twenty minutes away from the station and rushing through the teeming roads to get there on his foldaway bicycle. His dark curly hair stuck out every which way from his lopsided helmet and his face stung with the cold air. Small flecks of snow were gathering on his jacket as he cycled furiously, dodging slick manhole covers and inobservant pedestrians as he went. He was due to take a train north to an interview which would determine whether he stayed in London as an engineer or moved onto a different path training to be a solicitor at a corporate law firm. He had high hopes, and high enough qualifications, for the latter.

Nestled in a corner of the platform occupied by Sofia, the three Apollo Division agents stood talking softly and keeping a low profile, having arrived with only a few minutes to spare. They were easily overlooked, owing to their automatic ethereal cloaking quality that all agents possessed, but not entirely invisible, therefore were cautious about assembling and loading their bows too conspicuously.

Casey nodded excitedly towards the young woman eating a sandwich on the wall. 'That's her, I know it.'

Erron rolled his eyes, suppressing a smile. 'Is it because you saw her photo on the file you researched before coming here, because you *always care* and want to make sure she goes off truly happy in her little bubble of contentment this afternoon?'

Casey looked momentarily downcast.

'You know you're supposed to at least look at the file, Erron. At the very least to see their photo.'

'Why do I need to do that when I've got you to give me a complete *This is Your Life* moment for each of them?' Erron teased.

'Well, you could at least make an effort,' Casey complained before turning to Nikita. 'Anyway, this is a golden arrow assignment, which will cause a life-changing romance, resulting in the young lady Sofia missing her train to see her father, which means she will end up rescheduling to a later date because otherwise her father would have been stuck in the snow and had a heart attack because he was late to take his medication and—'

'Case, shhh.' Erron gesticulated for his friend to be quiet. 'Nobody cares.'

'I care. I always care.' Casey sulked.

Erron rolled his eyes. 'You absolute fridge magnet.'

Nikita raised one eyebrow at the pair and made a point at looking at her watch.

'Oh! Yes! We must get in position!' Casey exclaimed. 'I'll explain the rest in a bit.'

'Right, I've been assigned Sofia.' Erron checked his card while walking away.

Casey turned to the new recruit. 'Our target's name is Jagdev Ali. Look out for a young man. He'll have a bicycle helmet. He needs to stay in London.'

After a pause, Nikita turned to Casey. 'Has Erron always been so . . . nice to you?' She raised her eyebrows sarcastically.

'Oh, he's all right really,' he blustered. 'He's much nicer once you get to know him.'

'Hmm.' Admittedly she was still struggling to make accurate character assumptions as her normal sensibilities were still suitably fogged by the Apollo Flush. To her, almost everyone in the station was looking like a delectable dish on a buffet cart, and Erron was no exception.

'Have you worked together long?' she asked.

Casey smiled warmly, his eyes losing focus as he fondly remembered the past few decades. 'Quite a while now. Though I still clearly remember his first day.' He stared off wistfully into the distance, a myriad of micro-expressions playing out the memories on his face.

'So do agents always work in pairs?'

Casey snapped back out of his trance. 'Sorry, what?'

Nikita repeated her question.

'In short, yes. For two people to fall in love there needs to be two arrows shot. And it's not like the fables where an arrow can hit the wrong person and it makes them fall in love with whatever they see first. No, these are predetermined, so if they don't hit their mark the Fates will usually reschedule and put the people in each other's paths again later in life. But golden arrows are really important as they tie into one's entire destiny, so you won't be asked to do these until you have a proven track record in marksmanship. Don't worry, you'll be assigned your own partner once you're settled. Depending on how long that is will determine who trains you in marksmanship, but as you can see that's a key element of the job.' Casey placed down his kitbag and pulled out his custom horse bow, delicately made from white wood with inlaid gold accents scrolling from the limb tips. It looked like an iconic Cupid bow and he was a stickler for tradition. 'They stopped issuing these in 1892,' he explained, caressing the side of the bow in admiration. 'I've taken good care of her.'

'Eighteen ninety-two ... as in ... the year?'

'Yes. I hadn't been enlisted much over a hundred years then. This is my third bow, but the craftmanship on this one is exquisite.'

'You don't look a day over thirty,' Nikita observed, more with curiosity than out of flattery. She resisted the urge to prod his face to see if he was real.

'Why thank you.' He beamed. 'Perks of the job really. Technically I am for over thirty-three.'

It was true, the agency staff didn't visibly age and all had a youthful glow about them, owing to their new cosmic satsuma battery. There was no cosmetic surgery or skincare regime that could compare to having a newly implanted galactic energy source in your chest.

The cheerful smile stayed on Casey's face as he checked the arrow over and took position behind a pillar, relaxing the loaded bow against his thigh.

'So, what now? You just shoot him?' Nikita whispered, still conscious of being overheard, despite the general public being almost oblivious to them.

'It has to be timed right. When our other mark gets here, close enough that the two of them meet almost straightaway.'

'What about unrequited love?'

Casey furrowed his brow. 'I don't really like those assignments. They're half-sized arrows and you need a crossbow for those. Sometimes they change a person's life for the better, most often not. Luckily there aren't many that actually need to be shot. Most unrequited love falls under infatuation, and that's not real love.'

Stood on a platform above, Erron watched Casey and Nikita talking closely and smiling at each other, making h   is toasted sandwich turn uncomfortably in his stomach. He shook off the feeling, wondering why it bothered him at all, and shifted his focus back to the job at hand.

Jagdev arrived right on cue, flustered, red-cheeked and catching his finger while struggling to fold away his bicycle. He swore softly and sucked the blood from his hand while scrabbling in his pocket with the other, desperate to find his ticket before his train left. Sofia had spotted him chasing a ticket that was tumbling away from his grasp and stood to assist. She made her way down the edge of the platform through the throng of people and was barged by another traveller. Distracted momentarily by the push, she stumbled against a wall and dropped her bag.

Up above the crowd, Erron was watching intently, growing frustrated when his target was shoved out of his line of sight. Like a meerkat, she popped her head up once more, pulling her bag back over her shoulder. Relieved, Erron fired his shot.

Back on the platform, Nikita heard a soft whistling split the air above them, barely catching sight of the arrow before it struck Sofia harmlessly in the upper chest, bursting into a shatter of golden sparkles. Unaware, Sofia looked up abruptly as the train marched into the station.

'*Almost*. I just need an opening,' Casey muttered, poising the nocked arrow against his cheek, his bow arm outstretched in Jagdev's direction.

Sofia halted, as if transfixed by something, her eyes rolling back momentarily until they were little more than white globes. Nikita's gaze was drawn to the arrivals and departures screen, which fuzzed and crackled, the display going wild with distorted lines. Without warning, Sofia screamed and tried to run from an unseen force, before she stumbled over the yellow safety line and promptly toppled under the wheels of the approaching train. There was a moment of frosty silence before the air was shattered with the horrified screams of onlookers.

Casey lowered his arrow, eyes bulging, his jaw slack with shock. Within minutes, Erron was there, shaking him and asking him what happened, but he couldn't comprehend the question enough to answer. Erron glanced back to where a gathering of people were peering down at the mangled remains of Sofia and a train official was trying to forcefully usher them away from the grisly scene.

Seeing his friend utterly bewildered, Erron guided him away from the platform and asked Nikita to pick up his kitbag.

Casey's target, Jagdev, was at the front of the crowd spilling towards the yellow line on the platform; some people overwhelmed with the herd mentality of needing to see what had happened, others surging forward with the misinformed hope that someone needed saving. Jagdev, upon seeing the mangled remains of Sofia, pushed his way back through the crowd and immediately threw up in a nearby bin. Nauseous and disoriented, he was guided to the exit of the station for fresh air by another passenger.

'Case, it's OK. There's obviously been a mix-up,' Erron reassured him once he had finally regained some fortitude.

'I don't understand,' Casey whispered.

'Well, nor do I, but I'm sure there's a perfectly reasonable explanation. It's nothing to do with us. Let me get you a drink. A nice cup of tea.'

'So much blood.' Casey stared off towards where the remains of Sofia were still coating the front of the train. 'That . . . wasn't . . .'

'Wasn't in her file?' Erron queried, noticing how pale his friend had become. 'Hey, hey. Look at me.' He placed both hands on Casey's face and brought his gaze back to him, away from the carnage. 'Don't look at the train, Case. I'm here, look at me,' he spoke firmly. Once Casey had shifted his gaze to making eye contact with Erron, his shaking subsided.

'You OK?' Erron slowly took his hands away from his friend's face.

Casey took a deep breath and nodded.

'What about you?' Erron glanced over his shoulder towards Nikita, who seemed unfazed, if not a little curious.

'Oh me? Yeah, I'm fine. I guess I looked like that yesterday,' she responded matter-of-factly, nodding towards the result of the heavy impact.

Beneath them, a deep shuddering rippled across the platform. It's thunderous shock waves caused the crowd to scream and scatter, as loose items on the food stands fell all over the floor and hairline cracks appeared on the concrete underfoot. The quake lasted only ten seconds before the station fell quiet, leaving in its wake a trail of disarray and minor damage.

'What in the holy fucking biscuit was that?' Erron was still gripping the edge of a bench, expecting further quakes.

'I don't know, but I think we ought to get out of here,' Nikita reasoned.

Erron nodded, then caught hold of Casey's elbow to guide him outside the station to a nearby coffee shop. He sat him in one of the soft leather armchairs at the back. Nikita went to order, eventually bringing over a tray of hot drinks. They didn't speak much as Casey worked through the shock of seeing the young woman crushed under the approaching train, his expression vacant. Blue lights flashed outside in succession less than ten minutes later. There was a lot of murmured chatter about the quake in the coffee shop among those who had felt it.

'Did you see what happened to the woman before she fell? It was like she was being terrorised by something,' Nikita said, morbid curiosity sparkling in her eyes.

Erron was about to say he hadn't seen anything but glanced at Casey. 'Probably best if we chat about it later.'

Nikita shrugged and settled herself, sipping her latte. Having only just been told she herself had died not all that long ago, she'd reached the conclusion that she'd either effectively dealt with the news incredibly well or was still so much in shock that nothing else could possibly make it worse. Nevertheless, she replayed the image of Sofia tumbling on to the tracks in her mind, wondering if she had missed some key detail, or if she had just witnessed a murder.

'What happens next?' she eventually asked.

'We still have a second job to complete.' Erron rested back in his chair and warmed his hands on his own mug of coffee. 'Then back to the office to get these ... Well, we need to sort this mess.'

Casey was distraught and barely noticed his favourite type of tea (Assam, splash of milk, two sugars) steaming on the table in front of him.

Erron observed him for a moment, then pulled a mobile phone from his jacket pocket and dialled. Pressing it to his ear, he waited for his colleague to pick up. 'Freya, hi, it's Grover. Are you nearby? ... Yes, great. There's been a problem ... No, I can't explain right now. Are you in a position to pull off a job for us? It's in forty-five minutes, not far from here ... Sure ... I'll text you a picture of the assignment card ... It's not fussy no, straightforward ... Thanks, I owe you.' He hung up and took a picture of his card as promised before tearing the corner off another two sugar packets with his teeth and tipping them into Casey's tea.

It was against company policy to trade assignments, and it wasn't something Erron would do unless there was a real issue.

He trusted Freya, as he'd known her a long time and she'd covered for him previously.

'Back to the office then?' Nikita surmised.

'Back to the office . . .' Erron glanced at Casey. 'In a bit. No rush now.'

They sat in silence again for a short while, Nikita sipping her latte and Erron gulping his coffee with no regard for how hot it was. Casey still hadn't touched his mug and continued staring at the table blankly. Nikita excused herself in the realisation that her new body still needed to pee. Once she had gone, Erron worriedly picked up Casey's mug and pressed it into his friend's hand, still cupping it with his own. 'Talk to me, Case . . . I need you to be OK. Please.'

Erron withdrew his hands as Casey reluctantly gripped the mug and took a sip. 'I'm OK,' he whispered.

8

Lethal Temptress

THE SNOW WAS PILING UP in the streets when they returned to the comfort of the office. Casey slumped into his chair and rubbed his temples while Erron went to speak to their boss, Kendra. Nikita sat in silence, her mind gradually processing the events of the day and her new position. As she thought, her hand furiously wrote notes in her new notebook, snippets of things she wanted to remember, wanted to ask, everything she had learnt, all bundled in a chaos of biro. Clarity was returning to her as the heightened hormones of the Flush gradually subsided.

Half an hour passed before Erron re-emerged, sauntering over and sinking into the chair next to Casey. 'Right, Kendra has said she will look into it and not to worry, she'll speak with Lettie and find out if Hades had any crossed wires.'

'Who's Lettie?' Nikita asked, looking up from her notes.

'Merletta Crawford, she's the district boss for the Hades Division.'

She wrote it down.

'Kendra did mention there might be some fractures, owing to the unexpected twist of fate. That would explain the mini earthquake. Apparently, it's happened before and it usually causes some localised disruption as the natural order gets interrupted temporarily,' Erron explained, scratching the back of his neck in thought.

'I have heard of that but usually it's an agency error, a badly fired arrow or something.' Casey furrowed his brow. 'But the arrow didn't miss this time. It all seemingly went to plan so I don't know what happened.'

Seeing an opportunity to put her journalistic skills to good use, Nikita perked up. 'I could look into it, see if there's a previous record of these sort of things held anywhere?'

'I guess if they had any information on this kind of thing it would be held at the Eligos – it's an agency-only library,' Casey pondered. 'It'd be interesting to know when this last happened and what the result was. But I doubt you'll get a chance to go there just yet, what with all the new stuff you need to learn.'

'If I get the chance I'd love to.' Nikita made a few extra notes to find out where the library was and how to access it.

'Still hung up on it, Case?' Erron asked. 'I can't see it happening again for another millennia.'

Casey sighed and stretched. 'Nothing I can do about it now, I suppose. Just a crying shame. Such a waste.'

Erron eyed the clock on the wall: it said 6.49 p.m. 'We're pretty late finishing today. I'll show Nikita to her apartment. You get yourself home and changed, and I'll meet you at Nightjar at 8.30 p.m.' He stood to leave, picked up his coat and nodded for Nikita to follow.

'I don't know, maybe not tonight,' Casey answered.

'First drink is on me. One of those fancy-pants milkshakes you like.' Erron walked away before he could respond.

* * *

Erron and Nikita approached an impressively modern apartment block in Canary Wharf which, had she still been in her old life, would have been far out of her reach financially. They entered through a plush communal lobby with polished marble floors and bright spotlit ceilings and ended up in front of the lift doors. Another man in a suit and overcoat was waiting as the lift descended.

'What floor is my place on?' Nikita scanned the brass plaque on the wall with the apartment numbers.

'It's complicated.'

The doors slid open and they boarded the lift, the other man avoiding eye contact and pressing the button for the fourth floor. Erron placed his hands over the numbers and touched several at once, a warm glow emanating from them as if the buttons had been superheated. The lift juddered once, and the doors opened once again. Erron then gestured for Nikita to step out.

'We haven't moved?' she questioned, then noticed that the lobby had changed to a hallway as the doors closed behind them.

'We did. It's the other guy who didn't. He's still setting off from the first floor. That judder you get from a lift is usually an agent going into the liminal zones. You see, places made especially for us exist between the layers of reality and nothingness. It's like Dark Matter – no one can see it, but it's definitely there.

Your apartment is on a floor that no standard mortal person can access, and they don't even know it exists,' Erron explained as they dawdled down the long and softly lit hall.

'So that guy in the lift ... just saw us disappear into nothingness?'

'No, he doesn't even remember us going in,' Erron said. 'Most of the time our ethereal cloaking works to make people forget we existed the minute they can't see us.'

'A bit like déjà vu?'

'Very much like that. We're conveniently forgettable.'

As they passed several doors, Erron explained she was on a floor of apartments for mixed divisions, and most of her neighbours would also be new in service. Once outside her door, he handed her a key.

'Most agents treat these apartments like student halls at university. At some point they end up relocating to Elysion once they've severed the tie from their mortal lives and no longer feel the need to stay connected to the town or city in which they used to live. It's a transitional thing, mostly. It varies how long it takes, but the place is yours until you tire of it.'

'So, you and Casey live in Elysion then?' she asked, unlocking the door cautiously.

'Actually no. Casey has owned his house in Craven Street since his old life. He's a sucker for nostalgia so hasn't budged from there, plus the mortgage was paid off already and he had no next of kin so he somehow wangled it that he got to keep the place. As for me, I like to stay close to ... I mean, I've got no desire to level-up just yet.' He leant on the door frame as she tentatively took a step inside. 'My place is only up the road from here, four buildings away.'

'Oh, so similar to this then?'

'Well, similar. Anyway, you get everything as standard: basic decor, basic possessions. But here's the kicker: if you want to keep yourself in Earth luxuries, you'll need to sign up for some drudgery in the call centre to earn old money like we said before.'

'I had a feeling I wouldn't be able to avoid that for ever.'

'Uh-huh. You don't completely escape the need for old currency while operating on Earth. In the Apollo building, we have a room that functions as a call centre dealing with complaints for a dating site the agency runs for mortals. Ironic, huh? It's in that room we walked past to the locker room, if you want to check it out.'

'I wasn't told about having to do that when I signed the contract. They just said I *could* earn extra.' She half wished she'd chosen to wander the Oblivion Fields.

'Ha, they won't tell you that bit. You can pick up shifts ad hoc, depending on how much old money you want to earn. It's dull, soulless work but it's what furnished my apartment and keeps Casey in croissants.'

She huffed disapprovingly. 'I'll make do without.' She remembered the small allowance she'd been given by Jerry in recruiting and hoped she could make it last for as long as possible.

'You'll change your mind when you're dying for a coffee mid-shift.'

She ignored him and went further into the apartment to explore. She was pleasantly surprised by the apartment she had been allocated. High-rise, compact but modern, with a balcony view over the district.

A plain grey suit was hung on the back of a door and she had no recollection of owning it. She asked Erron what it was for.

'It's your trainee suit. Most recruits don't get many possessions when they start out, so the agency provides a basic outfit. There'll be a week's worth of underwear and shirts in the cupboards, I expect.'

'Huh. They obviously like grey.' She looked down at the drab tracksuit she'd been issued to leave the hospital in. 'It could be worse, I suppose. Though it's creepy they know my underwear size.'

'You'll be amazed what they keep in your file.' Erron raised an eyebrow. 'I'm just going to nip back to my place to get changed. Do you want me to meet you back here or are you happy to make your own way to the bar?'

Nikita thought about it. 'Actually, I'd like a little time to myself if that's OK? I'll make my own way over.'

'Sure thing.' Erron wrote down the address of the bar and left his phone number in case she got lost. He gave her detailed instructions on how to get back down using the lift, before leaving her in peace.

After the door closed, Nikita stood and admired the black polished kitchen worktops, the sleek grey bathroom tiles and the simple clean beige of the bedroom decor. Her meagre possessions from life that the agency had recovered for her were neatly stacked in six cardboard boxes in the corner of her living room. She eyed them cautiously, knowing she had time to look through them but didn't feel like facing the emotional roller coaster of seeing her memories from life just yet, so left the boxes mostly untouched apart from a few essentials. The longer she avoided them, the longer she had to accept that her old life was over and there was no going back. She'd done the same when her ex-boyfriend had left her for another woman. For months she'd left his stuff lying around her flat, knowing that when she finally got round to bagging it up, she'd be admitting that he would never be coming back. She had hated him for leaving her, but she couldn't hate the memory of having him there, the sound of him humming while making breakfast, the smell of his clothes, the surprise takeaways and the rainy nights watching bad zombie films wrapped up together on the sofa.

One thing she pulled from a box was her favourite dressing gown, which she hugged close to her body and breathed in the familiar smell of home.

She opened the balcony door and embraced the bitter January cold, wrapping the dressing gown around herself and watching the streets light up in Canary Wharf below. Flutters of snow swirled around her and caught in her hair, and she found herself feeling thankful that she had been given the chance to see snow again. She'd reached an unusual sense of calm, despite everything. She found that she didn't miss her former apartment, the run-down, mould-filled bedsit in Islington for which she could barely cover the bills, but she did miss her friends and the few family members with whom she had any kind of connection. Before long, tears were rolling silently down her cheeks as she pictured how people might have reacted to the news of her death. The thought of their despair and grief was more painful to her than her own sadness, and the fact she could offer no comfort or explain where she was felt like a guilty burden deep in her gut.

Wiping her face on her sleeve, she checked the time on the new agency-issue phone she had been given. She had a mere fifteen minutes before she would need to leave, so rummaged for something to wear and jumped in the new shower for a quick wash.

The act of showering shifted her sadness slightly as it was a familiar, and therefore comforting, thing to do. Though she couldn't speak to her loved ones now, she had to remind herself that, one day, they would know all about the afterlife themselves.

*   *   *

The Nightjar cocktail bar in Shoreditch was starting to fill with people when Nikita arrived, ten minutes late and wearing an old blue dress she'd found among her sparse boxes of personal belongings, poorly matched with a pair of black trainers. It seemed the Ghosters had neglected to bring most of her favourite clothes, and likely had to leave enough behind so her apartment didn't look ransacked after her death. She spotted Casey and Erron in a quiet corner away from the bar and raised a hand to them in greeting as she made her way over. In her peripheral vision she saw her new boss, Kendra, who was sat at the opposite end of the room with a couple of people she didn't recognise.

'How's the new place?' Casey asked when she reached their table, his chirpy tone restored. He was already sipping on a tall salted caramel and dark chocolate milkshake.

'It's actually really nice.' She placed her notebook and a pen on the small table.

'Still taking notes?'

'It helps me get things in order. Is that alcoholic?' She nodded towards his glass.

Erron cut in, 'Case doesn't drink, but we're such good customers here they make him that specially. He even has a special order at the Sky Pod Bar – that's where we go to play chess and Casey goes all sappy over the sunsets up there.'

'It's one of nature's most glorious creations,' Casey scorned. 'You should learn to appreciate these things.'

Nikita raised her eyebrow. 'Well, I haven't been to the Sky Pod Bar, and I'm certainly not one for chess, so I guess cocktails here will do just fine.'

'Anyway you won't need the notebook. You won't even know how to hold a pen by the end of the night.' Erron drained half his drink and grinned. 'Tonight is a celebration of your first day of semi-immortality, and we're going to drink like Dionysus himself.'

Nikita had wanted to discuss the earlier incident as she had too many questions, but Erron soon stopped her. He was conscious of the impact it had had on Casey and didn't want his stress levels to spiral again at the mention of it. Tactfully, he chose to use the excuse that they were in mixed company at the Nightjar, most of the mortal crowd enjoying the music were oblivious they were mingling with the reanimated souls of the agency and work-related discussions should be kept to a minimum. Thankfully, Nikita cottoned on and changed the topic.

A flickering overhead light nearby kept drawing her attention away from the conversation. It hung low over two mismatched men on the adjacent table, sitting out of earshot and nursing drinks. Something about them kept her gaze, and a misplaced feeling of unease lay in her stomach from looking at them. One of them lounged back against the wall; he appeared to be in his early sixties, dressed like an old rock star in tight black jeans and an open blazer revealing a satin blue shirt. He had a dirty blond ponytail and piercings in his eyebrow and both ears, his various rings glinting in the low light as he spoke animatedly with the other man across from him. His companion, a sombre figure with a shock of white spiky hair, wore an all-black suit and no tie, a long black overcoat, and a single, black-stoned ring on one index finger. His sharp blue eyes caught Nikita staring before he turned back to his tumbler of brandy.

'Ghosters.' Erron nodded towards them subtly. 'But you don't want to mix with them,' he warned. 'Those guys are senior agents, they don't have time for people like us. Besides, it looks like at least one of them is on assignment.' He gestured to the flickering light above them.

He explained that Hades agents on assignment often surrounded themselves with shadows, known as the *Umbra Noctis*, much like the Apollo benefits that came with the Flush. It gave them the ability to blend in or be as easily forgettable as the natural charm the Cupids possessed. But when electricity was invented, the *Umbra Noctis* inadvertently affected electrical relays and circuits, causing lights to flicker and electronics to play up when any Ghoster was nearby on an active assignment.

Nikita hugged her chest. 'They give me the creeps.'

'That's normal. It's their version of our Apollo charms. You aren't supposed to feel comfortable in the presence of a Reaper.'

'Duly noted.' Nikita couldn't help but be curious though and kept glancing over at them before Casey took her gently by the wrist and led her to the bar.

Erron watched as Casey laughed with Nikita and pointed out the various cocktails that the bar was famous for. Once again, Erron felt an unusual sensation bubble up within him, a certain envy that he struggled to shake off.

Erron recoiled as he saw Casey buy the new recruit a drink and she slung an arm around his waist in thanks, a bright smile flashing across her face. He was more confused when Casey brought a tray of three cocktails over and set one down for himself.

'Nikita said I had to try one, just this time.' Casey examined the drink a bit closer. 'Apparently it's not to be missed.'

'Did she now?' Erron muttered. 'You won't like it. You never have.'

Casey brushed off Erron's comment. 'Well, tonight is a special occasion.'

* * *

Half an hour later, after Casey and Erron had pointed out the agents they recognised among the crowd and introduced Nikita to a few of the friendlier faces, their attention was drawn to a young woman. She burst through the door in the full dazzling glory of a neon-meets-gothic pixie party girl that perfectly matched the attitude she oozed. Cropped black hair, heavy eyeliner and a skull nose ring did nothing to tone down the vibrant green vest and glittery black miniskirt that she wore. She waltzed up to the Ghosters' table and greeted Rockstar with a cheek kiss before ruffling the other Ghoster's hair. It wasn't long before she made her way over to the table occupied by the Apollo agents.

'Well hello, Erron, must be my lucky night, seeing you here.' She ignored the other two, seductively curled her arms around Erron and kissed him on the cheek, leaving a smudge of black lipstick.

He shrugged her off and wiped his cheek with the back of his hand.

'So is this a Cupid-only table or can I get a seat?' She rested her hands on her hips and pouted. 'Or I could always climb on your lap, Grover.'

'We're just having a quiet drink, Izzy. I'm sure you have plenty of other people to sit with … or on,' Casey said, his voice edged with tension.

'I wasn't asking you.' She threw him a cold look before smiling warmly at Erron once again.

'Leave us alone, Izzy,' Erron said flatly.

Her playful expression dropped, replaced by a cold smile. 'You don't know what you're missing, Erron. There's still time to take me up on my offer, but now I might just make you beg for it.' She pinched his chin and tried to turn his face to hers.

He jerked away and glared at her.

'Ah well, you know where I am when you change your mind.' She flicked her fringe off her face and sauntered off.

Casey sipped his drink, visibly uncomfortable.

'And she is … ?' Nikita asked. 'An old girlfriend?'

Erron spluttered, nearly choking on his drink. 'Christ, no …'

'That delightful young lady is Izobella Cain. She's from Hades Division and a little bit hung up on her teen party lifestyle. She was murdered at seventeen by Lucas Devine,' Casey explained.

Lucas Devine was a convicted serial killer who had murdered twenty-three teenagers in the late nineties. It had made national news when he was finally caught but the cases were kept quiet from the media for some time to avoid national panic. The wild child Izobella Cain had not been featured much in the press, in favour of the more homely and sweet-natured victims who had sold far more papers.

'But anyway, since Erron tried to be a good friend to Izzy a while back over something, she has it in her mind that they belong together. It started off as a bit of a teenage infatuation but she's not getting the hint.'

'I've cut all contact with her now.' Erron rubbed the back of his neck. 'I honestly don't know why she's so obsessed with me.'

'Oh I mean, I could probably come up with a couple of explanations.' Casey tilted his head to one side in thought. 'Show Nikita the messages, if you still have them.'

Erron reluctantly reached for his phone and opened a string of messages from Izzy. Nikita scrolled through them, noting how they went from a friendly exchange to Izzy becoming overtly flirtatious, then downright pushy. Towards the end, she had sent multiple messages which he hadn't responded to, clearly demonstrating she had no intention of leaving him alone.

Nikita read the texts, wide-eyed. 'You should report this. It's harassment. Wait, is there somewhere to report harassment in the afterlife?' she asked.

'It's fine, just leave it be. She'll soon get bored.' Erron took the phone back and tucked it in his coat pocket.

'I highly doubt that. She's been acting this way with you for over three years now.' Casey raised an eyebrow. 'Trying to avoid her isn't exactly helping.'

'What was her offer?' Nikita pressed. 'She said you could still take her up on it.'

'Actually, yes, what was that about?' Casey chimed in.

Erron waved off the question. 'It was nothing, forget about it. What she fails to realise is that I'd rather be obliterated than get involved with the likes of her.' He wrinkled his nose.

'Obliterated?' Nikita questioned.

Erron grimaced. 'Ah, yes. Nasty business. Imagine putting a strawberry in a blender, placing it on the highest setting, then pouring it down a drain into pure nothingness.' Nikita spluttered into her drink, but Erron continued, unfazed. 'It was a punishment devised by the Lord of Chaos, Elzifur, but it hasn't been used for several hundred years by the agency. The pain is unimaginable, apparently.'

'*Anyway*, anyone for another drink?' Casey took one look at Nikita's face and changed the subject quickly.

'Same again?' Nikita asked. 'And, Casey, don't you dare come back with anything that encourages sobriety.'

He nodded dutifully and went to the bar alone. A live band had started up, playing some original spins on some older jazz classics. Nikita took the opportunity to quiz Erron further about the Hades agents opposite while the music comfortably muffled their conversation.

Rockstar was Theodore Roscoe, collector of fine art, poker player, social on the music scene and passionate about his two pet cats, Castor and Pollux. He was stabbed to death in a biker bar brawl in the mid-sixties and was, by far, the friendliest Reaper the division had ever known. His companion held a much different reputation.

Darren Oliver-Alliott, known as D-O-A not just down to his initials but because he never failed to get the job done promptly. If he arrived, someone died, much like the common term used by first responders, 'Dead on Arrival', which fitted his initials perfectly. He didn't like the rain, cats, people or art but could agree on the appeal of music. He hated being touched and despised unnecessary newspapers, garden ornaments and children in general. Killed in battle in the fourteenth century, he once went by the name Sir Daryn of Dagworth and very little else was known about his early life, or much at all about his death. His length of service, however, was well known, and although he could have retired after the standard two hundred years, he was one of the most senior Reapers and of the mindset that no one else could do the job right if he left. He was stuck in a comfortable routine, and no one was brave enough to suggest he move on to pastures new. As with all agents, retirement was purely voluntary so long as there were no concerns with their performance, and many exceeded the two hundred years as they were too entrenched in their routine. Erron explained the only likely reason D-O-A was sat there socialising was because he was probably on a job nearby, as he wasn't one for keeping company.

Izzy was practically sitting on Theodore's lap, no doubt using her charm to get herself free drinks from the genteel old rocker who, despite knowing her ploy, was happy to accommodate provided she kept on her best behaviour. He was soft by nature but was no fool to be taken advantage of. She knew very well not to attempt any of her ploys on D-O-A, who watched her the way a hawk would observe a feckless mouse. She regularly stared over at Erron, desperately hoping to catch his eye. He grimaced each time he accidentally glanced her way.

'That girl is really bothering you, isn't she?' asked Nikita.

He slumped his shoulders and leant back in his chair. 'There's not much I can do about it.'

'I know it might not be my place, but I'm just going to ask Kendra if there's anything that can be done. It's really not right that you're putting up with that. Surely there's some kind of policy against harassment.' Nikita stood purposefully. 'She's only over there.'

'No, please don't . . .' Erron tried to catch the sleeve on Nikita's jacket but she had already disappeared into the crowd, emerging a few moments later.

'Kendra's going to have a quiet word with her. I asked her to keep it low-key.' Nikita sat back down and took a long sip of her drink. She caught Erron's intense look of concern and felt immediately guilty for letting her sense of justice take over before really thinking it through. 'I was careful how I worded it, I just wanted to see what could be done. I didn't mean to make it worse.'

Erron threw back the remainder of his glass of whisky and placed the glass down with a soft *thunk*. 'It's fine. I can't see it escalating, she's just a kid really. Maybe she does need a reality check from Kendra.'

'Well, don't put up with it if she continues,' Nikita said firmly.

Casey came back with a second fanciful cocktail, with a curl of lime wedged on the side and a little umbrella, not because the establishment usually provided umbrellas, but because he had shamelessly asked for one. He delighted in the little mechanism that opened and closed them and never lost the fascination, despite having collected numerous examples that he kept in a drawer at home. It was in Nightjar when he'd first discovered the little contraptions, when Erron had jokingly ordered him a ridiculously overdressed drink on their first visit, only to realise Casey didn't like alcohol. It hadn't gone unnoticed by Erron that Casey seemed to be drinking the cocktails to impress Nikita, as she'd been heavily encouraging him to steer away from his usual milkshakes.

Erron fidgeted anxiously when he spotted Kendra quietly speaking with Izzy a few moments later, the hushed conversation taking place near the bar. Izzy glanced over at Erron reproachfully before leaving the bar and Kendra left soon after without a word to the group. Erron only began to relax again as another hour slipped by.

The more concentrated the alcohol in their systems, the more diluted and wishy-washy the conversation turned. Casey's tolerance was non-existent and he was hopelessly inebriated with far fewer drinks than the others. Nikita, however, was just ecstatically happy that she was still able to get drunk.

'So ... what's ssis abou—about when I gets wings?' she slurred.

'You'll get 'em soon enough,' Casey answered, twirling his third mini umbrella between his fingers. 'Master the bow firsth, complete shum asshignments, get signed off, getss wings, float around a bit like a ... like a ...' He wrinkled his face in thought. 'Like a ...'

'... bird,' Erron finished for him. 'A birdy bird.' He'd had one too many double shots of whisky and was content watching the twirling umbrella. 'A big birdy bird though. Y'know. She knows. You know. Not little.' He distracted himself making his hands imitate a bird flying away.

'Awesome.' Nikita grinned wildly at the idea. 'Can I ... Can I fly to the moon?'

Erron snorted and nearly toppled off his chair laughing. 'Nah, that's way ... way over there.' He waved his arm floppily towards the sky. 'You can fly to erm . . .' his eyes narrowed in thought '. . . not so far places. Moon is for portal. Ice cream and shit.'

'You . . . You need t'get some sleep, mister.' Casey, though heavily intoxicated himself, propped Erron's head up with one hand as he was starting to slump over. ''Smonday, isntit? Or wassit Whens-day?'

Erron glared at his watch, seemingly unable to mentally configure the time from the display. ''S it late?'

Cascy yawned. 'Yah. 'S's late.'

As many of the people had thinned out for the evening, they noticed the Ghoster, Theodore Roscoe, had fallen asleep in the corner and D-O-A had already left. Noticing his absence, Erron tried to make a joke of sorts.

'Death waits for no man . . . no cab . . . no . . . shit.' He failed miserably but laughed anyway.

The frigid air outside met them with a sobering slap as they fell out of the door, giggling at everything and nothing all at once. Snow had built up considerably and was degrading into a grey slush on the roads. Casey was draped between the others, unable to walk unaided. Erron managed to hail a black cab and paid the driver to take Casey home while he and Nikita walked back to their respective apartments. They were both grateful of the extensively long, staggering walk back to Canary Wharf to sober them up enough to be able to work the liminal lifts back to their respective apartments.

The streets were mostly empty as Casey was dropped to his small townhouse on Craven Street, south of Covent Garden. He desperately tried to control his stumbling up the steps and took a little too long to put the key in the lock, his face inches from the keyhole in firm concentration. He was annoyed at himself for caving to the pressure of drinking, having never enjoyed the feeling of being drunk, and not particularly enjoying the taste of the expensive cocktails he'd managed to put away that evening. The familiar smell of cinnamon-scented candles and the leather of his worn reading chairs greeted him as he made his way into his lounge, easing his building nausea. The colour scheme was warm with Bohemian-accented furniture, awash with the deep greens of indoor plants and trailing ferns, colourful mosaic pots and tastefully matching rugs. Above his living room was a mezzanine floor, which he used as his master bedroom and led on to the roof terrace. An ornate wooden balustrade ran around the edge of the mezzanine floor and down the stairs, which were situated between the living room and the small open-plan kitchen. A small bathroom and a single box room with a pull-out sofa bed led off from the kitchen. The house was small, cosy and had suited Casey for the majority of his mortal life and the entirety of his afterlife. He'd never had neighbours long enough to notice his extended stay, but occasionally changed his name on the bills in case the post office started asking questions.

Lighting a fire in the log burner, he settled down in a high-backed chair with a cup of tea. Though he loved his home comforts, it had taken many years to get used to the emptiness that waited for him there, and he longed to have someone to share his evenings with. Too tired to climb the stairs to bed, he dozed under a cashmere blanket in the lounge, the crackle of the fire imitating conversations that he could only wish to understand.

Erron, on the other hand, had no trouble collapsing into the tangled bedding on his king-sized bed. His apartment, much like Nikita's, was in a prestigious location less than two miles from the Apollo building and boasted several in-built mod cons. He had a sleek flatscreen TV that descended from the ceiling by remote control, a whole host of pre-programmed mood lighting and his own pinball machine in the corner of his open-plan space. He had furnished the place in silvers and greys, brushed stainless steel and a bold black corner sofa, all paid for with months of gruelling extra shifts in the call centre, something he begrudgingly carried out to make his living space far more enjoyable. His prized possession was an entire wall made of an immense marine fish tank with a collection of rare and colourful fish, their neon shapes spiriting through the azure water and throwing ghostly shadows on the stark grey wood floor. He also enjoyed the company of a Roomba vacuum which he'd stuck large googly eyes on and named Roscoe, after the Reaper. His reasoning being that they both hoovered things up, one was errant Coco Pops, the other souls. Erron religiously put Roscoe on charge in such a way that it looked like it was peering out from under the bed.

On closer inspection, his apartment gave away his more unconventional interests; old comic books were tucked behind newspapers, the odd superhero figure perched on the corners of furniture and his bedroom lamp was designed to look like the Marvel character Ghost Rider, with light-up flames. Having switched the lamp off, he slept dreamlessly, his googly-eyed flatmate keeping watch in the shadows from under the bed.

9

Stole

CASEY WOKE WITH A START an hour before he was
due to be at work. His back ached from sleeping in
the chair and his head throbbed with the effects of
the cocktails from the night before. It was well known that
agents weren't afforded the luxury of those free-floating souls
in Heaven, instead they were still tied within their replicated
body, which had all the same needs as their original. Unfortunately
for Casey, this included a mint-choc-chip-ice-cream-level
hangover that he was definitely not used to.

It was part of his morning ritual to put on a pot of tea and
stretch out his wings in the kitchen. It was a conscious effort
and it had taken him several months to get the hang of having
wings, though after two hundred and thirty-seven years, they
felt as natural to him as his arms were. The kettle hissed on
the stove and he took it off the ring before it started whistling,
to avoid further irritating his hangover-sensitive ears. He
discovered that he must have drunkenly tried to make tea when
he'd gotten home, as he found the milk bottle in a plant pot
and the spider plant in the fridge.

With some caution, he glanced around the living room, half expecting to have broken or destroyed something else in his drunken state the night before. He had never liked alcohol and the last time that Erron had convinced him to drink was the 1998 agency Christmas party. That time, he'd mistaken the socks in his laundry bag for coal and burnt the lot in the fireplace.

Casey made it to the Apollo building first, suffering through every loud noise in the busy office and feeling like he'd been dragged under the wheels of a bus. The other two looked a little worse for wear when they arrived shortly after him; Erron was using the bright winter morning as an excuse for wearing dark glasses, his choppy dark hair styled by his pillow and a takeaway cup of coffee in his hand. Nikita turned up last, dressed in her agency suit, hair piled up in a French plait and carrying a bag of warm croissants which she dropped down in front of Casey.

'Thought you guys might like some breakfast.' She plonked herself down into a swivel chair. 'I didn't know what type you liked, so I got the works: all butter, pistachio, almond, raisin.'

'Easy there, Wolf, that's akin to a marriage proposal for Casey,' Erron jibed. He said it casually, trying to gauge her reaction, but Nikita caught the slight edge to his voice. 'But if it were me, I would have gone for the pain au chocolat, as they're his favourite ... you know, if you really wanted to run off into the sunset together.'

Nikita looked up at Erron and rolled her eyes. 'It's just a bag of croissants and I'm not the marrying type.'

Casey eyed the croissants as though they held the secret of life itself, until Erron handed him the coffee cup and his line of sight was averted. 'I picked that up for you. It's one of those fancy gingerbread lattes. No need to thank me; I had a coupon.'

'Oh well now, gingerbread latte, huh? Consider me propositioned.' Casey winked and plucked off the lid of the cup with glee, filling his lungs with the smell of the coffee, his eyes closing in ecstasy.

Erron stepped away, cheeks slightly flushed, and went to get a filter coffee for himself and Nikita.

An agent approached their desks carrying a newspaper folded in half. Freya Carthage, who had recently been promoted to assist Kendra in running the division, was tall with a flawless dark complexion, neatly braided hair, and a gold nose ring which drew attention to her bronzed cheekbones. She was the vision of a motivated morning person, wearing a striking white suit and a face that said, *I've been awake for hours.*

'You guys look like shit; too many shots on a school night?' She rolled her eyes. 'This was your hit, wasn't it? I had to pick this up from one of those newsstands. No one is talking about it here.' She dropped the paper in front of Erron and he picked it up to scan the headline:

UNEXPECTED TRAGEDY AT FARRINGDON STATION

'Freya, yeah, Kendra said not to worry about it, that she'd take care of things. But that's why I asked you to fill in for us.' Erron tossed the paper down and yawned.

Casey pulled it towards him and read the small print. 'The newspapers are indicating that it was a suicide, but that doesn't add up,' he muttered. 'Anyone could clearly see she was thrown or pushed.'

'Let it go, Case. She ain't gonna be falling in love anytime soon. Our involvement is over.' Erron leant back in his chair, watching Casey continue to scrutinise the text.

'Nikita Wolf?' Freya looked down at the red-haired woman. 'You're with me today. We're covering basic skills. Kendra asked me to step in for marksmanship training. Unfortunately I can't take you on full-time yet until I have signed off my last trainee, but that's only going to be a few weeks, if that.' She shook Nikita's hand with the conviction of a new prime minister ascending to office. 'I trust these fine gentlemen pickled your new liver sufficiently to celebrate your induction.'

Casey interrupted them, waving the paper. 'It says here that she left a note, but I don't believe it.'

'Newspapers get things wrong all the time.' Erron wrinkled his nose. 'But maybe she did actually jump.'

'I'm not convinced. If there is a note though I sure would like to read it.'

'You'll never get your hands on that. Just drink your coffee and forget about it.'

Casey looked mournfully at him.

'Oh . . . all right then, you absolute traffic cone.' Erron rolled his eyes. 'If you *really* need to see it, I know where they keep that shit. If that's what it takes to put your mind at rest about the whole situation, I'll get it for you.'

In his former life, Erron had been a police officer in the Met, where he dealt with a lot of tragedies before he died from complications relating to an injury sustained in the 1981 Brixton Riots. At thirty-one, he had been young enough to still enjoy his job but experienced enough to have built a sense of disdain for the general public. After three days of trying to recover from a bludgeon to the head by a flying Jack Daniel's bottle, his disdain had turned to contempt. Fortunately, he hadn't felt any lingering contempt for whiskey.

'Thank you,' Casey mouthed, taking a sip of his latte.

A furious rapping came from the glass at the assignments window, and Margie Murnard, the assignments clerk, was waving a selection of cards at them. She had often been likened to an angry gremlin, aside from the very few agents she had actually warmed to – Casey being the main one, owing to his natural predilection for being sickeningly charming towards her.

'Is she dead too?' Nikita asked.

'Yes, everyone at the agency is. I don't think she was ever alive, the miserable cow,' Freya murmured. 'Though it seems like she's been here for ever, no one really remembers when she started.'

Casey was the first to stand, volunteering to pick up their assignments despite desperately wanting nothing more than to sit *very still* and stay *very quiet*. When he returned, he sifted through their assignments and passed Erron two golden-edged cards.

'Two golds? So soon?' Erron was taken aback.

It wasn't completely unheard of for an agent to have a run of gold assignments in the same week, but it was exceptionally rare.

'Not just that, but look at the first one. Read the name,' Casey tittered excitedly.

Erron's eyes widened as he read the card. 'No way.'

Freya snatched it off him and read. 'How did you land this? After I covered your arse yesterday.'

'What is it?' Nikita tried to get a look at the name. 'KiaRia? The singer?'

KiaRia was one of the upcoming starlets of the UK rock music scene, a seventeen-year-old Japanese singer of a chart-topping soft rock band named after her. The girl had shot to fame a year earlier and was more popular among teens than sitting still was among Tibetan monks.

'Kendra's going to this concert apparently. I heard the tickets sold out in minutes.' Freya couldn't hide the envy in her voice.

'A celebrity, Erron!' Casey was clearly ecstatic. 'We don't get those often.'

'No, most rock stars end up with Hades early.' Freya raised an eyebrow. 'Grover, can I have a word with you?'

Sensing that the conversation would need discretion, Casey stood to leave. 'Nikita, let's get you your kit for your training this morning. I expect Freya wants to take you to the shooting range.' He shuffled off towards the locker room, Nikita in tow.

'What's up?' Erron looked confused and rested his elbows on the desk.

Freya pulled up a chair and softened her voice. 'Kendra told me you've put in another request to switch to Hades. Why keep on trying?'

Erron stared at the mess of paperwork on his desk and fidgeted in his seat. 'Every few years they let me reapply despite not making the cut.' He sighed and ran his fingers through his hair in frustration. 'I don't fit in here, Freya. We both know that. I think everyone in the office knows that. Love isn't something I care about.'

'Maybe you don't care about love like some of us. But you are loved here, even if you don't realise it. What about Casey? He'd be devastated. You're his best friend.' Freya leant over and squeezed his arm gently.

Erron glanced over his shoulder to where Casey was chatting happily to Nikita by the locker-room doors. She was laughing and pushing him playfully, her cheeks faintly flushed. 'I think he'll forget me easily enough.' His tone was bitter, especially as he knew the initial effects of Nikita's Apollo Flush would have worn off and she was still giggling like a schoolgirl around Casey.

She followed his gaze. 'You and I know very well that's not the case. And so what if he's getting close to Agent Wolf; that won't impact your friendship, will it?'

Erron exhaled and shrugged his shoulders limply. Not one to entertain childish nonsense, Freya fixed him with a stern look.

'Fine, if I can't convince you otherwise, I'm going to need your reason statement for division transfer when you've completed it. I'm on the review board with Kendra this year.'

'It's right here.' He pulled out a lever arch file with tatty corners from a tray on his desk. A small stack of papers slipped out and scattered by Freya's feet.

She gathered them up, pausing briefly when she saw what they were. 'Please tell me that you haven't been researching this stuff.'

'What stuff?' He grabbed the papers off her and turned them over. They were photocopies from an old book and the heading leapt out at him: *Blood Mixing of 1605*.

He was able to skim a few lines about a banned practice of blood mixing before Freya snatched the papers back. From what he could gather, it covered how different blood combinations of agency divisions resulted in almost superhuman abilities.

'Erron, this is serious. This kind of information is prohibited, you know that. Where did you get these?' she asked sternly, folding the papers in half.

'I've never seen them before. Honestly, I've no idea,' he blustered as he unclipped the Hades transfer statement and handed it to her.

'I'll have to raise this with Kendra, you know that.'

He sighed. 'Please don't. They're nothing to do with me. Someone is clearly playing some prank on me and put them there.'

Freya looked unconvinced. 'I'm your friend, Erron, but I've got a duty of care.' She left him at his desk, where, in his worry and confusion, he rested his head in his hands, wondering if his day could get much worse.

Casey returned, still ecstatic about their famous assignment.

Erron stared deadpan at his colleague, who was grinning from ear to ear and clutching the card against his heart like a schoolchild holding an autograph. Erron couldn't help but smile and shake his head, pushing his own worries out of his mind.

'Nikita has been telling me what sort of thing to wear for the concert,' Casey explained.

'Oh, has she now?' Erron raised an eyebrow. 'Can't we just go casual for this one?'

Casey's expression sank. It was their unspoken tradition to blend in the mortal way for big assignments by going clothes shopping for a disguise. They didn't need it as the Apollo cloaking ability could get them in almost anywhere unnoticed, but Casey revelled in choosing an outfit and pretending he was part of the crowd. For the best part, Erron didn't mind humouring him, despite having ended up in some outlandish costumes in the past. Though he resented the time they ended up in inflatable shark costumes for a charity event at the aquarium under Casey's insistence that it would be fun to be noticed for a change.

Erron glanced at his watch and sighed heavily. 'Oh, all right then. We can go pick something to wear.' He smiled as Casey's eyes widened in delight. 'Plenty of time yet, though. We need to complete the other gold first.' He scrutinised another two cards detailing the people who were due to be visited by Cupid's arrow before the singer.

'They've really started making these fancy now,' Casey remarked, holding the card up where it glimmered under an office light. 'They're even sticking our names on in gilded font instead of the usual biro. How posh.'

Erron couldn't say he noticed, or even cared.

Over coffee and another croissant, Casey perused the files of his day's targets, occasionally smiling, or folding his gentle features into a sad frown at some detail or another. Erron sipped his own hot drink and watched the theatrics of expressions play out over Casey's face, trying to guess the nature of the information he was reading. He would never admit it, but he admired Casey's ability to memorise such trivial details about a person's life and cling to them until his arrow had been fired.

Erron's phone buzzed several times in succession with a multitude of messages coming through. Casey glanced up, curious; his friend was staring at the phone, looking angry.

'Everything OK?'

Erron sighed and showed Casey the six texts he'd received. They were all from Izobella Cain, spitefully complaining about him involving his boss.

'What do I do?' Erron rested his head in his hands.

Casey stood and picked up the phone. 'Maybe we need to take this down a formal route and get Kendra to contact Lettie Crawford. Izzy should listen to her own boss.'

Erron vehemently protested and snatched the phone back. 'Absolutely not. I'm just going to ignore her. I didn't want it even going this far.'

'OK, but I don't like how she's spiralling.'

'She's just an immature kid. You know she'll never mature past the age of her death, and unfortunately she's still saddled with those lovesick teenage infatuations that most of us grow out of pretty quick. She might be annoying, but she can't do anything.' Erron went through the phone to delete her messages.

'OK, but if it gets worse then I am going to raise it,' Casey reasoned. He changed the subject, holding up the newspaper. 'Can we go and look for that note now?'

'The things I do for you.' Erron buttoned his black overcoat and slipped the assignment cards into the pocket. 'Let's sign for these arrows and head on out.'

Once they'd collected their gold arrows, they took the lift to the roof as it was an easy launchpad to fly from. It was a short distance through the frigid wind to the police station where Sofia Carter's death would be kept on file. Since he was recorded to be deceased, Erron didn't have access to the shared computer files anymore but would be able to extract the physical evidence with little difficulty.

It was times like these that Cupids could make use of their Apollo Flush, clouding people with a brief state of agreeability. It was a skill not to be taken lightly, and never to be used off the clock, but it easily earned Erron's entry into the police station evidence room without question and, more often than not, landed them free drinks at any bar in London. But that's strictly off the record.

'If there is anything else I can do for you, Inspector Kyler, please just say.' A burly officer with a patchy beard smiled broadly, fully enveloped in the charm of the Apollo Flush.

'No, no, this will be all.' Erron pulled Sofia's note from the file and took several photos before placing it back on the shelf. Casey watched through the skylight on the roof, as Erron pocketed his phone and shook the officer's hand before leaving.

A minute later, Erron joined him in the roof, settling down with his knees by his chest and lighting a cigarette. 'That was easier than I thought. I assumed there might be one or two questions, but the chap just bought the whole story.'

'Well, it is the whole reason for the Apollo Flush.'

'Nah, I think it's this pretty face you see; I'm just damn irresistible.' Erron smirked while drawing a lungful of smoke and handing Casey his phone.

'Quite ... but I do wish you would give up those things.' Casey huffed and waved his hands in the air, ineffectively trying to convince the smoke to go elsewhere.

Ignoring him, Erron turned over his lighter in his hands. It had been a gift from his late brother and was inscribed with a quote – 'Evil is powerless when the good are unafraid' etched into it across the dented pewter. It was the one thing he clung to from his former life and he liked having a reason to keep using it. He leant over and pointed at the second image on the phone. 'See here, I think you were right. It doesn't add up.'

The note itself was fairly similar to what Erron had seen over the years: some apologetic words to loved ones and a vague dialogue of internal struggle, but it wasn't the note that had piqued his interest.

'The train ticket?'

'Yes. A return fare. Bought less than an hour before the actual incident.'

'But why would she . . . ?' It dawned on Casey. 'She had every intention of getting on the train.'

'And coming back, it seems. We both know this was no suicide, but I expect the police are happy to wrap it up as one for convenience.'

Casey gripped Erron's arm with urgency. 'But there *must* be an investigation. They can't just ignore it; this is murder we are looking at here! Can't you tell PC Beardy Guy?'

'Casey.' Erron rocked his friend gently. 'There *is* an investigation. I took that from the *evidence* room. The file is open, but they'll likely close it soon enough. The note doesn't help matters. Besides, what do you expect me to say? *Hi, I'm an undead guy that walks around shooting people so they fall in love, and my friend sat on the roof wants me to tell you that yesterday's death was suspicious.* Come on, Case, the mortal world does its thing and we do ours.'

Casey hugged his knees and sighed in frustrated acceptance. Erron didn't like to say that the case would be No Further Actioned. The coroner would register the cause of death by multiple train-wheel-based traumas and the CCTV would be too poor or lost or overwritten for there to be any lead in that respect. Sofia Carter would be a newspaper tragedy that by next week would be part of a child's papier-mâché art project. Erron rested the cigarette in one hand and with the other he tugged Casey's ponytail playfully.

'You know your problem, Case?'

Casey looked at him expectantly.

'You care *too* much. I bet you any money when Kendra gets back to us, she will say it was a Hades mix-up. At some point or another these things get confused. Don't you remember that story of the famous ice skater who died during an assignment gone wrong a few years back? These things happen; don't stress.'

Casey thought about it, issuing a slow sigh before he nodded in agreement. 'I still want to make sure we find out what caused it. Like you say, it might be a mix-up, but I want to know either way.'

Erron changed the subject. 'Do you know much about this KiaRia girl then?'

'What do you want to know?'

'Ah yeah, of course, you know everything, probably right down to the name of her dog.'

'She's got a bearded dragon actually ... called Rusty.'

Erron couldn't help but laugh. 'Well, I did promise you a shopping trip, so shall we go and find something exotic to wear to this fanciful event?' He waved his arms in mocked extravagance. 'We could try Camden, but it's gone downhill lately, all hipster and no soul.'

'Well, there's no harm in trying. It'll still be fun.' Casey stood up on the sloping roof. He stretched out his huge white wings and Erron followed suit. Bracing themselves for the cold wind, they leapt from the roof and soared into the mottled grey clouds that promised more snow on the horizon.

10

Blaze of Glory

'THAT'S IT, HOLD YOUR ARM straight, turn your elbow a little. Perfect.' Freya stood close to Nikita as she instructed her with the training bow. The new agent was picking it up quickly and had a naturally good stance. The practice range was inside a huge warehouse at the London Docklands, cleverly disguised from the outside as a private gym but inside housing a whole manner of social, fitness and training facilities for staff of all the divisions. It was known as The Arena, and its shooting range was an impressive size with a variety of stationary and moving targets, all aimed to simulate real people.

'Why are my shots all off-centre?' Nikita asked, adjusting her foot spacing.

'Try aiming up to the right to correct the angle.'

She did as Freya instructed and was soon hitting right on target.

'Luckily, you haven't got to hit the heart, but close enough is good in the field.'

'I always go for the heart.' A voice came from the side wing, followed by its owner: a petite Chinese woman with long braided hair, carrying an oversized sports bag.

Lian Zhang, a senior agent of the Nemesis Division, liked to visit the range on a regular basis to let off steam. She was one of the longest-serving members at the agency and had moved from China to England in 1889 as a young woman, assisting her family in setting up a silk business. She'd never married, despite her father trying to encourage it, but she and her family were murdered as part of a hate-filled exchange with a group of drunken men who objected to the influx of Chinese immigration.

She was dressed in a pair of simple black tracksuit bottoms and a baggy hoody emblazoned with a band logo. She introduced herself to Nikita and asked how she was settling in over at Apollo, at the same time pulling out a black recurve bow from her bag and fitting a quiver to her hip.

'Watch this,' Freya whispered to Nikita as they stepped back a little from Lian. As she drew the string back on her bow, the whole bow burst into flames, bright and wild and crackling with intensity. Flashes of different colours flickered among the bright tongues of orange but swiftly died down once Lian had released the arrow.

'Nemesis Division,' Freya explained, 'are responsible for justice and vengeance.'

'I was briefly told about them in my induction.'

'You'll spot the bow first if you ever see them out on assignments. Or their flaming wings of hellfire and retribution, of course.'

'Erron said I'd get my wings when I'm a full agent ... how long will that take?' Nikita had been dying to ask.

'When you get your full licence. It's a slightly complex process, and they take a while to get used to, but you'll love them. You get signed off after three successful supervised assignments and a written exam.'

They watched Lian in silence for a short while before resuming their own shooting. Nikita had a good grasp of the new skill, and it was only a couple of hours before she was consistent and accurate, though the moving targets were taking time to get used to. After practice, Freya gave her a tour of the warehouse and its various facilities. The shooting range was upstairs, above a large indoor pool which was set up not just for swimming, but for complex assignment training involving water, high diving or various stunts that might require a soft landing. There was an assault course, sauna, games room, gym and a virtual reality room.

'This place is amazing,' Nikita marvelled.

'It was set up when they thought the old library was getting out of touch with modern life.'

'Library, is that the Elephant one or something? Casey mentioned it.'

'Eligos. The divisions used it as a shared space and it had a few extras behind the scenes, like a mini archery range and coffee shop, but we mostly use this facility now as it's a lot more up to date. There is, however, an underground pool at the library which is always worth a look if you like an ancient ambience. Personally, it gives me the creeps. Too much like the start of a horror film down there on your own.' Freya started to pack away her kit. 'Besides, when you get your wings it's a pain in the arse to dry them at the Eligos. At least here they have drying rooms with proper air jets.'

'I'd like to go there, just to see it.'

'Casey will take you one day. He's there a fair bit, he haunts anywhere that's older than him.'

* * *

Quite the opposite to an ancient library, Casey was wandering through the main shopping street of Camden Town, throwing the odd uncomfortable glance at the occasional person with implanted forehead spikes or neon green hair.

'Did you hear about the whole chlorinated chicken debacle?' he asked, looking down inconsolably at the sad cheese sandwich that Erron had bought for him at a corner shop while picking up his usual lottery ticket in the hope he could win the jackpot and avoid shifts in the call centre for a few decades.

'The what now . . . ?' Erron had been distracted by an array of colourful Doc Martens, while he munched through a curry chicken wrap.

'Well apparently, they wash them in it, or feed them it or make them swim in pools of it . . . I'm not *entirely* sure but . . . I mean, if that's the state the world is going to how will anyone be able to fall in love in the future?' He pulled a piece of limp lettuce from the sandwich and flapped it from his finger, where it was clinging on for dear life. It landed with a soggy slap on the grubby pavement.

Erron raised his eyebrows and faced his friend. 'I don't seriously think that the powers of destiny will be overly concerned about chlorinated chicken, Case. Anyway, you don't even eat chicken, that's why I got you a cheese sandwich.'

'It's all dreadful.'

'Stop worrying about the chicken.'

'No, I meant the clothes here. What am I supposed to wear?' Casey thumbed through a rack of PVC things that could loosely be termed as garments, held together with stainless steel rings and covered in studs. 'I don't even know *how* you wear this.' He held up some kind of harness with shoulders made of chain mail.

'For one thing, we're not going to some kinky bondage club, so you won't be wearing *that*.' Erron stifled a laugh. 'But if you want to wear it, I won't object.' He nudged Casey and winked.

'Oh, give over.' Casey hushed his friend and quickly returned the dangle of fake leather to the rack while his face burned with embarrassment.

'Besides you'd look better in this one,' Erron teased, pulling a black mesh shirt with a medley of studs and chains affixed to it off the rack.

Mortified, Casey took the shirt and hastily stuffed it back on the rail, then grabbed Erron by the scruff of his neck and marched him towards the market.

'You can let go now!' Erron had laughed all the way around the corner before shaking his friend off and sorting his collar out.

'Let's just get something and get going.' Casey was flustered, his colour gradually settling the further they got from the rack of bondage gear.

At the market, Erron was quite content picking out a rock-gothic outfit as he was more than comfortable in black clothes, lace-up boots and the odd vampire-inspired accessory. Casey was doing his best to be enthusiastic but was somewhat lost. Camden was no longer the lively hub of unusual shops and alternate clothing; it had been transformed into another lifeless cookie cutter collection of hat stalls and overpriced jewellery. The few clothing shops left offered very little range. Eventually, he found a small shop with the type of clothing that KiaRia fans would flock to.

'Oh, now that suits you,' Erron stated.

'You think?' Casey spun away from the mirror in the corner of the shop holding a quirky gothic tailcoat under his chin, trying to work out if it would look all right on.

'Try it on. Properly.'

Relenting, and holding the coat up once more in front of the mirror to double check, Casey disappeared into the changing rooms. He emerged somewhat triumphant, looking almost pleased with the coat, despite the fact it appeared like he was wearing a rucksack underneath without the necessary adjustment for wings.

'Don't you laugh,' he warned. 'This is not something I would ever wear again.'

'No, no I wasn't going to laugh.' Erron cocked his head to one side. 'Looks good. Just . . . not with the rest of the ensemble.'

'Well, I know that.' Casey looked down at his pinstripe trousers and charcoal tank top. 'What on earth do I put with it?'

'We are going vampire rock; this girl's following is all into that gothic steampunk Dracula mash-up stuff. Any of these will go with that coat.' Erron handed him a bundle of things off a nearby rail. Casey reluctantly picked out a few other things and disappeared once more to struggle into what he could fit over his wings.

'You look like you've stepped out of a Tim Burton film,' Erron mused when Casey stepped back out. 'All you need is the eyeliner.'

'Now that's quite enough. I draw the line at eyeliner.'

'I think that's generally how it works.'

'Enough already. You forget I lived through the era when these clothes were mainstream.' He'd picked an ivory poet shirt with a lace-up collar and a slight satin sheen to it. Though he was unable to try on a waistcoat, he had a dark purple one at home he was confident would go well with the outfit.

'Of course. When were you born again?'

'Seventeen fifty.'

'Sheesh.'

'Well, so long as you think it looks OK. I'll add the wing gaps when I get home.' Casey made a mental note to find his fabric scissors as soon as he got back.

They agreed to call into the office to collect their kit prior to heading home before the evening's assignments. Erron mapped the route to the concert on his phone.

'I'll pick you up at six in a cab as I'll be passing near you anyway,' he offered. 'We've got this first job to do on the way but it looks like that'll be straightforward enough.'

'All right then. It's the little house on the end, remember. Mine is the only one with the roof terrace.' Casey was especially pleased with his roof terrace. It was partly a requirement for discreet flight, but also a retreat where he spent many evenings looking wistfully at the stars (because unless you are looking at them wistfully, there really is no point). On special occasions he turned on the warm glow of festoon lights and danced around to Frank Sinatra, but only when he was in a good mood and the neighbours were away.

Having worked with Casey for over three decades, Erron was fully aware of where he lived, though he was embarrassed to admit he'd never been in the little townhouse when invited or seen the roof terrace in all its glory. Casey, on the other hand, had visited him at his flat at the Docklands on numerous occasions, turning up with barista coffee or croissants 'as I was just passing and thought you'd like a pick-me-up' or nipping in after work for a quick drink and a chance to admire the fish. Casey was particularly taken with Roscoe the Roomba (as most people born in the latter part of the 1700s would be), and Erron would set the little machine running just so his friend could watch it miraculously make peanuts or Coco Pops disappear. He also had a child-like fascination with the drop-down flatscreen and the remote-control mini helicopter that Erron would daringly fly around off the balcony. And though Erron teased him for it, he found it quite endearing.

* * *

Pacing back and forth in his living room hours later, Casey was getting restless. He checked his appearance for the umpteenth time in a long mirror behind the door, smoothing down the new coat and adjusting the open collar of the shirt. The purple velvet waistcoat he'd had since the sixties did, in fact, go very well with the rest of the outfit. The doorbell rang shortly after six and he grabbed his kitbag, and assignment cards. He opened the door to Erron, who was leaning casually against the door frame, making the gothic outfit look effortless and fetching. Simple black jeans, a full-length double-breasted black coat and a wine-red shirt underneath, nicely paired with his heavy lace-up boots. He'd slicked his hair back and even shaved off his usual two-day old stubble, pulling off a very convincing vampire look, complete with a pair of small red-lensed sunglasses perched on the end of his nose. It was a good thing Erron was responsible for making other people fall in love, because he scrubbed up to be quite the heartbreaker himself.

'Good evening, Mr Hart. Well, don't you look absolutely dashing!' Erron put on a posh voice and bowed dramatically. 'Your carriage awaits, my lord.'

Casey immediately felt the blood rush to his face when he caught a glimpse of authenticity in Erron's smile despite the playful teasing.

'Ready when you are.' Casey stepped out, no longer feeling quite so self-conscious.

Thirty minutes later, the cab dropped them a few streets away from the concert, where they were to complete their first gold assignment of the night. Erron tipped the driver, pulled out his first card and read it aloud.

'Quentin Smith, electrician, turning the corner in three ... two ... one.' Erron eyed his watch as a stout, fresh-faced man pulled up to the kerb in a battered white van. He answered a phone call and sat with the engine turned off, scribbling a few notes on a scruffy notebook.

'Lucy LeFarre, apartment three-nineteen, due to have her heart stolen by this emergency call-out to fix the smouldering wall socket in the living room.' Casey watched the window of a flat several floors up, having previously memorised his card.

The electrician, of Quentin Smith and Sons, was an optimistic and chatty divorced guy in his mid-forties, with two grown-up boys learning the trade. He was a stereotypical dad, with a good sense of humour and terrible dance moves, a slightly podgy belly and a love of football on Saturday afternoons. Lucy was a mum of one teenage boy, making ends meet by selling her hand-crafted wedding invitations online. She longed for a steady hard-working man around the house, as her son's father had ended up in prison and she no longer wanted anything to do with bad boys. Their romance was due to be an incredibly happy one leading to Lucy conceiving her second child, a girl who would grow up to be a world-class ballet dancer and key advocate of the women's rights movement.

'I'll make my way up.' Casey approached the apartment building and let himself in, using an agency skeleton key that could open just about any lock. Residential assignments were a little complicated, as they often required a significant level of ruse or stealth. Casey opted for stealth as he made his way up the stairs, then used the key to silently slink into Lucy's apartment. He listened for movement. He could smell the electrical burning from the dodgy socket and Lucy was pacing in the kitchen, on a speakerphone call to her mother.

The buzzer for the flat rang.

'Sorry, Mum, I've got to go. That'll be the guy now.' She hurried out into the hall and answered the buzzer. 'Yes? Oh, great, I'm so glad you could get here so quickly.'

The soft lighting in the flat was made up of several floor lamps against a warm grey and peach decor. They flickered in unison, the oven timer started beeping and the fire alarm went off. 'Bloody electrics,' Lucy muttered, rushing to find a chair to stand on to turn off the noisy alarm.

Casey watched her silently from behind a heavy drape, carefully setting the golden arrow onto his bowstring. Down on the street below, Erron had sent an arrow neatly between the electrician's shoulder blades, a shower of sparkles glinting in the streetlight. Quentin wedged open the building's door while fetching his toolkit. As he did so, the streetlights mimicked the electrical fault in Lucy's flat and dappled on and off in a wild panic.

'Hmm. Might be a bigger job than I thought.' Quentin decided to check the external cables in the transformer box first and unlocked the panel. Several cables had been tampered with and were dangerously arcing. He pressed his coat sleeve over his nose as the smell of hot wire and melted plastic snaked from the box. Reaching for the emergency isolator switch, he suddenly paused, a strange stillness coming over him. His eyes rolled back a little before he let out a bellowing scream, his arms flailing in front of him as if fighting off an unseen foe. In his terror, he stumbled forward, his hands grasping onto the arcing cables with a searing crack of electricity. He was blown backwards with an immense force, landing with a heavy thud, his heart as still as a stone at the bottom of the sea.

Erron's jaw dropped and his bow fell, just as Lucy LeFarre threw herself from the lounge window, landing in a crunched, bloodied heap on the icy pavement below, mere feet from her would-be electrocuted lover.

'Oh . . . oh fuck,' Erron whispered, just as Casey landed near the mangled body of Ms LeFarre, his wings quickly folding in, a cold sweat on his face.

'She just . . . screamed and ran backwards, falling right through the glass. Like she could see something I couldn't,' Casey said hurriedly, all colour gone from his face. 'One minute, she was on the phone with her mother, the next, leaping past me into the night. Where's your guy?'

Erron nodded his forehead at the still-smouldering lump in the doorway that was Quentin Smith, father of two, toucher of live wires. Sparks still pulsed from the electricity box, a macabre firework display to mark the love that would never be.

Erron pulled himself together quickly, noticing movement of a curtain in the flat across from them, followed shortly by a commotion at the sight outside. 'We can't stay here, Case. Coppers will be crawling all over this in no time and we've got our next appointment and this one is important. We'll handle this after.'

'Right, yes, of course.' Casey stood dazed, unable to take his eyes off the broken skull of the young woman, knowing full well she was beyond saving. His heart bled for the ballet-dancer child who would never be.

Just like in the train station the day before, a thunderous shock wave nearly knocked them off their feet, sending loose chippings from a nearby roof scattering over the floor. The sky seemed to impossibly darken, and a flash of crimson lightning crackled across the heavy clouds, leaving an acrid smell of curdled blood in the air. Nearby traffic lights rearranged their light patterns, throwing a disco of red, amber and green light across the buildings in a chaotic manner. Each crossing bleeped simultaneously, and the few cars that were attempting to navigate the junctions were nervously edging over the white lines while the lights partied like it was 1999.

'This is serious.' Casey's mouth was agape at the traffic light anarchy that had followed the quake.

'We can't be seen here, you know that. We leave no trace.' Erron tugged Casey's arm and got him moving. 'Remember, Case, death has no secrets for us. They've already gone elsewhere.'

'Where were the Reapers?' Casey mouthed to himself as they fled. There was only a short window for a Hades agent to release a person's soul prior to the death, and Casey hadn't seen anyone hanging around or inside the flat. It didn't make any sense to him. As he jogged away, he caught a glimpse of a twisted shape in the reflection of a nearby window, which disappeared with a flash of lightning overhead. He was moving too fast to pick out any features, though the image left an unsettled sensation in his gut.

A few moments later, Casey skidded to a halt and leant up against a wall, his chest heaving as he caught his breath, Erron slowing down and following suit.

'Did you see that thing in the window?' Casey waved a pointed finger back towards the building where he'd seen the reflection, his face pale with fear.

'What thing?'

'Like some kind of person, but all twisted up and . . . rotting?'

'Case, you're in shock. It's probably just all the lights or something. I didn't see anything.'

'Something is really wrong here, Erron. One unexplained death is one thing, but three in the same week? All gold arrows? We need to make sure it doesn't happen again, especially not at the concert.'

'Obviously. But we haven't got any time to go off and find out what's going on now, have we?' Erron impatiently checked his watch.

Casey shakily retrieved his phone from his pocket and was stabbing at the screen with one finger, going through his contacts. 'I'm going to call Nikita, see if she can look into what these fractures mean, and why this has happened again. There's bound to be a record of it. She said she wanted to check it out.'

'What good would that do?' Erron folded his arms and peered over at his friend's phone to see what he had Nikita's name saved under.

'I was thinking, maybe if she can find something before our next assignment, it might actually stop this happening again,' Casey explained, finding 'New Recruit 452' and pressing dial.

Nikita was in her apartment when her new agency mobile rang, making her jump at the unexpected sound. She had been forced to get used to her first couple of days without her normal phone pinging with notifications. Nobody texts you when you're dead. The sudden detachment from social media and messaging had really amplified her sense of loneliness in the times she would have aimlessly scrolled through her feeds or video-called her friends.

Casey was on the line and sounded stressed. He explained what had just happened, and that he was hoping she was still up for looking at the library to see if there were any records of this happening before. She agreed, sensing the urgency in his voice and reassuring him she would get back to him as quickly as possible. He thanked her profusely and told her how to find Eligos as she bundled her notebook and pens into a tatty bag, one of the few remaining possessions from her former life.

11

Don't Fear the Reaper

NIKITA SET OUT TO THE Eligos within minutes of hanging up the call. On the walk in from the nearest Underground station, she'd noticed some odd occurrences, mostly indecisive traffic lights and the odd rubber duck lying on the pavement, sparking her curiosity, but putting it down to a strange set of coincidences.

Just under an hour since she'd left, she stood outside a building of such archaic magnificence that she felt like she was in the presence of a greater power. It was lucky she had been given detailed instructions on how to find it, as it was a building tucked away on a crossroad on Hampstead Grove, just west of Hampstead Heath. Like her apartment, it existed between the realms, only accessible to agents in the afterlife, so getting there first time was no easy feat. She had to first locate the outer gate, which was only visible to agents, but still well hidden within the thick privet hedge surrounding the grounds. Once she'd finally found it, she had to turn the gate key in a particular sequence back and forth (six turns to the right, three to the left and then back to the top) before it released a set of bolts to let her in. When she closed the gate behind her, she watched in amazement as the heavy key reset itself to its original position.

The Eligos library was gated and guarded, only the heavy foliage of the evergreen trees could be seen below the gothic stonework of the roof. Demonic stone gargoyles lounged and sneered from their various high roosts, watching over every corner of the immense building. A long gravel path led to the huge oak doors, which were flanked by two immense statues of winged knights on horses, each holding a book in one hand and a sword in the other. The doors led into a marble vestibule with a gilded revolving door, through which lay the lofty heights of vaulted ceilings, propped up by stone pillars bearing scores of carved climbing demons and damned souls in eternal reach of the descending armies of Heaven above. She breathed in the cool air, its scent of brittle pages and leather bindings filling her senses. Droves of candles littered the alcoves and lecterns, bright soldiers guarding the endless shelves of books as far as the eye could see. It seemed no mythology had been left by the wayside, statues of Greek gods stood next to Eastern deities, neighbours to Christian busts and Satanic effigies. The floor was a detailed depiction of a hellscape of fire and demons, directly beneath a mosaic ceiling of the celestial heavens.

Nikita's footsteps echoed softly as she padded past the ground-floor shelves, her presence inviting stolen glances from the few other agents using the library. Struck by the need to explore and get her bearings, she climbed a spiral of stairs which were encased in a brass scrollwork of bright vines and leaves. As she reached the top, to her left lay a deep-set reading and relaxation area, filled with soft lighting and softer vintage chairs. To her right was a further landing full of bookshelves which circled a brass balustrade, so that those on the second floor could look down on the mosaic floors below, and those on the ground floor could still see the beauty of the ceiling artwork.

Nikita trailed her fingers lightly over the edges of books, the smooth wall carvings and oak shelves. The building felt alive with the souls of a thousand authors and craftsmen; it practically whispered with ancient magic. Peering outside through the dome, she spotted the shooting range, a long stretch of perfect lawn, ensconced in the thick privet hedge and overhung by even older trees.

To complete her exploration, she descended back to the ground floor and found the archway entrance to the lower floor. A deep spiral of stone steps led to the pool that Freya had declared gave her the creeps, yet Nikita found it anything but. The high ceilings gave the gentle lap of warm water a soothing echo, the swirling steam from the vast pool rising to meet the cold air, like ghosts in an ethereal ballroom, dancing their last waltz before ascending to the gods. Nikita half expected toga-clad goddesses to rise from the pool and languish on the towel benches, fanning themselves with nothing but the glorious ancient ambience that oozed from the whole building.

She took a deep breath of the heavily misted air before finding her way back up to the ground floor to seek out the index cabinets. She was stabbing in the dark but she was determined to help her new friends out before their next assignment. Glancing at the wall clock, she saw that she didn't have much time before Casey was expecting her to call back. There was a clear sign on most of the non-fiction bookcases that no books could be taken off site, though she had no intention of carrying heavy volumes back to Canary Wharf when she wasn't entirely sure what she was looking for to begin with.

First, she found a couple of books on the general history of the Fates and, without an afterlife version of Google, found a seat and started frantically paging through the books, scanning the text for anything related to fractures, desperate to prove she could use her investigative skills for some good.

After half an hour of brisk skim reading, she found a small snippet of text about the fractures, which referenced an older book called *Rifts of Fate*. Keen to find the original source, she hurried down to the lower floors of the library. A dusty shaft of light fell on a row of antique books, lined up on a shelf beside a life-size statue of Lucifer before the Fall. She paused briefly to admire the resounding beauty of the marble angel, her fingers finding the smooth curve of his neck and trailing along the rough textured feather wings. Her eyes fell on the shelf of books behind the statue marked as *Pre-1900 Agency History* and her gaze caressed the book spines until she found *Rifts of Fate*. Compelled, she pulled the book from the shelf in a rush, but it slipped from her fingers and hit the mosaic floor with a muted thud. A handful of aged pages spilled from their binding and onto the floor.

'Oh shit,' she whispered, scooping up the loose papers and tucking the book under her arm.

She glanced around. No one had noticed her accidental vandalism, so she hurried back to her library desk, hoping to put the pages back in order. She was immediately drawn to the first page she held. It was titled 'Fractures'.

Conscious of the time, she absorbed as much of *Rifts of Fate* as she could, taking fervent notes of its contents. Her hand gripped her pen with such intensity that her fingers began to tingle. The text explained that fractures were caused by unplanned ripples in fate and ultimately, if left to accumulate, the very structure of the mortal world would be compromised. But there was little information regarding the finer details of this undesirable outcome. Instead, they skirted around the topic by giving examples of previous fractures. All of which seemed to occur after a botched assignment. Pausing briefly to stretch out her arms, Nikita read over the pages of notes she had made. In the bibliography at the back, she had found reference to another book that she was keen to read, but there was no mention of it on the main index cards by the unmanned centre desk.

A dark figure caught her eye and she looked over her notes to see Darren Oliver-Alliott enter the library, carrying a heavy book and dressed head to toe in black.

Most of the time, D-O-A was used to the same reception. Wherever he went, people looked away, hurriedly busied themselves or started quiet conversations with their companions. His presence could be likened to a dark horror film; people with morbid curiosity wanted to look at him, but they knew that it wasn't worth the nightmares. Visually, he wasn't horrific to look at; he appeared to be in his early fifties, his silver-white hair framing his soft face and rounded jawline, his narrow eyes deep set and striking blue. But it wasn't his appearance that was unnerving, it was that he possessed an aura of sheer terror, a disquieting *something* that made you feel haunted. The thousands of years that he'd been escorting souls from the mortal plain had left him saturated with death. He was the fear that lingered in a dark alleyway, when you dare not look back, as it was his steady footsteps walking softly behind.

Nikita, however, met his gaze steadily and he wasn't entirely sure what to do about that. He was even more confused when she stood up and walked towards him. She felt herself tremble slightly, the hairs on the back of her neck instinctively rising, but she ignored it and pressed on. She remembered Erron's explanation for the feeling in Nightjar, the first time she had spotted D-O-A, that it was the Reaper version of the Apollo Flush, keeping anyone and anything at a distance.

'Excuse me,' she said politely, resisting the urge to ask him questions about her own untimely death. Which was in fact, timely, now she thought of it.

He looked at her questioningly, an expression which invited her to continue.

'Do you know where I would find this book?' She showed him a piece of paper with the title *Vaticinium De Tumultus* written on it. 'It's not in the index cabinet and there is no other reference to it. I don't even know if it is something that would be kept here.'

D-O-A, still slightly in shock at someone choosing to speak to him, thought for a moment. 'It will be in the vault.' He enunciated his words carefully, a medieval voice having had to adapt to contemporary speech, though clinging to the hope that one day people would go back to speaking poetically and using *thee* and *thy* all over the place like there was n'er morrow.

'Which is . . . ?'

Frustrated that the conversation hadn't immediately ended, he sighed and placed his book on the desk. Nikita glanced at the title and wondered why someone who killed people for a living might be reading a beautiful leather-bound version of *Lord of the Rings*.

'Follow me,' he said sternly and led her to the second floor, stopping in front of a small shelf unit labelled 'Knitting and Woven Crafts'.

'It's a book about crochet?' Nikita pulled a face.

'A little agency jest.' D-O-A pulled the edge of a book called *Timeless Scarves* and the shelf swivelled slowly to reveal a hidden passageway. 'Cliché, I know.'

'It's a little *Scooby-Doo*.'

'Is that ... a book?'

She raised her eyebrow, and he reddened a little.

'I assume you have your access card?' he muttered.

Nikita fumbled in her pocket for the library card she'd been issued with. It was holographic and had a terrible photo of her, when she had only just been told she had died.

'No, that won't get you in the vault. You should have been issued with a special access card. Only senior staff can access the vault or sign off permission for someone to access it on their behalf.'

'Oh, I'm new. I don't have a pass.'

'I thought you looked new. What do you need the book for?' he questioned.

'I'm helping a friend with something.' She shivered slightly under his gaze, not wanting to lie to him, but choosing to be vague in case she was overstepping any boundaries.

He paused, seemingly studying her. 'I'll accompany you, but books can't be removed from the vault by anyone, so I will have to stay and supervise you.' He stopped himself from adding a 'milady' at the end.

They descended into the passageway and down another spiral of stairs, the 'Knitting and Woven Crafts' shelf closing behind them. The vault room was accessed through a heavy steel door and, once inside, automatic lights flickered on to reveal a modern, temperature-controlled space. Cool air caressed Nikita's skin as she entered first, admiring the perfect black of the walls, floor and ceiling against the stark white spotlights that lit up an ancient and breathtakingly carved bookcase.

The books themselves gave off a heady scent of thick parchment and ancient inks that would have excited any bibliophile, a carefully managed layer of dust settled on them, just enough to coat the antiquated covers but not enough to cause any decay. They were separated into six topics with bold, wood carved headings: **Apollo**; **Fortuna**; **Hades**; **Nemesis**; **Fates**; **Chaos**.

'These are the rarest books, some of them as old as the divisions themselves. But they are here because the information they contain must never be in the mortal domain,' D-O-A explained.

'Isn't the whole library off limits to anyone but agency staff?'

'Yes, but these books are incredibly rare and ancient, so they have to be stored where there's an audit trail of who enters this room. Only a handful of copies exist, stored in other headquarters across the world, and you have to be in management to actually authorise their removal.' He gestured for her to approach the shelves. 'The book you seek will be in the "Chaos" section.'

She knelt to examine the titles, while D-O-A sat down on a chair in a shadowy corner of the room. Moments later, she muttered that the book wasn't there.

'It must be,' he said, his voice nothing but an echo from the darkness. 'They never leave this room.'

'Well, unless this book looks remarkably like a gap where a book used to be, then it's not here.'

He emerged from the shadows and crouched down next to her. 'No, no, it's not possible.' He sounded frantic, like a man who had lost his child in a busy shopping centre.

'This is where it would be, right?' She placed a finger in the gap. There was no dust. 'Looks like it was taken recently.'

He had zoned her out and was inspecting every inch of the shelves, then the room, and even the alcove above the door.

'Is there a librarian? Someone who runs this place?'

'Not so much a physical entity, but yes, sort of. He goes by the name of Dantalion and you would need to request discourse through the appropriate means,' D-O-A said seriously.

'Which is . . . ?'

'You'll need to leave a note in the library guest book. How he responds will be entirely down to his discretion.'

'This is . . . worth disturbing him over?' She checked the time on her mobile, she only had about fifteen minutes before Casey expected a call back.

'Indubitably.' D-O-A nodded and led her out of the room, swiping his access card and heaving the heavy steel door open.

The guest book was more of a huge ledger, balanced on the central desk near the index cabinet. A pen of goose quill with a needle-sharp point rested in a specially made stone fountain of crystal water.

'Where's the ink?' Nikita lifted the plume of black feather. She leant over the ledger and could see previously scrawlings, all written in a dark stain of red. 'Is that *blood*?'

D-O-A nodded solemnly. 'It has to be worthwhile to summon him. Dantalion is a Demon of the Balance. He's not a Chaos agent, nor does he work for the Fates, but he still requires cosmic blood in exchange for his services.'

'Why? What does he do with it?' She hugged herself and stepped back a little from the ledger.

'The cosmic energy in agency blood is incredibly potent. It's like pure stardust. Demons and chaos agents alike crave it and the power it holds. A few drops can summon one to the edge of the veil when used at a designated portal.'

'This book is a portal?' she asked, gently touching the ledger.

'No, the fountain is. Water, mirrors, glass. Certain reflective surfaces can be used as portals. But don't worry, the active ones are well established and very carefully protected. You won't summon a demon accidentally,' he reassured her. 'This fountain has been here for hundreds of years. There are only four key locations that Dantalion can be reached.'

She dithered nervously, her face slightly wrinkled with the thought of giving a gift of cosmic blood.

'Here, allow me.' Ever the chivalrous knight, despite his outward persona, D-O-A took the quill. 'Your blood would be a valuable offering as a new recruit, though I wish not to tarnish your fair skin when I hath . . . *have* got plenty of my own. And this matter concerns me also.' He drew the sharp nib of the pen deeply across his palm, bringing forward a bright line of blood. Disturbingly, the pen slowly drew the blood up into a small glass vessel at the base of the plume.

Nikita watched in awe as he wrote a message in the ledger in neat copperplate, making certain to mention that the response be sought at the earliest convenience. Once he had finished, he flexed his hand, the wound closing slowly in front of their eyes.

'It will be I that he contacts for it is my offering, but, alas, I do not know your name.'

'Nikita Wolf.' She somehow felt the need to curtsey but held back.

'Then, I shall ensure a message is passed to you when I hear from him.'

As he spoke, the pages of the ledger ruffled as if blown by a strong wind, the candles all simultaneously flickering out for a moment, before resuming their endless light.

'He has received our message,' D-O-A affirmed, placing the quill back into its stone basin. The crystal waters enlivened as if full of tiny unseen hands, drawing any leftover blood from the nib and making it disappear. 'It might be hours, or days, before a reply.' He bowed his head and went back to his heavy Tolkien volume.

'Thank you!' Nikita called after him, returning to her notes. A grandfather clock at the back of the hall chimed half past eight. She pulled out her phone and called Casey, relaying the information she had found.

12

The Show Must Go On

WHEN CASEY AND ERRON ARRIVED at the concert, hordes of fans were already gathering, a sea of black clothing dotted with studs, chokers, corsets and tailcoats. A heavy sense of dread lay in the agents' stomachs, but neither felt up to discussing it straightaway. Casey had just got off the phone to Nikita and relayed to Erron everything she'd said. Despite what she'd found, they were no clearer on the situation.

'I knew we should have gone for eyeliner.' Erron tried to remain calm as he surveyed the men in the crowd, the bulk of whom were done up with heavy makeup and numerous piercings.

'We're here to work ... Nobody is going to be looking at us closely anyway.' Casey wrung his hands nervously.

'Hey, remember that time you made us dress as Christmas elves?' Erron tried to ease the twisting feeling in his stomach as he thought about the candy-cane tights and curly-toed elf shoes they had donned while waiting to shoot Father Christmas in a shopping centre.

Casey managed a half-smile, but his face was still a sickly white. 'I have a really bad feeling, Erron. Do you think we should even go ahead with this one? We need to call Kendra and explain that it's happened again.'

Not one to admit his own fears, Erron just sighed. 'Give her a call then.'

Casey found a quiet corner and dialled their boss's number. Kendra picked up on the fourth ring. Shakily, he explained the situation and asked if she wanted them to pull out of the KiaRia assignment. Kendra was already backstage at the concert and sighed audibly at the inconvenience.

'Hart, I wouldn't worry about it right now. We haven't got a lot of time and I can't give you any explanation as I'm still waiting to hear back from Lettie Crawford at Hades. They must have had this sort of thing happen before and know a lot more about death than I do. Besides, the world isn't going to come crashing down after a couple of mishaps,' she reasoned.

'But what if it's a glitch with our assignments? Something could go wrong on this one too,' Casey raised.

'We haven't a lot of choice right now, do we? Stick to the job and we can discuss the other two tomorrow.'

Casey reluctantly agreed and hung up.

'I'm sure it's just a hiccup.' Erron shrugged after Casey relayed Kendra's response. 'Let's get it over with then. It's out of our control. We need to find the best place for the final act anyway,' he conceded.

Backstage was crowded with event staff and a small gathering of fans who were allowed access to the exclusive bar and costume room. It wasn't difficult for two Apollo agents surrounded by an aura of natural charm to make their way in unnoticed. Four team members were responsible for keeping the fans in check and making sure that they didn't wander into the restricted places. But the staff radios were playing up and causing a significant distraction, enough for Erron and Casey to slip past them and explore some of the restricted areas.

Erron had been given the KiaRia assignment, and Casey had been given the matching card for one of the starlet's close friends, a backing singer called Chloe Moore, stage name Ravenette. The Fates had decided that both would be catapulted into a new and wonderful direction in life by falling in love with each other at approximately 21.53 during the final song of the set, when KiaRia would catch Ravenette from falling off stage after she tripped on an amp lead.

They found an outdoor staff gazebo that had little foot traffic and seemed to be stacked with surplus sound equipment and excess boxes of fan merchandise. It was out of the way enough that they could talk comfortably over the noise of the warm-up acts on stage.

'Go on then, give me the rundown: their histories, favourite films, how long their hair was on their fifteenth birthday, or whatever other rubbish is in their files.' Erron was perched on a disused speaker, smoking and half listening to the surging excitement of the crowd out front. A couple of hours had passed since their ordeal, and he was trying to focus on the upcoming job.

Casey folded his arms defiantly. 'Not if you're going to be like that.'

'Fine, whatever, just making conversation.' He dropped the cigarette stub in a half-empty cup of lukewarm beer.

'You should read the files, really.'

'Have you read *my* file?'

126

Casey looked away awkwardly.

'You have, haven't you? Bloody hell, is nothing sacred and left to the realms of mystery?' Erron asked incredulously. 'Even *I* haven't read my own file. How did you even access it?'

'No comment,' Casey said with an apologetic smile.

'All right, I'll bite.' Erron dropped down from the speaker to face his friend. 'When was I born? What school did I go to? What was my first car?'

Casey coughed, avoiding the challenge.

'Come on, Sherlock, don't give me the silent treatment.'

'OK, OK ... Twenty-first of March, 1950. Grafton Primary, Islington, then Beacon High School. A 1962 Ford Cortina in blue.'

'Fuck me ... they really do have everything on file.' Erron raised his eyebrows in astonishment. 'I'm more worried you remember all that shit.'

'I wouldn't forget it,' Casey said quietly, his face flushing.

They were interrupted by a stressed staff member who blustered past in a flurry of static radio crackle. She was attempting to get a full response on her headset but was met only with whirring and hissing. 'These bastard things have never done this before,' she cursed, fiddling with the radio controls frantically, before noticing the two gothic Cupids. 'You ... you're not supposed to be back here. You need to leave.'

Erron held his hands up in guilt.

'Look, if you're part of the backstage lot, it only covers the exclusive bar mainly. The band are arriving in less than five minutes, so if you want to meet them before their first set, I recommend you head there.' She shooed them with her clipboard and bulging eyes. 'Go ... go!'

13

Tainted Love

THE BACKSTAGE LOUNGE AND BAR were a cleverly thrown together mix of neon lighting and black plastic panelling, succeeding in looking space age on a budget. The ceilings felt too low and the pulse of background music thrummed in such a way that it turned the stomach slightly, much like the sensation of stepping off a roller coaster. The staff were all dressed head to toe in black, as were most of the fans, so walking into the dark room was like navigating a black hole with sunglasses on. Erron forged a path through to the bar, in the hope of picking up a short measure before the show, but quickly retreated when he caught a glimpse of the prices. Kendra was at the bar, having snuck in with her own Apollo charms, and she waved them down. Erron's eyes bulged at the sight of her hair, which appeared to have twice the usual volume and at least six cans of hairspray holding it skyward.

'I can't stay here long as I need to get to the front row!' she shouted over the music. 'I hope it goes well for you guys. We'll talk about the other assignments in the morning, don't stress.'

Before either of them could answer, a surge of excitable fans rose up like a tide to meet the star of the show, followed by her band, as they entered the stifling neon void.

The singer was stunning, her petite figure poured into a black lace corset and thigh-high fishnet stockings, a spangly miniskirt barely covering her. Her long black hair had been pinned up in an eccentric style and coated in gold glitter and she looked every bit her young age as she kept close to her staff, like a fawn loitering in the shadow of its mother. She greeted fans graciously with a wide, perfectly white-toothed smile, signing autographs and shaking hands. Erron watched her sail through the crowd effortlessly, all the while spinning his pewter lighter in his hand and letting it catch the neon lights. He was accidentally shoved sideways and dropped it, sending it spinning under the bar. Kendra ducked down and fished around for it, her squat frame lost in the throng of people.

KiaRia was moving towards Erron, pulling out a cigarette from her tiny handbag, and gave him a mischievous smile.

'Got a light, handsome?' she asked with a giggle.

He looked round to where Kendra had stood up, brushed herself off and handed the singer his lighter. KiaRia smiled as she lit the cigarette before she was hustled away by her security guards.

Casey and Erron used the distraction to slip out of the room and find refuge in the costume closet – *closet* not being an accurate word as the space was almost bigger than Casey's entire house. A young girl with a striking bob of ginger hair was sat by a mirror applying mascara, dressed in a svelte red lace-up dress, something akin to what Dracula might have worn if he were a seventeen-year-old girl and had a taste for high heels that hurt just to look at. Casey recognised her to be Ravenette, the target for his assignment. She was startled by their sudden appearance in the room but soon warmed to them when she realised they were keen fans. More accurately, she warmed to them because Casey fixed her with a deep stare, exuding all manner of Apollo charm.

'Lovely to see you guys at the show tonight.' She stood, wobbled slightly on the heels, but regained composure quickly. 'I'm surprised you aren't in there with Kia.'

'Oh, we're huge fans, of course.' Casey grinned with feigned enthusiasm. 'We said hello to her first.'

'Of course. Well, I don't usually get the same following but that's the price you pay for being a backing singer.' She laughed delicately, but there was a sadness in her eyes.

'We couldn't waste the opportunity to meet you before you went on stage,' Casey enthused, his smile was warm and oozing with charm. Erron wondered if one day Casey might exude so much charm that he turned into a puddle of pink, glittery slime, around which people frolicked and fluttered their eyelids at him. He put the bizarre thought out of his head and played along.

'Yes, after all, no singer can make a show this good without her backup. I have no doubt that with your talent you'll soon be leading your own band.' Erron didn't enjoy the taste of his words as he never liked to tell a bare-faced lie. Not that he didn't mean it, he just had absolutely no clue who the girl was. Casey, however, had read her file and was intimately aware of her shoe size and where she went on holiday last year, among many other pointless facts.

'It's an honour to meet you, Ravenette.' Casey shook her hand excitably.

'Thank you.' She winked at him. 'Enjoy the show, guys. I must be going. I hope you are sticking around for the after-party.'

'Oh, we will, definitely.'

She walked with the care of a bomb disposal expert balancing a detonation device in her hands, her towering heels threatening to break her ankles with every step.

'You went all out with the charm there, Case,' Erron said flatly, his brow furrowed.

'Of course I did! You honestly think a seventeen-year-old girl would be enthusiastic about a thirty-three-year-old?'

'Plus a couple of hundred years.' Erron snorted.

'Thirty-three plus a bit then, OK … but they don't count because I haven't aged. I didn't exactly want her to scream about two old guys traipsing in on her alone while she was doing her makeup. Especially while I am dressed like *this*. Hardly says discretion.'

Erron seemed relieved. 'Anyway, I'm not old. I'm thirty-one.'

'Plus a bit. Technically, you're sixty-odd.'

People spend a lot of time and money trying to halt or even reverse the signs of ageing; if only they knew that death was one way to permanently preserve a good complexion and put to rest any aches and pains. Apollo agents were especially blessed with the glow of their division, a trace of the Apollo Flush remaining long after the initial hormonal effects had worn off.

The show was beginning, lights danced across the crowd and the heaving mass of bodies pulsed with excitement, the air muddled with the heavy smell of lukewarm beer and sweat. Up front in the crowd, who were hyping themselves up with cups of cider, Kendra was letting her hair down with a friend from the office, scanning for Erron and Casey. Screams erupted when KiaRia and her band took to the stage, wasting no time before bursting into their first song of the set – 'A Wicked Thunder'. Meanwhile, the two Apollo agents had taken refuge in the wings, tucked out of view in the folds of a hefty velour curtain. It was cramped and stifling hot as they stood chest to chest, desperately trying not to be seen. Despite the agents' cloaking technique, which allowed them to blend into a crowd, it couldn't entirely help to explain a moving, whispering curtain.

'You're standing on my foot,' Casey hissed.

'I'll stand on your face if you don't shut up.' Erron clamped a hand over Casey's mouth as a member of staff went by, muttering distractedly to themselves about the electronics control board playing up. Once they had both disappeared, Erron let go at the same time shifting his foot. 'We can't stay here all night, we'll suffocate.'

Casey raised an eyebrow and considered it. 'There are worse situations to be in.'

Erron looked up, in time to see Casey wearing the brief flicker of a soft, daydreamy smile and he wondered what he might have meant. Casey broke eye contact and fiddled with the buttons on his tailcoat in an attempt to steady the nervous tremble in his hands.

Erron thought best not to question it and fumbled in his trouser pocket for his assignment card. 'Right, we've got to time this really well. Ravenette takes a fall stage right after the final song and twists her ankle. KiaRia catches her. That's the moment; our arrows will practically cross. Damn, the Fates don't make this shit easy.'

'It adds to the fun.'

'I'm dying for a smoke.' Erron exhaled dramatically, shifting his footing once more to keep his legs from getting pins and needles. He was stood so close to Casey that he could see the missed stitching on his waistcoat and fought the urge to break off a loose thread.

The band were coming to the end of the first set, the heavy bass giving the two agents a sensation akin to a minor heart attack.

'Well, smoking is completely out of the question.'

'I know that. Do I look bloody stupid?'

'When you come to mention it, in that outfit ...' Casey teased, though deep down he couldn't help but admire how good Erron looked, but he was loath to admit it.

'Oh, shut up, you melon. I look great,' he said dismissively.

The concert had now reached an interval and a low-key supporting act was keeping the music going while fans fought through the bar and toilet queues.

'Hello, boys!' A chirpy voice interrupted them, its owner pulling a bit of the curtain aside to peek through.

With a face of pure innocence, blonde-haired and blue-eyed Ember Songfire smiled widely at them. She was an agent of the Fortuna Division, responsible for dishing out hefty quantities of either good or bad luck. She'd died in a rather unlucky accident in the 1960s, when part of a tipi had collapsed on her at a festival and she'd never deviated from her hippy fashions of bellbottom jeans, cropped tie-dye vests or shell peace sign necklaces. It worked for her, and she was such a sweetheart that no one ever pointed her in the direction of the current decade. Everything about her screamed *wholesome*. And gullible. Erron had once managed to convince her that you shrunk if you stood behind a fridge for long enough. The Fortuna Division lost her for three days while she tested the theory. She and Casey had been good friends for decades and she often joined them at Nightjar.

'I see you're getting cosy on the job there. Sorry to disturb, but I thought I would say hi.' Her voice was akin to sunlight on a perfect summer's day, warm and bubbling with sweetness.

'Oh no, we weren't,' Erron protested.

'It's quite all right, I won't tell head office.' She winked knowingly. 'What you do before a hit is no business of mine. Can't say I blame you. Peace and love, guys. I'm here for the backing singer, Ravenette? She's getting a whole host of goodness after you've pinged her with your love spell.' She grinned encouragingly, dropped the curtain and went skipping away to where she was planning to work her own agency art. Fortuna agents' work involved no bows or arrows, but simply a kiss of some sort to pass the luck on. In her belt of silver daisies and yellow festival shirt, she stood out among the throng of vampiric fans like a dolphin at a crime scene.

It was no surprise that she'd located them without so much as a search, blessed as she was with an afterlife of good fortune. Much like the Apollo Flush for Cupids, Fortuna agents were gifted with a heavy hand in good luck; for example, they never had to look where they were going, check a bus timetable or make a dinner reservation. Things just fell exactly right wherever they went. Of course, they weren't permitted to abuse these powers off the record, like buying lottery tickets but there wasn't a single Fortuna agent that hadn't, off the record, tried their hand at the grabber machines in the local arcades. Erron sometimes wished he could gain the favour of an agent like Ember, to make his lottery attempts more profitable.

Erron's face burned crimson after Agent Songfire's comment and he muttered about the heat of the stifling curtain. His wings were cramping and he arched his back to try and ease the ache. They still had around an hour to hang around before they could complete their assignments and the tension was building.

'Oh, fuck this, I need a break.' Erron fought his way out of the curtain, patting down his pockets for his cigarettes and lighter while the blood dissipated from his cheeks. 'Case, you seen my lighter?'

Furrowing his brow, Casey shook his head, but looked around his feet and the folds of the curtain, and even inside both of their kitbags.

Erron muttered a string of expletives and paced back and forth in frustration, realising that Kendra had given it to KiaRia before the show.

'I'm sure we'll get it back for you,' Casey reasoned.

Inhaling slowly and deeply, Erron calmed down enough to agree. They spent the next forty-nine minutes talking quietly to pass the time until eventually, KiaRia announced that her final song would be a new creation. The crowd screamed in anticipation as the guitars started their intro.

The petite singer, usually with a powerful vocal output, came in softly when the drum solo died off. Casey's ears pricked up at the last set of lyrics as an unwanted feeling of disquiet crept over him.

Yeah . . . I'm followed by shadows,
They are claiming my soul,
Like the fading of a TV screen,

Like the crackling of a radio,
When there's only static and no more show ...

Erron had assembled his bow and fitted his arrow before the singer got to her second chorus, and Casey wasn't far behind. They emerged from behind the curtain, arrows poised at half draw, tracking their respective targets.

'Oh, hey, I can see your lighter.' Casey nodded to where it lay at the front of the stage. It struck him as odd that KiaRia would have taken it on stage.

'Thank Christ, I'll grab it after the show,' Erron replied, relieved.

They both jumped in shock when a high-pitched electrical squeal reverberated around the stadium. Erron loosened his arrow, which sailed across the stage, unseen by the crowd, and shattered into a burst of sparkles as it hit KiaRia.

The stage lights flickered chaotically and KiaRia's microphone cut out in the last few lines of her song. She froze on the spot, her eyes drifting out of focus and staring vacantly ahead, gripping the microphone to her chest.

'This isn't ...' Casey started.

'... in the file?' Erron finished.

'No. What's happening?'

'Technical glitch, surely? They must have backup.' As Erron spoke, the sound and lights went back to their former glory and the backing singers repeated their string of 'oohs' and 'ahhs' to finish off the song. As the music reached an ear-bleeding climax, KiaRia, still seeming out of touch with reality, leapt forward in a frantic movement, her eyes filled with terror and a tortured scream escaping from her throat. She accidentally skidded on Erron's lighter, which sent her flailing like a deer on a frozen lake towards the stage front. In the same moment, a huge burst of flames exploded at the front of the stage as the end-of-show pyrotechnics were set off.

At the same time as the drums rose to a crescendo, the young singer stumbled into the flames, which roared with a volcanic intensity. She flailed her arms, her screams turning to a rasped gurgling before she collapsed into a burning hulk over one of the speakers. For a moment, everything stopped. Then the screaming from the band began, shattering the illusion among the crowd that it was a cleverly staged stunt. Applause turned to silence, which in turn morphed into a horrific wailing from distraught fans. Fire marshals and medical staff rushed onto the stage to put out the blaze and assess the extent of the singer's injuries. But Casey and Erron both knew that she was dead. They both had a terrible sense of déjà vu.

'What in the *Final Destination* was that?!' Erron exclaimed, horrified.

The concert grounds began to stink of acrid burning flesh and people were screaming to leave. Eventually, the surging of the crowds prompted door staff to allow people to escape into the night air, where a thick sleet was falling over the wet streets of London.

Right on cue, a violent earthquake rumbled through the entire stadium, shaking amps off the stage and causing cables to snap, sending sparks flying and light units crashing down, narrowly missing the band and stage staff. Microphones squealed and the speakers began playing a bizarre high-pitched version of a Johnny Cash song. Deafening crashes of thunder ripped through the sky, carrying intense streaks of multicoloured lightning that could have rivalled any laser show on Earth.

Casey instinctively shielded Erron beneath his arms as stage equipment crashed down beside them, a lighting unit glancing off Casey's shoulder. Once the quake had calmed, Casey released his friend and turned his face away from the horrific mess on stage, not being able to watch the medics go through the motions on the blistered and melted form of KiaRia. Erron placed his bow down out of sight.

'Oh god, are you OK?' Erron saw the blood seeping through a tear in his friend's jacket.

'I'm fine, it's OK. Are you OK?' Casey flexed his shoulder, knowing he would heal quickly if it was a simple laceration.

'Yeah, I'm OK thanks to you. But we need to help,' he stated, nodding towards the stage.

'There's nothing we can do for KiaRia.'

'Not for her, but . . . for *her*.' He gestured towards Ravenette, the hysterical girl in the svelte red dress, the makeup she'd applied earlier streaming down her cheeks. 'Casey, do your thing. Off the record, you know.'

'I can't, I can't.' He was in a panicked state, wild fear in his eyes.

'Casey,' Erron said firmly. 'This is what you do. You care. You help people.'

Taking a deep breath, Casey nodded and went to where Ravenette had been pushed off near the side wing out of the way of the commotion. The 'off-the-record' thing was something Casey had perfected when there was a time and a place. The time was when a person, so desperately in need of comfort, needed something equally irrational to shock their body back into control. The place was right there, at the concert, where Ravenette was looking at the girl she was supposed to fall in love with being hoisted onto a gurney.

Casey brought her into a hug, then let his wings unfold and wrapped them around her, completely enveloping her in softness and shielding her from the horror of the scene. It was forbidden for agents to reveal their wings to mortals, but he had discovered a long time ago that people in dire straits would easily forget, putting their experience down to shock, or a dream, or a brush with an angelic presence. To be embraced by the wings of a Cupid can only be described as floating in a bubble of ecstasy, where feelings of peace, love and harmony ripple around you like the lapping of a tide, where your heart is filled with a piece of music that your soul dances to.

The girl softened in his grip and her sobbing subsided. He released her slowly, allowing her emotions to gradually balance themselves, so she would not suffer the sudden shock of emotional collapse.

'Who *are* you?' she whispered, her face a Jackson Pollock of mascara.

'Just a friend,' he replied. 'Who are you staying with tonight?'

She explained she was staying with a few band members at a nearby hotel, her response sluggish, still heavily under the influence of the winged embrace.

'My friend here will call you a cab. You get back, take a hot bath. I'm sure there will be people who will want to speak to you in the morning.'

Erron was already dialling a taxi for the girl. She was nodding, blindly agreeing to the suggestion, unable to fully generate her own decisions. She provided the address of her hotel without a thought and allowed herself to be led to the rear exit to wait for the cab.

'I don't even understand.' Ravenette was mostly talking to herself, having lost the ability to engage with anything or anyone around her.

She would forget the sight of Casey and Erron the moment they left the scene and, if she met them again, they would be those vague familiar faces that you just can't place. One of the show staff had come out to find the backing singer and shepherded her to a private car instead to be driven to her hotel.

Fighting through swathes of people, a flustered Kendra appeared and grabbed Erron by the wrist. 'Did you see anything? What on earth happened up there?'

'I don't know. It looked like she slipped over. It was an accident.'

'OK. Get yourselves home immediately. We'll talk tomorrow.' Kendra turned on her black kitten heels and walked off, her big hair bobbing up and down like a space hopper as she went.

Casey gathered up their kitbags, struggling to understand how their assignments could have gone so horribly wrong.

'Let's get out of here.' Erron walked out into the accumulating slush of the cold night and checked his phone, his hands sweating despite the chill.

There didn't seem to be any disruption to traffic lights like after the last quake, but every so often they stumbled across rubber ducks scattered across the street, the largest of which was the size of a dog. The roads were relatively empty apart from a lone goose honking its way towards central London, the slap-slap of its feet audible in the cold night air.

Eventually, Casey put an arm around Erron and squeezed his shoulder. 'Are you sure you're OK?'

Erron shrugged him off. 'I'm fine.'

The earthquake had long since abated and the thunder had made way to a thick sleet, which was slowly soaking through their clothes and clinging in their hair as they trudged in silence. Casey dragged his feet a little, his hands pushed firmly into the pockets of his new coat. After a long pause he spoke.

'Are you heading straight home?'

'Not yet. I need to get my head around everything.' Erron pushed a flop of soggy hair out of his eyes, deep in thought. 'Chess?'

Casey breathed out a thin cloud of cold vapour, considering the deviation. 'I'd like that.'

One of their favourite places to go was the Sky Pod Bar with its expansive view over the city and legendary sunsets. They rarely ordered food there, but they were well known by the staff and had a small table reserved with a built-in Berkeley chess set, which was miraculously ignored by any other patrons. The perks of which meant they often stayed after closing hours, because it was remarkably easy for people to forget they were even there.

Casey always faced the window and played the white pieces on the board. Erron didn't mind sacrificing the view, as he didn't get anywhere near as gushing over sunsets as Casey did. When they reached the bar, they were greeted by Stefan, the lanky Greek bartender, who gave them a friendly nod and started on a strawberry and marshmallow milkshake for Casey and a straight measure of Kraken dark rum for Erron. Their first drinks were on the house, not as a result of the Apollo charm, but because they always left a healthy tip for being left alone to talk.

Casey kicked off with hopping a knight in front of a pawn. It was the starter move he usually chose, and though they had played hundreds of times, he still won nearly every game. Erron was much more suited to poker, or anything on a Sega Mega Drive.

'What did Kendra say again?' Casey asked.

'Not a lot. She just said we would talk tomorrow.'

'Are we in trouble?'

'Clearly these deaths are all linked somehow. And currently the only link seems to be that we had all the assignments,' Erron answered, dithering over the placement of a bishop. 'But did the victims know each other, do you reckon, or have something in common?'

'Sofia Carter had no connection with the singer. The other two, I don't even think they'd met each other before dying in the same very moment.' Casey snatched away the black bishop triumphantly.

'I don't get it. How could four assignments be wrong?'

'The Fates must be confusing the assignment cards. There's a crossed wire with Hades Division somewhere, surely?'

'Maybe, or ... and hear me out.' Erron decisively pushed a rook sideways. 'Perhaps, Ember Songfire's luck assignment was for Ravenette *because* KiaRia was supposed to die, which would make Ravenette's career take off following all the publicity.'

'So why did I get a card for Ravenette then? You can't tell me another card was generated for no good reason. And did you notice KiaRia's eyes before she slid over ... ? She seemed like she was looking at something no one else could see, same with Lucy before she leapt from the window.'

'Quentin Smith acted oddly too, but I still think you're over-speculating, Case. There will be a reason for all of this;

it's not our fault. There is something bigger going on, and I imagine it's all just a big corporate fuck-up.' Erron gingerly edged his rook closer to Casey's knight.

'No, not this time. Something is very wrong. That girl didn't want to die. Someone or something changed her fate when the stage power went all jittery ...' Casey gripped the knight in mid-air as he went inside his own thoughts for a moment.

'The fire alarm!'

Erron stared at his friend impatiently, waiting for an explanation. Stefan had brought over their drinks and left a small neon green cocktail umbrella on the table.

'The rest of the electrics in Lucy LeFarre's flat were playing up and I thought it was just an issue with the faulty socket, but the fire alarm went off too.'

'Your point is?'

'Fire alarms like hers are run on AA batteries. Why would that go off at the same time as everything else?'

'You know Ghosters affect electrics.' Erron rubbed his temples. 'They must have been there to collect the souls. Like I said, these were all Hades jobs and we got mixed up in it somehow.'

'No, it's too much of a coincidence. Hades agents aren't invisible to us, Erron. Even when cloaked, *we* can still see them.'

Erron sighed. 'The streetlights were flickering too, when Quentin Smith ended up playing cat's cradle with a couple hundred volts. It was already faulty, though, the cables were doing some crazy shit when he opened the box. But ... and this is a big but ... if there was a Ghoster there, then Kendra will find out who and why.' He took a long swig of his drink and rolled the taste over his teeth.

'OK,' Casey conceded. 'We'll leave it to them to sort. I guess it's not our problem.' He leant back in his chair and stretched. His cosmic heart jolted at the flash of an image in the reflection of the glass behind Erron. A hideous face, covered in teeth and pulsating boils, grinning from the gloom of the night sky outside. He swivelled in his chair to see if it was stood behind him, but nothing was there.

'Case?' Erron questioned. 'You OK?'

Casey rubbed his eyes and shook the image out of his mind. He was exhausted and stressed. 'I think I'm just tired.' He let out a long sigh.

Concerned by the troubled look on Erron's face, Casey changed the subject quickly.

'So, what do you think of our new agent, Nikita? She seems very lovely.' Casey smiled warmly. 'She's taken to things very quickly.'

'Yeah,' Erron answered bluntly.

'I think she's going to fit in really well. I mean, those croissants she brought in for a start,' Casey chattered on, pausing when Erron scraped his chair back swiftly and stood. 'Where are you going?'

'I'd love to sit here and chat about how you've got a crush on the new girl, Case, but I'm tired, and frankly, not interested.'

Casey sat wide-eyed for a moment. 'Oh no, you have it all wrong. I'm not after her at all.'

'Sure.' Erron's sarcasm was palpable.

'I think you need some sleep,' Casey chided and rose from his chair slowly.

They left the remainder of their drinks, a hefty tip and their game unfinished. Stefan smiled politely as they left, waiting a heartbeat or two before scurrying over for the money. Casey pocketed the neon umbrella away from the sleet that was turning to hail, pinging off cars and dancing chaotically on the pavement. Flight in heavy hail was exhausting and tended to hurt the eyes, so they opted for a night bus back to the Isle of Dogs, entering the Apollo building just after midnight, where they dropped their kit back in silence and went their separate ways home.

14

This Train Don't Stop There Anymore

K ENDRA HAD SPENT THE EARLY hours of the morning in a meeting with the other division bosses discussing the fatal assignments. Each death had caused fracture in the usual smooth running of the mortal world and, if the fallout effects of the fractures were left to continue, the worse they would become.

It was not a new phenomenon; fractures had occurred previously when assignments had been missed or gone wrong, but never multiple occurrences in a short space of time. They were best explained using the analogy of a scarf. The progression of time was like an endless scarf, forever being added to, stitch by stitch, by the Fates (who didn't actually knit the scarf as they were far too busy for anything like that). Each time a fixed point was missed or changed, it left a tiny snag in the scarf which altered the normal order of things in the mortal world, like politicians telling the truth or printers reaching the end of a document without running out of ink, paper or the will to live. The imperfections, if left to build, caused bigger fractures and eventually posed the threat of unravelling the entire scarf. And for Chaos, an unravelled scarf was a perfect excuse to sneak through the worldly divide and start, well, *causing chaos*. And nobody this side of the mortal veil wanted that. Life on Earth would become a hellish nightmare of nonsense, torn apart faster than Max Verstappen could get round the Monaco circuit.

It had been agreed that, due to the seriousness of the situation, the division bosses would summon Elzifur, the Lord of Chaos, to find out whether the fractures had travelled across the veil.

'We must know the extent of these fractures beyond the veil,' the Nemesis boss, Osato M'Raya, stated. Her voice, despite having spent many hundreds of years in London, still possessed the punchy undertones of her Benin and Togo heritage and demanded attention from the listening ear. She was the embodiment of justice, brimming with power and righteous fury, midnight eyes and the clean-shaven head of a Dahomey Amazon warrior.

To Osato's right sat Lettie Crawford, the Hades boss. She was petite, sleek dark hair with distinctive silver stripes framing her face, a pair of maroon glasses perched on her nose. Though she didn't take up much space in the room, her Hades aura gave her weight and presence like no other.

'Agreed. We need to know what we are dealing with.' Lettie stood and walked towards a large object covered in a red velvet drape. Beneath was an ornate full-length mirror on wheels, which Lettie carefully pushed to the head of the table before removing the drape. The mirror's surface was dark, reflecting the room with a strange haze that dimmed and distorted the images.

A fourth figure sat in the room, a strikingly handsome middle-aged man with silver-blond hair and a tweed suit. He was Emrys Taliesin, head of the Fortuna Division. He spoke in a soft Welsh accent. 'Who'll be summoning him?'

Kendra shrank into her chair. 'I'd rather not.'

'I will,' Osato offered.

'No, you did last time, if I recall. Allow me.' Emrys rolled up his sleeve and approached the mirror. Lettie passed him a penknife and he pressed the blade to his palm, wincing as it cut through his skin. 'Elzifur, we bid you come to the edge of the veil and consult with us.'

He smeared the reflective surface with his blood before returning to his seat. Osato offered him a handkerchief to press against the wound as the mirror began to react. The blood swirled and danced on the surface before it was sucked into the aether, leaving a residue of cosmic sparkles in its wake.

Darkness filled the mirror before an image shimmered to the surface. The Lord of Chaos scanned the room as he appeared. Bound by the laws of the Fates, Elzifur could not enter the realm of mortals and could only interact through a mirrored surface, summoned by a drop of cosmic blood and a spoken request, much like Dantalion, the library guardian. He presented as somewhat human, with long dark hair, deep red eyes and a russet face covered in otherworldly, tattooed runes. His ears tapered to points, the skin charcoal black at the ends, much like the tips of his clawed fingers. He wore an asymmetrical coat of mismatched dark fabrics, draping to the floor. Elzifur was responsible for keeping tabs on his agents of Chaos, and for centuries he oversaw their activities on Earth, where they were only allowed to cause minor disruptions, such as hiding keys or rejecting one in every ten coins at a parking pay point.

'Mmm ... the blood of Fortune ... a rich blend, not unlike honey and cinnamon, a hint of damson.' Elzifur licked his cat-like fangs and offered a cold smile. 'Though I much prefer Nemesis blood, all mercury, fire and rage.'

'Elzifur, have there been any changes in your realm?' Osato asked, ignoring the comment.

'I can feel the veil thinning,' he rasped slowly, his expression of concern mired by a slight smile. 'You know, if it tears completely, I will not be held responsible for my agents wreaking havoc in your world. This is the doing of *your* people, not mine ...'

The agency bosses were visibly uncomfortable at this news. They were not equipped to deal with the complete collapse of the veil between the worlds and no historical fractures had got remotely close to such disastrous consequences. After they dismissed Elzifur, it was quickly agreed that all efforts would be made to prevent such a thing happening. By their nature, Elzifur's legions were parasitic, otherworldly beasts that fed on despair, terror and rage. The mortal world would become a playground for their deeply unsettling games so the bosses decided to reconvene to form a plan once they had each completed their research and, as they all prepared to leave, a heavy cloth was thrown over the mirror, closing the reflective portal.

* * *

Around 8 a.m., Erron and Casey returned to the office, followed closely by Kendra, who had nipped home to grab a quick shower. As she walked into her office, several of the other agents did a double take at her gold sequinned suit jacket and matching dress, which caught the light from every mismatched lamp in the room and turned her into glitzy Christmas tree worthy of Times Square. She waved Erron into her office and closed the door behind him.

'What's the news then?' he asked as he took a seat at the desk.

'I need to ask you something, and I need your honesty here. Erron, are you involved in the murder of these people?' She folded her arms, her tired eyes searching his face for any reaction.

He sat up sharply. 'Excuse me?'

'Freya told me about those photocopies you had and I read through them before I came here. The use of mixed cosmic blood to enter a prohibited shadow state? As well as having highly addictive properties, the practice has been used in order to kill others in the past. Erron, I thought maybe you'd just been curious, but have you got mixed up in something sinister here?'

'I don't know what you're talking about!' he snapped. 'Those papers weren't even mine.'

'I'm just trying to get to the bottom of this, that's all.'

'You have to believe me; I have no involvement in this,' he pleaded. 'Check the office CCTV and see who put the papers there.'

She rubbed her temples and sighed. 'OK, don't worry about it for now. I will see if we have any footage on the security cameras that could show something, but without a definitive time frame, it's likely that would already have been overwritten.'

'What do I do in the meantime?' he asked.

Before she could answer, her phone trilled with some dreadful disco tune. 'I have to get this, but I will talk to you later.' She waved him away and answered the call, mustering up some fake enthusiasm for whoever was on the other end of the line.

Erron trudged back to his desk, where Casey pressed him about what Kendra had said.

'It's being investigated. She didn't really say a lot, it's out of our hands,' he said bluntly and slumped in his chair, checking the available shifts for call centre work on the rota system. Until they heard any more, he hoped to numb his mind processing pointless complaints instead of worrying about the new complexities of his job.

Sensitive to Erron's foul mood, Casey tried to be upbeat. 'Well, while you were in there, Mrs Murnard has given us an assignment. It's out of the city so hopefully it won't have anything to do with what's been going on here. She'll be back in a bit to sign out the arrows for us; she's just gone to fetch the files. Might be good for both of us to get out of London, don't you think?'

'Sign out the arrows? Is it another gold assignment?'

'It is, yes. You know gold assignments are non-transferable. Mrs Murnard has been waiting for us to get here.' Casey passed the card to Erron. 'If you say they are looking into it, what else can we do except business as usual?' he reasoned, not wanting to admit the whole situation felt very uncomfortable.

Mrs Murnard shuffled over as Erron inspected the card.

'This one is a fair way away.' He waved the card at the squat assignment clerk.

It wasn't unheard of for more senior agents to get special requests out of their usual district, especially for gold cards.

151

These were usually assigned by a much higher member of the division and preapproved depending on the skill of the agent.

Like the others, these cards had been stamped with Agent E. C. Grover and Agent C. E. Hart in gold foil typeface and were printed on exquisite quality paper.

Mrs Murnard went on to grunt, 'I don't make the rules. You were selected for this, so it's your job. You know these ones come from much higher up.'

Erron narrowed his eyes. 'Is there no one else that can fill in for us?'

'It's all prearranged. The target is an Austrian scientist, extremely high-profile and on the cusp of inventing a radical new technology to combat climate change, provided he falls in love with one of the members of the British Scientific Associates, a lady named Eva Lentern. Them being together has the potential to change the world.'

'I know this has come from upper management, but can you just check they still want *us* to do this? I mean, we haven't exactly had a good week,' Erron pushed.

'I've checked already. It's still going ahead. If they thought there was an issue, you'd have been taken off the assignment,' Mrs Murnard snapped. 'The approval has been ratified by higher up despite the recent issues. So, you need to undertake it.

'Here are the train tickets and instructions.' She handed them a small brown envelope and led them back through to the main office. 'Now there's nothing else on the books for you as you were on a late shift last night, so go home and rest up. Oh, and Grover, there's a letter in your in-tray about your transfer request. It came in with this morning's internal mail.'

Casey threw him a quizzical glance, but Erron averted his gaze. Outside the office, Casey tried to raise the topic.

'Transfer request?'

'I don't know what she's on about. Look, I'm just going to get home if that's OK. I'm shattered.' Erron's tone was abrupt and he started towards the exit, snatching up the post from his in-tray on the way out.

'Don't you want to go get breakfast or something?' Casey called after him.

'Why don't you go and hang out with Nikita? I won't get in your way,' he shouted behind him, an edge to his voice.

Left in his wake, Casey felt a mixture of confusion and hurt. He was being left out of the loop and Erron's usual cagey attitude had increased tenfold. The comments about Nikita disarmed him slightly as he had never known Erron to fall for anyone in the office before. Clearly, Nikita had caught his eye and he thought that Casey was interested in her too. This thought caused a wave of anxiety to wash over him, but he couldn't quite place why. He only thought of Nikita as a friend – a delightful friend, absolutely – but nothing more than that. And Erron, well . . . Erron was Erron.

Pushing these thoughts away with resignation, Casey left the office and flew home, landing silently on his terrace with the plan to spend the rest of the day reading by the fire.

* * *

The next morning, Erron's alarm went off at four o'clock like a siren of Hell wailing through the darkness of his dreamless slumber. He forced his eyes open and glared at the time displayed on the ceiling by his laser projector. His train was due to leave Farringdon at 6 a.m. but he felt no motivation to leave the warmth of his bed.

Reluctantly, he reached for the stereo remote by the bed and turned it on part-way through the soundtrack of *City of Angels.* Jimi Hendrix's 'Red House' was playing when Erron had made himself breakfast and, conscious of the time, he resisted the usual urge to play air guitar using the broom in the kitchen.

As he opened the door to leave, he was startled to find a small red gift box and a card on top of it just outside the door. The card had his name on it in swirly purple handwriting. Curiosity got the better of him and he took the box inside, setting it on the kitchen counter as he opened the card. His stomach fell as he read the note inside:

Dear Erron, please accept this small gift as an apology for the other day. I really think our friendship is special and could become so much more if we could just go back to talking again. I'm thinking of you always, Izzy xxx

Part of him wanted to throw the box away without looking in it, but he didn't have the self-control not to peek. Inside lay a small heart-shaped pebble that had been painted with red nail varnish and glitter, with the initials EG and IC drawn on with a marker pen. It was surrounded by a handful of chocolates. Conscious of the time, he stuffed the card and the box in his kitchen drawer and left for the train station.

There was no sign of Casey on the platform, and he imagined that he was probably still busy brewing tea, singing with the birds and making a perfect round of marmalade toast as he flicked through a newspaper. In reality, Casey had slept soundly

154

through the gentle dawn music of his alarm. It wasn't until Erron phoned him at 5.15 a.m. that he bolted upright in a panic.

'You're late. How far away are you?'

'Er . . . ten . . . maybe fifteen minutes.' Casey was haphazardly pulling on one of his most comfortable suits while running around the house throwing together an overnight bag.

'Liar. You haven't left yet.' Erron suppressed a smirk. He was stood on the platform, packed and ready to go. He'd even had time to get a coffee.

'I'm on my way,' Casey insisted. 'Have you got your arrow?'

'Yeah, yeah, I'm organised. Now hurry up, it's bloody freezing.'

Hanging up, Casey ran back up the stairs to grab his long winter overcoat and grey knit scarf. The coat, like all of his upper clothing items, had been adapted with long slits to allow his wings to unfold, should he need them to. He found a spare moment to glug a glass of milk and brush his teeth before leaving. He skidded down the steps onto the platform at 5.49 a.m., pushing out a dent in his grey trilby and dropping it on his head.

'You look a mess,' Erron observed casually.

Casey tucked his straggly hair behind his ears and tried to tidy his clothes. 'I made it, didn't I?'

'I thought you were a morning person.'

'I'm getting out of the habit. I hate that we have to get there so bloody early for these out-of-district jobs. It's not like we're going to miss anything by being there hours early.'

'I guess they are paranoid we'll be late for some reason, so they give us a whole shift for one job. At least the gold assignment qualification gets us a pay incentive.' Erron twiddled with the agency ear cuff on his right ear until it was sitting more comfortably.

Casey had to admit the extra pay for a gold assignment was worth the inconvenience. It wasn't a fortune, but it made a difference.

'Train is delayed anyway,' Erron stated with a smirk.

'What? How long have you known?'

'About erm . . . half an hour.' Erron tried not to laugh, masking his smile by sipping his coffee slowly. Casey's frustration was evident, so he thought it best to change the subject. He pulled a fiver from his wallet and passed it to Casey. 'Get yourself a drink, and could you pick up one of those cheap lighters for me? I'll watch the announcement board.'

Taking the cash, Casey left his kit and overnight bags at Erron's feet and did as he was told. He was mostly just glad Erron seemed to be out of his bad mood and back to his usual self.

When their late train eventually rolled into their destination town of Bedford at 8.03 a.m., they found breakfast in a run-down café and then went to check into their hotel. The agency had reserved them rooms at the Park Inn overlooking the river and the main bridge and even forked out for early check-in.

'Oh, Erron, look over there, couldn't we have got rooms in that one?' Casey pointed over the river at an old building named the Swan Hotel, with beautiful architecture and elegant bay windows.

'Bit fancy, isn't it?'

'I bet they do lovely croissants,' Casey said wistfully to himself, imagining a delectable array of breakfast items in the conservatory tearoom.

'Stop daydreaming, will you? Besides, we've only just eaten.' Erron tapped him on the head with the printed booking reference. 'The lady's going to check us in. She doesn't need you going all goo-goo eyed over the competition.'

'Sorry.' Casey spun around and followed Erron up to the check-in desk, where they were given their room keys.

In the lift, Erron reread the assignment instructions. 'So, this guy who we've got to shoot couldn't possibly have had his seminar thing in London and saved us all a trip, could he?'

'The organiser is based here and involved in some green energy park project that's local to the area. They have a tour of the project site the following day,' Casey offered as explanation. 'You know, he's come up with something absolutely revolutionary, a prototype nano-technology that can break down micro-plastics and turn them into a type of fuel that has no negative impact to the environment.'

'I figured you'd know why we had to come here.'

'Erron, there's something I want to talk to you about,' Casey said quietly.

Erron knew that tone of voice; it quivered with worry and melancholy, and he had been waiting for the conversation to surface ever since Mrs Murnard mentioned his transfer. 'Now isn't a good time, Case. Get settled and I'll call for you at ten fifteen.'

'It's about—'

'Whatever it's about, it can wait. We've got to be at the top of our game for this.' Erron knew he couldn't put it off for ever. 'We can talk after. We'll find something to do this afternoon, walk down the river or something. You can tell me then what you're worrying about.'

'I know but it's just—'

Erron sighed. 'We'll talk later. Look, why don't we both use the time to come up with a fancy sciency alter ego for the conference, and you can laugh at my bad acting skills? Then you can amaze me with the cover story you come up with. There will be plenty of time to talk afterwards.'

Casey gave him a half-smile. 'OK.'

'I bet I can think of a better character name than you.' Erron playfully nudged him.

Casey accepted the challenge reluctantly and went in search of his room.

15

A Little Less Conversation

NIKITA HAD TURNED UP TO work to find that Freya had yet to arrive. She had seen her briefly the day before, having had another session of tutoring at The Arena shooting range down in the Docklands. Nikita settled herself at the desk to which she'd been assigned and busied herself setting up the space how she liked it, though she only had a few basic things, such as an agency laptop, notebook and a basket of pens. She made a mental note to pick up a house-plant or two so the area didn't look so sparse.

Another agent, Tristan DeVangelo, sat on the desk opposite to hers. He was permanently twenty-seven, of Italian and Irish descent, with heart-breaking good looks and the kind of confidence that film stars could switch on in front of the cameras. His long dark hair tumbled in sickeningly perfect waves and his deep brown eyes sparkled like polished stones. He was born to be a Cupid and could have almost anyone falling at his feet without any arrow being fired. It's likely he would even have made the oversized cherubim nappy look good.

'New girl!' He greeted her with a bright smile. 'I trust that you are settling into this strange new world?'

'As best I can be.'

'I've been here for ages, but took me a while to get used to it. Have you had your first hit yet?'

'No, but Freya has shown me the ropes.'

'I thought you were supposed to be mentored by Tesco-value Maverick and Goose?'

Nikita looked confused.

'Grover and Hart,' Tristan added with a smirk.

'I haven't really had contact from anyone today. Not yet.' She ignored the subtle jibe even though she was a huge *Top Gun* fan. She glanced at the clock on the wall, it had gone 9 a.m.

'Well, it's probably because they're on the run together.' Tristan pointed a remote at a TV on the wall. He flicked through several channels before finding one running the morning news. 'It's all over the news, see. Another three suspicious deaths, coincidentally another three of Hart and Grover's targets. Rumour has it, they're involved somehow.'

'That's bullshit. They aren't killers.' Her eyes were drawn to the screen, where the news was recapping the horrific accident at the concert, followed by the bizarre double tragedy a few streets away, claiming the lives of an electrician and a single mother.

'You haven't known them long enough to say that.' Tristan left the news running, with sensationalised reports of KiaRia's untimely death dominating the airtime. He rolled his chair close enough to Nikita, so that when he spoke quietly, his breath moved the loose strands of hair around her face. 'I've worked here long enough to notice they don't socialise much apart from with each other. They spend countless nights talking quietly, *conspiring*, in a well-known Ghoster bar and they rarely work alone. It's like they're covering for each other all the time. And ... they like jazz.'

Nikita rolled her chair back and narrowed her gaze. 'So? I don't remember it being a prerequisite at serial killer school to enjoy jazz. I thought the sign was meant to be classical music.'

Tristan raised his hands in defeat. 'All I'm saying is the situation is a little odd, them being so closed off and secretive, and then these deaths happening within a week. Where are they this morning, huh?'

Nikita couldn't answer. She hadn't got to grips with the ad hoc assignment patterns yet, though Freya had explained to her how the call centre rota worked. She didn't need to attend that for a while as she was determined to avoid it for as long as she could. Although it was voluntary, very few agents could survive without the subsidised pay, especially with London prices.

Tristan wheeled his chair back to his own desk and went to the assignment window to pick up his daily tasks. 'You know, Wolf, you can come along with me and my crewmate for the day if the others don't turn up,' he called over to her, waving four cards.

She considered it. In the same way you might consider drinking your own urine if you were stranded in the desert. It wasn't a nice idea, but it was something that probably had to be done. 'If they don't show up, maybe,' she conceded.

Nikita was saved from answering further as Kendra called her into her office.

'How are you settling in?' the boss asked, having barely spoken to Nikita since she'd arrived at the agency.

'Fine, so far. I think.'

'I have to reshuffle who is tutoring you for a little while. There have been some complications with Grover and Hart around these assignments that have gone pear-shaped so they won't be working with you at the moment. I had planned to place you with Freya Carthage and her other student in the meantime but she's not due in until this evening and has some holiday coming up next week. In the meantime, I think it's best we just send you to study for the written exam that you'll have to pass before becoming an independent agent.' Kendra pulled out a list she had written up in haste. 'You can find copies of these at the Eligos Library.' She pushed the paper into Nikita's hand.

'When's the exam?'

'Oh, it's usually undertaken when your mentor thinks you are ready, but a bit of early study is always encouraged. Take as much time as you need; it'll be at least a week before we can either place you with Freya after her holiday or Grover and Hart again for practical training.'

Nikita scanned the scrawl of ink. 'Should I get in touch with Erron and Casey to let them know where I am?'

'No, don't worry, I will let them know. Just wait for me to call when we have a new mentor for you.'

*　*　*

Nikita, free of any further responsibilities at the office, decided to take a long walk to the Eligos and enjoy some of the winter sunshine that was peeking through the grey clouds. Ordinarily, back in her old life, she would have picked up a hot chocolate and cheese and onion slice as she walked, but she was conscious that she had to make the set allowance of old money she'd been given last. Alone with her thoughts, she dawdled along, pausing at a small junk shop with an array of old furniture outside. Among the drawers and cupboards stood a full-length mirror with an ornate frame. It caught her eye. Perhaps if it was cheap enough she could use it to add a little rustic charm to her sleek apartment. It would be worth sacrificing some old money to have something permanent to call her own. As she approached, the mirror seemed to swirl and darken, and she jumped back as a shadowy hand smacked the glass from the other side before disappearing back into the shadows. Once her heart rate had settled, she inspected behind the mirror and wondered if it was a Halloween prop designed for jump scares but could find no indication of a clever illusion. Needless to say, she decided to hang on to her money.

An hour later, within the calm sanctity of the library, Nikita took a deep breath and began searching for the books she'd been told to read. A short while passed before a cold shadow loomed over her as she rifled through the library index cards.

'I received a reply.' His voice was unmistakable. Subtle, well enunciated, and formal.

She spun around to see Darren Oliver-Alliott (D-O-A) holding out a slip of paper on which Dantalion had written his response. In beautiful cursive, she read the note:

Vaticinium De Tumultus, recent removal undetected. Please refer to secondary copy held at the Oriax.

'What is the Oriax?' She folded the slip of paper and tucked it into the pocket of her jeans.

'It's the agency reference building in Edinburgh. A vast place in comparison to this library.'

Her face fell. It wasn't exactly somewhere she could nip to over lunch. 'Was there any more to the message? If the book was taken undetected, there must be some concern over that.'

D-O-A hesitated. 'No. There was nothing more.'

'How would it be removed undetected?' she queried.

'Honestly, I don't know.'

'Well, is there a law or something preventing that? It wouldn't be in a vault if it wasn't important.'

'Dantalion is aware of it now. I don't know what higher authority there is for reporting missing books.' He furrowed his brow.

Nikita wouldn't begin to know who else to report the missing book to so accepted that it was out of her hands. 'Do you know anything about fractures?' she blurted out.

He froze briefly before answering. 'Any reason you want to know about them?'

She invited him to sit down and lowered her voice. 'I need to know if they are actually real, because I think they are starting to happen. And if that's the case, I need to know how to fix them.'

'What do you mean already happening?'

'There have been some weird goings-on, especially these earthquakes, that coincide with assignments that have recently gone wrong,' she said quietly.

He sat down slowly and rested his chin on his interlocked fingers. 'Fractures do exist. They are ripples in fate when a fixed point in time does not go according to destiny. It causes a small tear in the fabric of the universe, as such. But minor ones have happened fairly regularly, every few decades or so there's a hiccup or a missed assignment. The system isn't perfect; agents are only human, after all. Hard-boiled souls of humans, but still human, and mistakes do happen. Usually the effects subside over time.'

'But what if there are several in a row, quite important ones?' she pressed.

He pursed his lips. 'That's serious. But no one could make that many mistakes, surely?'

'Two Apollo agents have had four gold assignments derail and I think the fallout in the city is heading towards a catastrophe. But here's the thing: I don't think they have actually done anything wrong. I know I'm new, but I was there at the first assignment and the arrow hit the woman, but she reacted as though she was being chased by something terrifying before tripping up onto the train tracks. I can't see how that was a mistake made by the agent.'

'Grover and Hart,' D-O-A stated.

'You know about it then?'

'Not all the details. I saw you in Nightjar with them; it made sense that they were training you, and the train track incident was checked against our assignments for that day. Regardless, if it has happened that many times, with the same agents, it's either a major coincidence, or someone has engineered it that way.'

'For what purpose though? I don't understand?' Nikita scrunched up her face in thought.

'If one creates enough fractures, I gather that the disasters may never abate,' he mused with a solemn expression. 'I'm not sure, I have never had cause to look into this before.'

'I need to know how to stop the fractures happening.'

'Theoretically, were it a case of poor marksmanship, I would suggest extra target practice. But look for the cause. If the arrows are finding their targets, then you'll need to seek out another common denominator. But I would assume the heads of divisions are looking into this already? They may have already reached a conclusion.' D-O-A rose from the chair and pulled up his collar around his neck, ready to leave once more.

He left Nikita alone with her thoughts. She felt somewhat comforted by the fact that the whole situation really was for the bosses to sort out, but it wouldn't hurt for her to do some more research to flag her findings if they helped at all. Kendra had given her plenty of flexibility to study for her exam, so she reached the conclusion it wouldn't hurt to look into other topics with her time, provided she balanced the two. She thought over everything she had learnt about the fractures and what caused them, but it didn't explain Sofia Carter's death from what she had seen.

The missing book in the vault played on her mind and she couldn't shake the feeling it might be relevant somehow. She shuddered at the thought of making an offering of her blood to Dantalion in order to pry further. Instead, she went back to the book *Rifts of Fate* to check if it made reference to any other useful titles.

16

Bridge Over Troubled Water

THE CONFERENCE FOR SCIENTIFIC PROGRESS was being set up at the Harpur Suite, a small but grandiose building in Bedford town centre. It was treated as an aspiring edifice of ancient Rome despite its diminutive appearance, buoyed only by the large white pillars it sported as an entranceway. Selected delegates from across Europe were gathering for the conference, which was somewhat secretive in nature due to the unethical people who were keen to protest the scientific breakthroughs being discussed, as they posed a threat to the highly profitable fossil fuel and plastic industries.

The Austrian representative, an ambitious man named Gunther Hoffmann, was straightening his blue satin bow tie and excitedly practising his speech in front of the mirror in the delegates' lounge. He was early, well prepared, and very much hoping there would be sandwiches provided at the midday interval. His stomach grumbled in agreement, and to subdue it, he went in search of early refreshments.

Eva Lentern, the woman of whom he was due to become completely enamoured, was rushing through her own notes

back at her room in the plush Swan Hotel, completely unpre-
pared, her outfit thrown together and a croissant shoved in
her mouth (a delectable one she'd found on the breakfast
counter), but despite her dishevelled start, she had nothing
but utter faith in her own abilities to pull her speech out
of the bag at the last minute. She was a natural at public
speaking but the opposite when it came to being on time.
She put down the half-eaten pastry and tidied her curly hair
into a bun.

Meanwhile, a navy-suited Erron rapped on Casey's door as
arranged. Both had opted for smart, easy-to-blend-in attire,
each with a fake science associate name badge clipped to their
lapels.

'Go on then, who are you supposed to be?' Erron leant
forward to read Casey's badge. 'Professor Quentin Pidd. Are
you serious? Q. Pidd?'

'Well, you set the challenge, I merely came up with something
exemplary. Who are you, anyway?' Casey squinted to read Erron's
identification. '"Dr A. Pollo". You're as bad as me.'

Erron burst into laughter. 'I think it's a draw, don't you?
What are you the professor of then?'

'I'm Quentin Pidd, lead of entomological applications into
contemporary food chain processes, from Edinburgh University.
Essentially, it's using insect protein to bridge the gap in food
shortages,' Casey explained enthusiastically.

'Like cockroach bread?'

'Like cockroach bread,' Casey agreed. 'And you are a doctor
in what field, Mr Pollo?'

'Brainio-matology . . .? I don't know. I suppose I ought
to have some kind of spiel figured out. You may need to

help me with that. It took me all that time to come up with a name.'

Casey thought for a moment and then suggested Erron played the part of a fictional Swedish inventor of biomolecular fuels which he hadn't quite finalised, and therefore couldn't answer questions about because he didn't want anyone stealing the patents. That way he could give vague and dismissive answers while remaining aloof. He was very capable of aloof, incredibly good at vague, but disastrous at a Swedish accent, not for lack of trying. Eventually, he settled on being German, where he could comfortably muster a convincing '*Ja*' with an authoritative nod. Casey was, on the other hand, an excellent impersonator of the Scottish accent, and still managed to sound remarkably posh. He was hoping to avoid any particularly complicated questions by reverting to a full-on Scottish ramble, which could only possibly be understood by a fluent interpreter.

The conference was well underway when they entered via a side door. A Dutch scientist was giving an excellent demonstration of her plan for tripling the electrical output of existing renewable energy sources with a cleverly designed new electrical storage system. She received a standing ovation for her innovative work, and was followed onto the stage by Eva Lentern, the English professor delivering a speech in her field of nano-technology. She was captivating to listen to, even for the two imposters with their false badges.

'I can see why she will be the catalyst for Dr Hoffmann's world-changing invention. Just listen to her ideas. Genius,' Casey enthused, pressing a conference order of speeches booklet against his chin.

'Erm. *Ja*,' Erron agreed, completely out of his depth.

To Dr Hoffmann's immediate excitement, a table was filled with sandwiches during the interval and the delegates talked enthusiastically about the morning's presentations.

'Ah! Professor Pidd, so nice to meet you. I have heard a lot about your department, but I am afraid your name has not been mentioned before. Are you new to the board of associates?' A balding man with a tweed jacket enthusiastically shook Casey's hand.

'Oh . . . aye.' Casey went into his pre-prepared Scottish introduction into his field of work, and Erron watched on in amazement at the chameleon nature of his friend's acting talents.

The same balding scientist asked about Erron's expertise, and he fumbled his way through a half-German, half-Cockney response which, in normal social situations would seem suspect, but apparently in the scientific community it was quite normal for a person at the top of their field to be slightly off-kilter. The balding man was equally impressed by whatever rubbish Erron could vaguely throw together about his top-secret enterprise. Casey left him to it and boldly walked over to Gunther Hoffmann.

The young scientist was open and passionate about his ideas for a better future. He handed Casey a leaflet all about his presentation and only stopped talking when the conference staff announced the commencement of the second half.

Dr A. Pollo, the Cockney-German brainio-matologist, who apparently came from the small village of Biem-Dubbleyew, was busy putting together his recurve bow at the back of the room. The audience was rapt with Gunther Hoffmann's excitable insight into his vision of the future, where the planet was green and healthy, and all life was sustainable. His passion for

170

ridding the world of plastic pollution was inspiring, and his method of achieving it was groundbreaking. He was just what the world needed.

The lights in the room flickered, and the projector lit up the screen with crazed ripples of colour interspaced with black bands. The microphone squealed briefly, and people looked around in confusion. A few seconds passed and everything returned to normal, but an icy bead of sweat ran down Casey's back and a rise of panic swelled in his chest. He grabbed at Erron's sleeve.

'You don't think ... ?' Erron whispered.

'You can feel that, can't you?'

Erron could feel something, an unnatural weight in the air, a dimmer quality to the light in the room. Dr Hoffmann had paused his presentation while the lights had done their wild dance, but even now they were back on, he didn't continue. Instead, he stared with horror at something only he could see, before letting out a guttural cry and bolting for the back door, a flurry of research papers scattering in his wake. A handful of the lead speakers, including Eva Lentern, sprinted out close behind him, looking behind them as they ran, fearful of what might have terrified Gunther Hoffmann so badly.

'Follow him!' Erron hissed as he grabbed his arrow tube and bow and raced towards the exit.

Casey was hot on his tail, and they caught sight of the scientist as he pelted across the road by the church. Gunther was screaming and looking over his shoulder as if chased by the Devil himself as he turned sharply right before reaching the high street.

'He's heading to the bridge!' Casey yelled ahead to Erron, who had quickly overtaken him.

Erron knew he wouldn't catch the man in time but had an idea. He saw Eva on the other side of the road, calling after Gunther, her hair flying wild and her shoes long since discarded by the wayside. He figured that maybe by firing his arrow, he might be able to disrupt whatever trance Gunther was under, if he could just get the man to see Eva straight after. Erron was a decent shot but had never needed to hit a running target while sprinting himself. He needed to accelerate to close the gap so he could pause long enough to draw the bowstring and get an accurate fix on the target. While pushing his legs even harder, he unscrewed the arrow tube and discarded it, fixing the golden arrow to his string, desperately hoping he could save the man with a surge of pure love.

Bow loaded, he pushed himself to his limit and skidded into the bridge wall, raising the bow just as Gunther climbed onto the opposite wall, still desperately trying to escape his imaginary pursuer. Traffic raced between them, and Erron was forced to climb up on his wall to get a clear shot. Casey was running across the road, hoping to avert the situation by pulling the scientist out of harm's way. A moment of stillness was all it took. Erron exhaled, focused, and loosed the arrow, just as Dr Hoffmann leapt. The arrow sailed into his back, bursting into a firework of bright gold flecks against the cold grey sky.

Then Gunther plunged towards the murky water, where he landed with a significant slap against the churning river and disappeared under, knocked unconscious by the fall. Eva screamed in sheer horror, too shocked to comprehend what had happened. Casey, without thought, leapt after the scientist, the bitterly cold water stabbing him like a thousand knives and dragging him under. More delegates from the conference were catching up, some just in time to see Dr Pollo balancing on the bridge wall holding a bow, and Professor Pidd leaping into oblivion after the key speaker. They chose to ignore the bow-wielding German and focused on racing down to the embankment to see if either man had resurfaced.

Erron's heart raced as he frantically scanned the water for Casey. Nothing bobbed up from the blackness and he slung the bow over his back and took off in the direction of the flow, running towards the next bridge and an alcove where he could take flight without being seen.

Within fifteen seconds he was airborne, gliding high and keeping his keen eyes on everything below. A minute and a half elapsed before Casey burst to the surface just past the second bridge, far from the view of onlookers. Police and ambulance had been called, but unlike most American blockbusters, there would be no wailing sirens on the scene for some time, likely because there were no units free and the nearest backup was on lunch.

Casey was desperately clawing for anything to catch onto as he was dragged downriver, eventually pulling himself into a secluded spot by the Longholme Boathouse.

Erron dived down to land close by, wading into the swirling water to grab his friend's hand. Casey was blue with the cold and shaking violently and Erron had to use every ounce of strength to drag him from the water.

'I . . . c-c-couldn't f-f-f-find him,' Casey stammered, his blond hair plastered to his face and green river slime matted to his suit. His own wings were so cold and wet they hung open and limp, dragging behind him on the floor.

'This ... this is ... We're in deep shit.' Erron stared hard at the pitiful Casey. 'You need to get in a hot shower. And get your wings cleaned up.'

'I ... c-c-can't even f-f-feel them.'

Erron knew that heavy, waterlogged wings wouldn't easily fold away, and they were only a short walk from the hotel. With the state of both of them, he was afraid they would attract attention, and Casey's condition would dramatically reduce his ability to naturally cloak himself, including his wings. He guided Casey off the path and behind the boathouse while he came up with a plan to somehow make it back with Casey trailing his sodden feathers behind him. There was an earthly rumbling below their feet, and the embankment started to quiver.

'What the ... ?' Erron exclaimed, just as a huge tremor staggered him sideways. 'Oh shit. Let's go.'

Another tremor followed quickly after, and Bedford town was rattled by the violent quaking. Screams echoed from across the town bridge, where people were being thrown off their feet and bits of loose masonry shifted from the rooftops of the older shops. The fabric of reality was unravelling under their very feet. Deep jagged cracks were crawling across the roads and trees were toppling along the embankment as the earth shifted and heaved.

'The f-f-fracture in d-d-destiny is t-tearing everything ap-p-part,' Casey spluttered.

'I know. I know,' Erron fussed. 'But at least it might give us a chance to get back to the hotel without being seen.'

Even in the hubbub and panic, Erron couldn't see them being able to walk the distance to the hotel unnoticed. He'd have to carry Casey while he flew to the back door of the hotel and land in the private car park. Casey was shuddering dramatically, his suit still dripping wet and clinging to his blue-tinged skin.

'Er ... this may be awkward ... but it's our only option.' Erron held his arms open and wrapped them around Casey's chest. 'Hold tight.'

Casey did as he was told and leant his head on Erron's shoulder, his numb fingers interlocking around his waist, barely able to hang on. With a frantic beating of wings, they lifted above the treeline just as more tremors rippled through the town. The effort was intense. Erron's wings weren't designed to carry two; they were barely enough to carry him after a hefty breakfast, but he'd be damned if he was going to leave Casey in the state he was in. They reached the car park safely and got back to Casey's room without being spotted, as most other guests were clamouring to see what was going on outside. People were still shrieking, and cars were crashing into one another, trying to avoid the cracks in the roads and get off the bridge just in case it split in two. The lights in the town were going haywire, rolls of deafening thunder filled the skies above, followed by a deluge of tennis balls over the bridge which seemed to have appeared out of thin air. After several moments of chaos, the tremors subsided, leaving the town centre in complete disarray.

Erron wasted no time watching, but went through to the bathroom and switched on the shower to let the water run hot.

'Get in the shower. I'll wait in here to ... I'll just wait in here ... just in case.' Erron sat down on the edge of the bed, resting his head in his hands and staring emptily at the carpet, trying to contemplate their next move. He kicked off his sodden shoes and took off his own jacket, which was covered in river sludge from carrying Casey.

Cold sweat trickled down his back as the realisation sunk in that the bizarre deaths had indeed followed them out of London. He replayed each tragedy over again in his head, hoping to remember some detail that might connect each incident. He *knew* they weren't at fault, but it was going to take some doing to convince the management team otherwise. The common denominator was clear.

Meanwhile, Casey dragged his aching wings into the bathroom, which was filling up with steam. The heat of the water seeped into his bones and the ecstasy of being able to feel his limbs again was soon overshadowed by the horror of their situation. Like Erron, he realised that they had a lot of explaining to do, and there wasn't much that could be said in their favour. Another unexplained death that had caused a fracture in the weave of time would echo far and wide. Not to mention one of them running about with a bow uncloaked and the other taking a serious gamble by jumping into the river, losing the second gold arrow in the process. When he emerged, half dressed and his hair still dripping water down the back of his open shirt, Erron was peering out of the window to the streets below, transfixed by the scene.

'They've found him,' he said morosely, without dropping the curtain. Casey went to his side and looked out. An ambulance crew and several members of a water rescue team had pulled a body from the river and were attempting CPR.

'He was pulled out around three minutes ago. He's been dead for around fifteen, I reckon. No way they're saving him.' Erron dropped the curtain and turned to Casey, spotting his bare chest and quickly looking away, a faint blush tinging his cheeks. 'I'll head back to my room ... now that you're OK. Knock on the door when you're ready, and we'll talk about how to deal with this great big, colossal fuck-up. At least the tremors have stopped.'

'We should call Kendra. We ought to get a train back today.' Casey looked terrified.

Erron sighed. 'I'll call Kendra, but I think we should stay here for now, until told otherwise.'

'See what she says first,' Casey said quietly.

Erron pulled his phone out from his pocket, his fingers lingering hesitantly over the screen. Once he had summoned the strength to dial, Kendra picked up almost instantly, as if she was waiting for the call.

'Something bad is happening, Kendra, and it's not our fault.'

'Right. I assume another assignment went down the pan,' she replied bluntly.

'What do we do now?'

'You and Hart steer clear of the office for a while. I'll get to the bottom of this, but you best not undertake any more assignments until we figure out what's going on. I have no choice but to suspend you as agents. Do you understand?'

Erron paused at the mention of suspension. 'Sure, I understand. You better figure this out because I'm not getting hung out to dry for this. Do you want us to head back home now?'

'It's your choice, just stay out the office until you're contacted,' she reiterated.

He said goodbye and ended the call, explaining what she'd said to Casey.

'Shall I get my stuff together?' Casey asked.

'I don't know about you, but I think it's for the best if you get some rest after your swim in the river, plus there's no point buying extra train fare to leave early if we can't go back to the office. We might as well take advantage of the free breakfast, eh?'

'OK.' Casey tilted his head and wore a look of forced sincerity as he buttoned his shirt. 'We'll sort this out, I'm sure of it . . .'

Erron didn't lift his eyes from the floor but nodded and stood to leave.

'Erron, thank you, for what you did. I wouldn't have survived if you hadn't pulled me from the water. I'd have been dead by now.' Casey placed a hand on Erron's shoulder and squeezed it.

Despite their predicament, a comforting warmth travelled through Erron's body. After a couple of seconds, he gently shrugged off Casey's hand.

'It's fine. I need some sleep.' Erron picked up his wet shoes and jacket then left abruptly, returning to his own room, where his intrusive thoughts about the past few days plagued him.

He was physically exhausted, and mentally drained. The sight of his own bed was a welcome relief. He peeled off the rest of his soggy clothes and fetched a towel to dry himself off before collapsing onto the bed in his boxers, unable to think up any worthwhile explanations for what they had got themselves tangled up in. To make matters worse, his phone buzzed with another message from Izzy, asking if he had found her gift and if he had forgiven her. She'd picked the worst possible moment and he stabbed at the text keyboard angrily, demanding she leave him alone. There would never be anything between them. Exhausted, he ignored the following barrage of responses, closing his eyes and settling into the pillow.

17

Don't Speak

B Y THREE O'CLOCK, ERRON AND Casey were back out in the town surveying the damage. The earthquake hadn't brought about the kind of mass destruction seen in disaster movies, but it had become a talking point on a massive scale. Most of the damage centred around the area where Dr Gunther Hoffmann had plunged into the river. News crews were gathering, and the scientific convention had dissipated into the aether, keen not to be involved in the radical turn of events. The doctor had been pronounced dead at the scene despite the valiant efforts of the medical personnel.

'You know these fractures will likely cause a ripple as far as the influence their arrows should have had,' Casey theorised. He'd spent a considerable time trying to dry out his wings with the hotel hairdryer, which had about the same effect as getting someone to wave a paper fan on them. He had managed to fold them in, but they clung, damp and cold, to his overcoat as they walked.

'And I bet the influence of Gunther Hoffmann's would've been almost global, in time.'

'Yes. He was going to—'

'Spare me the details of his file. How are we going to deal with this?' Erron took a long drag on a cigarette and exhaled the smoke slowly into the cold grey sky, the odd ray of sunlight pushing through.

'It's not our fault. We didn't kill him. Or any of the others for that matter.'

'The agency won't look kindly on it, no matter whose fault it is. You know they would rather just bin us than complete a full investigation, it's less paperwork.'

'Don't be so cynical, Kendra will support us. She's not going to get rid of some of her longest-serving agents now, is she?' Casey ventured optimistically.

'That's all very well but you know we would be sent for obliteration for something like this, right? Haven't you thought of the consequences if they actually do think it's our fault?'

'Yes, no, I mean, OK, so if we *were* at fault—'

'Casey, I've seen enough innocent people go to prison for wrongful convictions in the mortal world to know that a similar thing could happen to us. What if they think they have enough to pin these deaths on us and we get obliterated? You know, put in the blender as such. Never to be seen again. Just snap, gone.' Erron grew increasingly frustrated.

Casey's face went pale. The thought of losing his job was bad enough, but being obliterated, having his cosmic satsuma juiced faster than a lemon at a cocktail party, was a concept that terrified him. Erron, sensing the horror had finally sunk in, continued.

'Exactly, Case. No more assignments, no more jazz nights, no more trips to Covent Garden to buy a new Christmas bobble hat ... No more croissants.'

Casey recoiled at the thought.

Erron huffed and kicked at a piece of crumbled masonry on the street. He carried on talking and was halfway down the street before he noticed Casey wasn't beside him. He was standing transfixed by a shop window. Half jogging back, he nudged Casey. 'I was talking to you and you weren't there,' he grumbled. 'You made me look like an idiot. What's caught your attention so badly?'

'It's beautiful.' Casey was gazing wide-eyed at a painting that hung off to the side in a small gallery. Clearly, he had selectively dismissed the idea of being obliterated.

Erron rolled his eyes. 'Go and have a look then. Might be your last chance before we're sentenced to eternal damnation.'

A little bell jingled on the peppermint-coloured door frame as they entered. The gallery owner was perched on a shabby-chic wooden stool, reading a paper and sporting a long grey ponytail. A young lad was busy clearing up a shelf of expensive abstract statues that had smashed during the earthquake.

'Afternoon.' The gallery owner offered them a wan smile, his neat white beard raising as he did so.

Erron hung back a little, unsure of the etiquette in galleries. He wasn't much for fancy things, and never really understood the purpose of buying stuff just to look at. Casey, however, couldn't pull his eyes away from the picture, and stood taking in every detail.

'What's so special about it then?' Erron finally came to his side and asked.

The image was of a vacant shore, with a solitary man stood facing away on a rippled beach. Within the reflections of the water, the man had dark wings. Underneath there was a small plaque reading *Liminal Zone* by Camillo.

'It's so utterly, desperately sad. The way he stands there, completely bereft from what he once was. A vacant land, the loneliness of his new position, a fallen angel learning how to walk without wings. Not just that though, the colours, the composition, everything ... it's breath-taking.'

Erron would have usually made fun of Casey's sentimental patter, but the sheer heartbroken passion in his voice silenced any quip Erron was tempted to spout. If he stared at the picture long enough, he could almost see what he meant.

'Get it then? If you like it that much.'

The gallery owner had walked over at that moment, hands behind his back, thick glasses perched at the end of his nose. 'Wonderful, isn't it?' He nodded towards the picture. 'The frame is included in the price.'

Casey tentatively caressed the handmade black frame which, in itself, was exquisite. Then his eyes fell on the price tag: £2,452. The agency provided well for them, free accommodation, food and certain allowances, but Casey hadn't done nearly enough shifts in the call centre to earn that kind of old money. 'I'll certainly consider it.'

'Well, let me give you a card.' The owner reached into the pocket of his natty seventies waistcoat and pulled out a business card. 'We can reserve pieces for up to a week, just give me a call any weekday if you change your mind.'

Casey thanked him and pocketed the card. Back out on the street, Erron looked at Casey questioningly. 'You could have used the old charm of the Apollo Flush, to get the price down a bit,' he suggested.

'It's not ethical. I mean, the artist needs to earn the money and the gallery owner needs to pay his bills. It's not exactly a few quid at the Nightjar,' Casey explained. 'Besides, aren't we heading for eternal damnation, didn't you say?'

'Probably.'

'What's the plan then, Detective?'

'Fucked if I know. You're the clever clogs.' Erron scratched the back of his head and sighed.

Casey inhaled deeply, letting the sharp air clear his mind. They had begun to wander down the Bedford embankment, where old trees bowed their naked branches over the gravel, the remnants of autumn leaves now skeletal and gathered by the exposed roots. They passed by the Iron Bridge in silence and didn't speak again until they reached the next one, the Butterfly Bridge, its white arching wings reflected in the dark waters as they crossed it, pausing briefly to take in the view and let some cyclists pass. A swathe of geese was waddling towards them.

'Erron … this … this is a *lot* of geese.'

'It's a riverbank?'

'There's way too many.' Casey began to wade through the honking chaos of birds.

'The quake probably got them all bundled up together …' Erron trailed off, peering into the distance as the sea of geese seemed endless and growing in number.

'Maybe.' Casey was unconvinced, and a little worried about the state of his shoes.

'I'm sure it's nothing.' Erron didn't like to point out that the geese were waddling sideways and backwards.

'This whole thing has got to be some kind of management issue,' Casey said quietly. 'There has been a mix-up somewhere, and it will get resolved soon. I know you think the agency will just get rid of us, but I have more faith in the system than that.'

'The Fates aren't likely to hold up their hands and go *Oops, my bad!* No ... they are going to find us responsible in all this mess and make an example of us.' Erron repeatedly flicked the wheel of his cheap plastic lighter, feeling a twinge of sadness at the loss of the inscribed one from his brother. Burying the memory, he cupped his hand round the flame and lit another cigarette.

He wasn't pessimistic, or optimistic. He just saw things in a realistic, logical way. And the logic he applied most often was Sod's Law.

Casey leant back against the bridge railing. 'Are you scared, Erron?' he asked softly.

Erron faltered briefly. 'Don't give me this emotional support bollocks, Case.' He didn't want to admit that beneath his blasé attitude, he was deeply unsettled.

'I'm just trying to be nice.' Casey kicked a stone into the river and waited for the soft *sploosh.*

A long pause hung between them. Erron would usually fill the uncomfortable void of conversation with a cheeky jibe or flippant comment, but he was all out of humour. He exhaled a thin cloud of smoke and tapped the ash of the cigarette over the side of the bridge, before turning to face his friend.

'Yes, I am. I'm scared,' he finally said, awkwardly running his fingers through his hair. He expected Casey to mock his vulnerability or try and get philosophical about it. But he didn't, he just nodded.

'I'm scared too,' Casey whispered.

'I won't let anything happen to you.' Erron edged closer to his friend and fixed him with a sincere look. 'I'll do whatever it takes to make them believe us.' Then, before he could stop himself, he grabbed Casey's hand and gave it a swift squeeze.

Casey looked down at their intertwined hands and squeezed back, gently. 'You know I don't want anything happening to you either, Erron.'

'Damn right, I'm awesome.' Erron broke into a smile, pulled his hand away and playfully nudged Casey.

'I mean it.'

Erron dropped his grin and nodded. 'I know.'

'Can we talk about what I was going to raise earlier?' Casey said quietly.

Erron watched as a handful of swans glided across the water towards them in the hope that they might suddenly reveal bread from their pockets, followed silently by a flotation of rubber ducks. He knew what Casey wanted to talk to him about, and he was dreading having to explain himself. He stubbed out the cigarette, not looking up.

'What's bothering you then?'

'What Mrs Murnard said, that you had put in an application to transfer. Is that to another district, or out of the department entirely?' Casey sounded bereft.

'Case, it's hardly worth worrying about now. We're going to be hauled over the coals, so there's no point even getting into this conversation,' Erron stated firmly, but his voice betrayed him, sounding more regretful than dismissive.

'Is it near London? Home Counties?' Casey pressed. 'You know, I could always change district with you?'

'I wouldn't want you having to leave your home, Casey. It's not far away,' he deflected.

Casey paused before asking, 'Is it because of me?'

Erron hesitated. It was enough for Casey to reach the worst conclusion, and the look of sheer hurt he wore tripled Erron's guilt. 'No, no, it's not you, Case.'

'Then why do you want to leave?'

'It's ... complicated.' Erron waved his hand as if trying to swat away the emanating sadness from his friend. 'Let's go get some food, huh?'

Saying no more on the subject, they walked until they reached a steakhouse at the Priory Country Park. The winter sun was just disappearing over the lake when they arrived, leaving a deep orange hue over the water and making the thin clouds glow a vibrant magenta. On any other day, Casey would have gazed at it lovingly, going off on a tangent about *the beauty of nature* and *how majestic a sunset truly was*, and Erron would have put together a string of light-hearted insults about what an insufferably soppy bastard he was. But instead, Casey quietly went to the door of the restaurant and asked for a table for two, not mentioning the perfect evening colours, or the serenity of the lake, or the picturesque moment when four hundred and sixty-five geese flew over in harmony. He didn't even make a fuss about the lack of vegetarian options.

Erron didn't comment on the blandness of his food or make joking comments about other customers which would normally have shocked Casey then made him laugh conspiratorially. Instead, the atmosphere was strained right up until they were walking back on the other side of the river, the twinkling lights of the town ahead and the trees lit up in blue and green. Festoon lighting hung between the Victorian lanterns and sparkled in the wavering river, and eventually, Casey couldn't resist.

'You know, I rather like it here. Look how the light plays under the bridge, and the swans. It's like a painting.'

'Well, it's not the Thames, that's for sure. You didn't like it all that much while swimming in it.'

'Not so much then, no.'

They watched as the festoon lighting flickered above the head of a dark shape on the other side of the river. As she moved, the flickering lights followed, returning to their steady glow once she'd passed.

'A Ghoster on the job,' Erron whispered. 'You gotta admit that *Umbra Noctis* shit is creepy.'

'"Death hides amongst the shadows deep, in darkness, the soul for ever sleeps."' Casey quoted from one of the old agency books of prose. 'Never doubt why people are afraid of the dark, you never know what might lurk in its depths.' He spoke distantly, no doubt still hurt by their earlier conversation.

'Reapers like D-O-A. Creepy medieval bastard.' Erron rubbed his arms to keep warm. 'I can't wait for summer, when the sun doesn't set in the middle of the bloody afternoon. It's not even 7 p.m. and it's like midnight.'

'You don't strike me as a summer person,' Casey observed.

'Since when?'

'Well, you're always so pale and ... moonly. Plus, all you do is complain about the heat,' Casey replied, folding his arms.

Erron snorted. 'Moonly? Case, that's not even a word.'

'It suits you, doesn't it? With all your black coats and mysterious lurking in jazz bars and stuff.' Casey stuck to his guns.

Erron thought about it. 'Fair. Though you lurk with me, dumbass.'

The light had faded while they'd been at dinner, leaving a sky clear as glass, and the stars overhead looked down on them with an icy gaze. In the distance, a throng of black clouds was moving slowly through the heavens, snuffing out the stars and threatening a bitter rain in the night. A lone rubber duck bobbed under the bridge and out of sight.

18

Devil's Dance

THE EARLY SUNSET OF WINTER had brought a darkness to the library that no amount of candles seemed to stave off, and Nikita was starting to wish she had taken some food with her. She was distracted by memories of the taste bubbles on Elysion and found herself craving chocolate cake or a family-sized four cheese and pesto calzone. She'd been told that mortal feelings such as tiredness, hunger and cold would disappear once she'd been finally promoted to Heaven, but their presence in her strange afterlife were comforting, as they reminded her of the humanity she was still tied to.

The familiar discomforts of hunger and cold continued to gnaw away at her as she went through book after book, looking for information. She grew frustrated at her lack of progress and once again her mind turned to the missing book from the vault.

D-O-A was crouched over another heavy classic nearby, having not spoken to anyone that had come and gone in the past few hours. Nikita hadn't wanted to quiz him any further with his knowledge of fractures, as it wasn't much more advanced than what she'd already discovered herself, though she'd occasionally glanced over at him to see if he wanted any company. Eventually, he had checked his watch, placed his book back on the shelf, and pulled a card from his pocket. He absorbed the details of the assignment and silently left the building.

Nikita's innate curiosity led her out into the street, where she followed him, trying to stay out of view and slinking around the corners, possibly making herself more noticeable than if she had walked casually behind him. The early evening had brought a misty rain which clung to her skin and flattened her hair as she progressed further down the tree-lined roads.

Darkness was closing in fast as the last of the blood-red tint of sunset faded above the buildings. The fog thickened, coating everything in a damp film and diffusing the streetlights into glowing orbs of orange. She caught up with D-O-A as he passed by a row of shops, the back of his black overcoat billowing as he marched along the wet pavement. He slowed before coming to a stop under a lamp by the gates of a church. Once he had reread the card, the light above him began flickering and a swathe of shadows curled around him like dogs coming to the call of their master. A figure dressed in clerical attire emerged from the churchyard, bolting a gate behind him and placing a worn fedora on his head, oblivious to the dark-ness-cloaked Reaper stood next to him. The old priest made his way along a narrow street, tailed by the rolling cloak of shadows and one very inexperienced Cupid.

The streetlights crazed and blinkered when the Reaper passed beneath them, only returning to steady light once he was further ahead. In the distance, the church bell announced five o'clock and D-O-A rested an arm on the priest's shoulder, sharing a word or two that Nikita couldn't hear, before he disappeared into the fog and the priest was left confused and alone once more. Moments later, a scruffy man with a shaved head and baggy hoody emerged from an alleyway, flicking open a menacing knife. In a flash, there was an exchange of words, the priest held up his hands and the assailant thrust the knife into the priest's stomach before bolting away. Nikita gasped and ran to where he slumped in the street on his knees.

As blood pooled thick and hot around the gaping wound, Nikita held the man, knowing in moments he would pass from this life into the next. Instead of wondering whether he would meet the god who he had spent his life praying to, she wondered if he would turn up as a new recruit in the agency, or whether he would be wandering the Oblivion Fields. Tears fell freely from her eyes as she watched the light leave his. His bloody grip on her hand weakened, his shallow, pleading breaths extinguishing as he sunk to the stone. She held him and cried long after his soul had flown, and when she looked up into the deserted street, she saw D-O-A watching her in the distance. He walked away slowly, the heavy fog weighing down his spiked hair.

She rested the priest's head on the pavement, loath to leave him alone, but knowing she could not be the one to alert the authorities. The land of the living was no longer where she belonged. Tearfully, she ran back to the library, allowing the chill of the night to permeate her clothes and take the breath from her lungs.

Once back inside the Eligos, she found the nearest bathroom and frantically scrubbed the priest's blood off her hands. After a moment of staring at herself in the mirror, she felt compelled to approach the library guest book with its black-plume quill. Her stomach doubled over at the thought of the offering, but she was desperate for an answer to a burning question in her mind. She hesitated the point of the pen over her cold palm before dragging it across her skin and watching the small glass vessel fill with her blood.

Satisfied with the message that she scribbled onto the aged paper, she waited for it to be received. Once more, the candles flickered and an unseen breeze moved the pages of the ledger, an eerie sensation quivering through her veins. She placed the pen nib back down and watched the water absorb the last traces of her blood.

*   *   *

Later, in the silence of her apartment, Nikita stood on her balcony with a hot mug of tea held against her chest. She'd made sure to change out of her bloodstained clothes, had thrown them in the wash the moment she'd got home. As the comforting rumble of the washing machine whirred away in the kitchen, she enjoyed the coldness of the night air pressing against her skin. The sheer drapes flapped, phantoms in the wind, tugging to escape their tether as the frigid night air flowed into her living space. London was awash with lights and colour; a plane glided overhead with a distant roar of jets before its blinkering lamps disappeared into the blackness and filled the air with quiet once more. People were finishing up their day's work and streams of traffic glowed in the streets below. A deep coldness filled Nikita's bones, a sudden, shivering ice that couldn't just be attributed to the January night. Without warning, a spear of lightning crackled into the corner of her balcony, brighter than the sun and as hot as hellfire. She had no time to leap back or cower before the darkness returned, leaving a scorched patch on the tile and an aged slip of paper in its wake. The wind threatened to steal the page that had started wafting around her feet, so she snatched it up and turned it over. Another answer from Dantalion in the same familiar scrawl:

Your answer is in book 4557, page 93, paragraph 12.

Though she was tired, she felt no urge to rest. Her mind was a spinning vortex of thoughts, always curious, always driven, as impatient as wildfire aching to get to the next dry field. She was keen to find out what book 4557 was, and if it provided a piece of the puzzle she needed ... but before she could do that there were a couple of things she needed to do, so it would have to wait until the following morning. Checking the time, she left a voicemail message on Kendra's phone and was surprised to receive a call moments later.

'Hi, Kendra, sorry if I have disturbed you at al—'

'No, no, I am here to support all new recruits. What can I help you with? How's the study going?'

'Well, I began studying but I got distracted thinking about the recent fractures. So I started reading into it to see if I could help in any way ... and I think that I've found something interesting. It's a bit much to explain over the phone but I wondered if I could chat with you when you are next in the office?' Nikita explained.

Kendra paused for a short time, leaving the line silent. 'Actually, I'm in the office right now as division management has a meeting shortly about this very topic. I'd like to hear what you have to say before that. Can you come in now?'

'Of course. I'll be there in half an hour.'

Feeling the most in control than she had been in her afterlife so far, Nikita closed her balcony doors, finished her tea and headed back to the Apollo headquarters.

* * *

Kendra ushered her into her office when she arrived. Nikita hoped to present herself as being a conscientious and interested employee, as opposed to a busybody, so she was careful to omit the finer details about the missing book, Darren Oliver-Alliott, and summoning the library entity with a donation of blood . . .

'Kendra, forgive me for going off-topic, but from what I have read, the issue with fractures and mysterious deaths has happened before, a number of times,' Nikita explained, while sat in the plush office.

Kendra sat up straight, her attention piquing. 'Go on?'

'I found a book in the library that detailed a history of recorded fractures and their consequences. The list hadn't been updated since 1772 *but* it mentions the devastation caused by bizarre earthquakes, weather changes, time shifts and ended with the Russian plague. What is interesting is, at the same time as the plague outbreak, the Russian Nemesis Division records four deaths that should have just been retribution assignments.'

'Well, the Nemesis Division *are* able to undertake assignments that result in death. It's called the *Caedes Justificatum*.'

'Oh yes, I know, I looked that up. But that's not a reaping, rather an act of retribution that results in the instant or drawn-out death of the target. I don't think that is what we're dealing with here.' Nikita's eyes sparkled with enthusiasm as she relayed her research.

Kendra waved her hand dismissively. 'Those records are very old and no one can definitively say that they weren't planned *Caedes Justificatum* assignments. It's a weak connection at best.'

'Well, maybe, but the fractures that followed were similar to the odd happenings since these current deaths. I was there when Sofia Carter ended up on the train tracks. It looked like she was spooked by something that no one else could see, something otherworldly maybe?'

'We aren't sure about the details of all of the current deaths yet.' Kendra pressed her fingertips together, her garish pink nails making a soft *clacking* noise as they met. 'While I appreciate you coming to me with this, I instructed you to study for your exams, Agent Wolf. Why do you think reports from the 1700s help us?'

'I know I have taken some liberty here, but this seemed important. There are other reports that may be connected too, even a situation where Hades targets have escaped death miraculously. Each time this has happened there has been a large-scale disaster, often taking years to resolve.' Nikita reeled off several events – major wars, economic collapse, going right back to the Black Death in 1346.

'You've gone on quite the tangent here. But did any of your . . . *research* explain how to stop these fractures?'

Nikita paused. 'No, but I was hoping you would give me a chance to work on that. I have nothing but study to do and this might prevent a huge disaster.'

Kendra shook her head slowly, her permed hair bouncing. 'I don't think any of this is relevant to what we are currently dealing with, and I don't want you being sent on a wild goose chase. You're not a journalist anymore, remember?'

Nikita's shoulders slumped in disappointment.

'How about I take your notes and look into them, just in case?' Kendra gathered up all of Nikita's papers and stuffed them into her desk drawer. 'But for now, just stick to the reading that I told you to do and stop digressing with ancient history.'

Nikita nodded slowly. She lifted her messenger bag across her shoulder and wrapped her thick scarf around her neck, fully intending to return to the Eligos Library the following day, after an important errand at the scene of Sofia Carter's death. She had hoped to get some of the CCTV from Farringdon, and knew there was an urgency to sort that before heading back to the library, in case the footage was recorded over. Leaving the building, she was incredibly glad that she had thought to make copies of all her notes.

19

Hammer to Fall

I N THE APOLLO BUILDING, KENDRA was in her late-night meeting with the heads of the other divisions. All of them had been made aware of the snowballing fractures, including the earthquake in Bedford that had rippled as far as Tring. Gunther Hoffmann's death had reached them via the standard news, and it hadn't taken long to identify that he was marked as another gold assignment for Apollo. Their combined fears about the catastrophic escalation of fractures were becoming a distinct reality and emergency action was needed.

A huge question hung in the air as to why Casey and Erron had been given the Hoffmann assignment.

'Well, it certainly wasn't me who gave it to them. I wasn't even aware that they had gone anywhere.' Kendra scoffed. 'They are fully aware they are now suspended pending investigation.'

'We need to consult upper management,' a stern voice of reason added, belonging to the head of the Nemesis department, Osato M'Raya. Though all of the bosses were equal in the room, Osato carried an authority that no one would question;

in meetings she naturally assumed a leadership role, and when she made a statement it was rarely challenged.

The Hades boss, Lettie Crawford, nodded in agreement. Her sleek hair was tied in two plaits, the silver streaks hanging loosely around her face. 'There are brief records of these sort of fractures happening in the past, and more often than not it's accidental, but once in a while there is foul play from someone within the agency itself,' Lettie said, pulling a stack of papers from her briefcase. 'I have gone through all our assignments and there are none that coincide, or even go near the areas of these recent deaths, so this isn't a crossed wire with Hades. I think it's important to consider that Agent Grover and Hart may have some involvement, owing to the circumstantial evidence we have. Though it is not sufficient to say they are guilty of any crime or misdemeanour at this stage.'

Kendra fidgeted in her chair, the garish polka dot of her pink dress making her look like a strong contender for a Mr Blobby impersonation contest. 'One of my new recruits is currently studying for her exam and happened upon some information about fractures. I went through it with her, but it seems like there is nothing more recent than the 1700s. It does link to some significant global and national disasters back then, but I don't think it adds anything to the current situation from what I read.'

Osato nodded. 'What do you think of the possibility of foul play, Kendra?'

The Apollo boss toyed with a plastic heart pendant around her neck. 'These are my guys. I know them. Grover and Hart aren't capable of causing this level of destruction on purpose. We need to conduct a fair investigation to see if there is any connection.'

'Agreed, we need to establish if these two agents have engineered these deaths and come to a consensus regarding
punishment if so,' Lettie said firmly. 'I would suggest that they
remain inactive to prevent any further fallout, if it is the case
that they are the cause by either mistake or design. The main
priority here is halting the fractures before they escalate out of
control, as the situation has clearly worsened since our last
discussion. It's quite clear that if the tears in fate continue, the
consequences could be as Elzifur described.'

'Just a handful of Chaos agents loose with their full power
would be devastating this side of the veil. But legions of them?
It's unthinkable.' Osato slowly shook her head.

'We can't let that happen. I agree with Lettie with regard to
Grover and Hart. We need to establish fault first, with our
main focus stopping any more wrongful deaths. We should
vote on who will lead the investigation.'

'My vote is for a continued suspension of both agents and
an investigation led by Hades Division,' Lettie stated.

'I object.' Kendra pursed her lips. 'Apollo should lead any
investigation on its own agents.'

'At Nemesis, we have long since been looked to for fairness
and justice, as is our very nature. I would prefer to lead this
investigation,' Osato said, her voice steady as a rock. 'Besides, it's
not recommended protocol for a division to investigate internally.'

Both Kendra and Lettie looked to where Emrys, the Fortuna
boss, sat quietly listening. He deliberated, pressing his fingertips
together and leaning into the long mahogany table. 'This affects
all of us. Without further evidence, I vote for an independent
investigation led by Nemesis, as they have the lead on all matters
of justice.'

'If the two agents are involved, then let us be clear, I don't think Execution of Contract is appropriate if they are found to have actively caused these deaths. Obliteration is the only rightful outcome,' Lettie added.

Execution of Contract, though almost as dreadful as obliteration, allowed the agents to enter the afterlife with an automatic entry to Hell for no less than four hundred years before they were eligible to be re-judged. Either option was only reserved for the most serious of charges, and neither had been used in decades.

'Agents Hart and Grover have significant service history. It is imperative that any charges are wholly proven before passing sentence,' Osato said.

'I don't agree with Obliteration. If they are guilty of causing wrongful deaths, I vote for Execution of Contract,' Emrys said firmly.

'Execution of Contract,' Kendra agreed regretfully.

'I stand with the notion of Obliteration. We can't give a lighter sentence to something this serious,' Osato voted sternly. 'But we will hold a fair trial. At this time, we have no solid evidence of any guilt, but the circumstances warrant continued suspension, if only for the prevention of further fractures.'

A cold silence filled the room.

'What about the lost souls, Lettie, have you had receipt of them?' Osato asked.

'They have not yet been traced. We are five souls down, but my clean-up team are working around the clock. Souls cannot stay loose for too long or they will become shadows, and that is not something that we want.' It was very uncommon for a soul not to reach its intended destination, but on the rare occasion they were lost by a Reaper, the person was never able to complete their rightful journey into the afterlife. They became shadows, conscious and trapped in between light and darkness, whispering their memories to any who were close enough to hear, their only apparent purpose was to leave blurry patches in the corners of photographs. A tormented existence, without any known resolution.

Osato had prepared a set of notes that she had pulled from the agents' files and stood to present them. 'Let us first discuss the suspects. Agent Erron Christopher Grover, formally a police detective killed in an act of violence on frontline duty at the Brixton Riots, has performed thirty-nine years of service with Apollo, with fifty-six thousand, nine hundred and forty successfully completed assignments. He is in the top tier of marksmanship and third tier for undercover special operations. He has, to date, fourteen counts of misdemeanours, five in-house complaints and has six service penalties for being caught fighting with other agents in a state of inebriation.'

She shuffled her pages. 'Agent Casey Hart, formally a physician murdered by vigilantes, spent fourteen years in Nemesis Division before requesting a transfer to Apollo. He has completed a full two hundred and thirty-seven years of service at the agency, with two hundred and fifty-nine thousand, five hundred and fifteen successful assignments. A trained mentor, in the top tier of marksmanship and top tier of undercover special operations. He has one case of a misdemeanour, relating to ... ah, of course ... helping his co-worker Agent Grover steal office supplies to make a giant rubber-band ball.' Osato raised an eyebrow. 'Is that true, Kendra?'

The Apollo boss sighed. 'Yes, Erron wanted to drop it off the London Eye to see how far it would bounce. Luckily, I caught them before this idiocy could take place. Casey confessed his involvement and paid for all the rubber bands.'

Osato looked bemused. 'Despite these misdemeanours, there's no indication from their service history that they have any intent to cause these fractures, or any attempt to do anything of a similar nature in the past. If there is any guilt, we need to establish motive. I have, however, considered that this might be opportunistic, as five gold assignments within the space of a week is exceptionally rare and has the power to cause the most destruction, if they did have any delusions of causing societal collapse. We will commence an investigation to determine whether these men have any genuine involvement in the deaths that have transpired. As they have already been suspended, we will need to ensure that they are detained at the earliest opportunity for questioning. Until then, this meeting is concluded.'

Lettie and Kendra made their way out of the room, going their separate ways.

Emrys stayed behind to speak with Osato.

'Anything you need assistance with, just let me know,' he offered gently.

'Thank you. I will happily allow you to contribute to this investigation. It would be useful to have a balanced perspective.'

Emrys had worked alongside Osato for many years and highly respected the way she'd conducted previous investigations. Their professional friendship was based both on sharing similar morals and an unspoken acknowledgement of their unique loneliness in the world. Osato had embraced it; she was, by nature, a solitary creature, highly focused and fiercely independent, rarely fraternising with anyone unless they had proven themselves to be completely worthy of her trust. Her sense of justice never swayed. It never bent rules; it never broke them. Of all the agency leaders, she was the most formidable, and had the presence of a powerful queen from a time of bloody battles and fierce kingdoms.

Emrys, on the other hand, was highly approachable. His strong moral compass and gentle manner made him an excellent diplomat, and he had a kindness which was well recognised across the divisions. Despite that, he never seemed to find a genuine connection with anyone, friendship or otherwise, owing to his quirky sense of humour and an awkward shyness that prevented him building on professional relationships.

'Should we look through what information we have on the two agents now and come up with a game plan?' he offered.

'No time like the present,' Osato agreed and gestured for Emrys to pull up a chair as she unfolded all her paperwork once more. 'The sooner we get to the bottom of this the better.'

20

Between the Bars

L ATE THAT EVENING, CASEY WAS sat by the window of his hotel room, a glass of water in one hand, and the other resting on the windowpane. Thick drops of rain had started to fall, and the crystal-clear evening had turned into a wet and cold night. His fingers lazily traced the drops as they trickled down the glass, distorting the colourful lights of the town several floors below.

He took a mouthful of water and leant his head against the window, worry twisting in his stomach. His mind kept circling back to Erron's transfer request. He wasn't angry that Erron had kept it secret, rather his sadness boiled down to the fact that he was afraid of losing him. The fear of being away from Erron rolled like a lead knot in his stomach. He couldn't comprehend the point of existing for all of eternity if you still had to contend with loss. Lost in these thoughts, Casey stared at the rain, feeling no urge to sleep but hypnotised by the lights of the traffic and lulled by the building storm.

Erron was stood by his own window, enraged, shirtless and open-winged. The scars of his old life were written on his skin, an old stab wound here, a laceration from a complicated rescue there and several burn marks. Although he was a mere replication of his first body, his scars had left marks of trauma on his soul. He slammed his fists against the glass, hot angry tears streaming down his face. He was angry that his comfortable afterlife was going to be ripped to shreds by the Fates for no good reason at all, but he was also upset with himself that he had hurt Casey.

Erron didn't make friends easily; he quickly discovered when joining the police that he didn't fit in with the bull-headed, power-hungry men who shoved their way to top ranks, took backhanded bribes in dark alleys or shook dirtier hands in the name of a secret brotherhood. He was outcasted almost immediately, but he did his job well, not caring to socialise with anyone from the office. Eventually, he took a detective position to concentrate on serious crime, where long hours and late shifts kept him away from the hustle of the parade room. He was an honest copper and was shunned for it. The public hated him equally; hate was all he knew, from every angle, every aspect of his life. After his death, he had been given a chance to start again at the Apollo Division and a new mentor who *valued* him, genuinely cared about his progress, his past and his place in the team. Casey had become his closest companion despite their differences, and though Erron hated himself for turning his back on him, he knew deep down that he would keep requesting a transfer until the day it got accepted. He needed to escape the warm, fuzzy embrace of Apollo, where love was such a complicated emotion for him and where his heart broke a little more each time he joined two lovers together. Joining Hades felt like his only option; he'd dealt with death and despair daily in his old life and, after the death of his brother, he'd long harboured a desire to connect with the agents who understood tragedy from the other side. He knew that his complex emotions were continuing to plague him because of his inability to confront them, and all he was able to do was keep running away from those feelings ... and from Casey. Eventually, he perched on the edge of the bed, his legs no longer able to carry the weight of his unspoken feelings.

Morning finally came, and it was bleak and wet. Neither agent had moved much, both slumped in their respective spirals of negative thoughts through the night. It was only the stifled sound of the dawn chorus that roused them from their places.

'A new day,' Casey whispered to himself, stretching his limbs and yawning. 'May it bring hope ... and breakfast.' His stomach growled, craving the comfort of food to chase the darkness from his heart. He tried to shake off the misery from the night before and began packing his bag to leave.

In the other room, Erron was lying on the bed, staring at the ceiling, his mind numb from a night of chaotic thoughts. He had barely slept, only passing out briefly around 5 a.m. when his brain finally shut down. He slowly and reluctantly swung his legs over the side of the bed, feeling like death warmed up.

21

Unforgiven

WHILE SAT IN THE SLICK top office in the Nemesis Division headquarters, Emrys pored over the written reports of the fractures and the summaries of the deaths. The futuristic office furnishings made Emrys look out of place in his tweed waistcoat over a shirt and tie, brown moccasins and tattered old briefcase. Everything had clean lines, with an emphasis on black and white decor, spacious and as neat as a pin. As he read, he discovered that the fractures, which had started off inconsequential, were developing at a disconcerting rate, with the effects of earthquakes and strange electrical storms causing havoc in the mortal world. Issues appeared to be spreading and getting worse the longer time went on.

In the corner of the room, Osato was stood stock-still by the bright, floor-to-ceiling window. 'Human order has always balanced on a pinpoint,' she said, 'and the tiniest shift gives way to chaos. Oppression, wars, religious crusades, slavery, torture, bigoted ruling classes that sell people by the pound. Humanity can conjure such devils all by itself, from small minds and poisonous views. These fractures could be a tipping point for society, even before they become catastrophic to the laws of physics.'

Emrys agreed. 'The larger fractures appear to be currently manifesting as natural disasters. We've now had reports of multi-coloured storms and earthquakes as far as Scotland. These things are dangerous enough without them spiralling out of control.'

Osato remained silent as she thought. She'd read everything to do with the case so far and was frustrated that immediate action hadn't been taken after the first missed assignment.

'Agent Hart was under my wing when he first joined. He was conscientious, loyal and had an excellent moral compass. I used to say his heart was too tender for retribution as I could see how he struggled to punish others and watch their despair. I encouraged his transfer to Apollo as, even though he had such a strong sense of justice, I could tell he would unravel if he ever had to issue the death sentence with a *Caedes Justificatum* assignment. I always made sure he never had to do those.' She turned to face Emrys. 'For the Casey I knew, these deaths would lie heavy on his mind and be a deep trauma to him. I'm sure of it. Though it has been many years, so I can't rule out that he has changed.'

Emrys nodded. 'Agent Grover, however, could be solely responsible; he could have influenced or manipulated him. I say that we focus our efforts on Grover, initially. I will conduct a full background check on him, while we await a reply from . . .' He pointed towards the sky.

'You will need to access his mortal records, too. I need to speak to both Hart and Grover personally, once they have been detained.' Osato strode to her desk and selected a remote control from a drawer. She clicked a number of buttons and a huge screen descended down the back wall, its edges lit with bright LEDs. 'Allecto, please bring up files from Apollo Personnel.'

The screen brightened and scrolled through files until it selected the Cross Divisional records.

Osato was already dialling a number from the personnel files. After several rings, the call was answered.

'Cassiel,' she said quietly. 'We need to talk.'

* * *

There was very little in the way of conversation between Casey and Erron on their train ride home. It was still very early. Rain streaked the train windows against the backdrop of a dim grey sky. Before leaving the hotel, Casey had received a call from Osato to inform him that they were now officially under investigation and the agency was looking to detain them for questioning. She had asserted that they make their way back to the office and turn themselves in peacefully to avoid being detained by force. She informed him that she would deploy a team of four Nemesis agents to locate them if they didn't return by that evening. Stunned by this knowledge, Casey had kept the information to himself as they left the hotel and now the busy commuter carriage was hardly the right place to raise it with Erron. Instead of wallowing in their misery, he suggested they visit his favourite tearoom in Covent Garden on the way home, as it had been far too long since he had any kind of French pastry. Erron had long since put Casey's youthful appearance down to consuming excessive amounts of good butter and all the exercise he did going from one tearoom to another.

Over a pain au chocolat and gingerbread latte, Casey broached the news.

'So, it's official then, they're looking to pin this on us.' Erron looked dismayed.

'Seems that way. If we hand ourselves in now, it might go in our favour. I mean, after all, we haven't done anything wrong,' Casey reasoned.

'I don't know. It all feels iffy to me, like a set-up. Why us? How do we know that we will be treated fairly and the investigation will be transparent?' Shuddering, Erron thought back to his early years in the police, when getting confessions and closing investigations were more about attributing the blame to someone, regardless of whether it was the *right* someone. Even though times had changed somewhat, he'd seen enough bad apples in the police never to fully trust an investigation.

'I worked with Osato once upon a time. She embodies justice and wouldn't allow us to be obliterated on false evidence or circumstance alone.'

'I haven't worked with her though so I'm the perfect scapegoat. You said she's planning to send people to arrest us if we don't hand ourselves in. I think they have made their minds up about our guilt. No one would give a damn if I got thrown in the blender.'

Casey looked hurt. 'I would care. You know I would.'

'Yeah well, it's no good you caring when we are both atomic mush and erased from existence. Even though I would probably still see your mutilated molecules munching on cake crumbs in the aether.' Erron smirked.

Behind the counter, a radio that had been playing a mix from the eighties crackled over to the news. Gunther Hoffmann's death was mentioned, causing Casey's ears to prick up.

'Yesterday afternoon an aspiring environmental scientist was pronounced dead on the embankment of Bedford River, having leapt to his fate off the iconic town bridge. Police are treating it as suicide, following a note found in his hotel room from the morning.'

'What if ... What if we don't go back just yet? Surely we can find some evidence to prove that we're innocent. What if we try and clear our names?' Casey suggested tentatively.

Erron pressed his hand to his mouth and feigned dramatic surprise. 'Case, you shock me. Suggesting we go on the run like outlaws.' He paused. 'I'm in. Let's do it.'

After a few minutes of hushed conversation, Casey came up with a vague plan.

'You want me to go and raid evidence lockers again? For what purpose?' Erron questioned, picking at his angel cake.

'I have a hunch. They just reported on the news that Gunther left a note, same as Sofia Carter supposedly did. What if we could compare the notes to see if there was any link, any similarity maybe? You have photos of Sofia's note, maybe we could get hold of Gunther's, and try and access the records for the other victims to see if there were any glaring links? It doesn't make sense that, if Gunther was planning to jump off that bridge, he would've turned up to the conference at all that day.' He paused, watching Erron prodding his cake. 'Are you going to eat that or just stab it with a fork?'

'Explain?' Erron pushed his plate over and dropped the fork on the tray.

211

Casey savoured the first mouthful of Erron's offering and went on. 'I don't know how they think we have done this, but the circumstances seem to point to us, right? If we can get hold of any other notes or even the files, we might be able to prove that these were actually accidental deaths *or* that there is someone else from the agency directly responsible for this. I am willing to bet that neither Sofia nor Gunther's deaths had anything to do with suicide. And I will be interested to see what they chalked the others up to.' Casey paused, looking up from the cake. 'I think it might be worth us speaking to the people who were close to the victims. See if they can piece together any anomalies prior to when we turned up on the scene, off the record. But to do that, we need access to the suicide notes and any evidence from the scenes.' He lowered his voice and leant forward. 'Essentially, I think we need to prove a Ghoster was there and operating outside of their standard duty. Killing for fun and framing us. It's the only explanation I can think of.'

Erron folded his arms on the table and lowered his head onto them in exasperation. 'I don't even know where to begin to prove that. This kind of meddling in an investigation could land us in the blender regardless, Case.'

'What choice do we have?' Casey had undergone a painful procedure to remove the optimism from his normal sunny perspective.

Erron looked up, his face tired, his hair a mess. 'OK. If you think this is going to help, then I trust you. But only you.'

They agreed that Erron would miraculously make the relevant evidence disappear from the various police stations, while Casey started the process of charming statements out of all the relevant people. After a few days they would meet on top of the BT tower in Fitzrovia, a place no one would be looking for them.

As they approached the nearest Tube station, Theodore Roscoe, the aged rock-star Ghoster, caught up to them.

'Hello, boys,' he said with a warm smile and one gold tooth. 'I heard about your suspension through the grapevine. How are you holding up?'

Theodore was, by far, one of the only Hades agents that anyone from other divisions was comfortable making small talk with. He was like the cool uncle, the one who had stories of travelling to Thailand and sharing a bottle of whisky with music stars in the back tents of festivals. The kind of uncle who had an abundance of lava lamps and would slip you a fiver for not mentioning to your parents that he was growing unusual plants in the loft.

'Could be better,' Erron answered.

'Well, I'm rooting for you both. If you pull through this, Grover, you would be welcomed at Hades, even if they have rejected you multiple times. You know how these things work, it's all office politics. Don't let it discourage you. I will put in a good word for you this time, see if it helps.' Theodore slapped him on the shoulder and nodded towards a man in a grey overcoat. 'Well, I gotta go. Take care, kids.'

They watched him approach the grey overcoat man, start up a light conversation, shake his hand and then carry on across the street. Within a few moments, the man collapsed to the floor, suffering a massive cardiac arrest. Erron pulled Casey away, conscious that the last thing he needed was to witness another death.

Casey tugged his arm away from Erron's grip. 'What did he mean?' he asked accusingly.

'What?'

'You know what!' Casey hissed. 'You being *welcomed at Hades*. You haven't requested a transfer to another district at all. You want to change *divisions*.'

'Leave it, Casey.'

'No. No, absolutely out of the question. I'm not leaving it. You couldn't be bothered to tell me, after everything we have been through. You're my best friend! You want to join the Ghosters? Of all the places you could go, you want to be one of *them*? And not just that, you have applied countless other times and never bothered to tell me? Instead of being able to witness beautiful moments when people fall in love, you would rather wallow in the misery of death day in, day out? I don't honestly know what's worse, that after nearly four decades working with me, you fail to mention you are hoping to jump ship, or that you choose some macabre glory of death over our partnership, bringing people happiness.'

'Casey ...' Erron exhaled slowly, knowing he couldn't hide from it much longer '... I don't believe in love like you do. I don't see the beauty of it, people being forced together to endure each other's company *day in, day out*. Until one of them decides that they are sick of the other and moves on. Love? It's just an easy way of getting hurt.'

Casey fumed. 'Maybe it's because you don't even know what it is yet.'

'Maybe you've just been lucky, Case? Maybe the rest of us know what a shitshow it really is. Tell me, have you ever had to pretend to love someone just so your family shut the hell up? Have you ever had to pretend to be happy because the truth hurts more than fiction?'

'Erron. I *died* for love. Isn't that suffering enough?'

Erron tried to answer, starting several sentences which were blown away like a leaf on the wind, leaving his mouth empty of words. Eventually, he managed a feeble 'What do you mean?'

'If you give a damn, Erron, why don't you read *my* bloody file.' When he faced a stony silence, Casey walked away, exasperated and hurt. Then he turned sharply and stalked back, pointing his finger at Erron. 'If ... If I find out that it's you who has something to do with all this ... you have no idea how ... how *disappointed* I will be in you.' His words cut like knives.

'Is that what you think? You honestly think I am the one causing all these deaths?' Erron raised his voice and got up close to Casey's face, standing on tiptoes to do so. 'I'm more than disappointed in you for even suggesting that. I thought you were my friend,' he hissed through clenched teeth. 'Maybe I am better off at Hades, they might even fucking trust me.'

'I trusted you all right, until you snuck off to join another division without telling me. Trusted you, befriended you, hell, I even wanted ... never mind.' Casey started to walk away again.

'You even wanted what?' Erron caught up with him.

'You know what, Erron, you wouldn't care anyway. I hope you find your happiness at Hades. If we're not obliterated before then.' Casey pushed him away and continued walking.

Erron stopped chasing him and slumped onto the nearest bench. He swore under his breath, then exhaled as if allowing his very life force to escape his body. He hadn't explained himself well enough, he hadn't defended his decision properly. He wanted to tell Casey about his hateful experience of love, how it had shaped every day of his adult life, and how seeing his targets become genuinely happy mocked him for everything he had suffered.

After several moments of self-pitying, he got to his feet and decided the only thing he could do to stop himself going insane was to stick to his side of the plan. After all, he wouldn't be able to fix his friendship if he was obliterated. He would need a few days to visit the evidence rooms in both London stations dealing with Sofia, Lucy, Quentin and KiaRia, and would need to make a trip back up to Bedford to seek out the information from the Dr Hoffmann alleged suicide. He'd try and get hold of any CCTV exhibits too, to prove that there was a Ghoster impacting the electrical items nearby. He knew it wouldn't be wise to draw attention to himself by travelling by portal or going near agency staff or buildings, so he made the decision to lie low and conduct his investigation as discreetly as possible. His first point of call was to withdraw all his savings of old money so he could operate under the radar and deal only in cash.

Casey, cooling off quickly in the light winter rain, went into the nearest department store to grab some food, clean under-wear and a small rucksack. He planned to embark on a long flight to Austria, to get the statements he needed from Gunther Hoffmann's family and friends. Wary of travelling on a plane in case he was spotted, he'd made a rash decision to fly himself, something that most agents wouldn't even attempt long distance. His wings had fully recovered from their swim in the river and he had no doubt that, with determination and favour-able winds, he could get across Europe and back in around three days with sleep. He checked the weather forecast for Belgium and Germany and neither predicted any heavy weather systems that would disrupt his flight. He took off once he found a safe place to extend his wings, soaring over central London and dipping low to check on his little townhouse. As he flew over Craven Street, he caught a glimpse of the black car that turned into the road and parked up outside his door.

*   *   *

Earlier that day, Nikita had returned to where it all started: the place where Sofia Carter's assignment had gone horribly wrong. She planned to get her hands on the CCTV footage of Sofia's death, and in order to do so, she needed to test out her newly acquired Apollo charms. She approached the train station help desk, putting on her warmest smile and tilting her head with a pleading look. The fifty-something lady behind the counter didn't return the smile but did seem briefly transfixed. Spinning a tale about how she had lost her wallet, Nikita explained that she wanted access to the footage of herself from their CCTV. She knew from her reporting days that the train company had an obligation to provide any captured images to anyone completing a Subject Access Form and provided the specific time, date and location that she needed.

'Do you want the form for the body-worn camera too?' the lady asked, without any resistance, seemingly unable to look away from Nikita's enthusiastic grin.

'Body-worn camera?'

'Yes. Graham the guard was on the platform that day so he likely had you on his vest camera,' she explained openly.

'Yes, absolutely. Now this is really important, so can this be processed quickly, please?' Nikita had already begun to fill out the forms that the lady had slid under the counter screen.

'I will put an urgent stamp on it. You should get it back within a couple of days.'

'Thank you.' Nikita stood in silence completing the forms and wavered over the section where photo ID was needed. 'Hey umm, this part about photo ID. I don't have mine with me right now ...' She tried to be as sweet and charming as she possibly could, not knowing if it had any impact on the lady or not.

The counter clerk smiled broadly, clearly fully absorbed in the Apollo charm. 'Oh, don't worry about that, my dear, not if it's urgent. I will say that I have seen it.'

Later that evening, Nikita returned to trawling through the library shelves methodically for book 4557, which was not where it should have been. She had had to abandon her search part-way through as Kendra had called to check that she was studying the correct material. She'd bluffed that she'd just got to the library and would call back in a couple of hours to recite what she'd focused on that day. When the clock chimed 2 a.m., the library was still aglow with soft candlelight, ever welcoming, ever warm against the stiff bite of winter. By that time, Nikita was alone, but she wasn't surprised or even frightened to hear the soft whispers of ghostly entities in the hallways and alcoves. She had already died once, and she was practically a ghost herself; there was little else any spooks could do to her. Tristan DeVangelo had warned her about them. *Shadows*, he had said, *haunt the late hours of the library. Ghosts of beings we don't need to understand. Harmless, but they like to talk.* He'd explained them as lost souls, those who still craved some knowledge or purpose after death. Souls that had slipped through the clutches of the Reapers. Trapped in an eternity between worlds. He had laughed and advised her to always take an MP3 player with her to drown out their murmuring voices if she was inclined to late-night library haunting herself.

Moments later, she broke the silence with an involuntary cheer of joy when she located book 4557 shoved between a pile of old maps on the second floor. She hugged it to herself and sat on the floor, exhausted, but excited to read it. The book was called *A Blood Romance*. She rifled through to the page that Dantalion had indicated. On first read, the opening heading meant little to her: 'The Umbra Amictus: Love's Cloak of Death and the Weave of Blood'.

She read on, her fingers tightening on the book as the realisation became clearer. In 1254, a Hades operative named Vladimir Dragos discovered that he could turn into shadow and move through objects, unseen as a ghost, when his blood had mingled on the battlefield with that of his lover, an Apollo agent named Lisbeth Hawke. This was back in a time when all divisions regularly had warzone assignments, and often got caught in the clash of swords or the odd stray bullet, depending on the era. Lisbeth had been severely wounded, and Vladimir held her as her cosmic life force seeped into the mud beneath them. Once her blood had mingled with his, he found that he was able to turn to shadow for a brief time, and even pass into the body of a human. From that point on, strict measures were put in place to ensure that agents were unable to mix blood, with a strict penalty for dabbling in the practice. As Nikita flicked through the chapter, she saw that large sections had been redacted from the text, which she assumed detailed the practice of blood magic.

She surmised that Dantalion had given her a vital piece of the puzzle. He had pointed her towards how an agent might make themselves a shadow that could pass through walls; all they needed was a mix of agency blood. Of one thing she was certain: there was an unseen force at work and someone in the agency was mixed up in it.

She flicked through to the index in the book and a torn page slid out from the dust cover that was clearly from another book entirely. She picked it up and read both sides; it related to the main blood groups of each division and something called a Cosmic Shift, but the information was ripped away at the bottom. From what she could gather, she no longer had O+ running through her veins, but Blood Type Corvus. Curious as she was to learn more, she wouldn't know where to begin to find the book the page belonged to.

Her first instinct was to tell Kendra about the blood mixing practices she'd discovered, but her second told her to keep the information quiet until she could narrow down some leads. The last thing she wanted was to add more weight to the accusations against Erron and Casey, not until she knew for certain whether they were involved. Nikita still wanted to visit the Oriax in Edinburgh to find a copy of the book that had been mysteriously removed from the Eligos vault. She had a feeling that whoever had taken the book was likely involved in the recent series of events, and it might reveal information vital to the case. But nipping to Scotland wasn't something that she could do unsupervised, and she likely wouldn't have the access needed to obtain the book anyhow. She knew that a good night's sleep would refresh her mind, so she began packing up her research and headed home. She finally crawled back in her bed at 5.15 a.m., her bones cold and her brain still trying to assemble the new information as the dawn birds began singing.

22

Who Knew

A GRAINY LITTLE TV BLARED IN the run-down hotel room where Erron was lying low. It was still early in the morning and he was in his boxer shorts, padding around on the grubby brown carpet barefoot and eating a bowl of Coco Pops with his wings outstretched. He had had no voicemails on his personal phone from Casey, asking him to meet for breakfast and talk through their fight, nor had Casey made any attempt to track him down at his hotel, with a cup of coffee and a sad puppy-dog look on his face in an attempt to reconcile. He was starting to worry that he really had lost the only person he truly cared about.

After their fight, he had gone to collect evidence on the London deaths, only to find that everything key to the cases had been removed. To his frustration that included his lighter, which had been removed from the scene of KiaRia's death. The items that were left weren't worth worrying about and he decided that his best option was to fly up to Bedford and see if there was any evidence left from Dr Hoffmann's river plunge.

Erron picked up the TV remote and flicked across to the news. It was flooded with one disaster after another. Not the usual headlines about stabbings and a traffic pile-up on the M25, but a tornado in Soho that was baffling scientists and mass rioting in Kensington over chlorinated chicken. His ears pricked up at the last report as he stood and watched the screen, a spoonful of Coco Pops poised mid-air. His first thought was to ring Casey and tell him he was right about the chicken, but his stubborn pride made him pause in his reach for the phone. He finished his cereal and drank the chocolate milk straight from the bowl, switching the TV off just as the national news was reporting a new disease sweeping across borders. Fractures were beginning to unravel the status quo, tearing shreds in the stitching of reality. He had to get a move on; time was ticking and he couldn't afford too many nights in a hotel relying on his savings of old money.

* * *

Meanwhile, Casey had made good progress on his flight over Europe, stopping late morning to savour the view on a breezy hill in Belgium. He wanted to push through until he reached his destination, but knew he would have to find a bed and breakfast for a few hours' sleep that afternoon to recharge. Wild grass danced against his legs in the cool air, the winter frost gradually melting away as the low winter sun hung on the horizon. He remembered a world when things were wilder, where the settlements of men weren't so far-reaching and electric pylons didn't stretch as far as the eye could see. He had never grown bored of the changing views, even when faced with the smog-filled streets of Victorian London, where he had wandered golden and cosmic among the sad souls of the poor, hoping his arrows spread a little warmth and comfort among their starving and desperate hearts. In his former life, he'd pioneered some of the newest advances in medicine and surgery, treating people without charge when he could and taking care of his neighbours as if they were family. Some of them had turned on him in the end, but he put their faces to the back of his mind. With every sunrise and sunset, the bright colours reminded him of the burning hope of those starved and helpless people who had loved him for his remedies and taught him how to value every day as if it were a gift. The beauty he found among the sorrow filled his heart and made him thankful for every moment he had left. He'd reached a stage where he no longer feared the threat of obliteration; he was just grateful that he had been given more sunrises and sunsets than most people would ever experience.

Casey wasted no more time, taking off at a run and letting the updraughts carry him into the thin clouds, where he could glide further east and enjoy the view from a far greater height. He planned to touch down in Frankfurt for a rest before pressing on to Salzburg through the evening into the night.

He didn't quite know what he might achieve speaking to the family of Gunther Hoffmann, but it was a start and he had nothing else to do while avoiding his inevitable detention.

Below him as he flew, an epidemic of geese was filling a number of small towns and villages, chaotically honking and waddling their way through the throngs of confused people. They were causing havoc on country roads and stuffing themselves onto bodies of water in such volume that each pond and lake looked like a fairground game of hook-a-duck.

'Geese ... of course,' Casey muttered to himself, gazing down as he flew. 'And I thought there were supposed to be horsemen at the end of the world. Who would've guessed?'

23

A Kind of Magic

'Hello?' Nikita croaked, the phone having woken her only an hour after she'd drifted off to sleep.

'Agent Wolf, my name is Osato M'Raya of the Nemesis Division. I need to speak with you regarding a case I am dealing with,' came the stern reply, with no apology about the timing of the call.

Nikita's heart pounded and she sat up with a start. She hated being in trouble and her off-the-record research must have put her there. A nervous sweat clambered down her back. 'Yes?'

Osato requested that she meet her at ten o'clock and gave the address of the Nemesis Division headquarters. By quarter to, Nikita stood outside the revolving doors of a tall, thin building near Southwark Crown Court, the large Latin proverb *Ut Sementem Feceris Ita Metes* (As you sow, so shall you reap) etched into the white stone mantle above the first set of tall windows. Above that, the building morphed into a mirrored glass mono-lith, boasting panoramic views and sophisticated architecture, a perfectly struck balance between antiquated and contemporary.

There was a crest on the wall by the doors bearing the Nemesis symbol, a winged set of scales within a circle of flame.

Osato, the elegant yet stern head of the Nemesis Division, collected Nikita personally from the marble lobby, with its brass flag poles and courtroom feel. The flags draped around the room were printed with symbols Nikita hadn't yet committed to memory, but were agency-related and nothing to do with any patriotism. After an awkward minute in the lift, Nikita was led onto the top floor, where she was offered a chair around the spacious centre table.

'You are probably aware of why I asked you here.' Osato poured Nikita some water into a crystal-clear glass.

Nikita accepted the drink gracefully but didn't offer any answer. Osato flicked on her wall-screen display and commanded Allecto to retrieve her current case file. It displayed two up-to-date ID shots of Casey and Erron against a white background.

'Agents Hart and Grover. You were assigned to them on your first day, yes?'

Nikita nodded, perching on the sleek plastic edge of the chair, her body too tense to relax.

'And you were present when Sofia Carter jumped on the line, yes?'

'She didn't jump; she was running from something and she tripped,' Nikita protested.

Osato observed her for a moment. 'She tripped then. Wording is everything when seeking the truth, Agent Wolf, as I see you are well aware.'

'The wrong words can bring down an empire.'

'The wrong words can do all kinds of damage, if used unjustly,' Osato agreed, her tone never faltering from its smooth, bold manner. 'Describe these two men for me.' She pointed at the screen. 'As best as you can, from your first impression.'

Nikita breathed out slowly and allowed her back to slump a little. 'Well, they were both welcoming and they both seemed very professional, kind. Casey, if I may say so, is a sweetheart. There is something inherently innocent and caring about him, I found. Erron has his quirks, but he didn't give me any reason to distrust him. They both seem like good, dependable people. Different to a lot of the guys I knew in life; the type who would do anything to sweet-talk you then grab you in the printer room or try it on in the taxi home after a night out.' Her thoughts flicked to Tristan DeVangelo with his flowing dark curls and Hollywood smile. It had taken her a long time to learn that she should avoid men like him.

'They both have a good service history.' Osato sat down across from Nikita. 'It is my job to decide whether they are guilty of intentionally causing or influencing five people to die. As I'm sure you've noticed, these deaths are resulting in a significant level of fracturing of which we have only begun to feel the effects. Let us go back to Sofia Carter. Tell me every detail of what you remember about that assignment.'

Nikita recalled everything that she could, Osato drawing out parts that she found of interest, typing it all up on a sleek laptop.

'Go back to that bit,' Osato instructed, fingers poised over the keys.

'What bit? That Erron shot and Sofia just . . . paused?'

'The bit about the departure screen. Describe it to me.'

Nikita tried to recall anything specific about the station's flickering screen that could spark some element of epiphany.

'A Hades agent was present,' Osato affirmed. 'But should not have been. Can you remember anyone there that stood out to you?'

Nikita racked her brain. 'Not in the slightest. I mean, I have seen a Reaper at work but ... no, I didn't see anything like that at Farringdon station.'

'Upper management have confirmed that none of the deaths were scheduled by the Hades department, so there should not have been any of their staff on assignment in these locations. Yet all of them have featured some *Umbra Noctis* disturbance.'

'So, you think that Casey and Erron are innocent?'

'We can't prove that, and it also clouds things that Agent Grover has been attempting to transfer for Hades for years. He has been rejected on a number of occasions and we must consider that he could potentially be trying to reap souls without permission. Listen, Agent Wolf, anything you know that could be relevant needs to be divulged. Is there anything else you'd like to add?' Osato made a point of closing the laptop and looking directly at Nikita. 'You understand that any failure to disclose important information will be taken very seriously.'

Nikita considered whether she should reveal her recent reading topics. Osato's gaze felt like needles probing her for answers. The sturdiness of her expression was enough to encourage righteousness in the worst of criminals.

'There are a few things,' Nikita found herself saying. 'It may not be relevant, but it might help in some way.' She explained her findings, offering Osato the list of books she'd skimmed through, the notes from Dantalion, the revelation about the forbidden *Umbra Amictus* about mixing agency blood from the story of Vladimir and Lisbeth. As she listened, Osato remained steadfast, her fingers interlocked and her face as professional as a doctor listening to how one managed to get a wasabi pea stuck in their ear without once challenging their lack of common sense. Nikita went on to show Osato her sketches and photos from the train station which, thankfully, she had thought to bring with her. She was careful to leave out the detail of requesting CCTV footage, as she wasn't sure how that fitted in with agency protocol.

'And I found this. Tucked into the book about the blood mixing.' Nikita reached in her pocket for the torn page she'd found. 'It refers to blood groups for the divisions and something called a Cosmic Shift.'

Osato took the page and studied it closely. 'This looks to be from a medical journal from what I can gather.'

'Is it relevant? What is the Cosmic Shift? Is that something to do with turning into shadow?' Nikita queried.

'No, it's nothing to do with the blood mixing. You see, we all have our division blood types, and these dictate our skills. Our reanimation stardust is all pulled from different constellations. For example, Nemesis is Blood Type Andromeda and you are Corvus and so on. But the Cosmic Shift is an incredibly rare occurrence when the Fates can change an agent's role on a whim when it can be wholly justified. Though it can only happen when an agent has previously transferred divisions, effectively having undergone blood reassignment.'

'What sort of situation would make that happen?'

'In all my years I only heard of it once, decades ago. A Fortuna agent who was previously from Hades. She was supposed to be on an assignment to hand out luck to a man at a casino, but as soon as she did, he tried to sexually assault her, hurting her badly in the process. The Fates intervened and gave the agent temporary Hades power to reap his soul on the spot,' Osato explained.

'I can't see how that would be relevant to this investigation though, if the Fates are the only ones that can do it.' Nikita took the page back and looked over it again. 'Unless whoever tucked this excerpt into the blood-mixing book was looking into the blood types of the agents?'

'That would make more sense.' Osato digested everything Nikita had told her before nodding slowly and rising from her chair. When Osato was deep in thought, she liked to take up her favourite place by the window, and as she watched the traffic shifting slowly in the streets below, she processed all the information she'd been given. Eventually, she faced Nikita again. 'We need to go to the Oriax. If you think the missing book is involved somehow, we need to get hold of a copy.'

'We ... as in me as well?'

'You've got a strong eye for detail, Agent Wolf, and you haven't been in Apollo long enough to form any alliances. I'd like to keep you on this assignment.'

'Well, I am supposed to be studying for my exam, seeing as I don't have a mentor at the moment.'

'Your study can be put on hold for a short while,' Osato stated, bringing up her digital assistant Allecto to book three plane tickets to Edinburgh for that afternoon and dial a number on the big screen. After four rings, a man's face appeared on the camera, slightly weathered but handsome.

'Emrys, we are flying to Edinburgh at 3 p.m. Pack an overnight bag and meet me at Gatwick.'

Emrys Taliesin yawned, showing off the silver fillings in his back teeth. 'Anything you say, ma'am.' He ran his hand through his messy hair and smiled a sleepy smile. 'Developments?'

'I'll brief you on the flight. Get some coffee; you look like you need it.'

He laughed. 'Rough night. These fractures have messed up a few of our assignments. You know how the Chaos love a bit of bad luck. All sorted now though.'

'You haven't lost any more agents to standing behind fridges to see if they will shrink, have you?' Osato teased.

Emrys rolled his eyes at the memory of the lost days of Ember Songfire.

'That was Grover's fault too. We should indict him on that alone.' Emrys rubbed his eyes and chuckled softly. 'But no missing agents, just the normal kind of chaos you would expect this time.'

In their limited power, the agents of Chaos would be having a field day with the fractures, backing up sewage pipes, adding unlisted phone numbers to company websites and loosening bolts on roller coasters.

'Good to hear.' Osato flashed a smile, a rare deviation from her usual stern expression.

'Where do we find these people, eh? Right, consider me packing a bag then.'

Osato ended the video call. She switched her screen to an email page and dictated a short message that would be sent to Kendra, explaining that Nikita would be absent from her studies for a minimum of two days. She mentioned nothing about the trip to Oriax.

'Well, Agent Wolf, I will see you at the airport. Thank you for your cooperation.'

Nikita nodded and headed for the office door, glancing at the clock on the wall. She had enough time to gather an overnight bag and stop off for some breakfast somewhere before heading to Gatwick.

* * *

Nikita arrived at the airport in good time, still full from a stack of Nutella pancakes she'd scoffed in a breakfast bar not far from the Nemesis headquarters. She hopelessly scanned the crowds of passengers for Osato but couldn't yet see her, her stomach churning a little at the thought of having missed them and the flight. The clock on the wall reassured her that she was there in good time.

'Nic ... Nicole? Is it Nicole?' She felt a gentle tap on her shoulder. Startled, she spun around to see the Fortuna boss, Emrys, looking back at her, an awkward smile on his face.

'It's Nikita.' She smiled and offered her hand to shake his.

'Oh, I am so sorry, I am terrible with names. Osato only texted me a few minutes ago to say you would be here. *Nikita.* That's a lovely name.' His cheeks flushed a little with embarrassment as he shook her hand warmly.

'My mum was an Elton John fan, hence the choice.'

'I do love that song as well.'

'It's not my favourite. Too many kids at school singing it at me, I guess.' She rolled her eyes.

'I suppose that does leave a lasting impression. I guess it's better than being named Rocket Man,' Emrys considered.

She snorted at the idea. 'I don't know, I think that's got a ring to it. Rocket Man Wolf ... I like it.'

'Had you been born a boy I expect you might have been Daniel then.' Emrys referenced another of Elton's well-known songs.

'Oh no, absolutely not. I would have been named Crocodile Rock.' She kept her face deadpan until he broke into a fitful laugh.

They made small talk for a short while; he asked about her former life and how she was settling in. The more he spoke in his gentle voice and seemed genuinely interested in her answers, the more she warmed to him. No longer under the powerful hold of the Apollo Flush, it surprised her when her stomach did a happy little backflip when he went to touch her arm, enthusiastically regaling her with a story of one of his assignments at an aquarium when he was a new agent. She zoned out briefly, finding herself admiring the sparkle in his eyes as he spoke and the excitability he showed when recounting his memories. She only looked away when she realised she was staring at him intently, and hoped she laughed at the right time when he mentioned having an octopus fall on his head.

She nodded and smiled as he chatted away, mesmerised by his mannerisms and scruffy hair. She only realised she wasn't paying full attention when he repeated a question he'd asked.

'What did you think of it?' He waited patiently for her reply.

'Oh, umm, well, what did you think?' she deflected, having no idea what he was referring to.

'I didn't like it much. I hate being underwater for a start.'

'Oh, yes. I . . . same.' She laughed nervously before realising he was referring to the soul replication tank.

She chastised herself silently for doing what she always did, becoming too quickly interested in a man of whom she had very little knowledge. In the past, it had never worked out all that well. Having grown up with emotionally absent parents, she was quick to latch on to anyone nice who showed her the slightest bit of interest. She couldn't deny there was something she instantly liked about Emrys, whether it was his gentle manner, his quirky humour or just that he had an exceptionally welcoming smile. She quelled the rising butterflies in her stomach and regained her composure, incredibly glad she was no longer in the throes of the Apollo Flush, or she would have embarrassed herself significantly.

'Anyway, I swear I have a dictionary possessed by a depressed alcoholic.' Emrys shrugged.

'Uhh, you do?' Nikita had fully returned to the conversation at that point.

'Sure. A psychic once told me to communicate with the dead through a dictionary. You ask a question, close your eyes, then turn to a random page and put your finger on it. Whatever word you pick relates to your answer. Well, I tried, and all the words I got were depressing, and when I asked what the spirit wanted, it would always give me an answer to do with drinking.'

'And this was ... when?'

'Oh, before I died.'

'I've always been fascinated with the afterlife, the occult, that type of thing. I bet that was quite creepy,' Nikita said. 'Though I suppose I never expected it to be this.'

'Ah, so you weren't thinking it would be a continuation of the daily grind and shopping trips to the moon then?'

'No, but if I had, I would have changed my name to Rocket Man a long time ago.' She laughed.

'Of course, going back to the dictionary, I don't really know if souls can actually possess things like in films.' He scratched his head in thought.

Osato finally joined them. 'Emrys, it was likely a Chaos agent messing with you.' She had caught the end of their conversation.

'That's highly likely. A depressed alcoholic one.' He considered the theory.

'Shall we?' She nodded towards the check-in desks.

Emrys nodded and gestured for Nikita to go ahead of him. 'After you, Agent Rocket.'

Nikita rolled her eyes and laughed. 'Why do I feel that name is going to stick now?'

He grinned mischievously.

'I expect at this short notice we will all be in separate seats next to crying babies.' Nikita glanced at the departure board.

Emrys cleared his throat. 'You're forgetting I booked the seats. By some pure luck, there were three seats all together Now I wonder how that could have happened.'

Nikita rolled her eyes and smiled. 'Of course, things just go your way in Fortuna, don't they?'

He looked incredibly pleased with himself.

Nikita was feeling particularly bold, so asked Emrys if she could sit next to him so they could continue their discussion into the supernatural. She liked how his eyes lit up and he agreed enthusiastically, giving her enough reason to believe that there was a chance he might like her too.

* * *

Several hours later, following muted discussions on the plane, the three took a pre booked taxi from Edinburgh to a tiny, ancient-looking hamlet that didn't appear to be on Google Maps. With Osato in the lead, they meandered down a dirt lane past a thatched roof church. Nikita felt like she had wandered back a few hundred years, looking around at the sheep that grazed on the hills and the old stone buildings that seemed frozen in time. She glanced at the diamond-leaded windows, enjoying the sight of the cosy-looking cottages and the glow of fireplaces adding warmth to the cold stone walls, though jumped when she caught a brief glimpse of a twisted, shadowy figure in the glass, horns protruding from its face and a mouth full of tentacles. She wanted to convince herself it was just a trick of the light, but it reminded her too much of the image she had seen in the mirror outside the antique shop the other day. She raised it with Osato.

The Nemesis boss was taken aback and asked her to describe both images she had seen. Nikita relayed the descriptions and where she had seen the first one.

'This is serious,' Osato stated. 'What you are seeing are Chaos agents in their true form; normally the veil is far too thick for anyone to see them, but if you have spotted two already, they must be gathering at the veil as it thins. It's only a matter of time before they manage to get through.'

'So I'm not imagining things then?' Nikita felt the colour drain from her face.

'No. Our world is in great peril. If they get through, it won't just be jammed printers and late trains, everything we know will become a hellscape of disorder and suffering.'

No more was said and the trio upped their pace to reach the Oriax.

At the end of the long lane, they reached a rocky ledge over a valley. The ledge was surrounded by a high stone wall and in the centre was a heavy wooden gate, with four agency symbols carved into it. Osato took out her Agency ID and passed it across one of the carved symbols, which glowed slightly, giving way to a low groan as the gate slowly swung open. Beyond it lay a narrow rope bridge across the terrifyingly vast and incredibly deep valley.

'We would fly, but you haven't got your wings yet,' Osato explained to the trainee agent. 'This is the flightless route to the Oriax.'

'You know, we could just carry her,' Emrys suggested.

'You know that's completely against regulation.' Osato frowned. 'You of all people should know better than to suggest such a dangerous deviation of flight rules.'

One thing Emrys did know better was never to question Osato when she brought up regulations. He raised his hands in submission. 'We'll walk across. Absolutely. Forget I said it.'

Osato gave him a stern look, before stepping onto the bridge.

Though Nikita wasn't that afraid of heights, she was distinctly aware that her newly baked body could still suffer catastrophic damage from a fall, so she opted to walk in the middle of the two agents with wings, should the bridge suddenly decide to disintegrate, there was a chance someone might catch her.

It took fifteen minutes to reach the other side, and there was another immensely high castle wall with an iron access gate at the end of it, all hidden in a thick forest of evergreen trees. Once inside, Nikita's mouth fell agape with wonder at the sheer beauty of the Oriax. It was immense, the long winding track to the entrance ran steeply up a sweeping hill among ancient oak trees that had watched agents come and go for hundreds of years.

The last of the light was fading from view, leaving a thin mist around the tops of the trees and countless twinkling lights glimmering from various walkways and woodlands. There were several agents milling around the grounds, all comfortably displaying their wings, walking through the beautiful frost-covered gardens and talking around the giant silver sundial at the entrance. Nikita's eyes widened at the sight, the angelic white wings of the Apollo agents compared to the black, shadowy wings of Hades, the smouldering and ember-glowing feathers of Nemesis next to the delicate, iridescent wasp-like wings of Fortuna.

'Something else, isn't it?' Emrys inhaled the cold Scottish air. 'Makes the Eligos look like an afterthought. Mind you, the Kimaris Castle near Cardiff is also impressive, it just lacks the sheer volume of books.'

'It's a world away from Islington,' Nikita agreed as they made their way to the front doors, enveloped by the clean, frigid air. Emrys and Osato both stretched out their wings. His were an eye-catching rainbow of crystalline membranes, hers were a daunting trail of smoky feathers that sparked and spat bright embers in their wake. Nikita felt naked walking among so many winged figures, their gazes turning to her like she was an imposter, or worse, a double-glazing salesperson visiting the castle without an appointment. As they wandered through, numerous people seemed to know Osato, as they looked at her in awe, whispering among themselves. Emrys was oblivious to flirtatious looks thrown his way. He had entertained Nikita on the flight with his many comedic stories of past ventures, his sense of humour shining through his soft outer appeal. She particularly enjoyed his slightly vague and eccentric snippets of advice that he peppered into the conversation, such as *Don't walk under seagulls* and *Turn over a new leaf, not the plant pot.*

Osato, Nikita and Emrys were signed into a guest book and allowed to roam freely around the castle and its facilities, including a library that would make any bibliophile believe in the miraculous. The Oriax resembled a holiday resort out of a fairy tale. As a new agent, Nikita was given a brochure, detailing every feature of the expansive castle amenities: archery in ancient woodlands trimmed with fairy lights, water sports, horse riding, language classes, swimming, night walks through lantern trails, falconry and many more enchanting hobbies to indulge in. There was even a luxury spa, where an agent could have their wings professionally preened.

'I'm moving to Edinburgh,' Nikita muttered, tucking the brochure into her messenger bag.

'I'm surprised you prefer this to Elysion,' Emrys remarked.

'I don't think I'm quite ready to live on the moon just yet, as beautiful as the city is.'

'Ah, well, if you change your mind, you could ... umm.' Emrys's shyness got in the way of the end of his sentence.

'I could what?'

He fidgeted slightly. 'I was going to say you could visit my place there sometime. Just, you know ... I could show you around.'

Nikita raised an eyebrow and smiled. 'Sure.'

She didn't fail to notice the slight flush that rose to his cheeks as he opened the door for them into the hall.

There was little time to explore what the Oriax had to offer as Osato headed straight to the vault. Owing to her status in the agency and the active investigation, they were able to lawfully remove the Oriax's copy of the *Vaticinium De Tumultus* for up to four weeks before it was due back. They were given a steel case for it, and a printed card with the combination number. It was an exceedingly small book, a reprint of something much, much older, and Nikita was itching to read it.

Once they had collected the book, they headed for a late dinner at The Turret Restaurant, which was just as enchanting as the other sections of the Oriax. In accordance with its name, it was in the westernmost turret of the castle, boasting expansive views of the dense woodlands. The circular room housed several medieval-style tables and was lit with ceiling candelabras and wall sconces bearing hefty church candles. The air was gravid with delicious smells that magnified each time the kitchen door swung open. Crystal stands full of delectable cakes lined the coffee counter beside a brimming bowl of free fresh fruit. Nikita picked up an orange to dull her hunger before they were seated.

'Oh, a strong choice. Oranges are not a starter fruit.' Emrys raised his eyebrows in approval. 'Definitely not for beginners.'

She didn't even ask but nodded as though she understood, wondering how he would've responded if she'd chosen an apple.

The waiter led them to a cosy corner booth, away from the twitching ears of the other diners. He gave them a few minutes with the menus before coming back to take their orders. Nikita was in awe of the mouthwatering options, and struggled to choose between peppercorn tuna steak with Lyonnaise potatoes or the gooey bowl of macaroni cheese. Her need for something heavy and comforting won, and she went with the macaroni.

Once they had placed their food orders, they leant in to talk quietly. Nikita peeled her orange as they spoke, conscious of her growling stomach.

'What's the plan then? Why the need for this book?' Emrys asked.

Osato had already opened the case and had started to move it towards Nikita. 'Agent Wolf discovered the Eligos copy missing from the vault. She was given indication by Dantalion that there may be a Hades agent employing *Umbra Amictus* and has used it to steal the book undetected,' she summarised.

'Remind me, what is that exactly? Cloak of darkness or something?' Emrys scratched his chin, where light grey stubble was beginning to show.

Nikita nodded and explained what she had found in the book, *A Blood Romance*, that Dantalion had pointed her towards: the blood mixing, and how Hades agents could employ *Umbra Amictus* if their blood mixed with that of an Apollo agent.

'So, that means we have a second guilty party then.' He nibbled at the complimentary mini Bourbon biscuit that came with his tea. 'This complicates things.'

'It might not,' Nikita began, pausing as her bowl of macaroni cheese was placed in front of her by a kindly-faced waiter. Once he had served them all and retreated to the kitchen, Nikita continued. 'The blood mix being used here creates the *Umbra Amictus* ability, which allows a person to become shadow and pass through objects, sometimes even possessing a living being. We know it can only be achieved by mixing Apollo and Hades blood. Think about it, we now need to examine which other agents have a close connection with someone at Hades Division.'

'Grover.' Osato narrowed her eyes. 'He applied for a transfer to Hades four weeks ago. He's been trying to transfer there for years. Each time it gets rejected for one reason or another. It's not a popular request, and he was on a knife edge where he would initially be recruited into, but he was chosen for Apollo as he'd lacked more love in life than he'd seen death. The decision was purely down to the Fates, but he's resented it ever since.'

'So, he's still a suspect.' Nikita was disappointed. She held off from opening the rare book in front of her while they were discussing Erron. 'Well, he does seem to have some connection to Izobella Cain, and she's Hades. She approached us in a bar the other night and mentioned something that she'd offered him. He refused to explain what the offer was though. But I got the distinct impression she's pushing for a connection that he doesn't want.'

'He might be playing it cool to distance himself from her in public,' Osato suggested.

Emrys rubbed his temples in thought. 'It doesn't look good, does it? I ran a background check on Grover. His service history is good, but he has struggled to fit in. Same in life, I went back through everything from the age of fourteen. He had a few brushes with the law in his early teens, nothing serious, typical of a boy in Islington from a poor upbringing with an abusive father. His brother, Ethan, committed suicide when Grover was twenty-one.'

'How did Ethan die?' Nikita asked.

'He leapt off a bridge into oncoming traffic. Apparently, it was particularly gruesome and Erron saw the whole thing.'

'I can't see why he would want to join Hades after seeing that.' Nikita pushed her macaroni around, deep in thought.

'Unless he feels like the more death he ushers people through, the closer he would be to getting closure on losing his brother or something.'

Emrys considered it while chewing a chip.

'Psychological assessment has its merits but what we need is evidence regarding the people involved in breaking a series of fixed points,' Osato added. 'I think it's clear that we are dealing with a rogue Hades operative, but there's an Apollo agent out there helping, either consensually or not. There have been no other deaths involving any other Apollo agents. We can look into this Izobella Cain lead and see if we turn up anything.'

Nikita could resist no longer and pushed her meal to one side so she could carefully examine the rare book.

'Isn't there reference to blood-mixing practices in the Division Leader Manual?' Emrys raised. 'About how to act on it from a manager's perspective?'

Osato furrowed her brow in thought. 'You know what, I think there is. In the Code of Practice section. I can pull that out of the Management Zone in the library. It might not be overly helpful, but it's worth a look.'

The waiter came over to offer more drinks and a dessert menu once their plates had been cleared.

'Is anything leaping out at you, Rocket?' Emrys asked Nikita, her eyes quickly scanning page after page.

'The common denominator is that this is all in another language – several, to be precise.' She was frustrated, but not deterred.

'So it's going to take longer than we anticipated then?' Emrys leant back in his chair and sighed.

'I'll spend a few hours on it this evening, see what I can do.'

Despite Nikita wanting to sit longer in the cosy restaurant and indulge in at least one slice of the chocolate fudge cake, Osato suggested they get settled in their rooms, to give Nikita some quiet time to work on the book. They were flying back to London at 8 a.m. the next day and had reserved guest quarters at the Oriax for the night.

Osato had insisted on being responsible for carrying the steel case with the book back to their rooms and handed it to Nikita at her door. 'You can let me know what you find in the morning, Agent Wolf. We'll all meet out front at 5 a.m. to leave.'

Nikita took the case gently. It wasn't nearly as heavy as the weight of expectation that came with it, but she was eager to prove herself. Emrys yawned and stretched his arms out. 'Try and get some sleep, Rocket, blankets make fools of us all.'

'They do?' Nikita raised an eyebrow.

'Oh, for sure.' He gave her a shy smile that could melt butter. He never once doubted his hard-won wisdom and loved to share it as often as he could, despite the multiplicity of confused looks he received back. Sometimes he threw in a few lines of nonsense just to see who would agree.

Osato and Emrys each went to their respective rooms and Nikita was left in the dimly lit hall. Stone archways collected the shadows of the night and formed blurred shapes of figures into the corners. Hollow echoes cast around the dark walls to breathe life into the imaginary monsters, and for every ounce of Nikita's rational thinking, her spine began to tingle slightly with disquiet. She felt like she was being watched, unseen eyes glaring through the stained-glass windows at the end of the hall. She felt a malice that was ripe and full, embodied by shadows in the thick fog. Backing into her room and closing the door, she exhaled with relief as the lock clicked home. She hid the steel case under her mattress before stripping off and letting the heat of the en-suite shower rinse away her sense of unease.

Once dried and dressed in her favourite pyjamas, she sat down with the steel case and opened it with the reverence of a starved man presented with a sandwich box. The thinness of the book was deceptive, as the print on each yellowed page was tiny, and would require some dedication to scour through. She checked the time; it was close to nine o'clock and she gave herself two hours before she would need to get some sleep. Peeling open the first page, she was deeply disheartened to find that most of the paragraphs were written in different languages. It would take her a lot longer to interrogate, as she would need to identify each language and translate it. Most pages were set out in stanzas of prose, each of varying lengths and attributed to different authors. She wasn't deterred however, picking through the pages to get a sense of the number of languages she was looking to translate, narrowing it down to six. There was definitely Latin, Arabic, Japanese and Russian, and two others she couldn't place. Those she recognised would be easy enough to translate online, though one page stood out to her. It was written in some form of runic language, though the symbols did not appear to match anything she'd seen before.

It was long past midnight before she gave up trying to find any relevant or familiar patterns in the runes and her bleary eyes forced her to put the book back in its case and climb into bed.

24

I Just Died in Your Arms

WINTER IN SALZBURG WAS BEAUTIFUL. Casey wandered the snow-covered streets while the lamps were still lit, the dawn still an hour away. He'd made excellent time since his brief stopover in Frankfurt, arriving a couple of hours before he thought he would. He ached from the exertion, but he'd been lucky with strong winds in his favour throughout the night.

He admired the Austrian architecture and the sweeping riverside walks while killing time, desperate for a cup of tea and something warm to eat. He was beyond tired, but the crisp air kept him alert. Gunther Hoffmann's parents lived ten minutes from where Casey paced back and forth, rubbing his blue-tinged hands together and regretting not bringing gloves. The sky was a deep azure expanse, a waning moon bright in the west and the first pale band of purple-dawn pushing up in the east. A lone bakery van trundled past, taking its first wares of the day to various bistros and restaurants for the morning trade. Casey's eyes followed it like a hawk, chewing his lip and imagining what pastry delights might be driving by, when he noticed a man-shaped heap in an alleyway. Snow had gathered on the dirty woollen blanket that was draped over him, and only a layer of cardboard kept the man from the icy stone floor.

Casey went over and knelt by the man, who, on close inspection, was painfully thin and wrapped in several layers of grubby clothing. He looked fifty-five but may only have. been forty, his wind-tanned face was mostly wiry beard and deep lines. He was shivering as he slept, his breathing shallow and fast, his lips blue and hands tucked under his chin.

'Hello?' Casey placed a hand on the man's shoulder. He eventually stirred when shaken gently, but his eyes barely focused on anything, and no words escaped his mouth. Looking out of the alleyway in both directions and seeing no one, Casey returned to the man, extended a wing and rested it across him, hoping the additional warmth would help.

He was startled by the figure of a young woman who appeared beside him, stealthy as a cat. She wore a fur-lined winter hat over her cropped auburn hair, and a beautifully tailored red wool coat. She spoke softly, but Casey didn't understand her. Too late to retract his wing, he was about to resort to using his Apollo abilities to ensure she forgot what she'd seen. However, she just repeated herself, offering no reaction to the sight of his wings.

'I'm sorry I don't speak much German,' he said, confused.

She tilted her head for a moment, observing him. 'Apollo?'

'Yes.'

The streetlights above her began flickering and she slowly pointed towards the homeless man.

'No. No, wait ... No. I'm a doctor. Please, let me help him, he has hypothermia ...' Casey protested, gripping the man's shoulder and shielding him from her. 'You understand? I'm a doctor. Medic?'

She knelt gracefully, like a dancer sinking to the stage floor at the end of her performance. 'No medic.' She shook her head slowly and pointed to herself. 'Hades. It is his time.' She placed her hand over Casey's and looked deeply into his eyes. 'You must let him go.' She spoke brokenly but with softness, carefully pushing Casey's hand away and resting her own on the man's shoulder.

The man shuddered violently, his eyes focusing briefly, showing a deep sadness and comprehension of his fate. The blue tinge of his lips darkened as he slowly slipped from the mortal realm. The Reaper didn't immediately walk away, she sat with the man's body, holding his limp hand, a solitary tear rolling down her porcelain cheek.

'You care for him,' Casey said quietly. 'I will remember your kindness.' He stood and folded his wings in.

A few moments passed in silent vigil for the unnamed man. Eventually, the woman stood and placed the dead man's hand back under the blanket.

'Your kindness, Apollo. He will remember. He will have seen an angel.' She held out her hand to shake his. 'Mia.' She introduced herself.

'Casey Hart.' Her hand was as cold as a tombstone.

'Where from?'

'London.'

She looked puzzled. 'On assignment? Or ... you are management?'

He shifted his feet and looked away. 'Oh no, suspended. Under investigation,' he said sheepishly.

'Oh.' Mia walked with him out of the alleyway, where it would be several hours before the man's body would be discovered and written off as another sad statistic of homelessness. 'You are hiding?'

'No, not hiding. I need to speak to someone here, to try and clear my name.'

'I see. You are hungry?' Mia guided him along a narrow street as the dawn birds began their chorus. The band of purple on the horizon was lightening to pink, giving the buildings long and sprawling shadows.

'Starved.'

She gestured for him to follow her, and they ended up at a small bakery just as the sun rose above the river. It was already open, awash with the warm glow of lamps and filled to the brim with the heady scent of freshly baked bread.

Mia explained in her relatively good grasp of English that she had two more visits that morning and was taking her breakfast to go. She invited Casey to walk with her through the local park as they warmed their hands on fresh cups of coffee. The snowy walkways and frosted trees looked magical under the glow of the lanterns. Sweeping areas of white lay untouched, broken only by meticulously-kept bushes of winter roses that lined the paths.

'I didn't want to be Hades,' Mia explained as they walked. 'I weep for them ... I weep for them all. Each man, I see my father; each woman, my mother; each child, my sister.'

'It is better to care than to feel nothing. I am so sorry you endured such terror and sadness,' Casey replied softly.

She curled her hand through the crook of his elbow as they walked. 'It is the last thoughts that I feel like needles in my skin.'

'Last thoughts?' Casey asked.

Mia explained that every Hades agent was responsible for recording the last thoughts of the dying souls that they reaped, and that those thoughts were kept on a confidential file only accessible to the agent who took the soul, and the Fates.

'The man just now, his thoughts, I share only with you as I feel you can be trusted,' she said. 'He thought, *Here is an angel come to take me to my mama . . . I am warm now.* This is why I cry.'

'I understand. But you said he would have seen an angel. How is that possible?'

'Those close to death can sometimes see us for our true selves. Our wings, the way Cupids glow with the warmth of love. To them, you are angels.'

'I didn't know that.'

'I have requested transfer to Apollo,' she said. 'I wish only to see joy. I wish to be someone's angel.'

Casey cast his eyes to the floor and sighed.

'You seem sad, why is this?' she asked, confused.

'My friend. My closest friend in this whole world . . . he has asked to move to Hades. It makes me sad that he doesn't believe in love; he doesn't want to see the joy he brings to others.'

She was silent for some time as they walked, the early birds twittering in the tops of the park trees. 'It's not that which makes you sad. You are sad that he is abandoning you, you are afraid of the space he will leave behind,' she answered softly. 'I sense these things.'

'It is a lonely world. You're perceptive.'

She stopped walking when she reached a recycling bin for her empty cup. 'I can sense you are a good person, Casey Hart.

The world is lonely, but only if you make it so.' She dropped her hand from his elbow and curled her fingers in his.

Realising quickly, he pulled his hand away. 'I'm sorry, I can't . . . I can't do that.'

'Don't be afraid. Your heart aches, and so does mine. Let us take comfort together. No one will know of it.' Her eyes sparkled in the early morning sun. She leant forward to kiss him, but he stepped back swiftly.

'Mia, I'm sorry, forgive me. I—'

She looked away. 'I understand. You are an Agent of Love, but you cannot feel it yourself. Much like I am an Agent of Death, but I take no delight in it.'

'I'm sorry, I just . . . it's not what I do.'

'It was lovely to meet you, Casey Hart. Perhaps, in your stay here, you might change your mind.' She handed him a card with the Hades symbol, a sword with black wings resting within an upturned crescent moon, four stars above the hilt. The card also showed her telephone number. 'We all get lonely at times.'

He took the card and watched as she spread great black wings and leapt upward, carrying herself on the wind to the next sad soul who she would usher into darkness, another mark on her heart that she would weep for at night in the loneliness of her apartment. Casey knew very well the need to reach out and be loved, to comfort another in the endlessness of eternity, but for all his years of solitude, it would not be Mia that he would finally reach for.

* * *

Francis Hoffmann answered the door at eight forty-five, his face forlorn and silver hair swept back over a bald spot. He wore a dark suit and house loafers, beckoning Casey inside once he was convinced the blond man was visiting as part of a police investigation into his son's death. Casey thanked his lucky stars that Francis spoke excellent English.

'I'm sorry to disturb you, Mr Hoffmann.' Casey sat at a wooden kitchen chair in the low-ceilinged homestead, the strong smell of hot coffee from a pan on the stove and a looming dresser full of decorative plates filling the space in the small room. Francis lived with his wife, Anna, a plump lady who busily tended to the laundry in the other room.

Mr Hoffmann waved his hand and mixed two cups of coffee with milk and sugar.

'Detective, there isn't much else to say. My son was gifted. He was going to make so many good things for this world; he was so *excited* about it. He phoned us every day, telling us about his work, how he could make such a difference. Asked us about our work, the plans we had for the garden. Normal stuff.'

'I understand that Gunther was exceptional. A fine young man.' Casey sipped the coffee that Mr Hoffman handed him and wrinkled his nose at the strength. 'Can you describe the last conversation you had with him? Did he say anything out of character?'

'My wife was the last to speak with him. The night before his big conference.' Francis called Anna to join them, and she bustled in, her hair still in rollers. 'The detective wants to know what you last spoke with Gunther about.'

Anna Hoffmann pulled up a chair to sit with them. Her face was of a woman who had lost her only son: tired, sad, sleepless. They both had the greyed look of grieving parents, a thin quality to their life force, as if they had died the day the news was brought to their door.

'He was a good boy, my Gunther,' she said, a quiver to her voice. 'So much energy, so much life.'

'I understand this must be terribly difficult for you,' Casey soothed. 'And I understand you probably don't feel like talking a whole lot right now, but I need to ask you both a few questions.'

Anna nodded reluctantly while absent-mindedly twiddling her necklace between two fingers.

'Did Gunther mention anything about the conference, or his trip to England?'

Francis answered, 'He was very excited about it. He was always keen to travel, to share his ideas.'

'He told us he was going to change the world,' Anna added.

'I'm sure he was a very aspirational young man,' Casey affirmed. 'When did you last see him?'

'He came by not long before he left. He wanted to borrow my best suit jacket, he said it was for luck.' Francis sighed heavily and massaged his eyebrows.

'And he seemed OK? Nothing worrying him at all?'

'He was my usual happy boy.' Anna's voice broke, a tear slid down her cheek. 'He said, "Mama, I am going to make you so proud." He was full of smiles.'

Casey nodded, jotting it down in a tiny pocket notebook. 'What about when he arrived in England, did you hear from him?'

'He phoned me when he got off the plane. He was tired, but happy to chat. He talked about plans for his cousin's birthday next month, as he was planning to pick up a gift in England,'

253

Francis explained. 'It doesn't make sense why he would have done what he did.'

'Was there anything he said, anything at all that gave you reason to believe he had intended to do something unexpected?' Casey gently pressed. His presence still exuded the subtle Apollo charm which had encouraged the parents to speak so freely.

Anna exhaled slowly and spun her silver pendant with a shaking hand. 'There was only one thing he said that, as a mother, worried me a little. He said that he was being followed by darkness. That he could see shadows moving, the day before he supposedly took his life. I told him to take vitamins and get a decent night's sleep. He'd gone to various meetings that week; I thought he must be tired. Now I wonder if he was sickly of something. He was still happy, you see? He couldn't wait to come home to visit and see us. It is why I believe nothing in this note.'

'Note?' Casey queried.

Francis stood slowly and pulled a letter from the drawer in the plate-laden dresser, jostling the china. He placed the letter in front of Casey and sat back down, his sorrowful gaze falling to the table. 'I just don't understand why he would have written it in English. Maybe you can shed some light on that, Detective. Apparently, they found it in his hotel room.'

Casey read the note, a cold sweat forming on his back. It was almost identical to the one Erron had photographed from the police station allegedly written by Sofia Carter. Even the handwriting was the same. 'Mr Hoffmann, I have reason to believe this note was not written by your son.'

'I know it wasn't. That's not my boy's handwriting. Nothing about it feels right at all.' Francis rubbed his eyes with one hand. 'With due respect, Detective, the police have done very little so far. I feel they are convinced this is a suicide. Witnesses say he jumped, so how can we argue with that? We're still waiting the coroner's report.'

'I can only apologise for the way this has been dealt with thus far. I would like to take this note away for investigation, if I may.'

The man nodded. 'Keep it, it is not my son's words. It means nothing to me. My son lives here.' He placed both hands over his heart. 'No letter will bring him back.'

Casey folded the letter with care and tucked it into the inside pocket of his peacoat. 'Mrs Hoffmann, these shadows you mentioned, did Gunther say any more about them?'

She thought for a while and chewed her lip. 'Not a lot. He laughed it off, said he must not have drunk enough water. But he was frightened, I could tell. A mother's instinct. He said he felt a presence, like a bad spirit hiding in the darkness everywhere he went. He didn't like his hotel room before the conference; he said it was worse there, the lights even gave him a headache.'

'How strange. Did he say they were flickering?'

'What are you getting at?'

'I have to cover all enquiries, Mrs Hoffmann.'

'Yes, I think so. I told him to get an early night.'

Casey finished the coffee and stood. 'I appreciate your time, Mr and Mrs Hoffmann, and I am terribly sorry for your loss. I have nothing further to ask you and will leave you in peace.'

'Detective, will we hear from you soon?' Francis asked, standing to show him out.

'If there is a significant reason, I will contact you myself.' Casey stopped just outside the door. 'Your son was a good man, and you should be proud of raising such a talented boy. I only hope that your pain will ease in time.'

'Thank you, Detective.' Francis closed the door and went back to his coffee, feeling that a little bit of weight had lifted from his heavy heart.

Casey decided to stay in Salzburg for the night and fly back in the morning, he was too exhausted from his trip to turn around that day. He found a small bed and breakfast in a converted church and paid for one night's accommodation before making dinner reservations at a nearby restaurant that boasted the best of Austrian cuisine. He busied himself by visiting the Rainermuseum in der Festung Hohensalzburg and taking a riverside walk after his pre-booked meal. Nothing he did, ate or looked at made him feel any better. No fancy cake or beautiful piece of art took the heavy sense of loss away that he had carried around since Sofia Carter had fallen under the train at Farringdon. The weight had become unbearable with every day that passed. All he could think about was the look on Erron's face as he had walked away and how nothing had felt right since.

As he meandered along the embankment, he reached for his non-agency phone to dial Erron's personal mobile. Even though they had parted on bad terms, he desperately wanted to discuss the new information from the Hoffmanns and find out whether Erron had come up with anything himself. His thumb hovered over the call symbol, his heart beating a bit faster. The night was bitterly cold but his fear was colder, and he put the phone away again. It wasn't long before he found it in his hand again, some sense of worry creeping into his mind. He gritted his teeth and pressed dial. The phone rang for a long time before cutting into voicemail. He hung up without leaving a message.

* * *

Two hours earlier, Erron was hunched in a hidden corner of Nightjar, miserable that he hadn't found any evidence to clear their names. His excursion to Bedford had proved somewhat useless as he'd learnt that a suicide note was found in Gunther's hotel room, but it had been sent to his family in Austria as the case had been closed. He wasn't in the best frame of mind since his falling-out with Casey, and he was finding it incredibly hard to think of other leads to pursue that would assist their case. In defeat, he'd ended up in one of his usual haunts, hoping a few drinks would numb the reeling thoughts of hopelessness that whirled around his brain. He knew it was stupid to go somewhere he might be recognised, but with Casey gone, he was desperate to be somewhere he knew and was even toying with the idea of handing himself in to end the whole ordeal. He hoped to remain unnoticed, dressed uncharacteristically in a grey hoody and tracksuit bottoms, a peaked cap shielding his face in the dark corner of the bar. He regularly scoped the crowds for familiar faces, ready to slip out the back door, but saw no one during the course of the evening.

He checked his phone for the umpteenth time. He had no missed calls, no messages, no voicemails inviting him out *to that lovely little place in Kensington that does the profiteroles, you know the one, I can never remember the name, what do you say?* Now he scoffed at all the times he'd said he'd rather get a burger and chips and visit a bowling alley than faff about in a twee little tearoom choosing a miniature dessert in the middle of the day. If he could turn back time, he would choose the profiteroles in a heartbeat.

Staring blankly into his fourth empty glass, he decided he would have one more drink then call it a night. The bar was busy with revellers, all shoulder to shoulder and three deep waiting for their turn to order, so by the time he had jostled his way to the front he was almost sober again. His last cocktail was a classic Dark 'n' Stormy but as he was reaching across the counter to pay, he was nudged hard in the side by a big man with a long beard.

'Sorry, fella.' The man raised his hands in apology.

The brief distraction was long enough for someone with a nimble hand to slip something in his drink, then disappear unnoticed in the crowd.

Ten minutes later, Erron was slumped in his corner seat, feeling very nauseous. The music in the bar slid off-key and a fog circled his vision.

'Darling, you don't look so good. Let me call you a cab.' A woman's voice, distant and strange, cut through his clouded hearing.

Erron shook his head, trying to regain focus but slipped further into a drunken haze, the room beginning to spin. He felt rough hands hoist him out of the chair and manhandle him out into the street. He felt like he was moving through treacle, an arm gripping his like a vice, his legs buckling and stumbling. A taxi was already waiting at the kerb. The last thing he remembered was someone pushing him into the back seat of the cab. Erron could sense motion, pressure and muffled sounds, though oblivious to where he was. He was plagued by dark and vivid nightmares, unable to wake from them, but he knew that something was terribly wrong. He was paralysed and helpless, only able to dream of horrific layers of lurking darkness and depravity. Suddenly, pain seared through him, dull, thudding, sharp and scratching. The smell of blood. Somewhere, in the depth of his mind, he could hear his phone ringing and ringing until it went to voicemail. Something told him he really needed to answer the call, to get help, but the agony and endless darkness persisted.

25

Headlong

ON THE FLIGHT HOME THAT morning, Nikita was secretly enjoying the cramped seating as her thigh was pressed up against Emrys's, causing all manner of tingling sensations to dance across her skin. She was glad the Apollo Flush had long since worn off, as she may have found it difficult to keep her hands to herself. Instead, she'd been left with the usual giddy sensation that any normal person felt when they were sat next to someone they had a crush on, and it was much easier to handle without being in a supernatural tempest of raging hormones. Emrys had thrown her the odd apologetic look each time the turbulence had squashed them closer together, occasionally blushing himself and making a point of looking out the window.

To distract herself, she showed him her notes about the *Vaticinium Tumultus* and a drawing of the strange runic language she'd found on one page.

His face paled. 'I'm not totally sure, but I think these are Chaos runes. Osato, what do you think?' He passed her the drawing.

Osato narrowed her eyes. 'You may be right. It's a language older than time itself. More of a code that deciphers the building blocks of the universe.'

Emrys took back the drawing. 'Nikita, I think we need to try and crack this code. When we get back, we can go over it together.'

She had burned crimson at the unexpected fantasy that flashed through her mind of them curled up in front of a log fire, sipping red wine and comparing notes from the book while lovingly gazing into each other's eyes. Of course, she realised Emrys was *actually* suggesting they sit in his office at a professional distance and remain clothed at all times, but that didn't stop her mind running riot.

'Are you all right? You're away with the fairies,' Emrys said quietly, jokingly waving a hand in front of her face.

Osato gave Nikita a knowing sideways glance which, of course, had made the new agent blush even more.

'I'm fine, it must be all the Scottish air,' she lied. 'I think you're right. I ran some of the other language sections through Google Translate and most of them were myths about the beginning of the world. Though one was a recipe for rye bread . . .'

Emrys suggested they meet that evening at the Eligos library, giving him time to catch up at the office first.

Osato had been quietly reading the Division Leader Manual during the flight and had found an interesting snippet about blood mixing which detailed the differing results caused by each combination. She knew a Hades agent was definitely involved in recent events as, on top of the electrical interference before the deaths, no other combination allowed for someone to take shadow form. She noted it in her investigation file and closed the book.

Meanwhile, fractures were still rippling further and further afield as a result of five missed gold arrows. The news was awash with mysterious sightings of rubber ducks flooding the flat lands of Holland, multiple wildfires laying waste to winter woodlands in Canada, and a conspiracy of broken washing machines was sweeping a large town in Italy. Not to mention the seemingly infinite volume of geese still cropping up just about everywhere over Europe. London was by no means exempt, and when they finally alighted at Gatwick, the airport was undergoing a mass system failure saved only by emergency generators. Several people were overheard complaining about their left shoe suddenly feeling tighter than their right and others were talking about a strange coincidence that all the books in the airport WHSmith were printed in Korean. The worst part was that nearly everything in the cafés and restaurants was starting to taste like Marmite, including the cupcake Emrys had picked up on arrival.

'You know the world's falling apart when everything tastes like Marmite,' he'd muttered, disappointed, as he chucked it in the bin.

'Oh, I *love* Marmite,' Osato purred.

'Knock yourself out.' He passed her a Mars Bar that he pulled from his pocket. 'I'm sure that's Mars-mite by now.'

She opened the wrapper and curiously took a bite. 'No, it's ... something else entirely.' She wrinkled her nose, only able to taste vinegar. 'These fractures are really spreading globally, and they are picking up pace. It's spiralling out of control.'

'It will be down to the fact the missed arrows were gold,' Emrys surmised. 'That's why it's getting worse, as the intended results of the gold arrows were supposed to ripple far and wide, such as the singer's career and the scientists creating a world-changing new technology. It's likely going to continue to get worse until we can come up with a way to fix it.'

'Why the gold arrows though? Surely every assignment has an impact?' Nikita queried, while noticing her left shoe was starting to constrict around her foot.

'As true love is so rare, it being missed has a huge impact. These botched assignments will have caused a huge tear in the course of destiny, not just to the individuals involved,' Osato answered gravely. She pulled out her phone and switched off airplane mode before dialling Kendra.

Kendra answered in four rings.

'Have Grover and Hart come forward yet?' Osato asked without so much as a greeting.

After a brief conversation she hung up and turned to Emrys. 'There's been no sign of the agents so now we need to actively treat them as evading us. I'm going to send out some of my staff in search of them; can you lend anyone from Fortuna to assist?'

'I'm sure I can spare some agents, or put out an urgent offer of overtime,' he suggested.

'They'll need to be detained and considered uncooperative now,' Osato confirmed, before she called her senior agent, Lian Zhang, to put the word out for the agents' arrest.

26

Is This Real?

L ATER AT THE LIBRARY, NIKITA was trying to find
books on Chaos runes and their meanings. She'd
managed to find a couple that made mention of them,
and another with photos of the runes from old architecture.
She'd been at the Eligos for six hours straight before Emrys
turned up in a woolly green scarf and beige overcoat. The night
outside was blowing bitter gales through the streets, and he
was visibly ruffled, but greeted her with a smile that took the
edge off winter and made her feel very warm inside. She had
made space for him at the old, polished desk where her notes
were spread, and he dragged the chair close enough so that
when he leant over to look at a passage, their shoulders brushed
together. She found concentrating almost impossible and several
times had to stop herself from staring at him. Ten minutes
later, he stopped, leant forward and smiled.

'Are you OK, Rocket?' He nudged her as she daydreamed.

'Sorry, yes, I'm fine. Just tired maybe? It's been a long day.'
She smiled at him, secretly loving her new, ridiculous nickname.

'We can leave it for now if you like?'

'No, no, I want to carry on. Sorry.' She stretched and straightened her back up, trying to look more engaged. 'It's urgent. We have to get this done.'

'Let me get you a drink,' he offered.

'Where from?' She'd explored the library before and hadn't seen any vending machine.

'I'll show you. What would you like? They have coffee, tea and juice.' He gestured for her to follow.

'Oh, a coffee would be nice.'

Emrys approached the statue of Lucifer and opened a discreet drawer at the base of the plinth, where a row of mugs was stored. He pulled two of them out and closed the drawer, then proceeded to draw two cups of coffee from a hidden spout on one of the wings by pressing one of the stone feathers.

'I take it you've been bringing your own drinks?' he asked, when seeing her stunned face.

'I'd never have guessed . . .'

'Ah, you get used to these things. The designers of the library didn't want an ugly vending machine ruining the atmosphere. The statue of Poseidon hands out apple juice, Eros is tea and Jesus is—'

'If it's not red wine I will be upset.'

'I'm afraid to say it's lemonade.' He shrugged with a grin.

She pretended to be dreadfully inconvenienced by the news and crossed her arms sulkily.

'Maybe . . .' he started, then faltered.

'Maybe?'

'Umm, maybe we could go out for a drink one evening, if you like? I mean, if you don't want a mug of fizzy Jesus-ade.'

He handed her the coffee with a slightly pained expression, waiting for her response.

Her stomach fluttered slightly but she saw no reason to be coy. 'Do you mean as a date?'

She saw a micro expression of panic cross his face as he contemplated how to answer. 'I mean, I'd like that, yes, but it doesn't have to be that if you don't want.'

She placed her hand on his wrist before he spiralled into an anxious spluttering of explanations. 'Emrys, I'd really like that.'

Caught off guard, he relaxed. 'You would?'

'Yes. I would. Actually, seeing as the world is falling apart, there's no time like the present. How about we grab a bottle of something fancy and do some more of this translation at my place?' she suggested.

'If you're sure? That would be brilliant.' He beamed enthusiastically. 'I'll drive us.'

Emrys was one of the few agency staff who still chose to drive. He owned a well-kept vintage Beetle in ladybird-red with beige interior and a custom walnut dashboard. During the drive back to Nikita's apartment, he told her more about his former life as an art teacher in Abergavenny and how he'd died in an unfortunate accident while on a school trip to the coast. He'd been chased by a particularly cantankerous goat which had essentially resulted in him being at the bottom of a cliff and the goat looking down from the top.

They picked up a bottle of Rioja en route before Nikita showed him to her door.

'If you don't want to start on the wine straightaway, I've only really got orange squash and about six tea bags as an alternative. But you are welcome to one . . . or all six if you like strong tea.'

He laughed and checked his watch. 'It's definitely late enough to start on the wine. Even if I could use that six-bag cup of tea after the long day we've had.' He closed the door behind him and admired her flash apartment. 'They didn't hand out places like this when I started at Fortuna.' He wandered around the living space and looked out of the balcony window.

Nikita rummaged frantically through her sparse kitchen cupboards trying to find anything to put the wine in. Eventually, she settled for the complimentary toothbrush holder from the bathroom and a chipped mug she had from her old Islington apartment. She led him through to the balcony, so they could take in the city lights below, hoping the wine would stave off the chill of the night. She'd picked up half a pack of Jaffa Cakes and offered him one.

'I love your taste in crockery.' He joked, taking a tentative sip from the toothbrush holder before accepting a Jaffa Cake. 'Fantastic view and everything. Nice little place to make home.'

'I do need to do some shopping at some point. But you should have seen the hovel I was renting in my previous life.'

'Do you miss it?' he asked. 'Your previous life?'

She took a moment to ponder the question. 'I do and I don't. If that makes sense.' She sipped her wine, deep in thought. 'I think the longer I'm here and I realise that death actually isn't the end of everything, the more I feel like this is an opportunity instead of some sad finale. What about you?'

He bit into the Jaffa Cake before making a face of disgust and placing it gingerly on the table. Confused, she tried one herself, finding that they too, had turned Marmite-flavoured. She laughed and apologised on behalf of whatever fracture had ruined her favourite snack.

He carefully placed his wine on the floor and leant back against the railing. 'Chaos sure has a lot to answer for ... but going back to your question ... I didn't really amount to much in my old life. I had a steady job that I enjoyed, but I think I kept everyone at arm's length. It was only when I was in my late thirties that I realised how lonely my life had become. I miss my cat though. His name was Mercury.'

'You never married?'

'No. I wasn't very lucky, or confident in love. Plus, I never wanted children, so that limited my options really.'

'Oh, I know the feeling. All my friends were having kids and I could never see the attraction to motherhood. In fact, I can't think of anything worse. Despite the fact society tells women that they have no value unless they sacrifice themselves to increase the population. One bonus of the afterlife is being told I am sterile.' She thought back to how relieved she was to learn her replicated womb was completely inactive.

'There are enough people in the world already. And you are valuable whether you had children or not.' He glanced away, a slight blush rising to his cheeks. 'It's getting really cold out here, shall we go inside?'

'Can we stay just for a moment longer?' Nikita set her mug down and stepped towards him. Tentatively, she placed her hands on his chest.

For a split second, he froze, before instinctively pulling her into a warm embrace. She slid her arms around his back and they stood in silence for a moment or two, enjoying the warmth and comfort of the hug in the bitter cold night air. Emrys eventually pulled back slightly and kissed her. She almost melted with how gentle he was. It felt like a stolen moment straight out of a Hollywood film. He pulled away and kissed her on the forehead before guiding her back into the warmth of the living room.

'Maybe I shouldn't have done that,' he said quietly.

'Why?' Nikita was confused.

'I'm supposed to be professional, as a manager.' He scratched his head.

'You're not *my* manager.'

'That is true. Am I too old for you?'

'It's not like any of us are ageing anymore. What are you, thirty-eight? Forty?' Nikita rested her hands on her hips.

'I'm forty-two. At least, I was when I died.' He looked like he was mentally calculating how many years he had been that age.

She rolled her eyes and grinned. 'Don't get hung up on the details; the world is one more Jaffa Cake away from disaster. Just kiss me again and we can figure it out from there.'

Laughing, he did as he was told.

27

Wicked Game

EMRYS HAD LEFT NIKITA'S APARTMENT late into the night and, the following morning, took her out for breakfast before dropping her off at the Apollo building. They had managed to figure out a few of the runes from the library books but were still a way off understanding the whole thing.

'Agent Wolf.' Tristan DeVangelo greeted her with a wolf whistle. 'Looks like you got *lucky*. Anyone might even say you were particularly Fortuna-ate.' He turned to three others who hid their laughter.

She ignored him and went to her desk.

'Oh, come on, Nikki, Emrys Taliesin? We all saw you kiss goodbye. Did you get to see his Welsh dragon?' Tristan dramatically flicked his divine locks and puffed out his chest. 'What's he got that I don't?'

'It's Ni*kita*. And he's got everything you don't. Like integrity for a start.'

'You know you can't get a promotion that way,' Tristan mocked.

Another agent, a petite, dark-haired woman, suddenly stormed over and shoved Tristan. He stumbled over his chair and landed in a heap on the floor. 'I won't stand for your bullshit, Tris, and neither will she.'

She left him looking humiliated, before pulling up a chair next to Nikita.

'I'm sorry about him. Nice to meet you, Nikita. I'm Bianca DeVangelo and that twat is unfortunately my younger brother. He's harmless but he runs his mouth far too much.' She pulled a bag of peanuts from her bag and popped one in her mouth.

Nikita smiled and shook her hand. 'I was hoping the patriarchy wouldn't continue its influence past death, but it seems that some men will never understand the word *no*.'

Bianca shared the same Grecian goddess looks as her brother, with a tumble of perfectly wavy hair and the kind of eyes you could get lost in. She was clearly fierce and passionate, and no doubt had countless admirers.

'Oh yes. Sadly, Apollo Division attracts that type. Did anyone explain the first parameter of recruitment? To be a Cupid you had to be unlucky in love during your mortal years. Unfortunately, that also means we also recruit from a pool of men with commitment issues.' Bianca huffed.

'I haven't met many agents yet. Does that rule apply to all divisions then?'

Bianca stretched and yawned. 'Nah. Hades agents either suffered great loss or were murdered. Fortuna were unlucky in life and usually had quite ridiculous deaths. Nemesis suffered great injustice, often leading to their deaths. You won't find self-centred pricks like my brother in Nemesis. It's mostly every oppressed community in history serving in that division. But they aren't the only things in the recruitment criteria.'

'Oh right, yeah, I didn't know any of that.' Nikita was keeping one wary eye on Bianca's brother, who was now grinning at her, bruised ego fully recovered.

'Is it true then, about Emrys?' Bianca teased.

'It was just a kiss.'

Bianca looked disappointed, hoping to have got some more gossip-worthy information from the new recruit. 'Well, I don't blame you. For an older guy, he's not bad. If you like that teacher look.' She popped another peanut in her mouth. 'Or guys for a start. Can't say I'm a fan.'

'Has anyone seen Freya?' Nikita changed the subject before anyone could ask about Emrys's *Welsh dragon* again.

'No, I haven't seen her for days. Are you training today?'

'I've been told to study for my exam, given what's happening with Casey and Erron. I was hoping to see Freya for some advice on what to expect.'

Bianca pursed her lips in thought. 'Oh, if she's likely to be mentoring you it's probably best you wait to speak to her about the exam. I think it's changed a fair bit since I took it. I would take you out myself today, but I'm tied up with a student already.' She finished off the bag of peanuts in one handful.

'It's OK. I'm checking emails and then getting picked up in a bit.'

'By Mr Lucky?' Bianca teased.

Nikita's blush said it all. 'Only for a project.'

'Hey, girl, if you like him, you go for it.' She winked.

When the little red Beetle pulled up again at the gates a few hours later, the Apollo agents pressed their faces against the windows of the second floor to get a look, like schoolchildren watching a fight in the playground. Emrys opened the passenger door for her and drove off in the direction of the Eligos.

'They love a bit of gossip,' he said. 'I hope I haven't given you a bad name.'

'Says the guy who calls me Rocket.'

'Would you rather Crocodile Rock?' He beamed at her mischievously.

'No, Rocket is just fine. I mean, after all, I have been to the moon.' She looked at him with a wry grin.

He held his left hand out to hold hers, intertwining their fingers over the handbrake as they joined a busy street heading towards the library.

28

Just Pretend

ERRON WOKE UP FEELING LIKE he had been run over by a herd of Highland cows. He couldn't remember anything from the night before apart from sitting alone at Nightjar. He staggered to the bathroom, where he desperately searched for painkillers. His whole body ached and there were strange marks on his wrists which he couldn't begin to explain. Bleary-eyed, he looked in the mirror and was shocked to see dried blood on his lip and a purple bruise forming around his left eye. He convinced himself he must have been in a fight at Nightjar and got knocked out before being bundled into a cab by a generous stranger.

He'd been in enough fights and had enough hangovers to put the whole bad experience to the back of his mind and turned on the shower. The heat of the water sluicing between his wings made him cry out with burning agony and he felt over his shoulder to find several nasty cuts. He stumbled out of the shower, now fully awake from the pain and wrapped in a bath towel. As he edged back to the bed and saw the sheer amount of blood he had lost matted into his sheets, he quickly realised that something much worse than a bar fight had happened. The sudden, crushing realisation hit him that he was back in his own apartment and not the run-down hotel he was hiding out in. However he had gotten home, it had been with someone that knew his address.

'My phone,' he muttered, suddenly remembering the noise had persisted through his nightmarish ordeal. But searching around, he couldn't find it anywhere.

He knew that he wouldn't be able to seek medical attention from the Raphael Sanctuary, the agency-dedicated hospital that patched up agents. To go there would be a very quick way to be detained and questioned. Erron would have to wallow in his pain and injuries until they knitted together naturally over time, reminding him of some of his most unfortunate escapades in the police force which had resulted in the scars scattered across his body. He tried to stretch out his wings but screamed when he realised one throbbing joint was broken. Instead, he did his best to fold them in, but the broken one hung limp at the joint, dragging behind him.

Panic was setting in. He knew that he had to get out of the flat and distract himself from the persistent throb of pain. He tore the house apart looking for his phone, every pocket, every cupboard and drawer, even down between the cushions of the sofa. Eventually he gave up when an intense wave of nausea overcame him, forcing him to kneel with his head over the toilet, retching violently. Since becoming an agent, he'd never been so sick or suffered such sheer agony. After twenty minutes, he managed to wrestle on some clothes and walk the painstaking mile to the hotel, keeping to the back alleys and shadows to avoid being seen in the state he was in. Once there, he carefully lay down on the bed until the tremors in his limbs eased. He knew he still had to come up with a plan to clear his name, but his body screamed for him to stay still, keep warm, and try to sleep off the discomfort and tiredness. He wallowed in regret for going to Nightjar and giving up instead of sticking to the plan. Now he was in an even worse situation and he couldn't even fly.

29

Make it Rain

EANWHILE, CASEY HAD MADE IT home in record
time. He had pushed himself through the freezing
cold, several rain and sleet storms and even a whole
flock of confused African parrots that had, for the first time
in history, decided to migrate to France. He stood on a roof
opposite his house for an hour, monitoring whether anyone
was watching or waiting for him to appear. There were no
people sat in cars, or skulking in the streets, so he risked entering
the house via his roof terrace. His home comforts greeted him
as normal, the silence of his living room doing nothing to ease
his persistent feeling of disquiet. He settled himself at a small
roll-top desk in his study and opened his laptop, careful not
to switch on any big lights or make too much noise. As the
place wasn't agency owned, they usually had no rights to enter
without his permission but could find good cause if they saw
activity within the house and he was wanted for arrest. He was
in no mood to rest, eat or sleep, only connect the dots where
he could. Finding KiaRia's official fan page, he scrolled past
the hundreds of sympathy messages, tribute videos and

investigation updates that her official representatives had posted. Several pages underneath, he found the details of her fateful concert, and below that, a fan had posted a link to a video which showed her final song, and her terrible demise.

Taking a deep breath, he pressed play and leant his chin on his folded hands as he listened once more to the last words she would ever sing:

Yeah, I'm followed by shadows,
They are claiming my soul,
Like the fading of a TV screen,
Like the crackling of a radio,
When there's only static and no more show . . .

He listened to it over and over, exhausted and struggling to concentrate. The lyrics bothered him, but he couldn't quite put his finger on why. He scrolled through the comments; one of the fans had written how sad it was that KiaRia had only just written the song, and it was the first time it had been performed.

Followed by shadows. The line jumped out at him. Anna Hoffmann, Gunther's mother, had said her son was being followed by shadows. Maybe KiaRia had written the song in a desperate attempt to put words to whatever she had been seeing. Casey was confident that whatever, or whoever, had terrorised the singer and the scientist was connected to the other deaths. He knew that he had to piece together everything from the beginning and, to do that, he needed to see Kendra's write-ups on the deaths. Perhaps they would spark a memory or highlight a detail that he had overlooked. He knew it was a huge risk to try and get the information, but he was in far greater danger of obliteration if he didn't get all the facts together to clear his and Erron's names.

It would take a significant amount of mental agility to get into the Apollo building while on suspension. Using any kind of charm or cloaking was pointless around other agents as they were immune to any of the basic skills. He racked his brain for a solution, finally deciding the safest bet was to walk there in case the agency could track him through his Oyster card. He was too exhausted to fly after his European trip. He hoped the fresh air would help him to think of a way to circumnavigate the building's security, and decided on a route that avoided the more well-known streets. His usual optimism was quickly waning and, in its place, lay a heavy fog of doubt and worry.

It was a two-hour walk to the Apollo building from his house on Craven Street. He made a point of dressing for the weather, which was the type of rain that made people run for shop doorways like they were made of rice paper. But he didn't mind the rain and dug out his oversized black umbrella so his wings wouldn't have another repeat of their soaking in Bedford river. The light of the afternoon was fading, and warm lamps were beginning to reflect in the wet streets like rivers of fireflies. Casey paused briefly near the Tower of London, where a clamour of voices echoed within and a gathering of sodden press members stood outside, looking miserable in their dripping anoraks and tinged blue with the cold. A reporter was giving a live speech in front of a camera, speaking loudly into her microphone.

'*Yes, this is Anna Jones, reporting live from the Tower of London, where reports have come in less than an hour ago that the famed ravens of the tower have all been replaced by wellington boots. No*

one has an explanation at this point, we are still compiling inform-
ation. There is no formal comment from the Tower at this time, and
they are looking into it.'

'Oh dear,' Casey whispered to himself. 'London may fall yet.'

Just as he spoke, a huge tremor rippled through the ground,
and a large crack in the pavement worked its way towards the
Tower. People screamed and scattered as the low groan of the
earth shunted paving slabs awry, and car alarms went off in
unison. Unlike the earthquake in Bedford, this one didn't quickly
abate, leaving minor damage. A sinkhole was suddenly forming,
growing wider and hungrier as it sucked in the surrounding
vehicles and lampposts, creeping closer to the historic London
landmark. A further immense tremor waged war on the pavement, and with a terrifying cacophony of tumbling stonework,
a huge section of the Tower of London collapsed into the earth.

Casey upped his pace to a panicked stride, moving quickly
away from the scene of destruction. Just past the King Edward
Memorial Park, a figure caught up to him, rosy-cheeked and
wrapped in a long multicoloured anorak.

'Hey, Casey!' the sprightly Fortuna agent, Ember Songfire,
called over. Her hair was lank and wet, tied in two plaits, but
this took nothing away from her bright smile. She'd jogged
across the road, blindly dodging traffic to catch up to him.

'Hi, Ember, are you on assignment?' He moved his umbrella
to cover her as they walked.

'Just finished up for the day. Hey, I heard you were in a bit
of a trouble. You need someone to talk to?'

He considered it. He'd known Ember for several years and,
if he was honest with himself, was feeling rather lonely without
Erron's company. 'Yeah, it'd be good to chat. Coffee?'

They walked until they found a small coffee shop tucked in a side street. Ember insisted on paying and Casey sat by the window morosely watching the rain as it drowned the sad-looking potted plant by the door. Cars splashed by and deep purple clouds filled the sky above them. People hurried this way and that, constantly aware of what little time they had in a day to get everything done. Casey remembered what that was like, back in the 1780s when life expectancy was much lower and healthcare was nowhere near what it was today. Although he'd been a doctor, he was all too aware of how fleeting life could be, and now, the same realisation pressed upon him. Even his supposed immortality had an expiry date, ready to be handed to him by the Fates at any given moment.

Ember returned with a tray with two hot drinks and two slices of flapjack. 'They don't do anything like gingerbread lattes, so I just got you a flat white, hope that's OK.' She took off her rainbow jacket to reveal faded dungarees and a colourful stripy jumper underneath. Her clothing matched her attitude, and both could cheer up the bleakest winter night. 'So, tell me all about it, or whatever bits you want to talk about.' She patted his folded hands.

Casey found himself telling her nearly everything. It came out as an unravelling spool of anguished words, his hands trembling, loosely wrapped around the coffee as it cooled. She listened without interrupting.

'So now I have to sneak into Kendra's office to find her write-up of our original reports. There might be something major in them that we missed. I may be clutching at straws, but I need to make sure,' he finished, dejected. 'I just can't think how to get in.'

Calmly, she placed her warm hands over his shaking ones and fixed him with a sincere look. 'If you are innocent of all this, then I believe it will work out in your favour. Let me help you, Casey.'

'You? How?'

'I can get you into the building, unseen. It just takes a little bit of luck.' She patted his hands reassuringly. 'And I've got bag loads of that.'

'I can't see how you can.'

'*Fortuna Diaboli.*' She folded her arms. 'You get your Apollo charm, we get our Luck of the Devil.'

'But it can't work on agents.'

'Oh, sweetheart, of course it does. Those in different divisions, that is. I couldn't use it against my own.'

'No, you can get in a lot of trouble abusing the system when you aren't on assignment.' He hung his head. 'I can't ask you to do that.'

'Consider it a gift, Casey. Besides, I have a feeling that I will have a lucky escape from any unwanted scrutiny.' She finished her flapjack and put the empty plate back on the tray, before checking her daisy-faced watch. 'It's six o'clock. I'd say most of the day shift will have gone by now, and the late turn will likely be starting their assignments, right? So, our timing is going to be pretty fortunate.'

He followed her back out into the rain, and they walked swiftly towards the Apollo building, stopping a few hundred feet away in the shadow of an apartment block.

'You know I have to kiss you, right?' she said, matter of fact. 'It's not as easy as arrows.'

He rubbed his neck, looking awkward.

'It's only a business interaction,' she stated but softened her voice. 'Will Erron mind?'

'Mind what?' he asked, confused.

'Mind me kissing you, in a professional capacity, of course.'

'Erron's got no reason to care about anything like that.'

'Oh, I thought you and him were . . . ?' She trailed off. 'At the concert, weren't you . . . ?'

His gaze dropped to his shoes, and he shuffled uncomfortably, shaking his head. 'No, we're nothing like that. How do we go about this?' He changed the subject.

She cocked her head to the side and smiled. She stroked his arm gently, speaking in such a way she might be comforting a child. 'Close your eyes, it'll be OK.'

He did so. She stepped under the umbrella and wrapped one hand around where he held the handle in a death grip of nerves. 'Relax, it's OK. I promise, it's OK.' Her other hand reached to his cheek, and she pulled his face to hers, kissing him with a sad tenderness of a wife seeing her husband off to war.

He felt a surge of sensation that could only be described as rolling a double six on two dice and finding a crisp twenty-pound note in an old jacket. It was laced with the high of winning a court case, getting the all-clear from an illness, passing a driving test and having a miraculous escape from death. Luck was something that could be presented in a million ways, and Casey felt sparkles of multifaceted joy passing between him and Ember as she kissed him. She pulled away and gave him a peck on the cheek. 'You've got about twenty minutes until that wears off. I'll wait for you out here.'

He came to his senses and handed her the umbrella. As promised, his timing was exceptional. He slipped into the main vestibule when the security guard had nipped away to use the toilet, accidentally leaving the building door ajar. The offices were deserted apart from two agents who both miraculously dropped a stack of papers and bent to pick them up as Casey walked past. Luckily, Kendra's office door lock had failed to engage as moments earlier she had left the room and dropped a single garish pendulum earring, which had wedged itself between the door and the frame. The desk drawer key she always wore around her neck was hung on the coat stand as it had gotten caught on her fluffy knit jacket that she'd slung over the hook, and it was pure luck that made Casey glance in its direction. He wasted no time in retrieving the envelope that had their reports sheets inside. As he headed towards the door, heart pounding, an intense feeling in his gut made him pause. He spun around and entered the back room where the arrow stores were. The gold arrow cabinet was ajar and Casey reached for the arrow sign-out sheet. He searched for their names but there was no record of either him or Erron signing the arrows out. Confused, he continued rooting around the cabinet. Buried at the back were two arrow tubes marked up for the Hoffmann hit, both with the name DeVangelo on. A glimmering gold arrow remained in each tube. He pulled out his phone and took photos of his findings before replacing everything as he'd found it. He made his way out of the building in a similar fashion, avoiding all scrutiny and feeling a rush of pure luck-filled adrenaline coursing through his veins.

Ember was waiting nearby as promised and handed him back the umbrella. He hugged her tightly. 'Thank you, I don't know how I could have done that without you.'

'I'm glad to be a help. I'm getting the Tube; you want to come along part-way? I've got to get my cards stamped before I go home.'

'I think I'll walk if that's OK. I need to clear my head.'

She cocked her head again. 'You two will be OK, I know it,' she said quietly. 'Whatever happens, look after yourself, Casey.' She smiled once, and walked out into the heaving rain, caring not a button for the weather as she hop-skipped to the nearest station. The Fortuna headquarters was nicely situated near the Natural History Museum and a lovely place that did excellent profiteroles which Casey could never remember the name of.

He made sure the stolen envelope was securely tucked inside his coat before embarking on the long walk back home, keeping a low profile and sticking to the back streets. By the time he reached Craven Street, he felt a little lighter from the walk and was glad to have had someone to talk to. But the buzz of the *Fortuna Diaboli* charm had fully worn off now, leaving him exhausted. He had to enter the house again from the roof terrace and creep down the stairs, still mindful not to switch on any lights. He shook off his umbrella and placed it silently behind the front door before setting the envelope down in the living room. He lit a tealight in a Moroccan lantern, the soft glow just enough to read by, intent on reading through the reports. But by the time he'd settled down in his armchair, exhaustion got the better of him and he drifted off to sleep. He'd turned the radio on low to play in the background, and as he dozed, the airtime was dominated by news reports of ever-increasing instability in the natural order of things, causing more environmental and metaphysical disasters by the minute. The radio host was speaking to a religious leader who was citing it as the precursor to Armageddon, claiming they were one earthquake away from a plague of locusts and widespread boils.

30

Lose Control

NIKITA AND EMRYS HAD SPENT a significant amount of time at the Eligos hunting down any more information they could find about the runes, only to come up empty-handed. Defeated, Nikita tilted her chair back and stared vacantly at the ceiling. The mosaic above depicted a beautiful heavenly scene and her eyes wandered from cloud to constellation until something grabbed her attention.

'Emrys . . . what's that?' She pulled at his sleeve and pointed upwards.

Among the images of angelic figures and celestial magic there was a depiction of a star with a symbol inside it.

Emrys squinted to make it out. 'It looks like a rune, but I don't recognise that one.'

'There's more!' Nikita exclaimed, finding a cluster of other stars bearing symbols on the other side of the mosaic.

'None of these match the poem though. They must be the Runes of the Fates. I recognise a few of them, the ones that are used in some of our agency symbols.' Emrys scratched his chin.

Nikita thought for a moment, before the realisation hit her. 'Of course!' She stood and pushed her chair under the desk before running up to the second floor. Confused, Emrys followed.

Nikita was leaning over the balcony, scanning the floor. 'This isn't a depiction of Hell at all. It's Chaos.' She was pointing at the mosaic on the floor of dark and twisting images, fire and darkness dotted beneath the desks. When she'd first explored the Eligos, she'd assumed the floor and ceiling mosaics were an artistic rendition of Heaven and Hell. Shadowy creatures appeared to crawl from under the bookcases, frozen in time, their claws and tentacles seemingly reaching for the sky.

'You know I never really looked at it that much.' Emrys came up behind her and wrapped his arms around her waist. 'You think the Chaos runes are there?'

'Yes. Look.' She singled out one of the demonic creatures. 'It's on his head.'

Sure enough, the rune was etched onto the mosaic head of the beast. After a few minutes they had found twenty-five more, all with runes that correlated to the ones in the *Vaticinium de Tumultus*.

'How do we figure out which letters they stand for though?' Emrys asked.

Nikita stood in silence for some time, flicking her gaze between the ceiling and the floor. She pulled out her small notebook and pen from her pocket and started to copy down the placement of the stars on the ceiling, then doing the same with the demon's runes.

Eventually, she turned to face Emrys and pointed at the sketches she'd made. 'The Runes of the Fates seem simple enough. They like order, see – the pattern is a spiral. I would be willing to bet it's alphabetical and runs either from the inside out or outside in.'

The demonic images were, of course, chaotic by nature and seemingly all over the place. Nikita rubbed her forehead, deep in thought. 'I think I need something to eat and some space to think about this.'

'I tell you what, take some photos of the mosaics and I will drop you back home so you can have a moment to yourself.' Emrys brushed the hair from her eyes. 'We can see who deciphers it all first.' He smiled at her softly.

'I'd prefer we worked through it together.'

Less than an hour later, they were poring over the photos and sketches together in Nikita's kitchen, a pan of spaghetti bubbling away on the hob. Nikita paused to taste some of the Bolognese sauce that Emrys had artfully thrown together with some bits and pieces from the local shop.

'Has anyone heard from Casey or Erron yet?' she asked tentatively.

'Osato's team have tried tracking down their last movements; neither of them has used their nova cuff to pay for anything, and they haven't been spotted either at their homes or at any agency buildings. They are aware of their suspension, and I suspect they will surface in a day or two, if they aren't found before then. They'll run out of old money soon enough and will be forced to show themselves.'

Nikita was concerned it didn't help their case that they were purposefully lying low, and she was worried that they might actually be on the run out of guilt. She was starting to question whether her attempts to find the real culprit were in vain. But she just couldn't shake the question that if they were really up to something so nefarious, why would they take her out on her first day, or get to know her over cocktails at the Nightjar? Surely the fewer witnesses, the better? The questions lay heavy on her mind.

'I'll be honest, I am starting to really worry about them. And whether they have done something awful or not.' She placed the spoon back in the pan, her appetite waning.

'Listen, Rocket, the quicker we can get to the bottom of all this, the better. If they are innocent, then they'll be just fine.' He gently caressed her upper arms and kissed her on the forehead. 'Let's dish up the food and get this mysterious book cracked.'

Nikita giggled as he haphazardly tried to strain the spaghetti and serve the sauce with limited crockery and only one small spoon. He made a show of it though, pretending he was serving her a dish worthy of *MasterChef* and describing the ingredients in increasingly daft and flamboyant descriptions.

'A nubbin of garlic mist, eh? I can't say I have heard that one before.' Nikita pulled a face of mock wonder.

'Oh yes. It goes exquisitely with the skin of a pretentious tomato,' he replied, his face deadpan.

Following their exceptional meal, two more hours of deciphering the book and more than a couple of mugs of red wine, they had ended up curled up naked together in a tangle of duvet. Nikita was not usually the type to move so fast, and Emrys had managed to put his shyness to one side once the wine had given him enough confidence to relax around her. But both of them had agreed that if the world order was collapsing around them, they might as well make the most of their time together.

'Do you think it's a waste of time, translating the book?' she asked, nonchalantly smoothing over the hair on his chest with one hand.

He took her hand and kissed it. 'No, I don't. I know it's a cliché, but you were led to it for a reason, and I really do believe that the message it needs to convey will become apparent at the opportune moment. Don't doubt yourself, as doubt is a fallen-down sock.'

She laughed. 'You say some bizarre things.'

'Think about it, you're walking along quite happy, then your sock starts to fall down and bunch up. It doesn't stop you from walking exactly, but you might choose to pause because the sock is bothering you, and before you know it, you've let a fallen-down sock stop you reaching your destination. Doubt is a fallen-down sock. It might not stop you, but it will make you think twice about continuing.'

She shuffled up the bed and kissed him, being careful not to lean too hard on his wings, which lay flat and shimmering with colour beneath them. 'I won't let my socks fall down,' she said with wide-eyed sincerity, tucking her head into his shoulder.

'That's the spirit.' He faced her and smiled, his hair tousled, and cheeks still flushed with their earlier exertions. 'I should let you get some sleep. I can always visit tomorrow after work if you'd like.'

'You can stay if you want?' She pressed herself closer to him.

'Are you sure? You don't think this is moving too fast? I'm normally a lot more old-fashioned about these things.'

'I'm sure. The way I see it, I only got twenty-nine years to live in my old life, and I spent far too much of that time waiting around for some fairy-tale romance that never happened. So now I think it's easier to just skip to the physical pleasure part and save on the heartbreak.'

He sat up slightly, looking hurt by her flippant comment. He leant forward and stroked her cheek, his voice gentle. 'I would have gladly romanced you in pursuit of your heart. I'm not the type that is interested in anything less than a fairy tale.'

'Oh, I didn't mean to suggest that this was meaningless,' she said quietly.

He wrapped his arm around her and pressed his forehead to hers. 'I will give you your fairy tale, if you give me the chance to show you how you should be treated.'

'So will you stay?' Nikita was dangerously close to forming a strong emotional attachment that she knew she would regret if he turned out like every other man she'd heard empty promises from in the past.

'Of course.'

Fate had other ideas, and his phone trilled on the bedside table. His work ringtone was Carl Orff's 'O Fortuna' and it came through as an ironic end to their evening.

He stretched across for the phone and answered before it reached voicemail. 'Emrys.'

Nikita sat up and wrapped the quilt around her, allowing him to sit up and unflatten his wings.

'You have? Where exactly? I mean, I can do. You may have to give me a bit of time ... No, I'm not home ... dinner with a friend ... yes, a late dinner.' He perched on the edge of the bed, hopelessly trying to tidy his wild hair with one hand as he spoke. He ended the call and faced Nikita again.

'One of the Nemesis agents has stumbled across Freya Carthage in the street not long ago ... She's in a bad way,' he announced. 'That was Osato. She's asked me to meet her at the agency hospital to question Freya. It seems she was attacked outside the Apollo building.'

'What's happened to her?'

'I don't know the full story. I better go but I'll update you later.' He kissed her before standing to get dressed. She couldn't help but admire his naked form, not quite a twenty-something Adonis covered in muscles, but well-toned, lived in, and comfortable in all the right places. She helped him find all the clothes that had been flung in various places around the flat and tidied his shirt collar for him before he left.

It wasn't late enough for her to go straight to bed, so she pulled on pyjamas and went to clean up the dishes from earlier, running the images of the library mosaics through her mind as she busied herself at the sink. Halfway through drying the spaghetti pan, she felt a pang of disappointment that she would be spending the night alone. She tried to focus her mind on deciphering the pictures of the mosaics on her phone, but she found herself glancing at her messages too often and wondering whether agents were capable of stable, incredibly long-term, relationships.

31

Carry You

THE CAPITAL'S AGENCY HOSPITAL, APTLY named the Raphael Sanctuary, was a top-of-the-range, highly secure high-rise building in the centre of London. Only accessible by agents and support staff, it housed a multitude of floors for specialist recuperative wards, a trauma unit and helipad. Generally, the helipad was reserved for the archangels, staff recruited from those mortals who had died while in roles of medical professionals, particularly paramedics and ER doctors, nurses and surgeons. They were given wings of glowing light and were responsible for all manner of unusual curative needs.

The hospital was rarely full as agents healed quickly from basic injuries and illness and rarely came across anything traumatic enough to kill them permanently, but there were always exceptions to the rule. The archangels dealt mostly with severe trauma such as broken bones, drowning, lost limbs, or mental well-being but those they did treat didn't often need to stay in the wards for long.

Osato marched Emrys down the sleek white-lino corridors towards the trauma unit on the top floor. It was by far the fastest way for patients to get into the hospital, as most were air-lifted in by a team of archangels.

'One of my team members found her wandering the Embankment with little recollection of where or who she was. She's coming round a little and details are slowly coming back to her, but doctors think she's suffered a head injury,' Osato explained.

'You said she might have been attacked?' Emrys queried.

'In a moment of lucidity she said she was leaving the Apollo building in a hurry though she can't remember why. But she was jumped and everything went hazy. She says she recalls fighting someone off then running away, but after that she goes blank. We're not sure at this stage if this is accurate, but we have to treat it as such until we know more.'

'Do you think it was a random assault?'

Osato sighed. 'I'm not convinced. Think about it: Freya would have been safe with her Apollo charms around normal people, agents in general go unnoticed. There hasn't been a recorded attack on an Apollo agent by a mortal for as long as I have been with the agency. That leads me to wonder if another agent has attacked her and, if so, why?'

'I can't think of any reason why an agent would do that,' Emrys mused.

'It's a very loose connection, but Freya covered an assignment for Grover and Hart following the first death, that of Sofia Carter. I checked with Kendra and two days after this botched hit, Freya didn't turn up for work. Kendra just assumed she had marked down her holiday dates incorrectly as she was supposed to be going on leave. That means there are four days where her whereabouts are unaccounted for. During that time Grover and

Hart went on the run. Something really doesn't feel right, and with everything else going on with these fractures, we need to rule out any connection. That's why I called you.'

They were met by an archangel, Dr Faro Alexus, dressed in green surgery scrubs and holding a steel clipboard. He was tall, Latino and in his late fifties with thick glasses and a sombre expression. 'Ms M'Raya, there's been improvement, but her memory is still hazy. Some things seem crystal clear but others she has no recollection of. I would say she's suffered a significant concussion with temporary amnesia as a result.'

They were led to where Freya lay in a sleepy state, a cold compress on the side of her head. She had bruising around one eye, a few scratches and scrapes but nothing too severe. Despite her exhaustion and memory loss, she clearly recognised her visitors and raised her arm in greeting. Dr Alexus left them to speak with her.

'Hello, Freya.' Emrys pulled up a chair and sat next to her. 'I hope you will be on the mend very soon.'

Osato stood rigid by the foot of the bed. 'Freya, I appreciate you are struggling to recall events clearly, but we need to try and find your attacker at the earliest opportunity. If you can answer any of my questions, it will be a big help.'

Freya nodded in understanding.

'Do you remember leaving work the night you disappeared?' Osato began.

'No,' Freya croaked, furrowing her brow, trying to force her memory to recall anything.

'The CCTV shows you leaving the building in a hurry. Do you remember why you were running?'

'I ... don't know.'

'Freya, you may or may not be aware that two Apollo agents have been suspended recently due to some serious circumstances that have arisen. We also know that you are close friends with both of them and recently undertook one of their assignments. We want to find out if the agents, or these events, are connected to your assault in any way.'

Freya nodded slowly.

'Has Agent Casey Hart ever threatened you, or committed any acts you consider to be against company policy?'

'No. Absolutely not,' she replied with conviction.

'What about Agent Erron Grover?'

'No. Well, he's had a few misdemeanours. Though I can't think of anything off the top of my head.' Freya rubbed her temple gently.

'OK. Do you remember anything at all during the last few days?' A long pause hung in the air before Freya said she wasn't sure. Osato pressed on. 'On the day of Sofia Carter's death at Farringdon station, you agreed to take two of Hart and Grover's assignments that afternoon. Is that correct?'

'Yes.'

'Was there anything suspicious, untoward or indicative of a Hades agent present at the assignments you attended in their place?'

'No ... it all went smoothly.' Freya was clearly becoming exhausted, and her heart rate was becoming fast and shallow.

Dr Alexus appeared, having been notified by the machines on a buzzer the next room over. 'I think we need to give her a break for now. She should be more stable in a day or two,' he said, adjusting the level of painkiller she had been administered.

'OK. Thank you, Freya. Get some rest and we will see you again soon.' Osato was a little vexed that she couldn't ask all the questions she wanted to, but knew her authority extended only so far, and the archangels had jurisdiction over the welfare of their patients.

Emrys had written down Freya's responses and was discussing them with Osato as they took the long ride down in the lift to the ground floor.

'There's nothing conclusive yet. We need to find out who she was running from, look.' Osato pulled an electronic tablet from her bag and loaded up the CCTV footage she had saved to it. Freya could clearly be seen exiting the Apollo building in panic, repeatedly looking behind her as she ran. It cut to another camera segment further down the road where she had opened her wings to take flight and disappeared out of view, but she never appeared on the third camera. 'One of my team, Lian, found a dried pool of blood here, around where she disappears. It seems like someone was waiting for her there and knocked her out when she was about to take off.'

'Which means, we are likely dealing with two people,' Emrys concluded. 'She was running from one and got knocked out by another.'

'What did you read into her expressions when we mentioned Grover and Hart?'

'Nothing detectable. She seems to be telling the truth. I say we give it another shot tomorrow if the doctors think she's up to it.'

'That's fine. I'm still following up the lead about this Izobella Cain from Hades, who we believe has a connection to Erron Grover. So far her presence has been accounted for during the

deaths of Sofia, Gunther and KiaRia, as her cards for assignments elsewhere were stamped as completed. Though she wasn't
working when the other two deaths occurred. We can't
completely discount her, but it does throw some doubt on
the situation. I'll keep looking into it; once I have more, I'll
call you.'

'Who stamped her cards?' Emrys queried.

'That's what I'm looking into. They have several clerks at
Hades and no CCTV behind the returns counter, so I will
track them all down in the morning and see who remembers
her returning the cards. Give me a lift back to Nemesis, will
you? I've got stuff that I want to get done before going home
tonight.'

'Sure.'

Emrys dropped her back to her office building just after one
o'clock in the morning. Once she was safely inside, he pulled
out his phone and checked the time, before sending a quick
text message. Nikita phoned back in less than a minute.

'Is the offer still open?' he asked, making an illegal U-turn
and pulling back into traffic without using his mirrors. He
knew nothing would hit him.

Less than twenty minutes later, Nikita greeted him at the
door. Emrys wanted nothing more than to collapse into bed,
but Nikita grabbed his arm and led him to the kitchen.

'I had a breakthrough.' She excitedly pushed a bunch of
papers towards him where she'd drawn out some extra sketches
of the mosaics from the photos they'd taken.

Exhausted, Emrys studied them, still none the wiser.

'So we know a few of these Chaos runes from our previous
research. I've arranged them against the sketch of the mosaic.

It took me a while to recognise it, but it seems to match up perfectly. It's not alphabetical, it's a QWERTY keyboard.' She beamed proudly.

Emrys couldn't deny that it seemed to match perfectly. 'But the library was built way before typewriters even existed. It can't be the case.'

'Do you think the Fates maybe played their hand here? Letting the tilers create what seemed to be a completely random pattern for the Chaos runes, knowing full well that it would make sense eventually … almost as if they planned for it to be figured out at the right moment?' Nikita considered.

Emrys was stumped. 'It's a good theory.'

'Maybe we'll never know. But what's important is getting this poem deciphered.'

'I need some sleep first.' Emrys ran his fingers through his hair. 'My head is pounding.'

Nikita agreed and shuffled the papers back together. 'We'll tackle this with fresh eyes in the morning.'

32

Poison

RRON WAS WOKEN BY A loud rapping on the hotel
door. He had slept fitfully all day and night, aching,
shivering and feeling utterly wretched. He glanced
towards the door, suddenly panicking that he'd been found.
The knocking continued until a gruff voice called through
the door, announcing himself as the desk clerk. Confused,
Erron dragged himself to the door and opened it a crack. An
untidy-looking man in a shabby hotel uniform handed him
a manila envelope.

'Grover, right?' The man grunted.

'Yeah, who left this at the desk?' Erron croaked.

'Some old woman. Was very specific that I delivered it to
you ASAP. Said it was your lost phone.'

The desk clerk wandered off before Erron could ask anything
else.

The envelope felt like it contained a phone and a wad of
paper. There was no return address, just his name printed in
small type on a crudely taped on label. Taking it to the bed,
he eased himself down before opening it and sliding out a

selection of A4-sized photos and a mobile phone that wasn't his own.

The colour drained from his face. Bitter bile rose in his stomach as he sifted through the pictures, the realisation creeping in that his injuries had not been from a bar fight in the Nightjar, but something far more sinister. A note fluttered to the floor from the back of the photo stack, and he bent to pick it up:

Call me. You will want to hear what I have to say.

A number was scrawled below the smooth handwriting.

He dropped the stack of photos on the bed with the note and ran to the bathroom to be violently sick. Curled on the cold tile floor, he sobbed until his body could produce no more sound or breath. An hour passed before he found the strength to return to the bed. First, he scrolled through the phone, finding only one number in the contacts, the same number on the note. Only then did he steel himself to look through the pictures again. Several of them depicted Erron in a vulnerable state of undress, and others showed elements of blood mixing between himself and another, unidentified agent. One that leapt out at him was a shot of him lying face down, shirtless, with several strange runes cut into the skin down his spine.

Clearly the photos had been staged to both humiliate him, as well as implicate him in the practice of blood mixing. He couldn't remember any of it and would never have consented to anything he saw in the images, though it clearly looked like he had. It certainly explained the strange marks on his wrists, and the cuts he had felt on his back earlier on. If Erron had anything left to throw up, he would have returned to the bathroom, but his disgust and humiliation were put to the back of his mind as a formidable wave of anger rose within him.

He would call whoever it was that had set him up. But not straightaway. First, he would try to piece together why anyone would do this to him. He and Casey were already under investigation for all the wrongful deaths, and it was too much of a coincidence that he was being framed for blood mixing at the same time. It crossed his mind that if this was somehow connected to the investigation, Casey might be in trouble too, and the thought of that terrified him. He had to think. He had to come up with something, anything, that would save him and Casey from obliteration.

For a long time, he forced himself to stare at the photos, desperately trying to remember the ordeal, or how he came to be in such a state. He didn't know much about blood mixing, but it abruptly brought his memory back to the papers that had fallen out of the folder in front of Freya. Kendra had mentioned the cosmic blood mixing could be used to kill or enter some kind of shadow state. It was no coincidence that neither he nor Casey had seen anyone suspicious at the scene of the deaths. If they could turn to shadow it made sense they could move around undetected, but clearly there was someone at each death with *Umbra Noctis* powers – nothing else could explain the bizarre electrical interference each time.

His head hurt too much for him to try and connect all the dots. Despite that, he had a sinking feeling that his attack was just another piece of the jigsaw that made him the perfect scapegoat for the mortal deaths. The only way to know for sure would be to call the number. He dropped the pictures at his feet and downed a small bottle of single malt from the minibar. Deep down, he knew that he was cornered. There was no way Kendra, or especially Osato, would look at those photos and believe he was innocent. The chances of finding the responsible person were slim. But he had one hope. If he could find footage of the crowd in Nightjar before he blacked out, he might be able to see what his last movements were, or who he had left with. It would be circumstantial evidence only, but it was the only lead he had. His afterlife was falling apart, and he'd done nothing wrong. Hot tears burned his eyes, but he refused to break down again. But then he thought of Casey, and once the tears came, there was no stopping them.

*　*　*

Across the city, Casey had been pacing around his kitchen since the early hours, having been jolted awake around midnight by a cacophony of geese honking as they passed by outside. The city had far worse problems than the geese; the bizarre and terrifying fractures were quickly spreading into every aspect of life in the mortal realm. Nothing followed a particular pattern, so emergency services and news crews were stumped at linking any cause of events together. Wild theories were cropping up online, and more than a few people had been severely injured in cases of exploding houseplants or rogue flying wheelie bins. Casey had followed the news whenever he could, hoping against hope that there were no fatalities as a result of the spiralling mayhem. He knew, however, with the escalation of the fractures, it would only be a matter of time before there were.

He'd checked his phone, ever hopeful that there would be a text from Erron waiting for him, his feelings of resentment having long been replaced with deep concern for Erron's welfare. He'd dialled Erron's number countless times through the night, but each time it had rang out, until it stopped connecting entirely around 4 a.m. They'd had fallings-out in the past but never to the extent that Erron wouldn't answer his calls. He considered contacting Nikita, but with her being so new in the agency, he wasn't sure if they would be monitoring her phone, expecting that he might reach out to her. Casey decided to spend the morning looking for Erron. Leaving the stolen Apollo file on the side, he flung on his overcoat and favourite grey trilby and took flight from his rooftop terrace just before dawn. His wings ached from all their recent exertion, but he pushed through the pain for as long as he could.

He first braved checking Erron's apartment, but there was no answer to his persistent knocking, and as dawn approached, he started to feel anxious about being found there by the agency. He slipped out the main door and took to the skies once more, heading towards one of their favourite places.

The sun was barely rising when he landed atop the dizzying peak of the BT Tower overlooking Soho. He and Erron had flown up there many times over the years to kill time between assignments or have lunch together on a day off. Casey smiled as he remembered the time Erron had accidentally dropped a pork pie off the top and it had dented a van below, but the nook in which they would shield themselves from the wind was now empty and soulless. He pulled a marker pen from his coat pocket and wrote in large letters on the metal cladding,

Erron, please call me. Casey, in the desperate hope his friend would return there sometime soon.

He stayed briefly to watch the thin streak of winter sun burn gold on the horizon before taking off once more to the next spot he could think of, knowing all too well that his attempts to find Erron in the city were futile, but he could think of no other way without alerting people in the agency to his whereabouts.

33

Sacrifice

'**I**'VE GOT TO SAY I'M impressed.' Emrys was leant up against the balcony window in Nikita's apartment, the *Vaticinium De Tumultus* open in one hand, an apple poised half eaten in the other. 'Your keyboard theory checked out.' He read their scrawled translations underneath the runes, his voice making it sound melodic with its soft timbre:

Rise of Chaos – 1337
The Iron Chariot bringeth first soul to fall,
On roads of metal, in stone-built wall.
The second be brought to Zeus's fire,
By lightning bolt in copper wire,
A third now needed in wingless flight,
To plunge through air in dead of night.
The fourth soul by Cupid's flame,
Will burn and smoulder in ashen pain,
Black water of a winter's day,
Claim fifth, he who has much to say,

Whence all souls pass before their prime,
The demons pass through breaks in time,
Stormbringer, he, with blackened knife,
Bring forth blood of cosmic life,
To rend the veil between the realms,
And thus the Earth be overwhelmed,
The land of Chaos born anew,
The end does come with skyline view,
Deathbringer, she, the chaos serve,
Disorder wilt now reign on Earth.

'That's beautiful and all, but we still don't know what it means.' Nikita was making pancakes in her underwear and an oversized T-shirt. Her wardrobe was still incredibly limited; she needed to visit Elysion with her first pay cheque to get some comfy basics and hopefully some wine glasses for the next time Emrys came over.

Emrys took a bite of the apple, chewed it, swallowed and walked towards her. 'My dear, let me read it again to see if anything clicks.' He walked around theatrically, reading the poem aloud as if rallying people to a noble cause.

He snapped the book shut to finish his performance and bit into the apple with satisfaction.

'Can you pass me the book a minute?' Her analytical mind was racing. She paused, deep in thought, Emrys coming to the rescue of the pancake that was starting to smoke.

'Anything you desire,' he answered, deftly flipping the pancake and finishing the last of his apple simultaneously.

She broke from her trance and raised an eyebrow. 'And they say that men can't multitask.'

They ate breakfast with the soothing sound of Eva Cassidy on the stereo, Nikita poring over the translation between mouthfuls of pancake. Once finished, Emrys stood to leave for work, before taking her hand and swaying her along to 'Songbird' while he kissed her softly goodbye.

Nikita dressed quickly and got straight to task, pulling apart the poem for any meaning. An hour later, she dropped her pen. 'Holy shit,' she whispered, grabbing for her phone.

Emrys picked up in three rings.

'It's eschatological. A recipe for the apocalypse. The poem,' she blustered. 'We need to speak to Osato. Now.'

Emrys was in his office facing a stream of Fortuna agents panicking that their assignments weren't going to plan due to the mounting disruption in the city. He'd managed to resolve a few significant assignments before Nikita had called. 'What do you mean? I'll call her now, unless it can wait until five o'clock. I'll be at the Raphael Sanctuary with Osato then to speak to Freya again. Can you get there?'

'Make it three o'clock if you can. I'll bring the book and explain everything then. Let Osato know about the poem. It might be the key to everything.'

He agreed and hung up. Nikita hurried through the rest of the verses, throwing any and every interpretation she could come up with at it. Then she packed her notes and the book into her bag and made her way out of the apartment, bracing herself against the chill outside. She needed to visit the Eligos again.

The streets were in turmoil: more sinkholes were opening across the district; people were claiming to have been caught in a time loop, repeating the same hour of their life over and over; and others reported seeing horrific, shadowy creatures appearing in various reflective surfaces. She fought through the crowds of unsettled residents and had to take a taxi to the Eligos as most Tube stations were out of action due to either electrical failures or goose infestations. The weather made no sense, she encountered gale-force winds that seemed to rage downwards towards the ground, forcing her to hunch over as she battled through them. Some streets were completely shrouded in an unsettling thick amber fog, and other areas on her route were covered in icicles that hung at odd angles all over the place.

Once inside the library, she finally felt safe and at home among the myriad of candles and ancient books, all guarded by the statues that lined the walls. It was a book-lined sanctuary away from the unfolding upheaval outside, but deep down she knew that it was only a matter of time before the fractures extended to every part of the world. The downward gales creaked the old timbers built into the roof and Nikita could hear the distinctive cracking of roof tiles with every strong gust.

She had urgent questions for Dantalion and needed them answered before she went to the Raphael Sanctuary. Her footsteps echoed as she approached the ledger, despite her soft-soled shoes. It was a Thursday lunchtime, and several agents were huddled in communal zones, as it's a well-known fact that few people die, fall in love or get lucky on a Thursday in January. Not even the Nemesis department were that busy, as they much preferred to carry out acts of retribution on a Monday morning, to add insult to injury. The atmosphere was tense as whispered theories about the fractures were being bandied around over cups of coffee.

She rolled up her sleeve and cut along her palm to fill the quill pen. She wrote two questions, refilling the pen twice, wincing each time:

Where is the skyline view?

Are we too late?

She spoke quietly under her breath so others could not hear her, the deep cut in her hand causing blood to drip down her fingers and start *tap-tap-tapping* on the mosaic-hellfire floor. 'I'm not leaving until I know.'

Nothing happened, the pages of the ledger didn't flutter, nor did the candles flicker. She waited and said it again.

Tap . . . Tap . . . Tap. A small tapestry of crimson spattered around her feet. 'I'm not leaving until I know,' she hissed, a little louder.

Nothing.

Other agents were beginning to look in her direction. She grabbed up the pen again and dragged the sharp nib across her hand, further opening the wound. Cosmically enhanced blood gushed freely from the cut, and she placed her hand in the water fountain. It slowly filled with scarlet, swirling and crazing as it soaked up her donation gleefully. 'I AM NOT LEAVING UNTIL I KNOW!' she shouted to the vaulted ceilings.

She felt herself begin to feel dizzy and she swayed a little on her feet but didn't move her arm. Whatever possessed the water seemed to suck hungrily at her offering, taking more than what gravity would have given. The candles didn't flicker but flamed wildly, intensifying with a glow that hurt her eyes to look on. The pages of the guest book rifled as if being read by a hurricane.

'Oh shit,' someone whispered, edging away from their work-station. Others moved away in panic.

The candles went out one by one, until the library was in darkness. A burst of sulphuric green fire manifested in front of Nikita and, like a lightning strike, a figure stood before her, fashioned in shadows with the amber glow of reptilian eyes.

'Six hundred years I hath abided by my realm. You summon me like a servant,' Dantalion hissed, his face a changing mask of darkness. 'Your answers are done. Summon me no more.' He exploded into a firework of burning green embers, returning the library to its candlelit stillness once more.

A pair of arms caught her as she fell, light-headed, towards the stone floor. She felt pressure on her palm and a grey fog crawled across her vision. Within a few minutes, she felt a rush of clarity returning to her and opened her eyes to see D-O-A knelt beside her.

'Stay still for a moment. You've lost a fair bit of blood.' He was holding a stack of tissues against her wound.

After a few moments, she wiped the cold sweat from her forehead and sat herself up slowly. 'Thank you.' She still felt a certain coldness towards him, as all she saw in his steel blue eyes was the murder of the priest who she had comforted as he died. To him, it was just a job; to her, it was a moment that would stay with her for eternity.

'Your answers.' He nodded towards the floor.

She clambered to her feet with his help and stepped back. Scrawled across the floor were letters in scorch marks almost a foot tall:

WHERE KINGS FALL, SUNSETS TURN BLACK AND HEAVEN SETS THE BAR HIGH.
IT'S NEVER TOO LATE, UNTIL IT'S TOO LATE.

She pulled her phone from her bag and took a photo of the burnt words. 'Well, that's just crystal clear.' She shook her head, exasperated, and inexplicably conscious that time was running out. She had under an hour to get to the hospital to meet Emrys and Osato, and she wasn't able to prepare for whatever spiralling chaos she would encounter en route, as the city was becoming a hotbed for destruction.

'Here.' D-O-A wrapped a bandage around her hand from the library first-aid kit. 'The world is unravelling,' he said solemnly. 'I would find out to where he refers as heaven setting the bar high.'

She agreed, gathering her things and leaving the library floor covered in black ash and blood.

'Wait!' D-O-A called and jogged to catch her up on the path outside. 'I shouldn't tell you this, but I think something significant is happening tomorrow night, into the early hours of Saturday.'

'What do you mean?'

He pulled from his overcoat a selection of assignment cards, all of them blank apart from the time slot he had given her. 'These are blind cards. We don't see them often, only when there are many deaths en masse.'

'Or when an agent might die,' Nikita interrupted him, her face pale. 'Casey told me about these.'

'Yes. An agent could die. I may need all of these; I may not need any. But chances are, something is going to happen tomorrow, and the Fates have little control when Chaos is involved.'

'How will you know where to go?' She stared at the cards, more unnerved by them than if they had a name and place attached.

'All Hades agents have been issued twenty blind cards each. We are on high alert around the city, probably much further afield. We likely won't know where to be, but when a body dies without the soul being reaped, we've got a limited time to get there before it's lost. If you figure out your answers, call me.'

'Let's hope I figure this out before you need any of those cards.'

34

Demons

ERRON HAD PHONED NIGHTJAR ASKING for any
possible footage from the night he was taken, and they
assured him they would give him a call back when they
opened. He'd provided a description of himself and the rough
timings he'd been there, though they did warn him it might be
hard to spot if anyone had spiked his drink. After hanging up,
he stared at the phone's blank screen for some time before he
picked up the note that had been with the images in the envelope.
His hands shook with both anger and hesitation when he dialled
the number that had been scrawled on the paper. After the third
ring, a male voice answered, smooth and calm, a smile tainting
the words. 'I've been expecting your call, Grover.'

'What's all this about?'

'We have you in a corner. Blood mixing is a very serious
crime, especially when it's used to erode the laws of physics.
You're facing obliteration for this.'

'I haven't done any of that, and you know it.'

'That's not what it looks like, though, is it? We've worked
hard to collect the evidence we need. With everything we have

on you, no one would believe your side of the story.' The honey-rich voice purred. 'But I can help you ... at a price.'

'What is it you need from me?' Erron kept his tone steady, employing every ounce of calmness he could muster.

'Not much, but under the circumstances I had to ensure your utmost cooperation, you understand. It's nothing personal.'

'Don't speak in riddles. What exactly do you want?'

'We will discuss it in person. You see, if you don't turn up where and when I ask you to, everything needed to convict you ends up on Osato M'Raya's desk.' The man gave out instructions on where to meet him, the following evening, which Erron wrote down on the note. 'If you want to protect yourself from obliteration, and maybe even save your pitiful friend, you'll do exactly as I ask.'

'And if I comply, then what happens? What is it you want from me?'

'Do as I say, and all this evidence disappears. I'm not asking for much in return, but I need to meet with you to explain. Ta-ta for now.' The line went dead.

He had just under a day and a half. Erron's first instinct was to try and get hold of Casey as he was desperate to know if he was OK. Erron's phone had been missing for over three days and they had never gone so long without speaking. But the thought of having to explain his humiliating ordeal, or even have Casey see the photos, filled him with complete dread. He wanted the whole thing to disappear so he never had to have that awful conversation with his best friend. He had been given a choice by the mystery person on the phone, and though he didn't wholly trust it, if he cooperated, he might be able to save himself and Casey from obliteration. He had no idea what demands he was expected to meet but, desperately, he wanted to save the little shred of dignity he had left. In his head, he made lists of things that he would do better if he could just save his job, *save his life*; promises to any and all gods that would listen in his hour of need. Promises that he'd give up drinking, that he'd be kind to strangers, that he'd learn to appreciate the beauty of sunsets, that he'd make time for people. That he'd make time for Casey. That he'd buy a big bag of peanuts and let Casey feed Roscoe the Roomba every day if that made him happy. That he'd go for the damn profiteroles in Kensington. That he'd stay at Apollo. That he'd say he was sorry. Oh god, he was so sorry.

He stared at the time and place he'd written on the note that came with the photos. A bell was tolling somewhere for him, and there was nothing he could do. Kicking himself out of his funk, he summoned his strength. Whatever happened, he had a day and a half, and he'd make the most of it. He strapped up his broken wing with a huge amount of effort and pain, folded in the other, dressed in his best suit and went out for a walk in the city he'd called home for seventy years. He lit a cigarette and gave the rest of the packet to a homeless man, along with the change in his wallet and a lottery ticket for the upcoming draw. It felt like a lifetime ago that he'd bought that while choosing an outfit with Casey for the KiaRia concert.

'I hope you win,' he said, exhaling a thin cloud of smoke. 'By the time they pick the numbers, I'll be a dead man.'

The man, bundled in his blankets and beer cans, shook his hand. 'Young man, if I win, I'll leave a bloody good bunch o' flowers on yer grave.' He gave Erron a toothless grin from under his filthy beanie hat.

'Glad to hear it.' Erron walked on, noticing the odd glances from passers-by that took in his nasty facial injuries and care-free demeanour. He looked like a bare-knuckle fighter, ambling down the road with his last cigarette pinched in the corner of his mouth. No one would be able to tell that he was in unbear-able pain, both physically and emotionally.

Self-disgust and humiliation still swam like sharks in his blood, but despite the violation he'd suffered, he wanted to give his last hours some semblance of redemption. He passed by Nightjar, taking a solemn moment to reflect on all the memories he'd had there, all of them sullied by the trauma of what he'd been through. He hoped desperately that they would find the CCTV, but time was swiftly running out. He stubbed his cigarette out on the pavement and briefly observed his battered reflection in the glass before continuing. The city was descending further and further into chaos. He passed by countless deep cracks in the roads, upturned cars, strange plants that were springing from the sides of buildings and tickling passers-by. Around a corner, a group of people were chanting and holding placards, saying 'The End is Nigh' and 'Repent your Sins', one even said 'Geesus Christ is the Second Coming', with a poorly drawn picture of a goose in a holy robe.

Finally, he came to a standstill. His subconscious had taken him to a church. A humble place tucked in a small parcel of land where, in life, he'd laid his brother Ethan to rest at a ceremony where only a few had gathered. Ethan had been a believer, not so much in the Bible, but in *something*, the parts of it that had mattered to him. He'd been a good man to those that he cared about, offering his street-earned wisdom to the lost souls who had gathered around him, in parks or under graffiti-covered bridges. He'd been no angel, but he'd always looked out for Erron growing up. Erron had nothing in the way of faith in life. His broken home and abject poverty had all contributed to his sense that life was terribly unfair. When he'd grown up, he'd suffered a miserable relationship with a woman just to prove to his mother that he was the good, stable son. The son who hadn't given up at the age of twenty-seven and leapt off an overpass.

Now, walking into that quiet space, the cloisters filled with the prayers of the hopeless and the spirits of the lost, he felt closer to heaven than he had any hope of getting. He knew from experience that there was no Almighty God, just the Fates, and some great Cosmic Sneeze that they were all part of, but the church still felt strangely comforting. He took a seat on one of the worn pews, the years of use having polished the wood to a dull sheen. The church was empty aside from a lone young priest, stacking Bibles near the font. He'd noticed Erron, but had given him respectful space, as it was not his nature to immediately meddle with the lost lambs who found their way in.

Feeling an odd sense of calm, Erron bowed his head, whispering a prayer that in most religious circles wouldn't have been read aloud. 'To whom it may concern. I know I've fucked up. But please, go easy on me. It's been a tough life.' He sighed. He knew all about the other side of death, and it was no Garden of Eden, it was a corporate entity of paper-pushing and destiny playwrighting. If anything, Erron's prayer was for his brother, wherever his troubled soul may be.

He sat for long enough that the priest hovered nearby, eventually deciding he ought to offer some counsel.

'Something troubling you, my friend?'

Erron reached for his cigarettes but remembered he'd given them away, so he wrung his hands instead. 'Something like that.'

'Talk to me, if you wish, but He is always listening.' The priest cast his gaze upward.

Erron paused. 'Even with your faith, you'd never comprehend what I really am. Tell me this, though, if you had a message you wanted to take to the big guy upstairs, what would it be?'

The priest thought for a while. 'I guess I already say to Him what I need to say, every day. Why do you ask?'

Erron rose from the pew and pulled up the collar on his black overcoat. 'Because I'm going to be meeting him real soon.'

'Oh, son, let me help you.' The priest picked up a leaflet for a suicide helpline and went to give it to Erron.

'Keep it, there's nothing they can do to help me.' Erron began to walk away.

'Then I would tell Him to welcome you with loving arms, and to ease your suffering so you might find a reason to keep going,' the priest called after him.

'Consider it done.' Erron waved without looking back and went back out into the chaotic, crumbling streets.

The priest's gaze followed the nameless man as he left and he saw a fluttering white object floating to the floor in his wake. He knelt and picked it up, amazed to find a large, blood-stained feather. 'Oh Lord, your angels walk among us,' he whispered reverently, taking the feather into the back office to be stared at in disbelief for an inexplicably long time.

35

How to Save a Life

C ASEY STOOD MOTIONLESS ON HIS roof terrace, having spent hours flying from place to place, leaving scrawled notes for Erron. His hand gripped his phone in his pocket, still clinging to the hope that it would buzz with a notification or call. He felt lost. His mind a tangle of possibilities, all without an answer. Part of him wondered if the agency had found Erron and were detaining him. Not wanting to waste any more time, he went downstairs to turn his mind to the envelope of statements from Kendra's office that he'd left on the side. He pulled out the papers and skim-read through his own. He was always thorough when writing up his reports, believing strongly that the devil was in the detail, even in the most straightforward of assignments. As he flipped through the pages, an unnerving letter caught his eye:

Statement of Confession, Agent Erron Christopher Grover.
    I hereby confess my involvement in the events surrounding the deaths of five Apollo assignments of January this year, resulting in the catastrophic fractures in the weaving of the Fates. Initially,

I did not realise the risks involved with using blood mixing. What started off as an experiment escalated beyond my control, and neither myself nor my accomplice realised the power of what we had discovered. My associate was using the power to possess mortals, soon learning they had ultimate power over life and death. They became insatiable, driven mad by their power. But before I could stop them I was already in too deep. This has gone far beyond my control, and for the safety of others I am coming forward to beg for mercy from the agency in exchange for the name of the person responsible for directly taking the lives of five innocent people. My esteemed colleague, Agent Hart, was completely unaware of my involvement and therefore should be returned to active duty without punishment. I will sign this confession in the presence of agency management in exchange for the information they seek about my associate.

With faith,

Erron

Casey read through the note several times, struggling to believe any of it. Erron had signed it, dated it and it was countersigned in red ink by Kendra. Though it explained the lack of contact, Casey found himself rubbing his forehead in utter disbelief, a queasy sickness somersaulting in his gut. He'd known that Erron had more to tell him, but he struggled to comprehend the depth of that truth. He could almost believe it; his friend had been quiet and subdued recently and seemed to be carrying around a secret that was weighing him down. He'd been closed off, more avoidant of any deeper conversation than usual. Casey's personal phone trilled loudly with an unknown number, breaking the intense train of thought that he had careening around the tracks in his brain. He was loath to answer, but curiosity got the better of him.

'Yes?' he answered curtly.

'Casey, I thought I might catch you on this number.' It was Kendra.

He didn't reply.

'This may not be the best news, but it has a silver lining,' she said cautiously. 'Erron Grover has confessed to his involvement in the deaths. All charges against you have been dropped. We need to speak with both of you for Erron's judgement tomorrow evening, nine thirty sharp.' She gave an address. 'It's important that you are there to give evidence.'

Clutching the envelope and careful not to reveal his knowledge of Erron's confession, he worded his response guardedly. 'I don't believe Erron was involved, not at all. And why isn't his judgement being held at Nemesis?'

Kendra sighed loudly, seemingly having expected Casey's resistance. 'The trial is being attended by a number of agency representatives and, due to the seriousness of the crime, they have chosen to hold the hearing on neutral ground. I didn't have any say.' She paused and Casey heard her draw breath slowly. 'Casey, you do understand what is at stake here? He's confessed to using the banned practice of blood mixing as an accessory in causing the wrongful deaths.'

Casey didn't want to say it, but he had to know. 'You're looking to obliterate him, aren't you?'

'Erron has provided us with valuable information in a plea deal to lessen his sentence. But it is for Nemesis to decide if they agree to the terms. They still seek obliteration at this stage, until all evidence is heard,' she confirmed quietly. 'I know this won't be easy for you, but if it helps, off the record I will send you evidence of Erron's guilt so you can let go of any last bit of loyalty you have to him. What I am about to send you will demonstrate exactly how Erron has been playing with blood mixing, and then hopefully you will understand our position on this.'

Casey sighed, his stomach a tight knot, wondering what other evidence Erron could have handed in. 'What evidence will I need to give? I haven't witnessed him doing anything wrong.'

'You only need to answer a few standard questions, nothing taxing. Mostly confirmation of his presence at each death. I'm sorry, Casey, truly I am. Let me send you this file and you can make up your own mind, but it likely won't change the result of the trial. We'll have you reinstated by Monday.' Kendra softened her voice. 'I know he was a good friend of yours, but we don't want you being in contact with him before the trial. You will get a chance to say any parting words tomorrow night. And, Casey, don't get any silly ideas about trying to protect him, your reinstatement relies on your full cooperation.' She hung up, not allowing him to answer.

Casey sat frozen in his armchair, his whole body drained cold until his phone buzzed with an incoming file. He had to sit very still and very quiet when he saw the photos of Erron.

36

Knocking on Heaven's Door

IKITA HURRIED THROUGH THE BUSTLING streets, her bag swinging as she dodged the crowds and the new infestation of tickling plants on many low walls. Her hair was a mess, wild Celtic locks tangling in the cold wind, her tatty jeans dragging in puddles. She reached the Raphael Sanctuary ten minutes early, fumbling through her bag for a hairbrush as she saw Emrys's red Beetle turn into the gated parking area. Her heart skipped a little and she tidied her hair but was in too much of a rush to worry about the rest of her dishevelled appearance. Osato got out of the Beetle, followed closely by Emrys, just as Nikita rushed to meet them.

'Agent Wolf, where's the fire?' Osato asked in her measured tone.

'Probably everywhere if we don't figure this out quickly.' Nikita held up her stack of notes. 'I have most of it, but the last bits are the key.'

Osato nodded for her to follow them up to Freya's room. The doctor was already coming to greet them. 'She's become quite lucid; she's been talking about shape-shifting but it's not clear what she means. Maybe you can make sense of it,' Dr Alexus explained.

They hurried to Freya's side. She looked much more alert and was glad to see them. In her still confused state, she was desperately trying to recall a name.

'Do you remember who attacked you?' Emrys was the first to ask. 'Or the person you were running from?'

She nodded as vigorously as she was able to.

With considerable effort, she explained that she'd been leaving the office late, and had heard a heated exchange between Kendra and another person, resulting in the Apollo boss sobbing. She'd tried to listen through the office wall but had been unable to hear the conversation clearly. A tiny gap in the blinds had shown a partially obscured woman from behind, who had shape-shifted in front of Freya's eyes into the tall, slender figure of a man. She paused through struggling speech to compose herself. After a moment, she went on to explain how the shape-shifting figure had turned to see her eavesdropping and she had run. Before she was able to take flight outside, she was ambushed, only just managing to escape, sustaining a significant head injury. Beyond that she had no solid memory of anything until she had been found wandering and cold by one of the agents.

'And you heard nothing said during the argument?' Osato quizzed.

She shook her head.

'Whoever we are dealing with must have some hold over Kendra.' Osato pulled out her phone and video-called Lian Zhang, her senior Nemesis agent. 'Lian, can you run a call-trace on Kendra Eckhart, please? Both personal and agency phones. Thank you. Let me know as soon as you get anything.'

Osato hung up and explained that if they could discreetly track Kendra and who she was communicating with, they might find out who was threatening her and, quite possibly, threatening the very stability of the world. The call-tracing was something she had the power to do for anyone she suspected as involved in the fractures, owing to that she'd been voted by all divisions as the investigative lead. In light of the situation they found themselves in, she was willing to try anything.

'Nikita, please go through your notes with us now. Freya, as you are directly involved, say if there is anything you need to add, or any ideas you have. It's important that we all understand what we are dealing with here.'

Nikita first went through the ideas she had written down from the poem, line by line.

'I was initially looking at this the wrong way. I assumed the poem predicted the future, but pulling it apart, it seems to be a recipe. Someone wants to bring Chaos to Earth, and to do so, they have to follow a set of rules. Each death appears to relate to an element, see: "The Iron Chariot bringeth first soul to fall, On roads of metal, in stone-built wall". Well, I surmised that to be the train, in Farringdon station. Sofia Carter was killed by the element of metal, or the stone being Earth. "The second be brought to Zeus's fire, by lightning bolt in copper wire". Zeus used lightning bolts, or electricity, and that had to be Quentin Smith, the electrician. "A third now needed in wingless flight, to plunge through air in dead of night". That was the woman Quentin was due to meet, who flung herself from her window, the element of air. "The fourth soul by Cupid's flame, will burn and smoulder in ashen pain". I considered for a moment whether an Apollo agent had shot a flaming arrow here, but while I was in the Eligos the other day, I heard whispers that the lighter KiaRia slipped on was Erron's and suddenly that section made sense.'

'Carry on,' Emrys encouraged.

'KiaRia burned to death, so that's fire. Finally, "Black water of a winter's day, claim fifth, he who has much to say". This one was easy. Gunther Hoffmann drowned; he was a particularly important man in his field and was giving a speech just before he died. Think about it, so many historical spells and potions involve these key natural elements, what if there is a shred of truth to that? What if, in order to bring Chaos to Earth, they needed these deaths to follow this pattern?'

Emrys chewed his thumbnail, deep in thought. Nikita handed him the book so he could lay it on Freya's bed for all of them to see. She'd photocopied the poem onto a large sheet of paper and scribbled annotations down the side.

'It's clear that all of these events have been leading us to the final line, which is the bit that I find truly terrifying. "Deathbringer, she, the chaos serve, Disorder wilt now reign on Earth". But I can't figure out the middle section about the cosmic blood. It's much easier to interpret in retrospect once the deaths have happened.'

Osato read the section of the poem that followed the fifth death. '"Whence all souls pass before their prime, The demons pass through breaks in time, Stormbringer, he, with blackened knife, Bring forth blood of cosmic life".' She took a moment before offering her opinion. 'The blood mixing maybe? Obviously cosmic blood relates to agents and we know they are involved. So maybe the knife relates to the blood mixing practices that have given rise to this.'

The room fell silent for a moment until Emrys spoke: 'I don't like the sound of where this is going.'

They stood contemplating Nikita's notes as it quickly sank in that the world falling into the hands of Chaos was becoming a very real, and irreversible, possibility. The world outside was not only becoming bizarre, unpredictable and full of geese, but as the effects of the fractures spread, it was also becoming dangerous to all life on Earth. And the worst was yet to come.

'Earlier, I did something that I shouldn't have, but I needed an answer,' Nikita confessed, pulling up the photos of Dantalion's answers. She explained that she had asked what the skyline view related to, and if it was too late, carefully omitting that she may have accidently, *ever so slightly*, summoned a demon. Dantalion's answer – 'Where kings fall, sunsets turn black and heaven sets the bar high' – captured their attention.

'"Where kings fall" just makes me think of a castle. Maybe the Tower of London? A lot of royalty fell there . . . or at least their heads did,' Emrys suggested,

'I think it was only queens executed there. Of the royalty, I mean.' Nikita doubted her recollection of GCSE History.

'Hmm.' Emrys shook his head, defeated. 'It could mean anything. There are a million interpretations.'

They puzzled over the answers and the rest of the poem for some time before Osato's phone rang.

'Lian? What have you got?'

Lian explained that both Kendra's agency and personal phones had been deactivated earlier on, but not before she'd placed a short phone call to an unknown number. Osato wrote this down on Nikita's notes before instructing Lian to try and locate Kendra without alerting her.

'I think Kendra is in trouble. Lian will get a team together to see if they can find her. Emrys, have you got any staff that can give them a bit of a boost ... off the record?' Osato didn't enjoy asking for favours that involved bending her usually very inflexible rules, but when such big things were at stake, she had to make an executive decision between doing the right thing and the good thing. Emrys placed a quick call to one of his most senior operatives.

Freya pointed at the number Osato had scribbled down frantically.

'You recognise it?' Nikita asked.

She slowly nodded and said with a rasping voice, 'Casey.'

'It's not an agency number; is it his personal mobile? The location pinged the call at a house in Craven Street. Remind me, is that his home address?'

Freya nodded. Osato immediately issued further instructions to Lian before turning her attention back to them. 'If he's home that will make things easier. We don't yet know Casey's involvement, but I've asked Lian to put out a few agents in a mile radius from his home address to see if we can find him as soon as possible. He might have a piece of the evidence that we desperately need to crack this.'

37

Judgement Day

LEGIONS OF REAPERS WERE GATHERING in the city the following morning. An excessive volume of fractures were rippling their way across the world, with London and the Home Counties as the epicentre, and time was running out. A river of pink lemonade had bubbled to the surface in Shaftesbury Avenue and was rolling its way towards Chinatown, leaving everything sticky and unpleasant in its wake. Localised hurricane winds were whipping up a storm surge on the Thames high enough to wash over the road on Tower Bridge. Even the DFS sale had ended.

Hades Division had been put on high alert by the Fates and were on assignment en masse to collect any lost souls, calling in neighbouring districts even as far as Oxfordshire, Essex and Kent in response to the scant information that the world may or may not be ending. The streets bloomed with the shadow of death, and the flickering disruption of Ghosters plagued every electrical connection across London.

As the most senior Ghoster in the city, Darren Oliver-Alliott was in charge of deployment zones. He'd assigned teams of delegates to their respective stations, efficient, prompt and industrious as ever. Death was his business, and business was about to boom. The heads of the other UK districts had all been officially notified to expect significant problems, ranging from traffic hold-ups and missed assignments to the general descent into chaos, depending on how things panned out. As expected, the Fates were not overly happy that things were out of their hands, but they were busy mapping out potential war plans against the Chaos in their hidden echelons. They were quickly running out of patience, faith in humanity and Bourbon biscuits.

Casey stared at his reflection in the hall mirror. With trembling hands he adjusted his dark grey tie and smoothed down the collar of his black shirt. Three days' worth of dirty blond stubble covered his usually clean-shaven face. His eyes were sunken and tired, and his heart was heavy as he pulled on a long black Chesterfield coat. He ran a comb through his straggly hair and tied it back, taking a deep breath before picking up his hat and heading for the door. He left the house at eight forty-five in the evening, walking purposefully towards his destination, holding his hat to combat the gale-force winds. Strapped between his wings, he wore his white horse-bow. He figured that he'd need it, alongside every ounce of mental resilience he possessed to undertake what he was planning to do.

Osato was still waiting for the Hades team to locate Izobella Cain's assignment cards from the key dates of the deaths. They needed to confirm her alibi for Sofia Carter, Gunther Hoffmann and KiaRia's wrongful deaths. It was no easy task: the cards were sent to a storage facility on Elysion and wouldn't have been uploaded onto the system for several weeks, so finding them was a manual task that was taking several days among the thousands of other deaths that had been completed over the past month. Osato had chased up the progress that morning, keen to have that piece of evidence to hand.

Nikita had convinced Emrys to head over to Casey's house to see if they could find him, or anything that might help them fill in the blanks. On the drive to Craven Street, Emrys's phone rang. He jabbed the answer button, his other hand spinning the steering wheel to narrowly avoid a giant turnip rolling down the road. For a split second he thought his luck was wearing thin as it almost grazed the paint of his prized Beetle.

'It's me,' Osato said sharply before he even had a chance to say hello. 'One of Agent Zhang's team thinks she spotted someone matching Casey's description heading east down the Embankment. She's going to follow to establish if it is him.'

'We can head that way, see if we can spot him,' he said, all the while eyeing the road with extra caution for any more oversized vegetables.

'That would be great, but try not to spook him until he's in a place we can easily detain him.'

Emrys glanced at Nikita, who frantically mouthed, 'Ten minutes,' pointing towards Craven Street.

'No problem, we are about fifteen minutes away. The roads are getting dangerous,' he answered calmly.

'Let me know if you find him.' Osato ended the call abruptly.

Emrys parked up at the end of Craven Street as chaotic storms raged around them, rocking the car and sending debris rolling down the road.

'If they have confirmed he's not home, there's not much we can do.' Emrys pulled up the handbrake and unclipped his seat belt.

'I'm going in. Which house is it?' Nikita began to open her door.

Emrys pulled her back. 'You'll be in a whole lot of hot water if you do that.'

'Look around, Emrys, the world is about to end if we don't find something solid soon. Casey could be going anywhere; we need to try and work out where he's going. Our best bet is to see if he's written anything down or left any kind of clue. You can stay here and pretend you dropped me off somewhere else, or you can give me a dose of good luck and help me stop a catastrophe.'

'You have a good point,' he conceded as a goose bounced off his windscreen, caught up in the raging winds. 'Ten minutes though, or Osato will have my neck.'

They exited the Beetle and broke the lock on Casey's front door, using the edge of a Blockbuster membership card that Emrys had had with him since 1997 and a whole bundle of good fortune.

'Don't worry, we'll make this quick,' Nikita whispered, creeping into the living room. 'Remember, we are looking for anything that might point to Erron's location, an address book of somewhere they might hide out, photos of any important locations, emails, even a calendar with the "End of the World" marked on it. I don't know for sure, but they are bound to have kept in touch, and if they are actually guilty of conspiring in all this, we could find something vital.'

Emrys rifled through piles of letters, newspapers and books, stopping short when he found the envelope with files strewn across the chessboard in the living room.

'This is a confidential management case file. I've no idea how Casey would have got hold of this.' Emrys showed her the stamp on the front of the file indicating as such.

Nikita went to his side and, together, they began reading through everything it contained.

'Interesting,' Nikita murmured to herself. 'Emrys watched her, admiring her focus and practically seeing the cogs turning as she tried to piece things together in her mind. After a long pause, she put the file down and pulled out her copy of the translated poem, scanning the lines she didn't yet fully understand, reading aloud one paragraph. '"Whence all souls pass before their prime, The demons pass through breaks in time, Stormbringer, he, with blackened knife, Bring forth blood of cosmic life".'

'I'm guessing the demons coming through breaks in time might be Chaos agents getting beyond the veil?' Emrys said, hoping to add something useful into the investigation.

'It's this bit about a blackened knife and cosmic blood that I don't understand. That's got to be an agent, right? Maybe they need agents to die for the veil to completely break down?' Nikita gripped his wrist, her sense of panic setting in. She was thinking about the blind cards that D-O-A had showed her.

Emrys's face drained of colour. 'Of course ... our blood summons demons. They feed off of it.'

Just then, Nikita's phone rang. It was the transport company dealing with her request for CCTV footage at the train station. It had been emailed across to her. She brought up the footage on her phone and scrolled through the various camera angles. Two minutes later her mouth fell agape.

'Oh my god,' she whispered, replaying the short bit of footage three more times. It captured a couple of seconds of a very familiar figure hidden away in an alcove opposite where Sofia Carter had stumbled in terror in front of the train. She showed the footage to Emrys, who was left speechless.

'We need to get a move on. This is huge.' Nikita nudged him, and he went back to searching.

'Wait, what was the library demon guy's reply again? Dantalion, is it?' Emrys asked with a sudden sense of urgency in his tone.

Nikita looked up; he was staring at the table and the muddled chessboard. She didn't have to open her phone. The words, and the experience, were burned into her memory. '"Where kings fall, sunsets turn black, heaven sets the bar high".'

'Where is the last section of the poem?' The continued urgency of Emrys's tone made her drop the paperwork and scrabble around in her bag to find the poem. She read it out to him in full.

'"The end does come with skyline view",' he repeated. 'Nikita, I think it's a bar.' He was holding up a small cocktail umbrella.

'What do you mean?'

He popped open the umbrella to clearly show a swirl of text reading the Sky Pod Bar.

Nikita's eyes widened. 'Where kings fall.'

She looked down at the chess set, where the king of the ivory row had toppled. 'They go there sometimes when they aren't at the Nightjar. They go to play chess and watch the sunset.'

'You know that for sure?' Emrys asked, his voice urgent.

'Yes, I remember. They mentioned it when they took me out for cocktails on my first day.' She clasped at the hope they might have solved Dantalion's riddle.

'Nikita, phone this number and ask if they have a chess set.' He read out the small print phone number under the name as she dialled. 'We need to make sure it's not a wild goose chase.'

'It's just ringing,' she mouthed. 'No answer.'

'Try again.'

A man answered on the third ring. 'Stefan, Sky Pod Bar, how may I help?'

'Hello, this is a strange question, do you have a chess set there?' Nikita asked hurriedly.

'Madam, we close in ten minutes. There's not even time for a drink, let alone chess.'

'Can you just tell me if you do?'

She heard him sigh loudly and then lower his voice.

'There's a table set up for two of my VIP guests. They requested a chess set many years ago, but it's not generally for public use.'

'Thank you. It means the world to know that.' She hung up.

'We need to get over there. If Casey has been tracked heading east along the Embankment, there's a chance he could be heading there. It's on Fenchurch Street.' Emrys grabbed her hand and they raced back to the Beetle. 'We'll beat him there if the traffic's light.'

The traffic was indeed light. Mortal residents of London were feeling an unusual amount of disquiet among the disasters and geese, and most had decided it was safer to stay indoors. With the sinkholes, the storms and earthquakes, most companies had sent employees home, schools had been closed and hospitals were overrun with casualties. There was a wide-spread sense of terror, and the explanations from scientists and religious leaders alike had started to dry up. The fear was to be expected with the sheer throng of Hades agents swarming in the streets, doing their solemn and miserable best to blend in as normal people. There was never an official uniform for Ghosters, and never an expectation to wear morbid clothing, but it turned out that Hades Division were rather good at recruiting people who wouldn't look entirely out of place if they picked up a scythe.

The little red Beetle squealed to a halt as near as it could get to the building on Fenchurch Street. Nikita had sent an urgent message to D-O-A as he'd requested she contact him with any developments. She then called Osato.

'We know who's involved,' Nikita stated. 'You need to get here ASAP.'

Osato picked up the call from her office. 'I'll get there as soon as I can, but a few of the roads are blocked and I can't fly in this weather, it's too dangerous. You'll have to keep me updated and I will meet you there.' Osato looked out of her window to see if any of the roads had cleared. People had abandoned cars and the local earthquakes had damaged the nearby infrastructure. No taxi would be willing to pick Osato up from her building in those conditions. She would have to run.

38

Losing My Religion

O NLY A FEW FEET FROM his favourite table, Erron was lying face down in a puddle of his own blood. He'd been ambushed the moment he'd walked into the empty bar, his shirt and tie crudely cut off, baring the wounds of his earlier attack. The friendly bartender, Stefan, had left moments before without noticing the agency staff enter the building.

'If you move again, I'll break the other one,' a woman hissed into his ear; the toe of a chunky boot pressed on the joint of his still-functioning wing. 'As soon as your little friend gets here, we can finish the show.' She rolled her toe, grinding the bones of his wing joint to show she wasn't kidding. He could feel the jagged edge of a chipped front tooth jutting against his tongue.

He'd been hit around the face with a blunt object before he'd laid eyes on any of the people there, but recognised the woman's voice; a vicious, vindictive snarl that could turn to honeyed charm in an instant. Izobella Cain. The tiled floor was bitterly cold on his bare chest, but nowhere near as cold as the realisation that he'd walked right into some kind of trap.

'Get him up.' Another voice swam among the pounding in his ears.

Two figures dragged him to his feet. He'd expected a whole audience, but instead he was met with the faces of Izzy and the Apollo clerk, Mrs Murnard. The rest of the vast space was empty but for a figure in the corner. She was standing half in shadow, the shimmer of sequins on her dress catching little pockets of light. Her obscured face was surrounded by a crown of back-combed blonde hair that bobbed as she slowly walked towards them.

'Kendra?' Erron spluttered, confused.

She appeared out of the gloom, her bold makeup glowing by the moonlight that thinly painted the walls and floor. The expression on her face was unreadable.

'You look surprised, Grover,' she finally said, her voice as cold as the floor beneath him.

'No shit,' he replied, coughing in an attempt to clear the blood from his nose and mouth.

'You know, it's nothing personal. You just fit the bill perfectly, and I have been waiting for this opportunity for a long time. You and Agent Hart of course. He'll be here soon.'

Erron's eyes widened in horror. 'Whatever this is, leave him out of it.'

Kendra smiled a cold, callous smile. 'I'm afraid I can't do that; you are both equally important. It's a shame. I actually liked Hart.'

Before Erron could react, he was manhandled onto an iron cross by Izzy and Mrs Murnard, where his wrists were cable-tied to the horizontal bar. A second, empty iron cross stood nearby.

'He'll be here soon.' Mrs Murnard checked her watch and spoke in a deep, masculine voice unlike her own. Erron's heart tightened. It was the same voice that had coaxed him to the meeting place.

'I should have known you were evil, you shrivelled, toad-faced bitch.' Erron spat blood at her.

'Good and evil doesn't even come into it, Agent Grover. The world has been under the governance of the Fates for too long now. It's time for a change.' Mrs Murnard's features began to alter, her body twisting and cracking as her spine elongated and muscles morphed in a grotesque rhythm. Erron felt nauseous at the sight of the transformation. Her skin stretched and bulged, shrank back and re-formed, the sound of crunching bones putting Erron's teeth on edge. Slowly, Mrs Murnard transformed into a seven-foot tall form with long dark hair, covered in tattooed runes. Beneath his asymmetrical coat, clawed feet protruded, and a long red tail rested on the floor.

The Lord of Chaos spoke, stretching into his new form and cracking his neck to get comfortable. 'I have waited centuries for this moment.'

'Elzifur. You are in breach of so many rules right now. So many.' Erron cursed himself for not saying something more badass, instead coming out with something Casey might say. Elzifur laughed dryly. 'Oh, I am *so* scared. If it hasn't escaped your notice, I happen to run the Chaos realm. Rules only apply in your world and, guess what, I am almost in charge of that too.'

As he spoke, Kendra and Izzy began wheeling tall panels draped in cloth over to the iron crosses. They moved them into

341

a wide semicircle surrounding Erron before removing the drapes, revealing seven full-length mirrors. A further one was laid out on the floor in the centre. Erron could clearly see himself in some of them. He winced at the sight of his battered body, as if seeing the injuries made him feel them twice as much. His face was a colourful tapestry of cuts and bruises, a stream of blood running down his face. He barely recognised himself, his limp wing hanging loose by his side, tugging at the raw skin on his back where the strange runes had been carved. But as he stared at the mirrors, his reflection grew darker as the seconds passed, swirling into an image of empty greyness. Kendra placed two plastic buckets on the floor by each cross.

'What the hell is all this?' he demanded, looking frantically at the half-circle of mirrors. A cold sweat was creeping down his back.

'You were such an easy target, Grover,' Kendra stated with a wry smile. 'I would have thought an ex-detective would have connected the dots a lot faster. But that doesn't matter now, it's you and Casey we have been waiting for, for so long. Months of planning, all amounting to this glorious moment.'

'Care to let me in on this grand plan of yours?' Erron struggled against his ties.

Kendra fell silent, picking at the peeling nail polish on one hand before she spoke. 'For decades I have been subservient to the Fates. Living some corporate half-life, toiling away for their mysterious grand scheme of destiny,' she said, not taking her eyes off her chipped nails. 'My previous life was so full of energy. I was wanted and adored by so many.' She wrinkled her face into a miserable snarl. 'Now look at me. I don't belong in this world full of boring rules and obligations.' She rolled her eyes. 'Then I met someone who made me feel alive again, who promised me the excitement of my former life by his side.'

Kendra smiled warmly at Elzifur, crossing the floor to cling to his arm. 'He gave me a glimpse of everything I could be again: young, beautiful, powerful even. But I couldn't be with him unless our worlds merged. It was a no-brainer, Erron. I could sacrifice a handful of people, and in return, I would get the life I deserve, and the man that everyone on the planet would envy me for.'

'You *stupid*, selfish piece of shit,' Erron seethed. 'Do you honestly think he would want *you*? A garish, bossy, shallow cow with plastic earrings and more sequins than a disco ball on steroids? Let's not forget the fact he is a whole fucking demon! He has a tail, for crying out loud.'

'He loves me!' she screamed, her eyes bulging. 'No one else could have done what I have done for him. No one else is smart enough, or loyal enough to change the world for him! He loves me because I would do anything for him. I have *killed* for him!'

Erron shook his head slowly. 'That's not love, Kendra.'

'Yeah? And how would you know, Grover? At least I'm able to admit my feelings. You're so terrified of yours that you became the perfect target.'

Erron scrunched up his face with confusion. Elzifur had walked away and was pacing by the window, clearly impatient for Casey to arrive.

'You think you just happened to be here? In the middle of all of this?' Kendra let out a mocking laugh. 'I've been watching

343

you for years, Grover. You and Hart, both incapable of outwardly expressing love. And yet so full of it. Your blood is coursing with it, unspoken and pure. The type of blood that will complete our ritual without fault. All I had to do was engineer events so you were ostracised from the agency long enough for us to make our preparations. With the focus on you and Hart, we were able to get everything ready without suspicion. Now we just need Hart to get here and we'll be ready.'

'So all that blood mixing rubbish, that was just an elaborate distraction?' Erron spat another mouthful of blood on the floor.

'Oh no, we needed that. In fact, that was what made it all work so perfectly! You see, a mix of Hades and Apollo blood allows the agent to turn to shadow and possess mortals, making it so easy to kill them. Of course, they see the shadow just before it takes over, just adding to the illusion they caused their own deaths,' Kendra explained with a smile.

Erron shook his head. 'What have you become?'

Kendra ignored him and checked her watch. 'Hart should be here by now.'

'Why go to such lengths? Why didn't you and Izzy just poison them all or something?'

Izzy, who had been leaning on the second cross, looked up and rolled her eyes at the suggestion.

'Ha!' Kendra scoffed. 'Do you think these things are that easy? No, we had to follow a specific recipe to get this result; those golden arrows falling in quick succession were everything we had been waiting for. Do you know how rare that is?' Kendra seemed to revel in the genius of her plan, almost expecting

Erron to applaud her efforts. 'It nearly unravelled when that stuck-up bitch Freya saw Elzifur in my office. Luckily, we got to her in time.'

Elzifur paced back over and stood in front of Erron. 'Oh yes, she was most unfortunate.'

Anger and bile rose in Erron's stomach. 'What did you do to her?'

'I just gave your little friend a tap on the head and threw her in the Thames. She must be out to sea by now.' He grinned, his eyes cold and empty.

'She deserved it,' Kendra seethed.

'I think he's heard enough,' Elzifur said. '... My darling,' he added through clenched teeth. 'Izzy, gag Agent Grover, will you?'

Erron turned his attention to Izzy, who was smiling sweetly at him, holding a piece of torn cloth. 'Izzy, you deserve to rot for your part in all this. I suppose you've got some grand plan of being all powerful too,' he spat.

Izzy thrust the cloth in his mouth and tied it roughly around the back of his head. She leant forward to whisper in his ear. 'I'll have all the power I need by making you pay for hurting me so many times.' She checked the knot on the gag and stepped back a little. 'It's a shame. We could have been great together, but you don't know a good thing when it's right in front of you. Maybe you'll come around in time.'

Erron made a face of disgust and pulled away from her as best he could.

'Izzy, the blade.' Elzifur held out one hand.

The Reaper pulled a foot-long black blade from her belt. It was shaped with a handle of goat horns, a gnarled and twisted pommel, and had a menacingly jagged edge down one side of the blade.

'You see, now we only need to kill you and Hart, and then the new world, *my* world, will begin,' Kendra said. 'We're so close now.'

'Wait, you're not actually going to *kill* him, right?' Izzy laughed nervously. 'You just said you needed some of his blood to open the portals.'

'Honey, if we only needed some blood we could have done that ourselves,' Kendra explained. 'Now hand over the blade.'

Izzy remained still. 'Can't you just use Hart?'

'It's not enough. We need both of them, to fill these with their blood.' She gestured towards the two buckets she'd placed down earlier. 'Izzy, listen to me. Erron doesn't love you and never has. Think of all those times he's ignored you. Why would you want to waste your time with a man that does that?' Kendra urged. 'We let you have your fun humiliating him, and it worked brilliantly to make him the prime suspect. Now we have to finish the job.'

'Izobella,' Elzifur hissed, taking a step towards the Reaper. 'I could snap your neck in a moment if you refuse to cooperate. Now ... let's keep this polite.' He opened his clawed hand to her.

Reluctantly, Izzy handed over the blade to him.

Elzifur approached Erron, his red eyes full of bloodlust. 'This is the part I am really going to enjoy. This dagger was forged before life itself, when Chaos ran the entire universe. Made from the very dark matter that sucks light from the stars. Ironic really, as it's the very same starlight that keeps that replacement heart of yours beating.' He pressed the flat of the blade gently across Erron's chest. 'Don't worry, I'm not going to kill you until your friend arrives. But I do need to raise my army with a small offering.' He grinned wildly, bearing hideous needle-like teeth.

The sound of hurried footsteps and voices yelling Erron and Casey's names echoed from the staircase. Elzifur snapped his attention towards the door to the stairwell. 'Looks like the cavalry has arrived,' he spat, turning swiftly back to Kendra and Izobella. 'Go and see who that is and hold them off. Nothing can go wrong tonight. Not now.'

'Anything for you, my love,' Kendra replied, fluttering her oversized lashes at him. 'Don't start without me!'

'Well, I can't do anything until Casey gets here, so don't worry about a thing . . . my love,' Elzifur replied through gritted teeth.

Kendra grinned like a besotted schoolgirl, hurrying out of the room and towards the stairs, Izzy close behind her.

Elzifur turned back to his prisoner and pressed the point of the dagger into Erron's upper chest, just enough to draw blood.

'My agents, they're like sharks. They can smell a drop of cosmic blood from miles away.' The Lord of Chaos flicked the blade at the mirror on the floor, leaving three small spatters of blood on the glass. Within a moment, the surface began to pulsate, gradually revealing the shadows of twisted and clawed hands pawing and groping from the other side, eager to escape. 'You are doing me a great service, Agent Grover. You see, no such thing as love exists in the Chaos Realm, and so your blood is so sweet to them. Yours and Casey's hearts are especially full to the brim of this ultimate delicacy. Unspent love, pent-up and concentrated, so I am told. You are the perfect sacrificial lambs, powerful enough to tear the veil completely.'

Erron sagged against the iron frame, feeling utterly defeated. He wanted to plead, bargain somehow for Casey's life, but nothing came through the gag but muffled noises of anger and despair.

39

Stay

THE LIFT HAD BEEN JAMMED so Nikita and Emrys were tiring as they climbed flight after flight of stairs, calling out for Erron and Casey in the hope they weren't too late. They heaved the weight of an archangel trauma kit with them that Emrys always kept in his car. The Sky Pod Bar was on the thirty-fifth floor, and at floor twenty-nine, Kendra practically ran into them. Izzy hung back, just out of view.

'Emrys, Agent Wolf!' Kendra exclaimed, clutching a hand to her chest as she caught her breath. 'What are you doing here?'

'I was about to ask you the same thing,' Nikita replied.

She clamoured for a reasonable explanation. 'I was tipped off that something bad was going to happen here . . . but there's no one here, it's all clear.'

Quietly, in the darkness of the next landing above, Izzy was attempting to prise open the emergency axe case on the wall.

'Why were you running?' Emrys asked.

'I was jogging down to save you the trouble of climbing any higher.' Kendra pushed her hair off her clammy forehead and straightened her dress.

'Drop the act, Kendra. I know you are behind these deaths. I've got CCTV footage of you at the scene in Farringdon,' Nikita said coldly. 'You've worked extra hard to set up Erron for all this, haven't you?'

'I have no idea what you're talking about.' Kendra's eyes narrowed.

'Oh yeah? We've got you at the scene of Sofia's death, we've got photos of the switched gold assignment cards, and not to mention the file with everything you carefully engineered to put Erron in the firing line, including a so-called confession written in the same handwriting as the fake suicide notes. We've got all the evidence we need to prove your involvement.'

Kendra stopped the pretence. 'It's too late anyway, the new world is going to shatter this one, and all your efforts will be in vain,' she hissed.

'It's never too late, until it's too late,' Nikita retorted. 'You'll be obliterated for this. I will make sure of it.'

Kendra's eyes widened and she made a dash to get past them, but Nikita blocked her, pushing her backwards onto the hard stairs. She yelped and tried to scramble to her feet, but Emrys grabbed her arm and twisted it to detain her.

The emergency lights in the stairwell flickered and crackled in unison. An unearthly silence fell, prickling the hairs on the back of Nikita's neck. Between the flickers of light, she could see a dark shadowy figure climbing the stairs, two at a time, but silent as the grave. D-O-A joined them, just as a feral scream pierced the silence and Izzy flung herself

350

down the stairs towards them, brandishing the axe. It whistled past Nikita's left ear and hit the handrail with an almighty crack, wedging itself momentarily in the laminated wood. Kendra had used the distraction to break free of Emrys and barrelled herself into him, sending them both rolling down the stairs.

'Emrys!' Nikita cried out just as Izzy pulled the axe free and started swinging it behind her head, ready to strike again. Nikita ducked and D-O-A dived towards Izzy, taking the brunt of her downward swing, the axe grazing the skin off his shoulder before glancing off at an angle. The young Reaper was flighty, and wriggled free of his grasp, making her way down to the landing, where Emrys was pushing Kendra off him.

'Nobody move!' Izzy bellowed, pointing the axe at Emrys's chest.

The Fortuna boss raised his hands slowly.

'Nobody move,' she repeated, her hands shaking with the weight of the axe. 'I swear, do not tempt me.'

Kendra pulled herself free of the tangle and stood shakily, touching her arm, which had been injured in the fall, with trepidation. 'Izzy, kill them now, be done with it!' she hissed.

Izzy raised the axe, Emrys braced himself, waiting for her to swing. Nikita launched herself down the stairs at the Reaper, landing on her with a sickening thud as they crashed into the wall. The axe clattered to the floor and Nikita was knocked out cold. D-O-A jogged down to them just as the dazed Izzy was frantically scrabbling for the axe. Unable to reach it, and pinned by the unconscious body of Nikita, Izzy grabbed Kendra's leg and plunged her teeth into it, drawing blood and causing the Apollo boss to scream and stagger backwards. She teetered awkwardly at the edge of the lower flight of stairs, before losing her balance and tumbling down the steps and landing in a bloodied, broken heap at the bottom.

D-O-A quickly realised exactly what Izzy was trying to do, as she bit her own arm to mix her blood with Kendra's. The only way he could intercept her, if she turned into a moving shadow, was to do the same. He bit his own lip hard, then ripped the bandage off Nikita's palm from where she'd drawn her own blood for Dantalion and pressed his mouth to her wound. Izzy began to evaporate into a dark swirl of shadow while trying to ascend the stairs. D-O-A followed, his body slowly changing into a roiling mass of shapeless dark, swiftly catching up to Izzy, and pulling her backwards with such force she was shocked out of her emerging shadow form. She found herself standing on the edge of a step, with D-O-A's hand gripping her hair tightly. He wasted no time and whipped her head back hard, throwing her down towards where Nikita lay. She skidded towards the wall next to the concussed Cupid, her body going limp as she smashed against it.

Emrys cradled Nikita, pleading with her to wake up, rocking her back and forth. D-O-A knelt beside them and examined the young woman's head and neck.

Urgent footsteps were heading up the stairs towards them, and Casey appeared, out of breath and pale after having had to step over the disfigured body of Kendra on the stairs below.

'Casey, we haven't found Erron. He must be upstairs,' Emrys spluttered.

'I know where he'll be,' Casey puffed.

'Get to him quick, we have no idea what's happening up there. We'll be there as soon as we can.'

Nikita was gradually coming round, her skin already swelling and darkening around one eye. D-O-A, having fully returned to his normal state, dragged Izzy to the banister, where he twisted her hands behind her and used his belt to secure her to the railings. Casey continued his climb, racing up the last six flights as fast as he could go, the stairwell far too narrow for his wings to be of any use.

He burst through the doors of the Sky Pod Bar with no degree of caution, somewhat hoping that Kendra and Izzy were all the resistance that he would have encountered. The blood drained from his face the moment he saw Elzifur. He was standing close to Erron, slowly dragging a dagger across his chest with a wry smile on his face. The demon was using the flicks of blood to spatter the glass of several mirrors, each filled with hideous shapes clawing and pushing their way to the edge of the veil.

The moment he spotted Casey emerge from the shadows, Erron desperately tried to shout through his gag, his eyes wide and bloodshot.

The demon spun around, eyes burning with madness. 'Well now, finally we can finish the show!' He cackled, pressing the tip of the blade against Erron's throat. 'Put your bow down, Hart, and come over here.'

Casey raised his hands slowly. 'Don't do anything stupid. I'll do as you say, just put the knife down.'

Elzifur narrowed his eyes and gestured with his free hand for Casey to approach. Casey steadily walked forward, despite Erron's muffled warning cries. He placed the bow carefully on the floor, raising his hands once more. The demon nodded towards the second iron cross.

'Loop your hands through the cable ties on the bar,' he barked, pressing the dagger into Erron's neck just enough to make him cry out. 'Do it quickly, or I'll slit his throat right now.'

'OK, OK, just go easy there.' Casey was trembling as he did as he was asked, desperately hoping for the others to come through the door in a righteous fury. He thought, perhaps, that he could stall the demon long enough for help to arrive. But Elzifur moved so fast, pulling the cable ties tight around Casey's wrists and securing him to the cross. Suddenly, he was just as helpless as Erron. Casey tried to remain calm.

'This all looks like some terrible type of magic trick,' he blustered, his nerves on edge. 'I don't know what you are planning to achieve here, but it's not going to end well.'

'Oh, but it *is* a magic trick, Agent Hart!' Elzifur laughed heartily. 'I get to change the entire world, in exchange for two pathetic Cupids. A very fair trade I would say, and what wonders the world will be witness to!'

'Oh . . .' Casey racked his brains for a suitable response, but he had none. He heard the imperceptible squeak of a door opening while the demon waffled on about how marvellous his new realm would be. Outside, the storm was building pace, ferocious winds whipping against the window.

'With each drop of blood you spill, reality shatters just a little more. Observe!' Elzifur spun back to Erron and ran the blade down his forearm, taking great pleasure in collecting the blood in his palm and smearing it on a nearby mirror. The glass was beginning to bulge with the ghostly hands, the grotesque images growing more three-dimensional as they clamoured against the veil. Outside, a great crack of thunder shook the windows, sending neon purple lightning crazing across the sky. A flurry of yellow rubber ducks on the wind slapped against the glass, all squeaking loudly as they had the air knocked out of them.

Ordinarily, Casey wouldn't have been able to resist saying something along the lines of *Strange weather we're having . . .* or *We don't usually get rubber ducks this early in the year.* But all he could muster was a quiet, and pitiful, 'Please stop.'

Meanwhile, Nikita, her head still pounding from the fall, had managed to creep into the room unnoticed. She crawled towards the bar, clutching the trauma kit in her hand, and tucked herself behind it. She'd left Emrys and D-O-A on the stairs securing Izzy and checking Kendra for any vital signs, and she'd promised Emrys she would only look through the window and report back. Worried for her safety, he bestowed a kiss of *Fortuna Diaboli* on her, and told her to hurry back the moment she had assessed the situation. As she surveyed the room from behind the bar, she caught Casey's eye. She gestured for him to stay quiet while she looked around for something that could cut the cable ties, eventually locating a small paring knife on the worktop. She could feel the gift of luck coursing through her. It was incredibly intoxicating and she was determined to use it to its full potential.

Elzifur had returned to tormenting Erron. 'You see, I am not burdened by love, or any of the structures that revolve around it. Think about it, what good has love done to this world? People go to war for it, they work themselves to death over it, they stay in horrendous places and situations for it. People do terrible things in the name of love, and it does nothing but ruin them. It's a force of destruction wrapped up in a sentiment of sparkly hearts. Humans are weak, driven by this putrid emotion. There will be no place for them in my new world.'

The rubber-duck storm was lashing against the glass and the lightning was a spectrum of technicolour. The odd jar of Marmite floated by on the wind, at a much slower pace than the weather would have dictated.

The demon lowered the blade and paused. 'I suppose, as you are giving me the gift of the Earth, Agent Grover, I ought to ask you if you have any final words. Apparently that's tradition in your world and I will honour that before my legions of Chaos lay waste to any such notions. A parting gesture, you might say.' He pulled the gag from Erron's mouth, just as the agent caught a glimpse of Nikita behind the bar. He needed to keep Elzifur distracted for as long as he could.

Erron coughed and inhaled deeply. The cuts on his chest stung and his mouth tasted like blood. 'You've got it all wrong,' he finally said. 'It's not love that drives people to war, it's greed, or hatred, or some false god that dictates people to kill in its honour. It's not love that causes people to stay in bad situations or work themselves to death, it's fear, hopelessness, poverty, abuse or this endless conveyor belt of disaster capitalism. If anything, love doesn't survive in this world, people are just slaves to an outdated system. And people who choose to love aren't weak, they are fighting for peace in a world full of hate and instability. With every act of kindness, every time they choose to walk away, every time they stand up for others, they show defiance in the face of evil. Love was never the problem.'

Without quite understanding why, Nikita grabbed a lemon from a basket on the counter and stuffed it into her pocket.

All she could do was trust the luck that Emrys had bestowed her with. Erron was still speaking, allowing Nikita to creep towards Casey and begin cutting his ties.

Suddenly alert to the movement behind him, Elzifur spun round and charged at Casey just as he was released from the bar. Nikita skidded out of the way as Casey instinctively reached for his bow, picking it up just in time to block the slash of the dagger as the demon collided with him, sending the blade skittering across the floor. Scrambling to her feet, Nikita wasted no time in helping Erron, working the blunt knife through the ties as quickly as she could. Elzifur and Casey tumbled to the ground, landing hard on the floor mirror, which shattered under their weight. They scrabbled for the upper hand, the pieces of mirror cutting deep into their skin as they tumbled over one another. Elzifur pinned Casey down and punched him in the face before pressing his thumbs hard into the Cupid's throat.

'Casey,' Erron rasped, nodding to Nikita to help his friend first as the ties were partly sawn through.

Casey was gasping for air and clawing at the demon, his bloodied nose blocking his airway further. The pressure on his throat instantly released when the demon was knocked sideways by a well-aimed lemon thrown with astounding force. He rolled to one side and went for the blade.

The terrifying figures that pressed themselves up to the veil became frenzied in the remaining mirrors. Their eerie wails began to resonate around the vast space, prickling the hairs on the back of Nikita's neck. She turned back to Erron and snapped the last tie on his wrist just as Elzifur raised the dagger over Casey's chest. Erron mustered the last of his strength and ran at the demon, letting out a blood-curdling war cry as he did so.

Elzifur instinctively turned and there was a sickening thud as Erron reached him. Time stood still and silence fell, as Erron looked down to see the dagger imbedded in his stomach. He staggered back as the demon pulled the dagger free, twisting it as he did so.

'Well, that wasn't exactly how I wanted to kill you, but I guess I can't complain,' Elzifur said coldly, as Erron collapsed to the floor, his hands powerlessly trying to stem the gushing blood from his wound. He paled, his skin glistening with a cold sheen of sweat as the cosmic lifeforce was draining across the polished floor.

Casey, seeing Erron crash to the ground, was overtaken with burning fury, a righteous rage that he couldn't contain. His blood felt like it was on fire. Something in him was changing rapidly. His usual passive demeanour was flooded with an overwhelming need for vengeance; it tasted hot and bitter in his mouth, his heart pounding hard against his ribs, each beat a drum calling him to war. He clawed his way to his feet, bruised and trembling hands pulling out the gold arrow he'd held onto since the Hoffmann assignment and loaded it to his bow. His wings opened violently, causing a rush of displaced air, and his feathers blazed black with the smoke and flaming embers of Nemesis. Elzifur stumbled back in shock. Casey's white wood bow blazed with bright fire as he shot Elzifur with such force that he sent the demon hurtling back into the row of mirrors, where he was absorbed through the glass as if falling into treacle, disappearing beyond the veil. Nikita wasted no time in picking up a nearby chair and smashing the mirror, sending fragments chittering across the floor.

Erron was gasping in short, shallow breaths as his stomach pulsed with blood. In a matter of seconds, Casey had dropped the bow and was at his side, screaming for anything to help slow the bleeding.

Minutes passed in a blur.

Emrys charged into the room as Nikita threw the contents of the trauma kit over the floor. Casey, drenched in blood, was wrist-deep in Erron's haemorrhaging stomach, putting pressure on the wound to stem the bleeding. Emrys had already made a panicked call to the Raphael Sanctuary but, with the storm raging outside, it would be nearly impossible to reach them in time.

D-O-A approached them slowly, respectfully, holding a card in both hands.

Sweat and tears stinging Casey's eyes, he looked up at D-O-A in horror. 'You get the fuck away from him! I'm a doctor. It's my job to keep you the fuck away from people.'

'Darren, please, give him a chance,' Nikita begged.

D-O-A looked down at the card bearing the newly inked name with the day's date: *Erron Christopher Grover. Time of death 21.17.* He looked at his watch, it was 21.10.

Emrys crouched beside Erron, shining a torch for Casey to see the wound better. Artfully, with trembling hands, he began packing the wound with medical gauze, attempting to stop the bleeding. But, for the second time in his existence, Erron was dying. Nikita was holding D-O-A back, frantically pleading with him to just wait a little longer. He raised his hands in submission as Casey performed CPR on Erron's limp body. At

21.14, a team of archangel paramedics arrived, their wings of pure light making the whole scene glow, as they set up a flight gurney to rush Erron back to their trauma unit. In a blaze of light, Erron and the archangels were gone.

Casey knelt in a pool of blood, shaking violently and sobbing into his hands.

'I'm sorry but I have to follow,' D-O-A murmured to Nikita, spreading his huge black feathered wings and jumping out of the window in the wake of the paramedics before she could stop him.

Nikita held Casey as if he would fall through the floor if she let go.

40

Who Wants to Live Forever

A N HOUR PASSED.
Casey sat wrapped in a blanket in the cold hallway of the Raphael Sanctuary staring at the floor. He clutched the shirt and tie that had been cut off Erron, holding on to it with such grim compulsion as if it might keep his friend tethered to the living world. Nikita sat with him in silence, her hand resting on his forearm. Osato arrived at the hospital a little later, having been caught up with the others dealing with the aftermath at the bar. It had taken her so long to reach Fenchurch Street through the chaos unfolding in the streets that she'd only arrived in time to deal with the destruction of the remaining portal mirrors. Kendra had been pronounced dead from the fall and Izzy had been taken away into custody by Lian Zhang so Osato could head straight over to the hospital. There was nothing that could be done with Kendra: she wouldn't be making any appearance in the afterlife and had ceased to exist aside from the crumpled replicated body that would need to be disposed of by Hades. They had a way of dissolving a replicated soul, using what was known as

the Ferryman's touch, and Kendra's consciousness would not live on in any way, shape or form.

Osato crouched down in front of Casey and reached for his hand. His face was battered and bruised, the dried blood crusting to his skin and clumps of his long hair hanging limply over his face. 'You did your best, Cassiel,' she soothed. 'I'm so sorry.'

Silently, he nodded, withdrawing his hand.

All three of them looked up when the hall doors swung open and D-O-A walked through. He approached Casey and handed him a card:

Erron Christopher Grover. Time of Death – INCOMPLETE.

'You're a good doctor,' D-O-A affirmed as Casey dropped to his knees, sobbing with relief.

* * *

Erron, on account of his severe injuries, took a long time to recover from the ordeal. He spent twelve days in ICU and another six on a standard recuperation ward at the Raphael Sanctuary. Casey sat by his bedside for every single one of those days, but only while Erron was sedated. He always left before Erron woke up, going home to sleep or read or wander aimlessly around the streets of London.

Freya had made a much faster recovery and was back in the office within a week, a little battered and bruised, but driven to return to active duty. She'd quickly started Nikita on her formal training to get her up to speed and, within two weeks, Nikita had undertaken her first few assignments under supervision and was showing real promise as an excellent marksman.

On her time off the clock, she visited Erron, giving him updates when he was lucid enough to hold a conversation, and reading to him when he was not. It was on a lucid day, when he was sitting up in bed, that he asked her to do him a favour.

'So, it turns out Elzifur had been playing the part of Mrs Murnard for years. She was never a real person at all; Kendra had made the job opening so she could legitimately have him in the office, keeping tabs on everyone all that time,' Nikita explained, as Erron lazily prodded at the hospital food on his tray.

'I should've known. Evil witch,' he muttered. 'And Kendra?'

'Kendra was just Kendra, but she was desperately in love with Elzifur and he'd promised her the world. She was convinced he felt the same. I think he had been manipulating her for quite some time; she was shallow, easily led, and he fed on her insecurities. She must have been under his spell for so long that she didn't even stop to think of the consequences. I pity her really; she didn't survive her injuries.'

'Maybe he was right that people do some terrible things for love,' Erron said quietly.

'No, that wasn't love. It was infatuation, obsession. Nothing more.'

They were both quiet for a bit, Nikita staring out of the window at the bright sunrise, its golden light sparkling off the many skyscrapers nearby.

'It's beautiful. I see that now,' Erron said, gazing wistfully at the early birds in flight, dancing among the pink and orange wisps of dawn cloud.

'You know, he visits you every day,' Nikita finally said.

Erron didn't answer.

'You need to talk. He knows you weren't involved. He knew you were innocent before he turned up at the Sky Pod Bar,' she pressed.

Erron exhaled slowly. 'I feel awful. I lied to him, said some awful things, never told him how I was trying to transfer. Then all this. He must hate me for that.'

'He doesn't, Erron, he saved your life. He knows you weren't to blame for the world nearly ending.'

'He hasn't been here while I've been awake. I don't blame him; I've been a terrible friend.' He pushed around the stodgy omelette on his plate.

Nikita placed her hand over his. 'What you went through is not your fault. Casey doesn't blame you, he just doesn't know what to say to you at the moment. He told me that you both fell out before all this, and I think he blames himself more than anything.' She paused for a moment, but he didn't answer. 'You should have seen him; he went full renegade with Nemesis wings of fire and everything. He was granted a Cosmic Shift by the Fates. And, my god, did he get revenge for you.'

There was a long silence.

'This food is fucking awful,' Erron finally deflected.

She sat back and rolled her eyes. 'It's so bad to make you get better faster, so you can go home and cook.'

The sun reached its morning height over the tops of the buildings, washing the hospital ward in a bright golden hue.

'Well, I've got to get going. I'm making good progress with Freya. It's a shame you guys aren't training me, I heard you were pretty good agents back in the day.' She winked at him and dropped a newspaper on his bedside table. 'Read some of the headlines about the fractures; the media are having a frenzy about the Marmite problem, of all things. They've come up with all kinds of weird and wonderful explanations. My favourite is a guy claiming the world will end with The Great Goose Invasion and they are after our souls. He's written an article called "The Four Hundred Geesemen of the Apocalypse". It's splattered all over the press. Needless to say, the media are covering up as much as possible to prevent any more panic. Oh, before I forget, since you asked so nicely, I managed to get hold of this.' She pulled a thick manila file full of loose pages from her bag. The front was marked 'Confidential – Personnel'.

He watched her tuck it under the newspaper.

'Don't take too long with it, I'll need to put it back before anyone notices it's missing.'

'Nikita, wait.' Erron shifted his position with painstaking care. 'I need to ask another favour.'

'Sure, but I'm not trained in sponge baths.'

He threw her a disdainful look. 'This is far more important. Do you have the key to my flat?'

'Freya has it. She's been going there to feed your fish. What do you need?'

He explained his request and she agreed to get it sorted, leaving him to paw at his omelette and take idle glances at the newspaper headlines between resentful mouthfuls.

41

Bleeding Love

ON THE THIRTEENTH OF FEBRUARY, Casey sat in the vast black and white office of Osato M'Raya, flanked by Freya Carthage and Emrys Taliesin. He was hunched over, worn out and thin, hands pressed together in a tight ball.

'Naturally, you will be reinstated in full with compensation, Agent Hart,' Osato announced, the file of evidence splayed over the desk. 'Unless you wish to opt for retirement, in which case you will be offered a range of staff positions or full retirement to the afterlife with immediate effect. The Fates look down on you with great pride, and your comfort in retirement is guaranteed. You were gifted the first case of a Cosmic Shift recorded in agency history in over two thousand years, it's very commendable.'

Usually, he would have firmly rejected any suggestion of retirement, but he wavered this time, still struggling to come to terms with the events of the past few weeks.

'You don't have to make a decision any time soon, of course. If you require it, you will be granted a six-month leave of absence on full pay to recover. You saved the world, Casey, I can't express to you how strongly we want you to stay.'

When he finally spoke, his voice trembled slightly with sheer emotional exhaustion. 'What about Erron?'

She exhaled slowly, pushing the papers in front of her into a neat pile. 'Hades have accepted his application to their division. He has not yet been able to respond, but either way he will still have a job with the agency. Given what one of the Hades agents did to him, I am unsure whether he will still accept their offer of a position. But all charges against him have been dropped, you'll be glad to know. I've also had word that he was released from hospital yesterday. Is that right, Freya?'

'Yes, I met him at the Raphael Sanctuary to help him home. He's still resting up.'

'And Izobella Cain?' Casey asked.

'Is under armed guard at our custodial facility in the Oblivion Fields. Lettie Crawford is holding a Hades trial to sentence her to her punishment. From studying the evidence, she was being heavily influenced by the other guilty parties so it's not yet clear if she will be granted a lesser sentence than obliteration. Upper management are dealing with the aftermath of what Elzifur left behind, in this realm and his own, but all the portals have been successfully closed.'

Nikita was waiting outside the office for Casey, leaning against the door pillar and pretending not to be eavesdropping. Once their meeting ended, she caught him as he was leaving.

'Casey, have you got a moment?' she asked quietly.

'Sure. What do you need?'

'I know you probably don't feel up to it, but I've got a couple of tickets to the "From Persia to Greece" exhibition tomorrow.

I've been told you like history. It would be good for you to get out.'

'Umm . . . I don't know.' He pursed his lips.

'Please? It's only an hour or two. I'll treat you to lunch.'

He looked at her pleading face and gave in. 'I guess it wouldn't hurt. What time and where?' He ran his hand through the back of his tousled hair and sighed.

'It's two o'clock at the Natural History Museum.' She handed him a ticket with the details. She stood on her tiptoes and kissed him on the cheek before leaving.

* * *

The previous day, Erron had faltered when he reached his front door, not wanting to see the bloodstains or the carnage left in the wake of his assault. Freya gripped his arm gently and took the key.

'It's OK.' She unlocked the door and led him in.

She'd taken care of everything ahead of his arrival. She'd binned anything damaged beyond repair and cleaned up any wreckage. Erron's bedding and sofa had been covered in dried blood, so she'd got rid of the bedding, put fresh sheets on and had hired a steam cleaner to remove the stains from the sofa. Most importantly, she'd kept his fish alive. Roscoe the Roomba was busy trundling around, hunting Coco-Pops.

'Right, tough guy, get yourself to bed,' she'd instructed. 'You look like shit. I've got an hour if you want me to make you some food?'

'Please. I could eat anything right now. Even the contents of Rosc— I mean, the vacuum, would be more appetising than hospital food.' He shuffled over to the sofa, each movement a stab of pain.

Erron's wings had been stained a rusty red with his blood, and he only noticed when he caught a glimpse of himself in the tall, mirrored cabinets that flanked the bathroom door. He'd had the broken wing pinned in two places but was still struggling to keep it from dragging on the floor. His face was a mosaic of cuts and bruises, a line of butterfly stitches running from his forehead to his temple on one side. 'I really do look like shit,' he muttered to himself.

Freya popped her head around the door as he was examining his injuries. 'The first rule of Fight Club is—' she teased before he interjected.

'You can talk.' He raised an eyebrow at her.

'You're in luck, I got you the stuff to make a half-decent fry-up before you came home.' Freya went to paw through the fridge. 'How's that sound?'

'Like a hug from Jesus Himself.'

In response, she grabbed the relevant bits from the fridge and heated up a large pan as Erron precariously lowered himself onto the sofa.

'You going to be OK?' she'd asked after he'd eaten.

'I made it this far.'

'Well, I took the liberty of getting you a lasagne for later. It's not a microwave one so you'll have to read the instructions.'

'I'll figure it out.'

'Read the instructions, Erron. I know you well enough that you will just throw it in at gas mark fuck-it and hope for the best,' she scolded.

'OK, I'll read the damn instructions,' he promised.

'Well then, here's your agency phone back. I've left your hospital bag over there, and your instructions from the doctor are pinned on the fridge. Twenty-eight titanium staples, mister. Don't do anything strenuous.' She gave him a stern look.

Freya still had the faint shadow of bruising around her eye, and though her dark complexion had reduced, the noticeable impact of her injuries, the memory of her attack had gradually come back to her, giving her nightmares she'd never suffered before. She left him to his own devices and made her way back to work.

* * *

The Apollo Division headquarters was buzzing on Valentine's Day. The new assignment clerk was a Benjamin Griffiths, a chubby young man with a cheerful smile, who had retired as a Fortuna agent and joined the support staff, opting for a change of division for a fresh challenge. He greeted everyone with enthusiasm and stamped completed cards while humming a cheerful tune, a huge improvement on the miserable toad who once growled at them from behind the glass screen. The rumours about what had happened changed on a daily basis, so Osato finally put out an official statement to all divisions, covering the key aspects of the investigation, the fractures and the guilty parties. She'd added a strong summary that any suspicious circumstances or missed assignments would be dealt with swiftly in future. Kendra's replacement was being selected from a pool of capable applicants and a temporary manager was in place.

42

Power Over Me

CASEY GOT BACK HOME FROM the exhibition at half past seven in the evening, having enjoyed it enough to stay out for pizza with Nikita afterwards. As he closed his front door, he breathed in the familiar smell of cinnamon and his medley of flowering houseplants. He dropped his bag in the hall and pulled off his overcoat, glad to be home. Then he noticed the living room door. He never shut that door. His feeling of calm evaporated, and with great caution he entered the room, expecting a gang of violent burglars or, worse, Elzifur back from beyond the veil to exact his own revenge.

Nobody stood in his living room, but there was something strikingly different. There, on his wall, was a painting. Not just any painting, but the breathtaking *Liminal Zone* that he had dreamt of owning since he spotted it in the small Bedford gallery. He gazed at it for some time, heart in his mouth. Finally finding the courage, he pulled his phone from his pocket and scrolled down to Erron's work number, aware he no longer had his personal phone. He dialled with shaking hands, jumping in fright when he heard a crash of a plant pot on his roof terrace. The phone pressed to his ear, he climbed the spiral stairs to his bedroom and crossed the wood floor to the door just as Erron's answerphone cut in. He hung up and dialled again, dropping the phone at the sight of a winged figure having crash-landed awkwardly, backlit by the glow of the streetlights.

'Sorry about the plant,' Erron groaned, shaking compost off his hands, the shattered terracotta pot beneath him.

'I ... I was just calling you,' Casey whispered. 'How did you ... ? The painting ...' His words trailed off, hot tears stinging his eyes.

Erron picked himself up with considerable effort, brushing the dirt off his knees.

'There's no way you should be flying yet.' Casey went towards him to help, but Erron held his hand up, determined to straighten up and catch his breath on his own merit.

'Yeah ... well ... Happy birthday, Casey,' Erron said quietly. 'Do you ... do you still love the picture?'

'I do, so much, I can't begin to say how thankful ... Wait. How did you know it was my birthday?' It was something he had never divulged or celebrated since joining the agency. A rumble of thunder brought with it a light rain, quickly forming puddles on the terrace floor.

'You read my file?' Casey whispered.

The rain became persistent, but neither of the men wanted to move.

Erron exhaled, leaning his aching body against the rail, his hair plastering wet to his face, fat drops of rain collecting and dripping off the end of his nose. 'Yeah, I read it. End to end ... Casey Hart, previously Dr Cassiel Ephron Hartlowe, born fourteenth of February 1750. Was killed in 1783 by vigilantes because ...' He couldn't bring himself to say it.

Casey joined Erron at the railing and leant over, gazing at the puddles of reflected lamplight gathering in the wet streets below. 'Because of James Warren. Trainee physician, my student. He was twenty-seven. I knew by the way he stayed late, the way he looked at me, that he saw me as a lot more than just his teacher. I'd kept myself to myself all my life, Erron. No one asked why I wasn't married; they knew how much I loved my work. But James ... he was different. He made me feel that there was more to life than work. The night we confessed our feelings for each other, our conversation was overheard by the bellringer at the local church.' Casey paused, closing his eyes for a brief moment. 'I died for love, and never even got to experience how wonderful it could be. All those people I had treated, cured their ills, they all turned on me and—' He pinched back the tears forming in his eyes and cleared the lump from his throat.

Erron took a slight step closer. 'Those people don't matter anymore. None of them. They sent you here, where you belong. Making people happy.' He smiled weakly and pulled an orange cocktail umbrella from his shirt pocket, then carefully tucked it behind Casey's ear. 'It's what you were born to do.'

'You think so?' Casey touched the small umbrella and tilted his head questioningly. 'You think that's how fate works?'

'From what I know about fate, it gradually leans towards justice. In the end. Did you ever find out where James went?'

'When I found out about the afterlife, I tried so hard to get the Fates to release the information to me, but I never saw him again. There's no file for him here. I just hope that, wherever he is, he likes the ice cream. I know now that he was never my destiny. I stopped thinking about him a long time ago.'

Casey pulled the soggy cocktail umbrella from behind his ear and tucked it into his shirt pocket.

Erron shifted his feet and stared at the floor. 'I'm so sorry I never told you about the Hades position. If you ask me to stay, I will.'

Casey swept his sodden hair out of his eyes and sighed. 'Erron, don't throw your career away because of me. I was selfish, and I'm sorry. You do what makes you happy. I'll always be your friend, no matter what division you work for.'

'That's half the problem, Case.' He twiddled with the buttons on his jacket. 'About us being friends.'

Casey's heart sank like a lead balloon. 'You don't think we can still be friends if you're working elsewhere? After everything that's happened? I know I said some hurtful things too ...'

Erron took a deep breath as flickers of lightning cracked overhead. 'No ... see, the issue is, I *do* want to be your friend. But I want to be more than that. It's why I needed to change division, because ... because it was getting so goddamn difficult. But I can't bring myself to lose you.' He looked up at Casey's unreadable expression, bracing himself slightly. 'Casey, you're my best friend. But I am in love with you. I always have been.' He searched Casey's face, waiting for a response of any kind, so that his heart could start beating again and his lungs might manage to breathe once more.

Convinced he'd made a fool of himself, he looked back down at his feet, the rivulets of rain running cold down the back of his shirt. 'It's OK, you don't have to say anything. I've been the worst friend lately. And this is the last thing you need right now.'

A silence hung in the air between the rumbles of distant thunder, before Casey stepped forward decisively, lifted Erron's chin and kissed him. The rain pelted them in droves, but nothing mattered in that moment. Their sodden wings tentatively curled around one another, their hands clutching at each other like their hearts might explode if they let go. Casey pulled Erron closer into his chest and held him for a long time, not minding the rain, the cold or the door he'd left swinging in the wind. He rested his chin on the top of Erron's head, and could feel his cosmic racing heart, a shared ecstasy that wasn't from any illusion, charm or hormonal imbalance, and he was rapt with its presence.

Erron relaxed slightly when he realised Casey was trembling just as much as he was. All the fear he had harboured for so many years was evaporating. He had carried its leaden weight like a chain, and link by link it fell away with every touch of Casey's hair, every gentle pause for breath.

'Erron, I have loved you for longer than I can remember,' Casey said quietly. 'Good or bad, guilty or not, I wouldn't have let anyone take you away.'

'Apparently not even death.'

'Especially not death.'

Casey kissed Erron's forehead. 'Let's get you in the warm.'

* * *

Casey latched the terrace door against the hammering rain and offered Erron a blanket.

'You need to know something.' Erron shivered, pulling the blanket around his shoulders. 'Izzy ... the photos ...'

'Were not your fault, I know. Don't think for a moment I doubted you.' Casey wrapped his arms around him protectively.

'How did you know I was innocent of the blood mixing and all that?'

'I just knew. I knew you weren't capable of anything like that.'

Erron didn't know how to respond.

'One thing is puzzling me though; how did you get that painting in my house?' Casey asked.

'Ah, Nikita and Freya. They sorted it all for me. Why do you think you had to be out of the house this afternoon?' Erron was starting to feel dizzy, having gone against every bit of doctor's advice. 'I ... need to sit down.'

'Stay the night,' Casey said softly.

'I ought to get going really ...' Erron said, suddenly overcome by nerves and swaying a little with the pain.

'I've got a spare room; I didn't mean to rush anything. I won't make you stay, but you're not really supposed to be doing anything until you're fully healed, especially not late-evening flights in winter storms. I really wouldn't want to put you in a taxi either.' Casey helped him sit on the edge of the bed.

Erron pushed his rain-soaked hair out of his eyes and raised a quizzical eyebrow. 'Is that doctor's orders?'

'Doctor's orders,' Casey affirmed, gently placing a hand over Erron's sodden shirt and feeling the patchwork of surgical staples that adorned his stomach. 'Just for once, let someone take care of you?'

Erron brushed a few beads of rain from Casey's cheek with his thumb. 'I do need to be kept under observation,' he whispered.

Casey smiled shyly. 'Purely for observation only. I swear.'

The storm howled outside the bedroom window as rain lashed the glass, and bright forks of lightning blazed through the dark sky. Within the room, only the soft glow of candles illuminated the walls, where, among cosy blankets and nestled into a wing that wasn't his own, Erron slept.

Epilogue

THE FOLLOWING EVENING, ERRON AND Casey sat across from each other at their favourite table in the Sky Pod Bar, talking over the events of the past few weeks. As the sun set over the teeming streets of London below, Erron nursed a short measure of Scotch over the game of chess. The most serious fractures had subsided once Elzifur had been forced back into his realm but the after-effects were still fading, and the world goose population was still a matter for concern. Osato had discovered an old notebook in Kendra's office detailing a gruesome ritual allowing her to create a portal for Elzifur. The book was destroyed, and the veil had been restored as the natural order re-established itself. Elzifur would not be able to return to the mortal realm without an accomplice willing to sacrifice a lot to do so, though Osato had put stronger precautions in place to prevent any recurrence. She'd hoped to have been able to exact revenge on the demon herself, but the Lord of Chaos was once again banished and outside the reach of the Fates and any chance of justice.

Casey lifted his glass, a smile spread across his face, warm with the glow of the dying sun. 'To your new venture at Hades, Agent Grover.'

'Cheers.' He clinked glasses together. 'Never thought we'd get through this. But here we are. So, I've been meaning to ask, seeing as I read files now. Why did you change your name?'

Casey sat his drink down, moved a rook across the chessboard and folded his hands under his chin in thought. 'Cassiel is the angel of solitude. I've been lonely for long enough . . .' His gaze drifted to the skyline outside. 'Anyway . . . the sunset tonight is amazing, so much colour. You want to switch seats? You never sit and watch it.'

'Nope. I've always preferred this view.' Erron looked at him deeply, leaning forward, his hand deftly moving his queen sideways as he held Casey's stare. 'Checkmate.'

Casey looked at the board in horror. 'Bastard!'

Acknowledgements

In no particular order, my endless gratitude goes to the following: Gyamfia, my incredible agent, who saw through the chaos of my writing and found something sparkly to work with. You have been the most enthusiastic, hilarious delight of a human being to work with, and I owe you so much for putting up with every Zoom call that a dancing cactus answered. I wish you the best croissants life has to offer.

To my beloved Phil 'Noodle', who not only has my entire heart but will have my cosmic satsuma in the afterlife. You kept me motivated and continue to cheer me on relentlessly. You gave me hope that there is love among the ruins, you are the Frank to my Jane, this is our hill, and these are our beans. May we have eternity in Arcadia.

To my amazing editor Kelly and the publishing team, thank you for joining this goose-driven journey of after-living madness, I hope this venture proves worthy of your time and dedication. Your enthusiasm and extreme eye for detail over cloud types across counties is to be celebrated without question. I have nothing but admiration for all the effort you have put in to make this manuscript as masterful as possible. Sorry about the stolen chocolate orange, I will replace it.

Thank you to the family and friends that have been endlessly supportive of my journey. With special mention to Sarah Moret-Bevan, who gave me so much confidence to stand up for justice and inspired the creation of Osato M'Raya. Sarah Wilson and Jaime Holmes, the most awesome friends anyone could wish to have, we've been to Mordor and back and evil wigs will never conquer us, just steer clear of Kettering. Thank you to Dad for your exceptional enthusiasm about the book and for pushing me to develop writing through workshops at Bedford library. I only went because of the sticky buns from Baker's Oven. To Mum, Emma and Tash for helping me get where I am in life and for being part of my spiritual journey. My cat, Salem Saberhagen, the most loving and formidable familiar, who keeps my lap warm and my fridge empty. For Pluto, you are still a planet to me.

I owe my love of writing to the readers of this book, those who have already given me glowing feedback have really given me the confidence in myself to keep moving forward. I hope my words take you on an adventure that will stay with you for years to come. (For any hardcore fans, the book's original name is *Apollo Division* but we'll keep that between us.)

Lastly, I must mention my mechanic, Dean, who has had to fix my van more times than I can count and has listened to every update with the book. I hope one day I will be rich enough to bring a car in that doesn't cough out black smoke and gets through an MOT without a week's worth of repairs.

Acts of Cupidity
Chapter Playlist

I'd like to acknowledge the music artists who have inspired the chapter titles of this book with the following songs. I find my best inspiration from music, and this is a mix of old favourites and new discoveries, all wrapped up in the distinct emotion or theme which loosely links to each chapter. There were so many more songs I could have included, each finding me in the lamplight of a late night at the laptop, but there are more books to write and more melodies to motivate me.

With obvious special mention to Nickelback – without you, the reanimation chamber wouldn't quite bake souls as perfect as they do now, and you've saved my life enough times it only seemed right you could bring anyone back from the dead.

Chapter 1 – Bleeding Heart – *Jimi Hendrix*
Chapter 2 – Under Pressure – *Queen*
Chapter 3 – Two Out of Three Ain't Bad – *Meatloaf*
Chapter 4 – Cupid's Dead – *Extreme*
Chapter 5 – Fly Me to the Moon – *Frank Sinatra*
Chapter 6 – Passengers – *Elton John*

**Read on for an exclusive first look at the
next book in the Afterlife Agency series**

Fortune Favours the Grave

For the agents of the Fortuna Division, being lucky isn't just their blessing, it's their business. Responsible for handing out doses of good fortune to oblivious mortals, they are known for being invincible to disaster. However, when agents of luck begin to turn up dead, it is clear their own fortunes have taken a turn for the worse.

Fearing what this means for the Afterlife Agency as a whole, a small team are thrown together for the sole purpose of unravelling this mystery. Agents Erron Grover and Nikita Wolf face an almost insurmountable challenge, but it transpires they are hunting a mortal man, one who has developed an uncanny ability to see the auras of agency staff and piece together their role in controlling destiny.

It isn't long before they uncover an underground network of similarly gifted individuals who are more than willing to risk publicly exposing the agency's existence in a bid to take back control of their fate. This is one problem that maybe croissants and ice cream cannot solve. Has the agency's luck finally run out?

Coming soon

1

Gold

SAM RIVERA WAS SQUASHED UP on a foul-smelling train on the eastbound District Line. The man beside him, a pasty, bulging-eyed student with a shaved head, was busy telling him about his theory on escaping destiny, a conversation Sam had neither engaged in nor invited. The student's tartan shirt was covered in pin badges, and he smelled like pickled onion flavour Monster Munch.

'You see, fella, everythin' is written out for us. But we can change it y'know? All you gotta do is be able to *see*.' The man clenched his jaw as he spoke. 'There are these guys called Oracles. They see the gods that walk among us, sorting everythin' out and shit. We don't have a choice in it, but if we could see them, y'know, we can change our own fate innit.'

Sam had mostly zoned out, not all that interested in the mindless conspiracy theories, but he offered the occasional nod to seem polite. He tilted his head so his long dark hair would provide a subtle shield between himself and Monster-Munch Man.

'You hearin' what I'm saying, fella?' the man spat, rudely waving his hand in front of Sam's face.

Sam raised his palm slowly. 'No, I don't speak English. I haven't got a clue what you are saying,' he said drily.

'Sarcastic twat,' the man grumbled. 'Don't you give a shit about who's controlling your destiny, mate?'

'Not much I can do about it if that's the case.'

Sam was not new to the crazies on the train; more often than not he would get some odd looks for his most distinctive feature, a milky-blue eye that had been blind since the age of five. He never felt the need to cover it and was used to the hurtful mutterings of others. Instead, he wore his hair long and a red paisley bandana to frame his face and help give him a sense of identity.

'Well, one day we will all open our eyes to them. There are green ones, and gold ones and red ones . . . and dark grey ones, stay well away from them,' the man rambled on, his bulging eyes scanning the carriage as if he were surrounded by enemies.

Sam's ears pricked up. 'Sorry, what?'

'The gods!' The man hissed in a low voice. 'They have glowing auras, some of the Oracles say they look like wings. We call 'em Fireflies.'

'Do you see them?' Sam queried. 'You're one of these Oracles?'

'No, I don't have the gift. But there's a website of people who do. It's all happened since the Goosening.' The man tilted his phone screen towards Sam, his hand jittery as he scrolled the web page. It was on the dark web, and mostly seemed to be a forum of bizarre conversations between anonymous usernames. Sam made a mental note of the page name just as the carriage began to whir to a halt.

The train abruptly pulled into Victoria Station and the man thrust his phone back in his pocket. 'Gotta go, man. Look me up on the site, I'll explain everythin',' he stated, handing Sam a grubby scrap of paper before exiting the train among a throng of other passengers.

Sam watched the man leave and breathed a sigh of relief as the doors closed with their usual hiss and clatter. He had heard the term 'Goosening' a few times it seemed to be gaining traction, hashtags online of the Great Goosening were being used when videos of the bizarre, apocalyptic-like occurrences of late had been uploaded to social media. It had only been a few weeks since the whole of London and beyond had been plagued with the strange incidents, everything from a huge sinkhole taking out half of the Tower of London, to the DFS sale ending. Though the city was quickly returning to normality, the Great Goosening was the hottest topic of conversation almost anywhere you went.

Sam wasn't one for wasting his time scrolling news feeds online, but the conversation with the man on the train had turned his blood cold. He knew exactly what the Oracles could see, as he had been detecting faint colourful auras around certain people ever since the Goosening. He shook his head, putting it down to a daft theory and nothing more than a symptom of his damaged vision and wild imagination.

He decided to walk from the next station as it was a bright day at the end of February, and the daffodils were beginning to bloom – his favourite time of year. He arrived outside a shabby little shopfront in Pennyfields a little while later, pulling a key from his pocket and unlocking the drab red door.

The soft hum of the neon 'Open' sign seemed enough to keep evil at bay from the spiritual shop that he now owned. A sun-bleached list of services was hung in the window, while the shop sign, *Path of Destiny*, had been hand painted by his father and hadn't seen a coat of varnish in years. Usually, he'd eat lunch at the counter, but he'd had to run a few errands that morning so decided to get them over with before the shop got busy. He pulled a note off the door explaining his absence and started tidying the shelves, hoping to encourage some afternoon trade.

Sam had been left the shop in recent months after his mother had passed away from illness and his father had been killed in a violent altercation not long after. It had always been their passion, filling the shelves with all sorts of magical paraphernalia and offering various services from tarot readings to Reiki massage. Sam had coped with the crippling loss of his parents by working hard on revamping the shop and keeping the doors open, despite being thrown in the deep end having to learn how to perform most of the mystical practices they'd previously offered. It was a steep learning curve for a man in his mid-twenties, but he'd thrown himself into the challenge.

A few customers came and went, mostly browsers with the odd knick-knack being sold. As the afternoon wore on, Sam found himself thinking over the one-sided conversation he'd had on the Underground. It nagged at him, making him wonder if it was actually destiny of sorts that had put him in the path of the raving pickled-onion student to learn more about his so-called ability to see something others could not. A recent visit to the optician had assured him his remaining vision was still healthy, but Sam was beginning to wonder if the auras might not have a medical explanation. He fished in his pocket for the scrap of paper the man had handed him and unfolded it, seeing the website name and a way to access it scrawled in green ink.

Curiosity got the best of Sam, and he made his way to the back of the shop and down a dark stairway into the room below. He'd moved into the basement a few weeks before, owing to the fact his previous flat-share had ended due to 'goose-related complications', according to the landlord. He had everything he needed and wasn't one for living in excess. He relished in the freedom of his own place, despite the fact it smelled of mildew and had previously been used as a storage and kitchen for a butcher, before his father had bought the building. His parents hadn't ever used the basement, so it still had some of the old steel tables and tools from its previous owners. The cold tiled floor was easy enough to mop, and Sam had set up a small metal framed bed in the corner opposite his desk, which held his prized MSI gaming computer.

Safe in the knowledge he would hear the shop bell ring if a customer turned up, he flicked the light on, the dim bulb giving off just enough illumination to help him see his desk. He switched on the computer and patiently waited for it to load before navigating his way to the mysterious website. It took him a long time to finally gain access, despite the fact he was pretty au fait with the dark web. In no time at all he was scrolling through the stories on the Oracles' website. There were wild claims that gods walked among the living, controlling the course of events or even killing people off, depending on their aura. Some argued they were angels, others, aliens. There were any other number of wild theories, but all reached the consensus that they were meddling in human lives. Normally, Sam would have scoffed at the idea, but the more he read, the more he was convinced. Undisturbed by any customers, he was absorbed for over an hour, the people on the forums claiming that some veil had been lifted, allowing a glimpse of a completely hidden world, but only for those who'd once been denied the gift of full sight. Each self-proclaimed Oracle had damaged vision in one or both eyes, setting them apart from the forum members who were unable to detect the auras but were fully invested in the lore.

Sam thought back to when he first saw one of the auras. It was very hazy at first, subtle tints of emerald-green that emanated from a man in Covent Garden, a few weeks prior. He hadn't paid much attention at the time and had put it down to tiredness.

A faint tinkle of the bell brought him out of his rabbit-hole. He climbed the stairs to the shop, in time to greet a young woman who was browsing the array of crystals on one of the shelves.

'Have you anything that's for good luck?' she asked, turning over a few polished stones in her hand.

'Aventurine is a pretty solid choice,' he said confidently. 'Though it depends on the purpose. Are you wanting good luck in money, work, love?'

'I have a job interview next week,' the young woman said.

'Perhaps one of these then.' Sam walked over to her and lifted a small citrine pebble from a small bowl. He glanced out the window, the breath catching in his throat.

A man in a long black coat was stood across the street, seemingly minding his own business. Sam was transfixed at the image of the man: a golden aura seemed to glow and ripple around him, pulsing like a heartbeat and extending like wings from behind him. It had been a week or so since Sam had seen a gold one, but this time he paid attention. He pulled out his mobile and snapped a quick photo. The man outside answered his phone, and turned on his heel, walking in the direction of the Noodle Street Chinese restaurant around the corner.

'Sir, are you OK?' The customer gently nudged Sam, bringing him back to reality.

'Sorry, yes. Is there anything else I can help you with?' Sam handed her the crystal.

'Just this please.' She smiled.

'Take it, it's on the house.' Sam replied, hurriedly guiding her out the door.

'Oh, thank you.' The woman looked confused but quickly left, with Sam following her outside.

He fumbled for his keys to lock the door of the shop before taking off in the direction of the man with the gold aura. He was bursting with curiosity, and very much convinced the morning's events were starting to line up in a strange twist of fate.